THE NIGHT OF THE TRIFFIDS

The Night of the Triffids

Simon Clark

NEW ENGLISH LIBRARY
Hodder & Stoughton

A CIP catalogue record for this title
is available from the British Library.

ISBN 0 340 76601 8

Printed and bound in Great Britain by
Mackays of Chatham plc, Chatham, Kent

Hodder and Stoughton
A division of Hodder Headline
338 Euston Road
London NW1 3BH

To the memory of John Wyndham (1903–1969)

CONTENTS

PROLOGUE

It is now twenty-five years since three hundred men, women and children withdrew from the British mainland to establish a colony of survivors on the Isle of Wight.

There, in every library and in every school, is a mimeographed typescript of William Masen's account of the Great Blinding, the coming of the triffids and the fall of civilization.

Comprising little more than two hundred quarto pages, it is bound between covers of stiff orange card. Inside you will find no illustrations and not so much as a single photograph.

It is a vivid enough story nonetheless.

This is the final paragraph of William Masen's book:

So we must regard the task ahead as ours alone. We think now that we can see the way, but there is still a lot of work and research to be done before the day when we, or our children, or their children, will cross the narrow straits on the great crusade to drive the triffids back and back with ceaseless destruction until we have wiped the last one of them from the face of the land that they have usurped.

That is the end of William Masen's testament. What follows now is the beginning of another — in a world that still lies in thrall to the dreadful triffid . . .

CHAPTER ONE

World Darkening . . .

When nine o'clock on a summer's morning appears, so far as your eyes can tell, as dark as midnight in the very depths of winter, then there is something very seriously wrong somewhere.

It was one of those mornings when I awoke instantly alert, refreshed and ready for a new day. I was, as my mother Josella Masen would have put it, bright-eyed and bushy-tailed.

Only, for the life of me, I didn't know why I felt that way. Raising myself onto one elbow, I looked round the bedroom. It wasn't just dark. That's too tame a word for it. There was an absolute absence of light. I saw nothing. Not a glimmer of starlight through the window. No lamplight from a house across the way. Not even my hand in front of my face. Nothing.

Only darkness in its inky totality.

There, I remember telling myself firmly, *it's still the middle of the night. You've been woken by some cat giving voice while following its natural instincts. Or perhaps the old man in the next room had to get up for some reason. Now, go back to sleep.*

I lay flat on my back and closed my eyes.

But something was wrong. A mental alarm bell jangled faintly yet with some urgency deep inside my head.

I opened my eyes. Still I saw nothing.

I listened suspiciously, with all the intensity of a householder hearing a floorboard creak beneath an intruder's stealthy foot.

Now I was certain that it was the middle of the night; there could be no doubting the evidence of my eyes. I couldn't see even the faintest glimmer of dawn beginning to filter through the curtained window. Yet at that moment understanding at last dawned on me: the sounds I could hear were those of a summer's morning, when the sun should have been streaming across the island's fields.

I heard the clip-clop of a horse passing the cottage, then the brisk rap of a stick on the pavement as one of the Blind went about their business. There came the clatter of front doors. Water rushed down a drain. And, perhaps most noticeable of all, there was the wonderful sizzle of bacon being fried for breakfast, accompanied by its tantalizing wafting aroma.

Immediately my stomach rumbled hungrily. But with those first pangs of hunger I realized that the world, somehow, had gone all wrong. Profoundly wrong.

This was the moment when my life, as I had known it for the last twenty-nine years, ended. Right there, on that Wednesday, 28 May. Nothing would ever be the same again. There was no tolling of a funeral bell to mark its passing. Only the sounds that should not be – indeed, *could* not be! – those morning sounds so strangely out of place here in the dark heart of the night: the sound of a horse pulling a cart to the beach; the smart tap of sticks as the Blind went up the hill to the Mother House; the sound of a man's cheery goodbye to his wife as he set out for his day's work.

I lay there hearing it all perfectly. But, I confess, none of it made sense. I stared up at the ceiling. I stared for a full five minutes – five seemingly endless minutes – in the hope that my eyes would adjust to the gloom.

But no.

Nothing.

It remained as dark as if I'd been sealed into a box and buried deep underground.

I felt uneasy now. And within seconds that uneasiness spread like the very devil of an itch across my body, until soon I could lie there no longer. Quickly, I sat up and swung my feet out of bed onto cool linoleum.

Now, I was not at all familiar with the room, unsure even of in which direction the door lay. Sheer fate had placed me there. I'd been taking a flying boat on a short hop from Shanklin across the four-mile stretch of sparkling sea to Lymington on the mainland where I was to pick up a foraging party.

I'd been flying the single-engine plane solo – those little hops from the island to the mainland were no more dramatic than a local cart journey after all these years. The sky was clear, the sea flat calm, mirroring that flawless blue; my spirits were high with the prospect of a trouble-free flight on such a perfect summer's day.

However, fate always lies in wait to trip the complacent, with results that are either comic, irritating – or lethal.

The instant I overflew the Isle of Wight coast a large gull exchanged its earthly existence for the chance of some avian paradise by the simple expedient of flying into my aircraft's one and only propeller. Immediately the wooden blade shattered.

And a flying boat without its propeller is about as airworthy as a brick.

Luckily I managed to tug the nose of the aircraft round in a U-turn as it glided downward, the slipstream whistling through the wing struts.

The landing, while lacking any elegance whatsoever, was at least adequate – that is to say, I damaged nothing when the flying boat flopped onto the surface of the sea just yards from the beach.

The rest of that particular incident was without drama. A fishing smack towed me to a jetty where I moored the plane. Then I walked to the little seaside village of Bytewater where I radioed back the news that I'd been downed by a seagull.

After the obligatory laughter and leg-pulling I was told that a mechanic and a new propeller would be dispatched to Bytewater the following morning. Meanwhile, I should find myself a bed for a night.

I then spent a messy hour or so removing what remained of the carcass of the bird from the plane's engine.

But I should have saved a feather from that bird as a good-luck charm, I really should. Because, unknown to me, the bird had just saved my life.

And without its sacrifice you certainly wouldn't be reading these words now.

My predicament showed no signs of improving as I sat there on the bed. My eyes still told me it was the middle of the night.

Yet my ears — and my nose — retorted emphatically that this was well after sunrise.

There were sounds of people working. Sounds of people moving around outside. All the buzz and murmur of daylight hours.

Then, suddenly, I heard a burst of unintelligible shouting in the distance. It was perhaps nothing more than some contretemps between a man and his wife, I thought. I even waited for the slam of a door to indicate the dramatic finale of the disagreement.

The voice became abruptly silent.

Indeed, the sound of the tapping stick stopped as quickly.

Seconds later the steady clip-clop of the walking horse became a sudden clatter of hooves against the road surface as it bolted.

Then that too faded to eerie silence.

And this all-pervading darkness . . .

It was really too much.

I was a pilot. A man of steady nerves. But this dark was beginning to eat into me, unsettling me more than I could say.

I called out the name of my host.

'Mr Hartlow . . . Mr Hartlow?'

I waited, expecting at any moment to hear the door

open and Mr Hartlow's kindly voice saying, 'Now, now, then. What's all the fuss, David?'

But there was no Mr Hartlow who, after thirty years of blindness, could find his way around his house with as much assurance as a young man with twenty-twenty vision.

'Mr Hartlow . . .'

That hungry darkness greedily devoured my voice.

A nasty feeling began to run through me. Powerful. Undeniable. The resurfacing of those childhood fears that you put away as you mature into adulthood. Suddenly they were racing back.

That dread of the dark. When the silhouette on the wall can become a cruel, nameless beast that is waiting to pounce and rip at your throat . . . and that creak of a floorboard — it heralds the arrival of a madman coming through the door, wielding a bloody axe . . .

At that moment I realized: those fears don't disappear with age, they merely hibernate. They only need the right environment and back they come, loping like phantom hounds from the recesses of your mind . . .

And the reason I can't see, and the reason I can hear people moving about as if it's broad daylight is because . . .

A deep shiver ran through me as the words came slowly yet inexorably from somewhere deep inside my head. I cannot see because: *I am blind.*

As a newly blind man I had none of the self-assurance of one of the old Blind who'd lost their sight when the strange green lights had flooded the night sky three decades ago.

Instead, I must have made a pathetic, shambling figure as I crossed the bedroom, my hands stretched out in front of me. All I could hear now was the loud pounding of my heart.

'Mr Hartlow . . . can you hear me?'

No response.

'Mr Hartlow . . . Mr *Hartlow!*'

No reply.

I moved through the door onto the landing, still engulfed by that all-encompassing darkness. Now there was soft carpet beneath my bare feet. I shuffled forward. My fingertips pressed against the rough textures of wood-chip wallpaper, then there was the cool hardness of a door frame, followed by the door itself.

I opened it, calling, 'Mr Hartlow? Are you there?'

There was no answering reply. My terrified breathing, which overlaid the thump-thump-thump of my heart, was far too loud to allow me to hear any subtler sounds that might be stirring the air.

I struggled on, opening doors. Calling.

By now I was becoming disorientated, not even sure in which direction my own room lay.

So this is what it is like to be blind, I told myself. A world of endless night.

An ominous thought struck me.

Had those mysterious green lights that had blinded more than ninety per cent of the population all those years ago returned to the skies? That strange cosmic firework display that had entranced so many people on the same night that my father, Bill Masen, had lain in a hospital bed, his eyes bandaged after triffid poison had sprayed into his face?

I cast my mind back.

I'd gone to bed after a pleasant evening listening to a piano recital on Island Radio and chatting with my host, Mr Hartlow. He'd poured me a glass or two of his excellent parsnip brandy to speed me on my way, so to speak. For the life of me, I couldn't recall seeing anything amiss with the night sky.

Perhaps, however, one didn't even have to see the green lights — (if they *were* responsible for my lamentably sightless condition). Maybe they had flitted across the sky during the day, unseen by people going about their work across the island. Was it possible that an *invisible* radiation they emitted was responsible for burning out the optic nerve?

Ouch.

I had just found the stairs by stepping off the end of one. My foot slipped down at least three more before I managed to grab the banister rail. Although I'd stopped myself from pitching forward and breaking my neck, my ankle had taken a painful wrench.

Yet, in a way, that jab of pain along the arch of my foot did my nerves some good. It encouraged me to stop my imagination roaming restlessly, and fruitlessly, over what might or might not have happened to me, to stop wallowing in self-pity, and to damn' well do *something*.

When I reached the level floor below I stopped and listened, the stone slabs of the kitchen chillingly cold beneath my feet.

No. I could hear nothing.

Limping slightly from the sprain, I moved across the kitchen, hands outstretched to detect obstructions (and all the time irrationally expecting my fingers to touch the soft hollows and contours of a living human face). I stubbed a toe on a stool leg and for a few seconds the pain made me lose interest in pretty much everything else, provoking from my lips a few words that I would never have uttered in the presence of my mother, unshockable though she was.

Again I reached a wall. Tentatively, as if the wall might suddenly sprout sharp-toothed mouths to snap at my fingertips (my blindness had certainly unleashed a hundred irrational fancies!) I moved slowly along it. First, I reached a curtained window (the Blind still draw curtains through habit); quickly I tugged open the curtain, vainly hoping light would cascade dazzlingly into the room.

I sighed.

Darkness – still darkness.

I moved on, touching pans hanging from hooks, a row of knives, bunches of dried herbs. Somewhere a clock ticked with a ponderous, doom-laden rhythm.

Tick . . . tock . . . tick . . . tock . . .

An insufferable noise that I hated – again irrationally – with a passion.

Tick . . . tock . . .

If I should happen to lay my hands on the clock I would smash the damnable thing against the floor.

'Mr Hartlow?' Then I added, rather illogically, 'Can you hear me?' Because if he had heard, he would have answered, surely.

Tick . . . tock . . .

'Mr Hartlow?'

Tick . . . tock . . . tick . . .

As I reached a doorway my hand brushed against an

electric light switch. In a small village like this there would of course, be no electricity. Electricity, after all, was a precious commodity reserved for workshops, hospitals, clinics, communications — and for laboratories like my father's. Nevertheless, I gripped the switch eagerly. The thing obviously hadn't been used for decades; metal contacts grated across an accumulation of grit as it clicked downward.

No light.

With the rational part of my mind I had expected none. But a tormenting voice inside my head sang out loud and clear that light — lots and lots of lovely brilliant light — had cascaded from the bulb to flood the kitchen. *But you can't see it, because you really are blind, David Masen . . . sightless as any three blind mice . . . three blind mice running after the farmer's wife . . .*

Stop that, I told myself sharply, fighting down the wave of panic rolling dangerously through me. *Stop that at once.*

Once more I fumbled my way across the walls. Now there were worktops.

A sink. Cooker.

More cupboards, with plates from—

I stopped.

A cooker?

Quickly, I groped back through the cloaking darkness until I found the burners and the iron stands on which to set the pans. There I could feel the round gas-control knobs, hard beneath my anxious, searching fingers.

Gas. Yes — *yes*.

I fumbled for a lighter that must, I thought, be close by.

After a few moments' fruitless search I began cursing — an equally fruitless occupation.

I realized too that there must be candles and lamps nearby. Not for Mr Hartlow's use, of course, but for any sighted guests he might entertain.

But, for me, these might as well have been hidden on the dark side of the Moon as I groped sightlessly through what seemed to be endless racks of plates, cutlery and vegetables in baskets. A candle might have been right there in front of me, only I couldn't, for the life of me, find it.

As it was, my characteristic impatience rescued my ailing sanity.

I found the cooker again.

Or rather, I located it — by blindly putting my hand in the hot bacon grease in the frying pan. I turned the knobs at the front of the cooker, instantly hearing the methane as it hissed odourlessly from the burners.

Right, this was crude . . . but if it worked . . . well, that would be just tickety-boo by me.

I reached out again to the worktops. My fingers found a pan — one that was satisfyingly heavy — and picked it up. Then, with the gas hissing from the cooker vents, I brought the pan down hard against the iron stands.

The impact clanged mightily.

I struck the top of the cooker again.

And again the metallic clang rang loud in my ears.

Then, at the third attempt — this time swinging downwards with all my might, shattering the wooden pan handle — my plan worked.

The two metal surfaces crashing together produced a single spark.

With a loud pop, followed by a *whoosh*, a ball of flame blossomed under my nose.

I reeled back from the smarting rush of heat, the smell of singeing telling me that I'd been too slow to save my eyebrows.

But I didn't care. I didn't care the tiniest bit. Because something wonderful had happened.

I could see.

I saw in perfect detail that brief blossom of orange and yellow fire. Within a moment it had died back to four discs of blue flame where the gas jets burned from their vents.

They were anything but bright. Yet they cast a faint bluish light across the kitchen, revealing the stairs, table, radio — and here were Mr Hartlow's pipe and tobacco pouch on a shelf by the window.

And, more importantly, I could see on the wall the clock from which issued those lugubrious ticks and tocks. For a second I thought my eyes really were playing tricks.

The clock, if it was right, told me it was ten minutes past nine o'clock.

I looked outside.

That was the moment when I realized that either I had in some way gone spectacularly mad and was imagining all this — or that it really was the end of the world. For all I could see beyond the window was absolute darkness. That tormenting voice of unreason wasted no time before murmuring: 'You're right, David Masen. The sun is dead. And this is the beginning of everlasting night.'

CHAPTER TWO

An Old Foe

What should have been giddy relief at being able to see again gave way immediately to a sheer, stunned perplexity.

This was a May morning after nine o'clock. The village and surrounding fields should be awash with daylight. Instead there was only that velvet black. So, where had the sun gone?

The idea that it had simply just not risen hurtled across my brain. Could it be that during the night some disaster of cosmic proportions had knocked the Earth from its orbit? Or that the Earth had stopped revolving and from now on would present the same face to the sun in the same way that the Moon eternally presented only one side to the Earth?

But that was too fantastic. A disaster of those proportions, such as a comet plunging into our planet at thousands of miles an hour, would have caused tidal waves, earthquakes, continent-shattering explosions.

But here on the Isle of Wight everything was quiet, peaceful as a summer's morning should be.

My mind was a confused whirl. Because I remembered waking to hear people starting their working day as if nothing was amiss. But why had they gone about their business as if everything was normal? As if the world hadn't gone topsy-turvy? And hadn't been left in total darkness?

The resoundingly simple answer to that, I realized, was that Bytewater was a community of the blind.

How could they know there was no light?

After all, darkness doesn't impress itself against your skin; it can't be smelled, can't be tasted. If a man is blind there's no way he can tell the difference between light and dark. Unless, that is, he's standing in sunlight strong enough to warm his skin. Instead he must rely on the chiming of clocks and the word of the sighted.

So the Blind of Bytewater had simply woken into total darkness, then unwittingly started the day, believing it to be like any other.

After staring through the window out into the dark for a full three minutes I shook my head. I had to do something; I couldn't wait in the simple hope that the sun would suddenly return in a blaze of glory. The first obvious move was to put some clothes on.

Now, there was no difficulty at all in finding a candle. And that light – that beautiful, wonderful light! – a miracle in the darkness, lit my way back to the bedroom.

Once dressed, I made a quick recce of the house. No Mr Hartlow to be seen. Perhaps he'd gone to feed his rabbits. He must have thought me an Idle Jack for snoozing away the morning while others worked.

Exchanging the candle for a brighter oil lantern, I left

the cottage, carefully closing the door behind me, mindful that my host wouldn't thank me for letting every cat in the neighbourhood into his kitchen. Once I'd done that, I set off along the road that led inland.

The lamp cast a yellow smudge in front of me; nothing more than a speck of light in this all-encompassing darkness. But I remember thinking then that this postponement of the dawn could be nothing more than a freakish pall of cloud that had temporarily blotted out the sun, and that it should pass soon enough.

I paused every so often to raise the lamp, looking for one of the Blind who might be tending his or her cattle in a field, still oblivious to the dark.

I saw no one.

At the edge of the road were the white-painted guide rails that the Blind villagers would follow. The rails were made of wood and ran at waist height. Here and there, signs in Braille directed the Blind to turn right or left to reach a particular cottage, the inn, or the Mother House. The Blind would always keep the guide rail to their left, so avoiding colliding head-on with a neighbour. But, in fact, they were so well adapted to their condition that they moved briskly around their territories with hardly as much as a fingertip brush of the rail.

I walked faster.

The oil lamp had no reflector plate to focus its light; instead I walked in the middle of a soft-edged glow. Consequently I could see no more than a dozen feet in front of me at any one time.

So when I came upon Mr Hartlow sitting alone on a roadside bench it was something of a surprise.

Mr Hartlow was a well-built man in his mid-sixties with close-cropped white hair. Long ago he'd been a London solicitor specializing in copyright law.

He looked up even though I'd stopped and the sound of my footsteps had ceased. His keen hearing must have picked up the sound of my breathing.

'Who's there?' He sounded immensely tired.

'It's David Masen,' I said, walking forward.

'Ah, David . . . come here, please . . .'

He held out his hand which I took in mine. Immediately he clasped it in a surprisingly fierce grip.

'What's happened, David? Something's gone wrong, hasn't it?'

'It's dark. All dark, as if the sun hasn't come up.'

'Dark. Ah . . .' His voice sounded hoarse with exhaustion; as if he'd just come through the grimmest battle of his life. 'For a moment I wondered . . .' He shook his white-haired head. 'I wondered if the green lights had come back.' He raised his own sightless eyes to the sky. 'I heard Tom Atkinson shouting earlier . . . oh, you don't know Tom, do you?'

I told him I didn't.

'He's one of the few Sighted here in the village. He's a fisherman – and he's one of the biggest grumblers I've ever met. He's always too warm or too cold, or the fish won't bite, or the wind's blowing in the wrong direction . . . Ah . . .' He broke off. For a moment I thought he was simply going to nod off there on the bench. I raised the lantern to look at him, but his head hung down wearily.

'Mr Hartlow?'

He seemed to pull himself together. 'Sorry . . . I don't know what's come over me this morning. I tripped into the hedge back there. Must have fallen over my own two feet. Clumsy devil I'm becoming. Never done that before . . .' He suddenly seemed to shake himself awake. 'Yes, I was telling you about Tom Atkinson, wasn't I? He was shouting out in the street that he couldn't see. At first, as I say, I thought the shooting stars or whatever they were had come back — those damnable things that burned out our eyesight thirty years ago.' He paused, then took a deep breath. 'You know, David.' His grip on my hand tightened further and he began to speak in a low voice. 'That fear came back to me. Just like it did after I stayed out in the garden that night all those years ago. My God. We even made a party of it with the neighbours because they said it was something we'd never see again.' He gave a colourless laugh. 'Never see again. How right they were. Because in the morning we were all blind. And of course I never saw my family again, even though they were in the house with me. But I could hear them screaming. Oh, by Heaven, I could hear that all right, just . . . just screaming with panic as their eyesight faded away.'

The grip on my hand, which had relaxed slightly during Mr Hartlow's sad reminiscence, tightened again. He turned his sightless eyes to me. And even though I knew he was one of the old Blind, at that moment I believed he not only looked *at* me but right *into* me, into the depths of my soul.

'David. You know, I had a beautiful, intelligent wife. I had two pretty daughters — just ten and thirteen they were. And thirty years ago, suddenly blind . . . stone blind . . . I stood every day in the doorway of our house and called for help. And I listened to my wife and daughters cry themselves to sleep every day for the next three months. You see, we ran out of food. I couldn't find any more . . .' He shook his head. 'I hated myself, David. I was too weak to find a way of helping them. My God, I wish I could turn the clock back . . . I wish I had just the one chance to help them; stop them suffering . . . because . . .' His voice failed him.

'I'll take you back to the cottage,' I said gently.

'Maybe in a moment. You know, I haven't an ounce of strength left in my body. What on earth's happened to me, David?'

'Don't worry, Mr Hartlow, it must be the shock of the fall, that's all.'

'Falling over into bushes? Time they put me out to pasture, eh?'

'You'll soon be fighting fit again, Mr Hartlow.'

'Maybe, David. Maybe. Now, do you see any sign of that old moaner Tom Atkinson?'

'I can hardly see a thing. This lantern doesn't cast an awful lot of light.'

'But how in heaven's name did it get so dark? It doesn't feel like rain so there can't be so much cloud that . . . ah . . .'

The grip on my hand suddenly loosened. His head hung forward again.

'Mr Hartlow?'

'Oh . . . uhm? Sorry, David . . . I'm just so light-headed. I feel as if I've put away a jug or two more of ale than I should have. Now, this darkness . . . what do you suppose is responsible?'

'I don't know — cloud, maybe. But it must be incredibly dense. Without a lamp I can't see my hand in front of my face.'

'Now that kind of darkness is a great equalizer between the two of us, isn't it?' There was no maliciousness there; the old man sounded as kindly as ever.

'Mr Hartlow, I'll help you back to—'

He waved my helping hand away. 'No, David. Not yet.' He took a deep breath. 'David . . . you know, I've always suspected something like this would happen. All these years I've sat in my cottage and thought about the terrible calamity that befell the planet, and how people like your mother and father and Ivan Simpson worked their miracles, how they saved so many people — Blind as well as Sighted — and how they embedded a tiny sliver of civilization in this island.' He sighed. 'But long ago I came to the conclusion it was all a waste of time and effort. Three decades ago Mother Nature, fate or God Himself decided that Man had ruled this planet long enough; so an attempt was made to wipe Man out; render him extinct. Very nearly succeeded, too. Still, as I said, due to the brave efforts of the Masens and people like them we cheated extinction. But I tell you this, David.' He looked at me, those sightless eyes once again seeming to pierce my soul. 'I tell you, God will not be cheated. Nothing Man can do will thwart His plan. We are all going to die. He has decided. The last twenty-five years here have been nothing more than a peaceful interlude. An intermission between two halves of a titanic catastrophe that will destroy all human life. Now He—' Mr Hartlow pointed skyward '—is going to finish the job. Remember the Bible's Book of Exodus. One of the plagues to afflict Pharaoh was darkness. The Lord said to Moses "Stretch your hand toward heaven that there may be darkness over the land of Egypt, a darkness to be felt".' Eyes glittering strangely, the old man lifted his hand as if to touch the encircling darkness. 'In every culture darkness precedes Armageddon. The Vikings predicted the end of the world would begin when the monster wolf, Fenrir, swallowed the sun, bringing darkness. The ancient Sumerians told how nearly all the people of the Earth were killed "when daylight turned to darkness" and their god "smashed the land like a cup . . ." Mark my words, David. Mark them well . . . this is the beginning of the end.'

'Mr Hartlow, you're tired. Let me get you back home.'

'Thank you, perhaps . . . Oh . . .'

'What's the matter?'

'My face is sore. I must have grazed it when I fell.' He touched his cheek.

'Let me take a look at that . . . Mr Hartlow . . . *Mr Hartlow?*'

His head sagged forward and I had to grip his shoulder to stop him falling. Not that it mattered to Mr Hartlow now. As I lowered him sideways onto the bench I instinctively knew he was dead.

I raised the lamp to look into his face.

There, in the glow of the lamp, I could plainly see the bright red streak across the old man's cheek.

Now I knew what had killed him.

I stooped quickly, using the back of the bench to shield at least part of my body. Then, raising the lamp as high as I dared, I looked at the dark shapes of the bushes and trees. But the light was too weak to identify individual species. They might have been everyday alders, sycamores, immature oaks, young chestnuts — but they might have been something entirely different. Something infinitely more sinister.

I knew there was nothing more to be done for Mr Hartlow. What mattered now was that I should warn Emergency HQ at Newport.

Keeping as low as I could, I ran at a crouch.

And even as I ran it started. A hollow drumming sound of wood on wood. A sound that every child on the island had been taught to recognize.

Something rustled in the hedgerow beside me.

Ducking my head still lower, I hurried on.

In front of me lay the dark form of a horse. The animal was stone dead.

A little further on, I saw a pair of waders protruding from the long grass at the side of the road. That would be Tom Atkinson; silvery fish from his basket lay scattered across the ground. He'd landed his last catch.

The drumming grew louder. A maddening tip-tap-tip-tap.

Ahead I saw a cottage from which hung a post-office sign. I raced for it, seeing from the corner of my eye a monstrous shadow moving jerkily through the gloom.

My voice rang out into silence as I burst into the building.

'Hello! Anyone home?'

Silence — as oppressive as the darkness.

Now it seemed that I was alone in the village. With the lamp casting shadows that leaped crazily up the walls, I searched the post office until I found the room that served as the radio cabin. Here I sat myself before the small set and switched it on. Seconds later valves glowed yellow through the ventilation slots.

Something tapped at the open window above my head.

Using the radio set's Braille instruction booklet as a makeshift shield to guard my face, I jumped up at the window, shoved it shut, then locked it. Now at last I could make that call for help.

I pressed the transmit button. 'Hello, this is an emergency transmission on frequency nine. Emergency HQ, Newport, do you read me, over?'

Static hissed.

For a moment I was convinced I'd receive no reply. Already I was too late — the island had been overrun.

I tried again, tension making my voice sound higher: 'Emergency HQ, Newport, hello, do you read me, over?'

'Caller on frequency nine. We read you; please stay off the air.' Weariness permeated the radio operator's tones. It sounded as if he'd had a long night.

'But I need to report an emergency. Over.'

'The darkness? Oh, yes, thank you, caller, we know all about that.' The man had clearly written me off as a dim-wit. 'Now, I'm waiting for a number of fire reports. I have to keep this frequency clear. So, caller, please go off air. Over.'

'Good grief! You can't be serious,' I shouted, forgetting on-air etiquette.

'Sir, I appreciate you must be anxious about the darkness. The official line is to stay put. It's probably an unusually dense cloud layer that has obscured the sun. So, kindly switch off—'

'No . . . listen to me! I have something else to report. Over.'

'Go ahead, caller,' came the voice, reluctantly.

'My name is David Masen, calling from Bytewater. I wish to report a triffid incursion.'

There was a pause. Static crackled on the ether.

At last HQ responded in a voice that came close to stunned disbelief. 'Say again, Mr Masen. It sounded as if you used the word "triffid". Over.'

Something lashed against the window.

'You heard correctly. And until someone can tell me anything different, I'd say we've just been invaded.'

CHAPTER THREE

Eye of the Storm

More than twenty years ago my father, Bill Masen, sat down at his desk and during one long, snowbound winter wrote a deeply personal account of what happened to him during the aftermath of the Great Blinding and the coming of the triffids. By now, it must be a familiar-looking book to all colonists, not only on the Isle of Wight but on the Scillies and the Channel Islands as well. That mimeographed quarto publication bound within its bright orange covers is instantly recognizable.

Along with Elspeth Cary's *History of a Colony* and Matt and Gwynne Lloyd's documentary films that continue to chronicle the day-to-day lives of the colonists, it is an invaluable record of how we came to find ourselves on our island fortresses when the whole world fell under the dreadful sway of the triffid. This was the botanical freak once trumpeted as 'the miracle plant that walks' that in a few short years became Man's nemesis – his destroyer.

Naturally, I read my father's account when I was a boy. How strange to rediscover my father as Bill Masen the complex individual in his own right rather than simply the cheerful, mostly optimistic – if sometimes preoccupied – 'Dad' I'd known since birth.

I never thought I'd write anything to compare with his book. Until now my writings had been restricted to pre-flight notes to do with weather reports, wind-speeds and navigational calculations, jotted on the backs of old envelopes and sandwich wrappers, as often as not picturesquely decorated with an oily fingerprint or two.

Now I find myself sitting here at a table, a dozen blank notepads in front of me. I tap a pencil against my lips. My brow furrows as I wonder just how on Earth I can recapture in the written word all those strange adventures – those sometimes nightmarish adventures – that have dominated my life since that fateful 28 May three decades after the fall of civilization.

That was the day I awoke to a world of darkness. And that was the day the triffids once more invaded our hitherto safe island home.

Some say the second coming of the triffids at that same fateful time when night refused to yield to day was too much to be pure coincidence. Some saw another hand behind it all – perhaps the divine hand of a vengeful god. Alas, I can cast no light on that (if you will excuse an unintentional pun). However, I remember a passage from my father's book wherein he contemplates the sudden blinding of the global population occurring at the same time that countless triffids escaped from farms and gardens. He wrote: 'Of course, coincidences are happening all the time – but it's just now and then you happen to notice them . . .'

And so, coincidence or not, I now sit here in a very different world from the one in which I grew up.

A colder wind than I have ever known before is blowing against this tower. Again and again the banshee shriek of the gale reminds me that, although I might have no natural literary abilities, I *do* have all the time in the world to write my book.

Therefore, I shall write down what happened to me. And I shall begin at the beginning . . .

My childhood was idyllic. I grew up amid the rolling chalk downs and green-clad hills of the Isle of Wight. A tract of fertile land that only became an island some six thousand years ago when the sea level rose to flood a valley that is now known as The Solent. Since then the island has played host to prehistoric hunter-gatherers, to Roman farmers who named the island 'Vectis', to Saxon immigrants, and then eventually to Victorian holiday-makers, including Lord Tennyson who declaimed that 'the air on the Downs is worth sixpence a pint!' And, more recently, we few survivors from the mainland. I'm surprised I remember these facts from some history lesson of long ago when Mr Pinz-Wilks tried so hard to instil into me a little academic learning. In fact, I'm certain Mr Pinz-Wilks (who must surely have gone to his final reward by now) would be astonished, too. I remember only too clearly how he raised his blind eyes in frustration to the ceiling so many, many times. Sadly, I retained historical facts as easily as a sieve holds water.

There, in the heart of the Isle of Wight, I shared a large house in the picturesque village of Arretton (population forty-three) with my mother, father and two younger sisters.

As soon as I was old enough I roved away across the poppy-strewn fields, exploring and looking for 'Mantun'.

This was the name I gave to my imaginary lost fairy city — a childhood fantasy that often perplexed my parents. And when rain or parental punishment for my deeds of natural mischief confined me to my bedroom, I'd grip a pencil in my chubby hand and draw pictures that showed a host of buildings as spindly as bamboo canes. Of course, when my parents asked me what I'd drawn I'd proudly reply 'Mantun'. My imagination was young and supple then. Entertaining for me, yet puzzling to others.

My father worked mainly at home in his glasshouses and laboratory. He grew triffids with scrupulous care, then dissected them with that same painstaking attention to detail. When I was five or six I'd watch him mixing nutrients, which he dissolved in water, before feeding the plants from a watering can. He'd stroke the leaves, as you or I would stroke a cat, and sometimes he would murmur to the plants as if they were his closest friends.

For a long time I believed that he loved the plants — as if they were some cherished branch of our family — so it was something of a shock when, at the age of eight, I learned that he was trying to find a way to kill them. Bewildering stuff indeed. Even more so when he told me he wasn't content just to kill those triffids that were in our glasshouses but that he wanted to destroy every triffid in the world. Running his fingers through a handsome head of greying hair, he'd speak to me of defoliants, growth hormones, cellular degenerators, pollination inhibitors, mutant triffid species with guaranteed nil reproduction capability.

More bewildering stuff. Double Dutch, as the old saying goes.

Then I'd tug the sleeve of his white lab coat, demanding that he come and help me fly my kite. More often than not he'd flash his big good-natured grin and say, 'Give me ten minutes, then meet me up on the hill.'

All this should really have given my father at least a good hint of where my future lay. Viz.: no comprehension of botany (evidenced by my lack of interest therein) plus no head for academic subjects meant that my following in his footsteps was extremely doubtful.

No doubt my father cherished dreams of my pursuing a career in applied botanical science — one specifically devoted to the eradication of the triffid menace. But love him as I did, and try as I might to master the baffling language of botany and the Byzantine complexity of test tube, retort and Bunsen burner, I must have been something of a puzzle to him. But to say I was a disappointment to him would have been putting it too strongly.

Because, quite simply, Bill Masen loved his children. He allowed us to cultivate our own interests; not for a moment did he wish for us to be mere facsimiles of himself or our mother. (Although my sister Lisabeth did inherit my mother's literary abilities — and a mischievous appetite to shock — with her steamy stories of *affaires d'amour* that appeared in the *Freshwater Review* when she should, according to her disapproving headmistress, have still been a blushing seventeen-year-old.)

My total ineptitude at laboratory research came to a head one Tuesday evening after school when I was 'helping' my father. I was twelve years old. I managed, quite inadvertently, to concoct an explosive blend of the familiar pink triffid oil in its raw state with an equal amount of wood alcohol. Father told me to leave the glass beaker somewhere warm for the alcohol to evaporate. I had a brainwave. I'd speed up the process by boiling off the alcohol with the flame of the Bunsen burner.

Then I sat back to watch, beaming proudly at my own brilliance.

The explosion that followed was as impressive as it was loud. It was even heard by the Mothers up at Arreton manor. I lost most of my hair in the fireball. And lost – permanently – my part-time job as my father's lab assistant.

My hair did grow back, although it acquired a pure white fleck in its otherwise jet-black fringe, which earned me the nickname 'Snowdrop' at school. (And, oh, how I'd cringe whenever friends teased me with *that* one.)

Later, that same day of the explosion, after my father (and his more competent assistants) had remedied much of the damage I'd wrought, he visited me in my bedroom. He stood there, a candle in his hand, the light shining on his greying hair. For a while he gazed down at my bandaged head, thinking I was asleep; I heard him exhale audibly through the white bristles of his moustache.

I had expected an extremely colourful, not to say high-volume description of my inabilities.

Instead, I realized that as he looked down at me he was thanking heaven I hadn't taken my head clean off in the explosion. (After all, Dr Weisser had had to tweezer half a dozen slivers of glass beaker from my face.)

My father pulled the blanket up around my shoulders, then affectionately laid his hand on my arm.

'I didn't mean to wreck the lab, Dad.'

'I'm sorry, David, did I wake you?'

'No. I can't get to sleep.'

'Does it hurt?'

'Not really.' I said this as manfully as I could. 'Just stings a little around my eyes.'

'Don't worry, the stuff Dr Weisser gave you will numb it soon enough. It'll make you sleep, too.'

'Will you ever be able to repair the lab?'

'Good heavens, yes.' He gave a chuckle as he set the candle down on my table. 'It took us a good couple of hours to undo what you managed to do in two seconds, but it's fine now. In fact, I've managed to wangle some replacement equipment from the old general, so it's not only as good as new, it's *better* than new.'

'I don't think I'll be much use to you as an assistant, will I, Dad? Perhaps Lisabeth or Annie would do a better job?'

'Now don't you worry about that. You're in one piece; that's all that matters. And you're not to bother yourself about your hair: it will grow back, you know?'

'Maybe I'm not cut out to be a scientist, after all.' I sat up in bed. 'Perhaps I ought to think of some other career?'

My father smiled and crinkling lines appeared around

his bright blue eyes. 'Now, my father, bless him, was an accountant for the civil service in the old days when the United Kingdom had a much-disliked institution called the Inland Revenue. He took it for granted that I'd follow him into what he called "the family firm".' Still smiling, he shook his grey-haired head. 'Alas, I was no good with figures.'

'Like I'm no good with test tubes and stuff?'

'Quite. I could manage well enough counting on my fingers but if you asked me to divide one hundred and twenty-one by seven I'd make a pitiful sight, scratching my head, counting on my fingers. My father would never criticize me for my ignorance if he sprung a surprise piece of mental arithmetic on me. But as he watched me floundering away his face would go redder and redder and redder. However, I did eventually find my vocation in life. So: believe one who speaks from experience – *experto crede*, as a certain Roman gentleman put it. You'll find yours one day if—'

At that moment his voice trailed away as he suddenly seemed to notice for the very first time what littered my room. Papering the walls were photographs of aeroplanes and dirigibles, while all over the room were models, from incomplete skeletons to finished aircraft complete with tiny engines, and fuselages and wings covered with tissue paper that had been wonderfully transformed into a hard, lacquered shell by modeller's dope. Hanging by lengths of fishing line from the ceiling was a handsome biplane, painted a brilliant strawberry red. I'd successfully flown this machine from our orchard, over the Mother House to a distant field on the far side of Downend. There were also kites and blueprints, as well as aero-modelling books and ancient aviation magazines printed before the end of the Old World. And on the table by the window was my pride and joy — a plywood rocket plane of my own invention that would boast a seven-foot wingspan when it was fully assembled.

As I said, my father looked at all this as if the scales had fallen from his eyes and he was seeing it for the first time (even though he'd often heard my mother complain about the state of my room).

That was the moment when, as the old saying goes, the penny dropped for my father and for me.

A pilot. That was what I would do with my life.

Of course, I was far too young then to begin training as a pilot for the island's meagre air fleet. But the seed was sown. In my mind's eye I saw myself in the cockpit of a fast jet, soaring through the clouds high above land and sea.

On a more practical level my father encouraged me. He found more aviation books and magazines for me. He also gave me my own workshop where I could work on my beloved model aeroplanes. Wisely, he chose one well away from the house when he learned that my rocket plane was fuelled by a substantial quantity of gunpowder that I stored in a biscuit tin beneath my bed. I singed away the downy black hairs of my adolescent moustache on more than one occasion when test-firing that rocket motor, I can tell you.

Meanwhile, I continued my studies at school — a bit more enthusiastically now that I realized I would need at least a few academic qualifications before enrolling on a pilot's course.

However, one of the core subjects at school was the study of the triffid: its origins, life-cycle, attributes; its dangers.

In the early years of the colony the triffid had been demonized and held responsible for the destruction of the Old World in the middle years of what was then known as the twentieth century. Then the only talk was of how evil the plant was, how it could be kept off the island. How it could be annihilated.

Now a more balanced view had developed. With an irony that any satirist would have found delicious we had come to depend on the triffid for oil, fuel, cattle fodder and about fifty other commodities. While the only triffids grown on the island were a few docked specimens for research purposes, we harvested vast numbers on the British mainland where they grew wild and unchecked in their millions. After being felled by heavily protected 'logging' teams, the plants were shipped to the Isle of Wight for processing. Of course, every child was still taught to recognize the plant from infancy.

As the son of Bill Masen, the world's greatest expert on triffids, schoolmasters would always — or so it seemed to me — ask me all the toughest questions about that peripatetic plant. (As if knowledge of the triffid could be transmitted genetically from father to son. Or perhaps more appropriately, considering the botanical nature of the subject, via some mysterious process of osmosis — some hope!)

'Masen,' Mr Pinz-Wilks might begin in those grave Oxbridge tones that would rumble out from beneath his handlebar moustache. 'Masen, would you please describe the triffid plant to the class?'

(This question was asked repeatedly despite the many posters of the plant that hung on the wall.)

'The mature plant stands around eight feet tall,' I would recite, parrot-fashion. 'A straight stem grows from the woody bole; er, at the top of the stem is a funnel; inside that is a sticky liquid that traps insects upon which the plant feeds by dissolving and drawing the nutrients down through the stem in a solution of sap; its sprays of leaves are green and leathery. The triffid possesses a sting that is curled into a whorl — something like a gigantic pig's tail.' (Laughs from the class; I'd shoot a grin at my friends.) 'This it can uncurl at high speed to whip at its prey. Er . . . uhm . . .'

'And what else, Masen?'

'Er, the sting is poisonous. Lethal if it strikes the exposed skin of a man or woman.'

'Indeed, they can fell a cow or a horse. Any other pearls of wisdom, Masen?'

I could tell that Mr Pinz-Wilks was less than impressed by my pedestrian recitation. By that time, moreover, I'd be shifting uncomfortably from foot to foot.

'Perhaps, Masen, you could have begun with the plant's origins. After all, was it present when the Emperor Claudius conquered the British Isles in AD 43? Can we be so fanciful as to imagine its discovery was splashed across the front pages of Rome's *Acta Diurna*?'

'No, sir.'

'Or did it arrive on this planet from outer space, perhaps hitching a ride on the tail of a comet?'

'No, sir. Er . . . it is thought that triffids were developed by scientists in Russia, after, er, World War Two, sir.'

'That is correct, Masen. A hybrid created from many different species. But have I ever mentioned that Ur is the ancient Sumerian city in Iraq that flourished two and a half thousand years before the birth of Christ?'

'Sir?' I was confused.

'It is just that you have such a fondness for punctuating your sentences with the name "Ur" that I thought you might be contemplating some deep and rigorous study of that fabled city of Sumer.'

My confusion got a whole lot worse. The schoolmaster's legendary wit was often as impenetrable as it was sarcastic.

As I said, botany was a weak point, a very weak point in my somewhat lacklustre portfolio of academic abilities. Often, at times like this, the schoolmaster would point unerringly with his white stick at a boy he could not even see, then ask that so much brighter individual to continue.

Crisply the boy would canter through the facts. 'The triffid, or more properly *pseudopodia*, takes around two years to develop the lashlike sting that can strike at a victim ten to fifteen feet away from itself. The sting is generally fatal to humans unless an antidote can be administered by hypodermic to the carotid artery. What is most unusual about the triffid, compared with other plants, isn't that it is a flesh eater – the Venus flytrap feeds in a roughly similar way – it is that the plant can walk. It walks by using three bluntly tapered projections that extend from its lower part. At first thought, mistakenly, to be roots, these support the main body of the plant and raise it perhaps a foot above the ground. It walks rather like a man on crutches. Two of the blunt legs slide forward, then the whole plant lurches forward as the rear one draws level with them. At each step the stem whips violently backward and forward. As William Masen, the expert on triffids, put it, "it gave one a kind of seasick feeling to watch it". The effect of the motion is irregular and jerky but the plant can cover the ground at an average walking pace.'

'Excellent, Merryweather. Excellent. Anything else of note?'

'From the plants we extract oil that can be used in the manufacture of certain foods and refined to make fuel for motors. From them we also get raw ingredients for plastics and for a variety of drugs. We use their fibres for rope, and the dried remains of processed plants, mashed into cakes, are fed to cattle.'

'Well done.'

'The plant can produce a rattling noise by striking small sticklike growths against its own stem. William Masen considered that they might be communicating with each other but, as yet, there is no evidence to support this.'

'Superb, Merryweather. Please sit down. Now, to history, noble history . . .'

Occasionally it did irritate me to hear my father being quoted as if he were some long-dead scientist. But, more often than not as the bright students efficiently gave their condensed lectures, my eyes would be drawn to the window where I'd gaze dreamily at the clouds floating through a deep blue sky as lightly as feathers. Then I'd imagine myself sitting snugly in the cockpit of an aeroplane, listening to the sweet hum of a pair of Merlin engines and feeling the vibration of those throbbing cylinders running through the joystick to tickle the palm of my hands. Yes. Adventure was in my blood.

And so, as always, my daydreams would take me far away from the classroom to a world beyond my safe but mundane island home.

Speaking of home, it might be interesting for anyone who should happen to read this to know something about the island community. When my family arrived on the Isle of Wight some twenty-five years ago, after their dramatic flight from Shirning in a triffid-infested England, the island's population stood at a mere few hundred.

The population, however, steadily increased as more refugees reached the island from the Irish Republic, the British mainland and even from the continent of Europe where waves of triffids spreading from the Russian steppes drove human survivors westward until their backs were to the Atlantic.

In Western Europe the most sizeable communities were based in the Channel Islands, the Isle of Wight and the larger Scottish Isles, while the Faroe Islands in the North Atlantic formed the northernmost community. Mainland Britain and Europe were largely no-go areas. Triffids extended in vast ambulatory forests, choking open fields and city streets alike.

From exploratory flights and careful monitoring of radio broadcasts we learned of a few small communities hanging on by the skin of their teeth on the mainland, permanently besieged by the triffid armies. Besides the Western European groups, there were other communities throughout the world, all as fragile as one another. Many were lost to the triffids, natural disasters, disease, famine – even, ludicrously, to wars that pitted man against man.

The great bulk of the world's population died in those first few months of Year One of the catastrophe. It was estimated that the entire population of the globe now might not number above one million men, women and children. Perhaps a third of those were unsighted.

In the light of such a dizzying drop in the population it was no wonder, then, that our island council placed such a priority on repopulation. After all, those first few hundred who had made their home on the Isle of Wight all those years ago must have been rattling round its one hundred and forty-seven square miles like the proverbial pea in an oil drum.

Women of childbearing age were encouraged to have as many children as possible. Half a dozen was considered the minimum. But Mother Nature herself would often override with ease any plans made by humans.

My mother, for instance, lost the ability to have any more children with the birth of my youngest sister by Caesarean. (This left my mother and father with a total of three offspring.)

The most radical initiative was the creation of the Mother Houses. Even though I'd been born on the mainland, I'd come to the island as a very young boy.

So I was really a child of the colony myself, didn't care a fig about the morals and social conventions of the Old World, and didn't find the idea of the Mother Houses at all strange.

But when the idea was mooted more than twenty years ago there was outrage; many left the island to join communities on Jersey and Guernsey that adhered to what some considered a stricter moral code. Simply, the plan was that unsighted women of childbearing age would be invited (some said coaxed, others claimed coerced) into becoming professional mothers.

Initially, the project stipulated that a sighted man would have a 'harem' of unsighted women as well as a sighted wife.

Uproar!

But the idea didn't go away.

Instead, under the guidance of 'Matrons' (these were older women, mainly unsighted and all above child-bearing age) professional mothers took over many of the larger country houses. They made it quite clear that these would be governed democratically, yet with strictly no involvement by men — administrative involvement, that was: human biology hadn't yet reached a stage where the female of the species could reproduce without needing at least the bare necessities from the male.

In a nutshell, Mother Houses functioned as self-governing communities of women who were dedicated to producing babies fathered by men *they* chose. Soon the Mother Houses overflowed with new babies. Buildings nearby were converted to nurseries, then, as the children grew, yet more buildings were turned over to schools.

Mother Houses, without a doubt, were here to stay. And I must say I rather liked them. They were always cheerful places, if a bit noisy. And they produced happy, robust children who counted every child in the Mother House as their brother or sister and every woman as 'Mother'.

One development that caught even the Council by surprise was that rather than becoming ghettos for unhappy blind women who couldn't find a sighted husband, the Mother Houses and their occupants were treated with the same kind of respect and admiration as holy orders of nuns had been in the Old World. So much so that many sighted girls who were born on the island elected to join them, even at certain times symbolically 'blinding' themselves by covering their eyes with scarves.

Some of the older members of the community, particularly the narrow-minded, grumbled darkly about the Mother Houses, referring to the Mothers as 'those bloody reverse nuns' or the local House on its hill as 'Mothering Heights', while hinting that the places were hotbeds of sex. But, oddly, that wasn't true. In a strange way the Mothers were mainly perceived as extremely pure and chaste (even though they might bear ten children fathered by ten different men). And they certainly didn't sponge off the rest of the community; in fact, they soon became 'exporters' of produce. My old schoolteacher Mr Pinz-Wilks (who I rather suspect considered that the only civilization of note fell with the departure of the last Roman emperor) commented rather admiringly that the Mothers appeared to him as earthly embodiments of the classical goddess Artemis who was revered not only as the goddess of hunting but also incorporated the apparent dichotomy of opposites in the fact she was worshipped as both divine protector of chastity and of motherhood.

The Mother system worked. It worked beautifully.

The birth rate on the island was strong. Together with the welcome flow of immigrants it helped to swell the island's population to a healthy twenty-six thousand. This was perhaps a quarter of the island's original population before Year One.

Pretty good work, you'd allow, all things considered.

There comes a time, at least once, when father and son speak to each other not as parent and child but man to man. As equals.

For me, this came just a few hours before the whole world was plunged into darkness on that fateful 28 May.

It began as many conversations with my father began. In his greenhouse, as he took a break from those things that had rooted themselves so firmly, and inextricably, into his life.

He poured me a coffee from the thermos, asking 'Tin or china?' while indicating two cups on the work bench.

'Tin.'

'Good choice.' Then he poured the dark liquid, shaking his head wistfully. 'Oh, for the aroma of Colombian coffee beans once more, or maybe a smooth Kenyan blend. Roast acorns . . . whatever new tricks we might learn to flavour them they'll never taste like real coffee.' He filled his pipe with a few shreds of that pale brown Jersey tobacco grown on our largest Channel Island, gazing dreamily at the triffid plants growing in line in their brick troughs, the sunlight shining through the glass onto their leaves. These triffids had had their stingers safely docked and they'd been chained to stakes to prevent them from walking. Even so, they would still give an occasional experimental tug on their chains. Every now and again, a *chink-chink* could be heard as steel links rattled.

As a child I had sensed that there was something thrilling about this place – the smell of the plants under the glass, the warm, almost tropical atmosphere even in winter. I liked to come here and watch my father handling a sharp knife with all the dexterity of a surgeon as he pruned branches, or nicked the stem to gauge the quality of triffid oil that would 'bleed' from the bark like blood that had been diluted to a pale pink.

After a moment spent contemplating the plants he scratched one of his bushy white eyebrows and said, 'You should have heard them talking last night.'

'The triffids?'

My father nodded, and shot me a sidelong smile. 'I've not heard them so active in a long, long while; their sticks were rap-rapping away against their stems like some botanical version of Morse code.'

'Do you think they really can talk? Intelligently, I mean, not just like birds calling to each other?'

'Well, birds and other animals *do* communicate with their own kind – send messages, squawk warnings, whatever.'

'But in a purely instinctual way: they're either sounding a predator alert or trying to attract a mate.'

'True. But I do wonder whether triffids have mastered the art of conveying more complex messages to their own kind.' He pulled deeply on his pipe before exhaling a cloud of blue smoke that swirled up into the sunlight. 'Perhaps they can even explain concepts and ideas to their neighbours.'

'You mean, that triffid over by the door might be passing on a message to one at the other end of the greenhouse along the lines of "Just listen to those two humans, they're talking about us again".'

My father chuckled. 'Maybe, maybe. But I did once work with a man called Lucknor who seemed to develop an intuitive understanding of triffids. He was convinced that they did actually talk to each other and, moreover, that they had a highly developed intelligence.'

'You think he was right?'

'I think he was damn' close.' He scratched that white eyebrow again, an old habit when he was in a contemplative mood. 'But, you know, David . . . I must have dissected thousands of those things and I've yet to find any trace of a nervous system, and I've certainly not had so much as a whiff of anything that could remotely be described as a brain. Still . . . I *have* watched how those plants operate, watched for the last forty years. They move with purpose. They communicate by tapping their sticks against their stems. When they lash out with their stings they "know" to aim for a human's unprotected face. And I've watched them move across the countryside, whole legions of them like infantry on the march; I've seen how they home in on a community, how they lay siege to it.' He sipped his coffee. 'Well, maybe I am stopping short of saying that they are intelligent, but if something has four legs, wags its tail and barks you'd say

44

it was a dog, right? Now those plants there act and react and plan and attack and kill just as if there was some cool intellect hiding somewhere inside them.'

'But can we beat them?'

'Oh, indeed we're going to try. Try our damned hardest.' He gazed at the plants again before shooting a sideways glance at me. 'After all, I don't believe they should inherit the Earth, do you?'

The plants replied for me. Until now they'd been silent, but suddenly they began to tap their sticks against their stems. It sounded like mischievous schoolboys deliberately trying to irritate their teacher by drumming their fingers quickly on the desks as soon as 'Sir' turned his back to chalk a homework assignment on the blackboard.

My father looked at me with a smile.

'And there they go again . . . my children of the soil. Talking.'

I listened to the plants drumming their little sticks. I thought I could hear their rhythm and I sensed a tempo that communicated an urgency now, as if each triffid was passing on a secret message to its neighbour.

At that moment I would have sworn that a sense of excitement had rippled through the twenty or so triffids shackled there in the greenhouse.

My father recognized it, too. When he spoke this time he addressed the triffids themselves. 'What have you heard, then? Has one of your armies conquered another of our human communities? Is Triffid High Command planning to march once more? Are you eager to join them?'

It might have been coincidence, or it might have been their response to my father's questions that he'd delivered in a manner half flippant, half serious, but the rap-rap-rap of stick against stem suddenly swelled into a wave of noise. There was a powerful clamouring; chains rattled as the plants tugged against them. Stems whipped from side to side like corn being blown this way and that by a sudden gale.

I could well have believed at that moment that somehow those plants had just been stirred by a rousing call to arms from one of their kind across the sea. Now, in their own inscrutable way, they responded. The rattling of sticks was their ecstatic applause, their side-to-side swayings were waves of jubilation.

They sensed impending battles. Imminent victories.

I could believe this as easily as I believed that the sun would rise tomorrow.

My father watched this display of triffid noise, movement and – maybe – even emotion. His grey hair caught the sunlight as he shook his head slowly. His face betrayed not one iota of what he himself might be feeling.

After a moment's silence he began, 'David. At the centre of me there has always been this iron-hard core of optimism, but lately . . . I'm beginning to have doubts, you know?'

'But surely we're safe, here on the island, from the triffids?'

'We're holding our own, son. But every now and again I wonder. Perhaps we're really living in the eye of the storm. Secure for the moment, maybe.'

'Then you think that this is some kind of fool's

paradise?' I'd not heard my father express these kind of doubts before; it troubled me. 'That we can't make a go of this community after all?'

'What I will say is this: by sheer good fortune we've been given a breathing space after escaping here from the mainland. A respite. The last twenty-five years have been a lull – a peaceful, even prosperous lull, I'll grant you. But I think we must face a harsher reality: that at some point in the future we shall encounter our greatest challenge yet.'

'But we *are* succeeding here. We have order, commerce, transport, homes, a growing birth rate.'

'Indeed we have – and that is a miracle in its own right. But we've grown complacent. Here we are, safe on our little island. However, we've largely turned our back on the outside world, with the exception of the other English Channel island communities.' He looked at me levelly for a moment. Then he began to speak to me in a low but grave voice. 'David, listen to me. We are a society that has become brilliant at the art of repair. Recycling, refurbishing, renewing. But we are not building from scratch. We don't dig ores out of the ground in order to smelt them into refined metals. If we're not doing that, how can we possibly even begin to build brand new tractors or cars – or even to cast so much as a humble teaspoon? These days, if we can't find a half-decent tractor that was built before the world went blind we cannibalize half a dozen clapped-out old tractors and cobble together just one that will do the job. Those aircraft you fly? The newest one is over thirty years old – *thirty years*, David: they should be museum pieces by now.'

He made a slow chopping motion with his hand to emphasize his words. 'David. Whatever we are achieving isn't enough. We must move forward from scavenging on this – this carrion of a dead civilization. We must begin to invent once more, to develop new machines. And we should be able to do all that from scratch: by mining ore, by smelting, by casting new components – because one day there will be nothing left of the old world to scavenge. Then, without a shadow of a doubt, we shall decline into a new Dark Age. One from which we might never emerge.'

It was suddenly clear to me, startlingly clear. My father foresaw a future devoid of the light of civilization; one engulfed by all the dark terrors such a time of chaos and anarchy would bring.

Later that morning I drove in a carefully maintained forty-year-old boneshaker from the car pool through the sunlit Downs to Shanklin where my flying boat was moored, ready for the short hop across to the mainland. (A flight, you will recall, that would be cut short by the gull's suicide dive.) As I eased the car along the narrow country lanes I thought about what my father had told me. And I wondered what form that new Dark Age would take.

As it was, my contemplation of an impending meta-phorical nightfall was far off the mark. Because the black horrors to come were literal. The darkness actual.

And absolute.

CHAPTER FOUR

Nightlands

I left the post office at a hell of a run. In my left hand I held the lit lamp. In my right, a cupboard door that I'd broken off its hinges, which would, I prayed, serve as a shield if I came within range of a triffid's lashing sting.

The radio operator had told me to sit tight in the post office. But as triffid stings snapped against the panes, leaving spittle-like streaks of poison upon the glass, I realized that to hide myself there in a cowardly funk meant that I would be guilty of manslaughter by default.

The triffids had invaded our island. That much was clear. They had already killed. They would kill again. And nearby must be dozens of unsuspecting islanders. I knew that I had a duty to warn them.

Now I moved as quickly as I could, carrying my light and my shield.

The day was still as black as—well, as night. I could see no more than a few paces in front of me. I realized only too clearly that I wouldn't even see the triffid that might kill me, striking as it could with its ten-foot sting from the darkness beyond the little circle of light cast by the lamp.

An additional problem: I didn't know this area at all well. I did, however, recall that up the hill from Bytewater ran a narrow lane. And that lane ran up through open fields to one of the Mother Houses. There, triffids would find easy targets. Children playing in the grounds; the mothers, some of whom were blind, pushing babies in carriages, or going about their chores.

So I ran through that all-encompassing darkness, my breath rasping in my throat, my heart beating thunderously. All I could see were my pounding feet and a few square feet of road surface beneath them.

Every so often, lying there on the road would be a felled bird or cat that had been taken by the stingingly accurate poison tendril of a triffid. What was more, it became rapidly clear to me that the lethal plants' behavioural patterns had altered. Instead of making a kill and then taking root by its victim in order to feed as putrefaction set in, a triffid would now kill and move on straightaway in a relentless search for new victims. Just what had brought about this new response was anyone's guess but it did mean that they were now even more dangerous.

I ran, straining my eyes to scan ahead, looking for the distinctive eight-foot-tall swaying shape of a killer plant as it sought new prey.

With my nerves stretched taut, I was acutely sensitive to every sound, every movement, every shape glimpsed no matter how fleetingly from the corner of my eye. More than once I ducked, simultaneously raising the cupboard door across my face, only to lower it and discover that I was protecting myself from a road sign or a common hawthorn bush.

I didn't allow myself much pause. In my mind's eye I could see with dreadful clarity those murderous plants moving on their jerky tripedal stumps into the grounds of the Mother House, the stingers whipping through the air to lash the faces of children and grown women alike.

I dreaded reaching the house and standing there with the lamp raised, impotently looking about me at dozens of corpses lying with their arms thrown out, their faces frozen in post-mortem expressions of agony.

Something whistled through the air. Quickly I jerked the cupboard door up in front of my face. A split second later I felt the smack of the stinger strike the other side with enough force to rock me back on my heels.

I heard sticks drumming against stems in the cold certainty that they had found another victim.

But I wasn't going to fall victim to them so easily. Shielding myself with the door I ran on. Another stinger lashed out but missed me as I zigzagged away up the lane.

I was panting hard. My foot ached abominably from when I had slipped down the stairs earlier in Mr Hartlow's house. More than once I nearly dropped the lamp.

And the lamp – that tiny, fragile lamp with its rag wick – was my sole light source. If I should accidentally break it I would be left helplessly blind in those nightlands. I risked a glance at the sky. Even though it must be mid-morning there still wasn't so much as a glimmer of sunlight.

Struggling for breath, grimly carrying the cupboard door that seemed to grow heavier with every step I took, I reached the top of the hill.

The wall that surrounded the old manor house seemed to roll out of nowhere, so feeble was the light of the lamp.

I heard a scraping sound. Heart pounding, I paused, trying to process that sound in my head, striving to match it with an image from memory.

Scrape-scrape . . .

It had to be the movement of a triffid upon the gravel drive.

I pressed my face to the cupboard door, waiting for the blow of the stinger.

'Yes? What do you want?' came a no-nonsense female voice.

I was so surprised at hearing human speech that I froze.

'Hello? Oh, don't be silly. I know there's someone there.'

Then it came again: *scrape-scrape*.

I raised the lamp.

There in the light stood one of the Blind Mothers, recognizable by the distinctive white headscarf they all wore. She was vigorously raking the gravel on the ground, flattening it where carts had formed ruts. Every so often she 'looked' in my direction with eyes that, although sightless, nonetheless revealed a keen intelligence. And while she may have been in her seventieth year she still had a robust energy; the white limestone chippings fair fizzed beneath the tines of that flashing rake.

'Mother . . .' I panted, finding my voice at last and addressing her formally by her title. 'Mother, you must get back into the grounds and close the gates.'

'I must, must I, young man?'

'Yes. There are—'

'And who is giving me such impudent orders?'

'I'm sorry. My name is David Masen.'

'Masen, uhm? Any relation to Mr Bill Masen?'

'Yes, I'm his son.'

'So, Mr Masen junior, why so much dash and breathlessness?'

At that moment my lamp dimmed to a feeble glow. I'd been in such a rush to leave Mr Hartlow's cottage that I'd neglected to check now much oil — triffid oil, ironically enough — remained in its reservoir. Darkness instantly rushed in to within a yard of me, like air pouring in to fill a vacuum. All around me lurked the humped and monstrous shadows of bushes, trees and who knew what else.

'Please, Mother.' I looked this way and that in alarm. I could see nothing now with that lamp. 'Mother. There are triffids coming this way.'

'Triffids?' She sounded astonished and immediately stopped raking. 'This had better be no joke, young man!'

'It isn't, Mother. Please . . . we need to close the gates. They will be here any moment.' I shot a look back the way I'd come. There was nothing behind me but darkness — dreadful darkness.

'Quickly,' she said, realizing the danger. 'You take the left-hand gate. I'll take the right.'

The light from the lamp was dying quickly as the oil

became exhausted. I could barely make out the ornate iron gates that stood a good eight feet high. Nevertheless, when they were closed they sealed the gap in a brick wall of about the same height. I prayed that the wall ran round the entire property – and that there were no more open gates. Triffids, after all, were shrewd enough to follow a barrier until they found an opening. Then they would be inside: poisoning, blinding, killing.

Somewhere in the distance I heard the high, excited voices of children.

As the Mother snapped the padlock onto the gate I said, 'Mother, is there a way to get the children into the house right away? If they get too close to the walls they might still be within reach of the triffids' stings.'

'I'll ring the bell for school,' she said as, with an unerring sense of direction, she hurried along the drive-way. 'Come along, young man, you can help. The children are in high spirits; they say that it is still dark.'

'It is.'

The Mother paused. 'How dark?'

I told her that without a lamp I couldn't see my hand in front of my face.

She considered for a moment. 'First darkness, then triffids . . . it strikes one as being rather a sinister omen, doesn't it?'

At that moment the light from my lamp finally died. Even though we should be safe – for a time, anyway – my stomach spasmed painfully. I had lost the power to see again.

I swallowed. 'Do you have a two-way radio? We need to get in touch with the authorities. I've already warned them about the triffids but we should let them know we're safe for the moment.'

'Indeed we should, Mr Masen. Follow me — we'll go up to the house. It lies just beyond those trees across there.'

'Ah, excuse me, Mother.'

'Why sound so nervous, young man? What's wrong?'

'My lamp has gone out.'

'You mean to say it is so dark that you really can't see a thing?'

'It is, yes.'

'Hmm, this really is rum, isn't it? Well, Mr Masen, allow me to take your arm and I shall be your guide.'

Then that old lady who'd been thirty years blind walked briskly along the driveway, her arm through mine, leading me through the inky dark, our feet crunching on the gravel.

I walked with one hand held in front of me, level with my eyes. Like all people suddenly deprived of sight I was wary of walking into something hard and hurting my face.

'Mr Masen, do you see the lights of the house yet?'

'No. Not a thing.'

'You should in a moment. Perhaps they are still screened by the trees.'

Or perhaps, I told myself fearfully, *the triffids have already slipped in by another entrance to exterminate everyone with their lashing stings.*

'Now, Mr Masen. I hear plenty of news stories about your father's laudable work to root out those bloody plants. However, I've not heard *your* name mentioned at all.'

'That's because I don't work with my father. I haven't his head for science.'

'What do you do, then, Mr Masen? If that doesn't sound too damn' nosy?'

'I'm a pilot.'

'Ah, one of our brave few. But you must find those cockpits awfully cramped. I can tell you're a tall man, well above average height. Six foot two, perhaps?'

'Six foot four.'

'How exceptional.'

She chatted to put me at my ease, knowing as she must have done how uncomfortable it was, to say the least, to be suddenly deprived of one's sight. But the truth of the matter was that I was anything but relaxed. I didn't like this unnatural darkness. I didn't like it one little bit. And, moreover, I knew that the triffids would be hurrying to the house as fast as their woody stumps could carry them, like a pack of starving dogs drawn by the scent of roasting meat.

'Are you married, Mr Masen?'

'No.'

'Not found the right girl?'

'Partly. But sometimes I'm away from the island for weeks at a time. It wouldn't be fair to a wife.'

'Ah, a man of sensitivity as well as of heroic stature. We really must talk later. You're a greater asset to the island than perhaps you yourself realize. Now – how is your mother? I remember long ago reading her novel *Sex is My Adventure* with enormous avidity.'

'She's very well, thank you. Although her writing is now confined to lab reports and the—Wow! I hadn't expected that.'

'The "Wow," I take it, indicates that the floodlights have been switched on?'

The first thing I saw in the wash of light blazing from electric lamps set on posts along the driveway was the Mother's smiling face. The next, as we rounded a dense barrier of bushes, was the grand three-storeyed mansion and children playing on a quadrangle to one side, which was illuminated by a series of more humble electric lamps.

'Well, now you can actually see again perhaps you would help me get these children indoors.' She clapped her hands. 'Timothy, Lucy. Out of that tree at once.' How the devil she could identify individual children playing in the tree mystified me. Then she reached something like a telegraph post set in the ground beside the driveway. Attached to that was a rope. I couldn't see the top of the post as it was lost to the dark. But the moment she tugged on the rope I heard the sound of the bell ringing across the rolling lawns and away into the nightlands beyond the walls.

The children responded to the bell obediently enough. They ran past me, calling in those high, excited voices, thrilled rather than frightened that the sun hadn't risen. As far as I could tell they were streaming into one of the wings of the house where lights shone through the windows.

The Mother still pulled hard on the cord; the bell continued to ring out. It told the children to return to their classrooms. Yet it also sent out a clear signal to the triffids roaming the fields. For them it could have been the peal of the dinner bell. I knew it wouldn't be long before they'd cluster about the gate, pressing against it, testing its strength.

A sighted Mother about twenty years old walked lightly along the drive toward us. 'All the children are indoors now, Mother Susan.'

'Thank you, Mother Angela. Best that you go indoors yourself now. And please ask all the Mothers and auxiliaries to gather in the refectory, I need to speak to you all.'

'Yes, Mother.' After an appraising up-and-down glance at me she returned quickly to the house.

There was nothing else to do now but wait.

Every gate into the grounds had been locked. They'd withstand the triffid assault for an hour or so at the very least, which would give the anti-triffid squads ample time to arrive. Besides, the doors of the house itself were stout enough should any of the plants break through into the grounds.

With nothing else to occupy me I mooched around the ancient building for a while. In the library I noticed above a Jacobean fireplace a stone tablet that had been set into the wall by the builders of the house. There, deeply chiselled, were the words *Sol lucet omnibus*. Helpfully for me the translation had been inscribed below: *The sun shines for everyone*.

Well, no . . . not any more, it didn't.

The world outside was as black as Hades. And who knew how long it would stay like that?

After the library I retraced my steps along the corridor.

From one schoolroom I heard the class singing an old hymn:

> *All things bright and beautiful,*
> *All creatures great and small,*
> *All things wise and wonderful,*
> *The Lord God made them all . . .*

The sound of the children's voices at that moment sent an icy prickle across my skin. They sang, feeling safe and secure in their familiar world. But beyond the walls, out there in the darkness, triffids would hear the rising and falling of the melody. In my mind's eye I saw them. Those grotesque plants, their stems swaying with all the menace of cobras moving to the sounds of a pipe. Only these vicious monstrosities would be far from charmed by the music. Given half a chance they would lash their ten-foot stings into the infants' faces.

The mental image unsettled me. If I'd been in charge I would have been inclined to herd the children into the relative safety of the cellar.

Mother Susan, however, had thought it best not to alarm them. So, with the exception of the darkness beyond the windows, it was business as usual – although I did suggest the precaution of posting a number of sighted Mothers as lookouts. These now patrolled the flat roof of the building. Occasionally, they would report back to a Grand Mother that slender stalks could be seen moving in that characteristic jerky motion beyond the walls.

Later, Mother Susan unerringly tracked me down to

the refectory where I was being fortified with tea and toast. Joining me at one of the long tables she said briskly, 'Mr Masen, I usually find it best to ask this straight. Are you registered with any of the Mother Houses?'

'Registered?' I asked, deliberately playing dumb.

'Now, now, don't be coy with me, Mr Masen, you know perfectly well what I mean. Come now, are you registered?'

'No, I'm not.'

'But the island's population would benefit enormously from such fine blood as yours.'

'Well, I don't know if—'

'You have no philosophical objections to eugenics?'

'No, but—'

'Well, that's settled then. After this storm in a tea cup has blown itself out, and once we've returned to our proper routine you must call on us as our guest for dinner.'

'I'm due to fly out to—'

'Oh, there'll be no pressure, Mr Masen,' she said with a bright smile. 'Would next Friday suit?'

'Er, I'm not sure . . .'

'Excellent! Next Friday it is, then. And just you remember: the oats you sow needn't necessarily all be wild ones. Right, I'll leave you to your toast. And do try the gooseberry jam – it is sublime.'

As she climbed to her feet she smiled before adding breezily, 'Now, it's not every day you're invited to contribute in such a physical way to repopulating the world, is it?'

'Er, no . . . no, it's not.'

She left me feeling a trifle dazed and with her extraordinary invitation still hanging in the air. I would certainly have to think *that* one over for a bit.

At that moment, despite the shock of finding myself in darkness when there should have been daylight, and my alarm at the incursion of triffids that had crossed the Solent to land on the beach at Bytewater, I still believed that my life would, sooner or later, go on as before. I would continue to ferry passengers by air to the Scillies, Jersey and Guernsey, and make rarer forays deep into the mainland. I had no idea when I woke to the nightlands that all of that was over – the future I had envisaged dashed to pieces and then swept away like so much broken glass.

Later that day the anti-triffid squads arrived in their protective gear, armed with triffid guns. These teams of men and women were mustered from every walk of life. As soon as the triffid alert sounded they would have dropped whatever they were doing and rushed to their designated assembly points, ready to deal with any triffid attack. With their appearance I remained convinced that life would soon return to normal.

From an upper window of the Mother House I watched as vehicles closed in on the plants, their head-lights blazing. Within minutes the triffids were being efficiently decapitated, thus depriving them of their ability to sting. Then, one by one, they were toppled and their stumpy timber legs were hacked away. After that, the stems and woody boles were hauled off to be processed and pulped as if they were nothing more sinister than bales of waste paper.

Within a few hours the island had been cleared of the triffid invasion. Triumphant radio broadcasts trumpeted the news.

But there were still ominous question marks hanging in the dark skies above us.

What had happened to the daylight?

Just where had the triffids come from so suddenly, and so murderously?

But as things fell out, I wouldn't have to wait long for some answers. That afternoon I received an urgent message to report to my airbase at once.

Little did I know that the short trip there was to be the first leg of the most remarkable journey of my life.

CHAPTER FIVE

To Dark Skies

By three-thirty that afternoon the pace of events was hotting up.

A weather-beaten but mechanically sound staff car brought me back from the Mother House at Bytewater to my airbase on the other side of the island.

With the world still immersed in inky darkness floodlights blazed, illuminating the aircraft hangars and the runway.

I was greeted by the airbase commander's PA who told me to suit up immediately. I was to take up our only Panther jet fighter and determine just how far the cloud cover extended.

'Heard you were taken out by a seagull, Masen!' The cheery voice of 'Mitch' Mitchell greeted me the moment I stepped through the door into the locker room. He was a tiny man, yet had long wiry arms that sometimes earned him the extra sobriquet 'Monkey'. From a radio in the corner a selection of jaunty Noël Coward show songs rattled the windows. Island Radio was doing its bit to raise spirits. An ironic 'A Room with a View' was followed by a hastily composed pastiche called 'Don't Let's Be Beastly to the Triffid'.

Mitch Mitchell lobbed a biscuit at me, then returned to pouring boiling water into a teapot. 'This seagull, then. What was she toting? Thirty-millimetre cannon or air-to-air rockets?'

'Very funny, Mitch.'

'Much damage?'

'Smashed prop. She'll be airworthy by tomorrow.'

'So you get the hero's job, I hear?'

'I don't like the sound of that.'

'You'll be front-page news tomorrow, sunshine.'

'For all the right reasons, I hope.'

'The girls will be queuing, old cock.'

'You really think so?'

'Dead cert, mate. Then chocks away, open your throttle and you'll be into the wide blue yonder with more skirt than you can shake a stick at.'

'But heroes have a habit of winding up very dead, very quickly.'

It was our typical kind of banter. I'd gone through pilot school with Mitch, and by now we'd developed a kind of patois of our own that outsiders often found baffling. As we knocked one-liners back and forth like tennis players enjoying a sustained rally I changed into my pressure suit.

Made of vulcanized heavy-duty cotton with neoprene collar and cuffs it fitted as closely as a second skin. From the hip dangled a length of hose that would be connected to the aircraft's air supply.

'Any news on what's causing the blackout?' I asked.

'There've been bulletins on the radio, suggesting it's just a thick layer of cloud—'

'Heck of a thick layer.'

'Tea?'

'Thanks.'

'Only, if you ask me, David, this thing's got the boffins foxed. Which machine are you taking up?'

'The Panther.'

'Lucky devil; the gods are smiling on you, old son.'

'Let's hope so.' I finished pulling the heavy-duty zip across my chest.

Just then the commander's PA poked her head around the door.

'Are you decent?'

'As he'll ever be,' Mitch quipped.

'Change of plan,' she told me. 'The Old Man's ordered ground crew to pull out the Javelin.'

'The Javelin? That's a two-seater. What made him change his mind?'

'Don't ask me.' She flashed a cherry-red lipsticked smile. 'I only work here.'

'Maybe they want me to hold your hand, David.' Mitch grinned. 'I can shoo away all those big nasty birds that keep attacking you.'

'Maybe,' I agreed. 'Perhaps you'd better suit up, too.'

'Wow, they're going to make me a hero as well,' he exclaimed. 'Those girls are gonna flock around me, just you wait and see, mate.' As he began to loosen his tie he called across to the pretty PA who was just leaving. 'Hey, gorgeous. I've got an idea: why don't I pick you up around eight tonight?'

'I've got a better idea.' She shot him a smile. 'Don't bother.'

Mitch shrugged, then winked at me. 'Well, she didn't exactly say no, did she?'

Mitch's efforts to wriggle into the pressure suit were wasted. When we presented ourselves at the Old Man's office it was to hear that I would be taking a passenger with me in the two-seater jet fighter.

By then it had started to rain. The sound of raindrops drumming on the corrugated-iron roof was somehow ominous.

Commander Reynolds, better known as the Old Man, was sixty-five if he was a day and so heavily jowled that he looked like an old bulldog just roused from a deep sleep.

'Masen,' growled the Old Man. 'This is Mr Hinkman.'

A bright-eyed young man standing by the desk bobbed his head and held out his hand. There was an eager air about him; he looked like a fresh-faced student who'd just been awarded his first assignment.

'Mr Hinkman is a meteorologist,' continued the Old Man in his characteristic slow growl. 'That means weather's his forte. He'll be taking the navigation seat.'

'Yessir,' I said, a little reluctantly. 'But can I ask if Mr Hinkman's had any experience of flying in a jet fighter?'

'Not that—'

Even though the eager young meteorologist had begun to speak the Old Man growled over the top of his reply. 'None, I dare say. Not that he needs it. He'll sit behind you in the cockpit, Masen. Make notes, photograph what needs photographing, that kind of thing.'

'Yessir.'

'Any questions?'

'No, sir . . . well, that is . . .'

'Yes, Masen?'

'Do we have any idea yet what's causing the darkness, sir?'

The rain drummed harder against the roof as the Old Man thoughtfully scratched one of his pendulous jowls. 'Personally I've never seen anything like it. Too dark for normal cloud; the closest I've come to this kind of blackout in daytime was in Suez. Damned sandstorm blew up so hard you couldn't see your hand in front of your face. Mr Hinkman?'

Mr Hinkman realized he was being invited to contribute to the discussion. Eagerly, eyes shining, he launched in. 'Commander Reynolds may have hit the nail on the head. The clouds we are familiar with in this part of the world are composed of water or ice particles that don't entirely obscure the light. However, sandstorms are composed of, ah, naturally enough, *sand* particles. These make a far better barrier against light, and quite literally block out the sun.'

The Old Man looked surprised. 'Sandstorms? On the Isle of Wight? Surely you're not serious!'

'Well, not sandstorms as such, Commander. But for daylight to be reduced by . . . well, ah, by one hundred per cent, then we're looking at a pretty unusual phenomenon.'

'And your job, Messrs Masen and Hinkman, is to solve this particular mystery.'

Hinkman had begun speaking again about airborne particles but the Old Man was peering gravely at his watch. 'Sixteen hundred hours. And if I'm not mistaken I can hear the engines of your aircraft. Godspeed, gentlemen.'

A man of few words, he shook Hinkman's hand, then mine. 'God-awful weather, Masen. I'm sorry to send you up in muck like this, but needs must and all that.'

Rain drummed against the roof and through the window I fancied I glimpsed a blue-white flicker of lightning.

Although those dark skies were far from friendly, I had an appointment with them that would not wait.

At a little after four-thirty we were ensconced in the cockpit as the jet plane sat on the runway waiting for take-off clearance from the control tower.

As I sat in the pilot's seat, Hinkman, sitting behind me, hardly paused for breath. Although he was similarly clad in helmet and flyer's pressure suit, which must have been strange to him, his chatter was fluent and rapid.

'There are ten principal cloud forms,' he said. 'From the nimbostratus that forms at a relatively low level up through to the high clouds of cirrus and cirrostratus and so forth that can exist at an altitude of 16,000 feet.'

I continued my pre-flight checks as he talked. Meanwhile the rain rattled fiercely against the perspex canopy of the jet. Already the odour of aviation fuel hung in the air. A distillation of triffid oil, it smelled sweet, like pears baking in a pie.

'I fully expect the obscuring layer of cloud will begin at low level,' Hinkman was saying. 'But as it is clearly the variety of cloud known as cumulonimbus that is producing this thunderstorm, it may well extend upwards to a height in excess of 20,000 feet.'

As if the elements wished to concur with the meteorologist's observation a fork of lightning tore across the sky. A moment later a peal of thunder buffeted the aircraft as it stood on the runway.

'Mr Masen?'

'Yes?'

'Our plan is elegant in its simplicity. You're to fly the plane up through the cloud until we reach unbroken sunlight so that we can determine the extent of the blackout layer.'

'I understand.'

'This aircraft can reach an altitude of twenty thousand feet?'

'It has a ceiling of about *fifty* thousand feet. Will that be high enough for you, Mr Hinkman?'

'Yes . . . yes, it will be.'

I now detected a certain falling-off in Hinkman's enthusiasm.

Another burst of lightning flooded the landscape with electric blue light. Trees, momentarily in silhoutte, looked like great shaggy beasts massing for attack. A potent image. Chilling, too.

'Ah, Mr Masen . . .'

'David, please.'

'Oh, yes, quite, quite. Then please call me Seymour.'

'Yes, Seymour?'

'The thunderstorm, I can't help but noticing, seems rather severe.'

'It's a real humdinger, isn't it, Seymour?'

'Ah . . . yes.' I heard a pale imitation of a laugh in my earpiece. 'It is that, David. Uhm, I just wondered . . .'

'Yes?'

'Should we actually be flying in this weather?'

'As Commander Reynolds said: Needs must.'

'Ah, yes, he did.'

'And we *do* want to get to the bottom of this infernal blackout?'

'Yes, yes, of course. Uhm . . . but isn't . . . isn't it possible our aircraft will be struck by lightning?'

'No. I'd say it's not a possibility, Seymour. I'd say it was a certainty.'

'Oh, my goodness.'

'Don't worry. I crashed a plane yesterday, so I don't think I'll be that unlucky for it to happen again today, do you?'

'I . . . uhm . . .'

'There's the green light. Hang on tight, Seymour. This baby can really move.'

I thought he'd begun to say something; it may even have been a prayer. But the roar of the engines drowned out his words. A moment later we soared towards whatever lay above us.

CHAPTER SIX

Recce

When all was said and done, I had expected a routine flight. What I discovered a few short moments later gave me ample food for thought.

True, these were no ordinary conditions. The weather was atrocious. And, true, I'd taken off in absolute darkness with Seymour Hinkman, the now extremely introspective – and oh-so-silent – meteorologist. Nevertheless, this plane, the Gloster Javelin, was an all-weather and night fighter designed to cope ably with sorties even in the midwinter Arctic.

So, up and up I soared.

Five thousand feet, six thousand, seven thousand . . .

And still darkness seemingly everlasting.

Periodically I radioed base. But there was little to report.

Ten thousand, twelve thousand, fourteen thousand feet.

By now I was taking the plane in long, twenty-mile circles around an invisible Isle of Wight below. I continued to soar upward, the engines howling. What little water remained on the canopy was scoured away by the six-hundred-mile-an-hour blast of air.

Eighteen thousand feet.

The altimeter raced, higher and higher figures rolling across the counter.

I heard a small voice in my ear.

'David . . . uhm, D–David . . . we came through it all right?'

'The storm? Yes, no problems.'

'We weren't struck by lightning?'

'We were hit six times.'

'Six?' His voice suddenly sounded strangled. '*Six?*'

'Six,' I confirmed calmly. 'Don't worry. It made the instruments a bit lively. But because we weren't earthed there was no damage.'

'Thank heaven,' he breathed.

I couldn't see his face when I glanced back because of his helmet, visor and oxygen mask but I could see his head turning from left to right. Evidently he'd now mastered his fear enough to take an interest in his surroundings once more. 'How high are we, exactly?' he asked.

'Coming up to twenty thousand feet.'

'We should be nearing the top of the cloud any moment now.'

'See anything?'

'Not a dicky bird. And you?'

'Nothing. I'll continue ascending.'

'You'll be . . . uhm, able to find your way back?'

'Don't worry, I'm in radio contact with the ground

and they have us nice and square in their radar screen. We're directly above Winchester now.'

'Winchester,' Seymour echoed. 'Good grief. My father was sports master at a school there. You know, he escaped the Blinding because he took a dive from a polo pony the day before the lights appeared in the sky. Knocked him cold for forty-eight hours.'

I found myself warming to Seymour. The little dose of fear inculcated by our taking off in a thunderstorm had humanized him no end.

'I'm banking to the right now,' I told him. 'That will take us south toward the coast again. How're you feeling?'

'Fine, thanks. Well . . . a little queasy around the gills but I think it's passing.'

A moment later the white numerals clicked past the twenty-five thou mark.

'Seymour. Twenty-five thousand feet.'

'I dare say we've found ourselves some record-breaking clouds, David. We should be . . . wait . . . just wait a moment.' His voice became hushed. 'I can see cloud shapes — we must be nearly above it.'

I looked upward, searching for a milky glow of sunlight penetrating the cloud. There was nothing yet. Increasing the thrust of the twin Sapphire turbojets I climbed still higher.

Twenty-six thousand feet . . . twenty-seven, twenty-eight.

Any moment now, I told myself. Any moment we'd erupt into a vista of sunlight cascading onto a cotton-wool cloudscape.

Thirty thousand feet: I pulled back the stick and piled on the power. Now the plane sat on its tail while hurtling straight up like a skyrocket.

At thirty-three thousand feet we were free of the cloud.

'Oh . . .' Seymour's voice in my earpiece was one of puzzlement, even disappointment.

We'd left the cloud, but we'd found no light.

At least, not the kind of light we'd expected.

A profound transformation had been wrought upon the world.

'What . . . I . . . I don't understand . . .'

I was hearing Seymour's voice. But my attention was focused on the light in the sky.

Imagine a dying ember. Imagine it just moments before the glow goes from the ash. There is a redness, but it is a dull, dull red that promises nothing but the dying of the fire.

The light I saw reminded me of that kind of dying glow. For all I could see – from the edge of one horizon across the full arc of the sky to the next horizon – was that same musky red. It gave precious little illumination. And it looked cold. Even more deathly cold than it was anyway at that height. The air moaned over the wings of the plane in a near-funereal dirge. One that gave voice to my own suddenly apprehensive feelings.

'I don't understand,' Seymour said. 'The cloud lies below us. So where is the sun?'

For half an hour we circled high in that sombre sky. Its profoundly muted redness gave forth little light.

I glanced along the metal wings of the plane. Above the clouds in daytime sparkling sunlight would usually dance along its length from root to tip. Now the light turned the once silvery surface to the colour of rust.

'So, it can't be ordinary cloud that's responsible for the darkness,' I ventured at length. 'At least, not thunder-clouds.'

'No,' Seymour agreed. 'They've exacerbated it, there's no doubt about that. But there must be another cloud layer even higher up that's obscuring the sun.'

'But you said the cloud would probably be no higher than twenty-five thousand feet?'

'Yes, that is true. But fly higher if you can.'

I did take the plane up higher. In fact, right to its maximum ceiling of fifty-five thousand feet where no audible engine noise reached the cockpit through the rarefied atmosphere. Here the sky should have been near-black rather than blue. But there was only that gloomy red.

Even if we'd somehow mistaken the time and flown after sunset we would have seen a brilliant display of diamond-bright stars. It was as if the gods themselves had grown weary of the Earth and drawn a red shroud across its face.

For some moments I talked to HQ; I half fancied I could hear the Old Man in the background, growling instructions to the ground controller. Every so often a splash of static sounded in my ear as lightning played merry hell in the heavens above the aerodrome. Behind me, Seymour made his notes and took his photographs.

I glanced at the fuel gauges. The needles indicated the tanks were a quarter full.

Our time was up. I told Seymour to stow the camera. We were going home.

I eased back on the power and allowed the plane to descend. Until the very last moments of approach I would be landing blind. The control tower would have to talk me in until I could see the strip's landing lights.

Already in my mind's eye I could see the radar controller poring over his screen, watching the fat blip of light that was our signal.

Behind me, Seymour was a little livelier and, although I imagine he was thinking aloud rather than talking to me, he was speculating about the cause of the loss of sunlight. 'Volcanic eruptions can fling out debris into the higher atmosphere, resulting in some sunlight blockage. But never to this degree — at least, not in living memory. The eruption of Krakatoa significantly reduced the amount of sunlight reaching the surface of the Earth: this in turn resulted in lower temperatures globally and that meant a succession of fearful winters and cool summers. But *this* is unprecedented. To go further, we might speculate that—'

In my earpiece I heard ground control. 'Reduce altitude to fifteen thousand feet, continue your speed of four hundred knots, maintain course setting of—'

Again there was a rush of static in my ear that sounded like a wave breaking against a sea wall.

I waited for the return of the ground controller's steady voice.

Static still hissed.

'. . . Therefore,' Seymour was saying, 'clearly neither water nor ice particles are responsible for this acute diminution of sunlight. If volcanic eruptions aren't responsible then we're forced to—'

'Ground control,' I said quickly. 'Am no longer receiving. Over.'

A rush of static. But no voice.

'Ground control. Do you read me? Over.'

'The quantity of debris in the upper atmosphere must be phenomenal. One could—'

'Seymour,' I said sharply.

'Uhm?'

'We've a problem.'

'What kind of problem?' He spoke almost dreamily, obviously still running through his own mental calculations.

'I've lost contact with ground control.'

'Is that serious?'

'Yes. Very.'

'Try again.'

'I have. They're not responding.'

I opened the throttle and the sharp cone of the fighter's nose lifted. The altimeter reversed its downward progress as we regained height.

'We're climbing,' Seymour said unnecessarily. 'We need to land, don't we?'

'We do. But preferably on the runway – not in someone's cabbage patch.'

'You mean we can't land until we re-establish radio contact?'

'Something like that,' I said tightly. 'I'm going to circle for a few moments while they — I hope — cure their technical hiccup.'

And so we circled for ten minutes . . .

Twelve minutes.

Fifteen, sixteen.

The fuel gauges crept towards that ominous red zone. Still no radio contact.

And still no light beyond the canopy. Not even that dreary red sky. It lay high above the cloud we now swam through. The Javelin was like an eel slithering through the silt bed of a particularly mucky river.

After seventeen minutes I told Seymour, 'If we stay up here much longer we'll have to get out and walk.'

'Pardon?'

'Don't worry, an old flyer's joke.' I eased the stick forward and the plane descended. I was going to add something about how to use the ejector seat if the fuel ran out. But in this murk, and bearing in mind that Seymour was a complete novice at flying, it might have been kinder simply to put a pistol to his head.

With radio contact lost I'd have to rely on some dead reckoning to get me within eyeball contact of the runway lights. Before take-off I'd seen a couple of rocket flares fired that showed the clearance between ground and cloud was about a thousand feet.

If I took this crate down carefully I could skate in on the underside of the cloud without any real danger of flying into the side of a hill or anything. While an altimeter at that height is no longer a precise instrument, the Gloster Javelin did have a brace of extremely powerful landing lights. Even at a thousand feet I'd be able to see if we were over dry land or water.

Steadily, I took the plane down to the thousand-feet mark.

I had perhaps seven minutes' fuel left.

Any kind of landing in those circumstances would, inevitably, be a rough one.

I had worked out that I'd flown in a large circle in my climb above the clouds. In the centre of that circle, along a line of radius of some fifteen or so miles, lay the Isle of Wight. It seemed to me that if I headed along that line at an altitude of around a thousand feet I would see the runway lights, and if not those at any rate the lights of towns and villages.

But I hadn't counted on the weather being even filthier than before.

Raindrops rattled against the perspex canopy like machine-gun bullets. The aircraft's own landing lights only revealed swathes of yet more rain that twisted and curled like smoke.

It *seemed* that I had three options — at least, when it came to flying.

Option one: to fly through the swirling rain and turmoil of winds that buffeted the plane.

Option two: to fly in the utter darkness of the clouds.

Option three: to eschew the clouds and darkness altogether for the dull red heavens above. (I use the word 'heaven' in the sense of a realm high above your head — if anything, that region above the clouds was more reminiscent of hell: a chillingly gloomy hell, at that.)

But, in fact, my airborne options were rapidly decreasing. With my fuel indicators nearing zero and still no resumption of contact with ground control I actually had no choice but to continue skimming the underside of the storm clouds. I flew for a good thirty seconds or so at around three hundred knots, the turbulence buffeting the plane like a breeze would a feather. The sheeting rain dazzlingly reflected the plane's lights. Slipstream howled mournfully over the wings.

My heartbeat increased; perspiration slid unpleasantly down my chest.

I now abandoned options two and three. I descended. Still I could see no ground below. And yet at this height (the altimeter was at all but zero) I could easily bury this thirty-year-old aircraft into the side of one of the Isle of Wight's gently rolling hills.

'David . . . David, can you see the runway yet?'

'No.' But then, I could see damn-all anyway.

I throttled back again, taking the airspeed down to two-fifty. The plane's nose dropped a little, and we were a few feet closer to terra firma.

'Good grief,' I gasped.

'What's wrong?' Seymour called.

'Sea,' I said tersely. Just feet below us I had suddenly seen waves.

They were white-flecked; the sudden gusts of wind had stirred up the sea into a boiling mass.

I had to keep a steady nerve. There was no point in taking the plane higher. Our fuel was all but gone in any case. Besides, if I lost sight of the sea I wouldn't know when we did reach land. I banked left, the plane's port wing-tip almost top-slicing the waves. A moment later the nose was pointing north. Now I must reach land. Either our island or the mainland. Not that it mattered now.

I'd have to land the plane in the next sixty seconds or we risked getting more than our feet wet.

'David, I think . . .'

'Please, not now, Seymour. I'm going to have to do some concentrating for the next minute.'

He clammed up.

In the lights beneath me, the sea raged. I fancied I could even see individual spray droplets flying up towards the aircraft.

A red light winked on the control panel beneath the fuel gauge. You didn't have to be an aviation expert to know what that meant. I eased the throttle back, trying to conserve the precious splash of fuel that by now could barely have wetted the bottom of the tank.

Nice and easy does it . . .

Ahead. A darker mass. One that didn't reflect the lights.

I told myself that if it wasn't land I'd eat my hat, with my plimsolls for pudding.

I could see no outcrops of rock, no trees or houses. It looked like flat pasture down there. There was no chance of going in with the undercarriage lowered. If the nose wheel hit so much as a rut or a rabbit hole we'd cartwheel. We'd have to slide in on the plane's smooth belly.

'Hold on tight,' I said. 'We're going in.'

The landing made me lose interest for a while in pretty much everything this big, wide world had to offer.

Eventually, I opened my eyes and thought I was waking in bed.

But I could hear rattling sounds against my skull. Gingerly, I probed my head with my fingers. It was numb – no sensation whatsoever. My fingers were numb, too.

Then, in a sudden moment of clear awareness, I realized that I was still sitting in the aircraft. The rattling sounds were rain drops falling on my aluminum flying helmet. Someone had raised the cockpit canopy.

My neck ached. And the way pains were shooting up my shins didn't bode well, either. I released the harness and groaned.

'David,' a voice shouted above the sound of the tapping rain. 'Are you all right?'

I nodded. That made my neck ache, but at least everything moved as it should have. 'Seymour?' I called back.

'Yes?'

'Are you still in the plane?'

'Yes. I thought I'd wait here until you came round.'

'Good God. How long have you been sitting there?'

'About half an hour.'

'You idiot. There might still be enough fuel in the tanks to blow us sky-high. Why didn't you get out?'

'I didn't realize. Sorry.'

Now that my senses were returning to normal I saw that although it was still as black as Hades outside the plane the rain was easing. I reckoned we had much to thank it for. It had damped down any fires and cooled hot metal that might otherwise have ignited what fuel remained, burning us to cinders.

I went through the motions of checking the radio, but my pessimistic suspicions were soon confirmed. It had been well and truly busted by the crash landing. I told Seymour to climb out of the plane. Still in our helmets we slithered over the metal surfaces and onto the ground, every movement making me wince and groan.

Not only was that ground soggy, it squelched softly underfoot. Evidently I'd put us down in a marsh. But where we were on the island – or, indeed, the mainland – was anyone's guess. Normally, I'd have suggested that we should wait until first light. But since first or any other light might not come we had little choice but to slog on by foot to the nearest farmhouse or cottage and get word to the airbase from there.

For a moment I carefully tested my legs. Although my shins ached like fury they certainly weren't broken; I was pretty sure that when I came to get undressed I'd find an attractive marbling of bruises in eye-catching shades of blue and green.

I glanced back at the Javelin. The cockpit light was still on so there was enough light to see that the plane was more or less intact. Admittedly, one wing did lie back flush with the fuselage and greenery bearded the pointed nose. But it hadn't been a *catastrophic* landing, considering. Seymour and I were intact, at least.

'There are torches in the emergency kit,' I told Seymour. 'I'll get those, then we'll start walking.'

'In which direction?' He pulled off his helmet and stood there, looking lost in the light thrown from the cockpit. 'We don't know which way to go.'

'Due south. If we're on the mainland that will take us

to the coast. If we're on the island, there's still no harm done. We'll probably find an inhabited house *en route*.'

Seymour wiped his forehead. I expect there was a good bit of perspiration mixed with the rainwater. 'I think I could do with a cup of tea,' he said in a small voice.

'I'll second that, Seymour.'

With that, I went to collect a pair of torches from the plane. When I returned I found that Seymour Hinkman, the eager young meteorologist, was dead.

CHAPTER SEVEN

Isolation

In the morning I opened my eyes to find that I was no longer alone.

There, through the cockpit canopy, I could see sinister swaying shapes. Dozens of triffids had congregated around the downed plane, eager as a pack of hungry hounds at feeding time.

More joined them. I could see their forms lurching across the marsh toward me, their leaves shivering and shaking with every step.

I watched for a while, hypnotized by the sight of so many of these ambulatory plants on the march. Perhaps at that moment I experienced a certain empathy with a mouse transfixed by the gimlet stare of a cat. For I knew, without a doubt, that these plants had targeted me as their next square meal.

Already the body of the young meteorologist, Hinkman, had vanished beneath the triffid greenery. What had happened to him there was something upon which I chose not to dwell too closely.

That I'd managed to sleep at all in such circumstances – hunched up in the cramped confines of the cockpit after the crash landing, horrified at the manner of Hinkman's death, and besieged by triffids – was remarkable. I put it down to the after-effects of sheer trauma. In the direst of straits the human body will seek respite in sleep. A rested body, after all, is in far better shape to survive than an exhausted one.

As I looked round at the *things* that now crowded up against the grounded Javelin it suddenly occurred to me that a marvellous thing had happened. *I could see.*

Light had returned to the world.

I stirred myself; my heartbeat speeded up.

At least I had a little more to be optimistic about. True, the sun only revealed itself as a dim disc no brighter than a piece of foil pasted against the sky. A dull red sky, at that. But at least I could see my surroundings. The upper atmosphere was mainly free of cloud, with the exception of a few streaks of high cirrus – which, peculiarly, revealed themselves as parallel black lines across the sky.

The sudden turning of my head to look this way and that excited the triffids into action. Instantly they smashed their stingers down on the jet's transparent canopy in a rain of vicious blows; each stinger left a smear of sticky poison on the perspex until I could hardly see through it at all.

The aircraft's ammunition magazines had been left deliberately empty to reduce weight and so extend the flight's duration. A pity: I would have dearly loved to press that red button on the flight-stick and blow those murdering plants to merry hell.

For a moment I sat still, controlling my furious breathing. I had to think clearly and decide what my next plan of action would be. When I stopped moving, the blows against the canopy subsided.

Soon there was silence, apart from a light tapping as the triffids exercised their stumpy little 'finger' sticks against their boles.

I found myself thinking about what my father had said. *The plants are talking,* he had told me. *They talk to each other, exchange information, make plans, perhaps even give voice to their dreams of world domination and the extinction of Man.* For the first time, I really understood what he had told me. And I believed.

Those infernal plants were intelligent. Even now they were singing out to their neighbours.

Here is Man.

Come, join the feast!

To remain there was death.

I had no doubt about that as I sat in the jet's cockpit, surrounded by thirty or more triffids, the reddish light of day glinting dully on their leaves.

Clearly, the plane had come down on the mainland. Equally clearly, I couldn't simply just wait to be rescued. The community's resources for mounting a search for a downed plane were severely limited. If the thunderstorm had knocked out the island's radar as well as the radio link then they would have only the haziest idea where to begin looking – in poor light amid hundreds of square miles of overgrown countryside, too.

Outside, the triffids' tapping grew a little faster, a little louder. It was almost as if they sensed I would have to act soon.

I had to think my plan through logically.

First, I must leave the plane so that I could begin my walk south to the coast.

I was sure that the triffids would strike at me the moment I opened the canopy. However, I was still wearing the all-in-one pressure suit. It was made of a thick rubberized cotton, and once I'd donned my gloves and helmet with its full-face perspex visor there wouldn't be so much as a tenth of a square inch of skin exposed.

In theory I was as safe as houses. But what if the poison should soak through the material? Or what if I should feel stifled and be forced to raise the visor?

If I thought about this any more, I reckoned, my nerve might fail me. There was nothing for it but to slip on my helmet and gloves. Then take a little walk.

After carefully fastening my helmet (the visor locked into the 'down' position) and making sure that my gloves made an airtight seal with the rubber cuffs of the flying suit, I cracked open the cockpit.

I found myself holding my breath as I swung myself out of my seat and climbed out of the plane. I moved as if I was trying to steady my nerves for a leap into icy water.

In a flash, the stingers whipped at me. Even though the poison couldn't penetrate my heavy-duty pressure suit the force of the blows against my body was enough to make my skin smart, while strikes to the helmet set the crash-strained muscles of my neck throbbing unpleasantly.

In a moment I was on the ground and pushing through the fleshy leaves like an explorer forging through virgin jungle. My visor was smeared in seconds with splashed venom as stingers struck, reducing the world beyond to a blurred red tableau of moving shadows.

I glimpsed the boots of the dead man, the legs already shrunken. Modern triffids made short work of their prey.

Then, thank Heaven, I was through the crush of plants. Even so, I felt the stingers crack against my back like whips as I fled.

I wiped poison from the visor with the back of my glove. With a slightly better view I could move faster, so I lost no time escaping the cluster of triffids around the plane.

The landscape in front of me was flat – very flat – and surprisingly springy underfoot. It was as if I was walking across a giant mattress.

The reason for this was depressingly simple – or so I thought. I knew that much of the low-lying land of southern England had been marshland long ago, only being drained in the Middle Ages or even later. With the disappearance of electric drainage pumps and with ditches becoming blocked by silt, the water table was creeping back to its original levels, slowly but surely returning farmland to bog.

I paused for a moment to check my revolver, as well as the emergency rations that I carried over one shoulder in a canvas satchel. After that, I turned my attention to the pocket compass. When I had due south, I sighted it on the murky red horizon and began to walk.

There was precious little to see close by as I walked. Only scrubby vegetation – no proper trees, no houses, no roads. With the horizon obscured by a rust-coloured mist and my smeared visor not helping visibility one jot I saw nothing in the distance, either.

I'd been walking for barely five minutes when I saw where land ended and sea began.

Just as I was telling myself that this must be the Solent that separated mainland England from the Isle of Wight it struck me that I couldn't be further from the truth.

Here was something I'd never seen before.

The land didn't end at a cliff and there was no beach. Oddly, the land just frayed away at the edges, looking as if it had decayed into fibres – fibres that were being washed this way and that by the surf.

As I walked, slowly now, towards its edge, the ground became even more springy beneath my feet. Now and again my boot broke through the turf into liquid beneath.

Once more I wiped at the visor. Although this made it only a bit cleaner I saw now that this ragged shore extended to my left and right perhaps a hundred yards or so before running back behind me. I might have described this as a headland, but now I realized that the word 'land' was, at best, an approximation.

This 'land' was counterfeit. It was a freak of nature.

Cautiously, I moved on towards the sea. Its waters glinted with dull oranges and reds, reflecting that sombre sky; even the foam whipped by a fresh breeze was the colour of rust. Crabs the size of dinner plates, with dull green shells, side-scuttled across the weed.

In heaven's name, what kind of world had I been thrown into?

I asked myself this again and again as I carefully

worked my way towards the shoreline, hoping that soon I'd see a stretch of sand or rocks.

But no.

I watched as a larger wave hit the shore. It didn't break so much as pass beneath the 'land' I stood on. I felt the huge, slow ripple as it moved under the soles of my flying boots and on inland.

It happened again. Then again. Good grief. This wasn't solid land at all. It was an undulating mass of vegetation. A huge one, floating on the sea, rising and falling in harmony with the waves.

I returned 'inland' to where the vegetation might be thicker and hence more likely to support my weight. For this was nothing more than a colossal raft formed from driftwood and held together by a thin layer of turf. Beneath it lay only cold salt-water depths.

Still, I cherished a hope that this vast floating mat of vegetation *might* still be attached to solid land. But investigation, carried out during an hour's walk around its outer edges, soon gave a pretty clear picture of the truth. My 'island' drifted freely in the sea.

Now, I could see how a mainland Britain largely untenanted by human life would become overgrown; silted rivers would alter their courses; cities might sink into waterlogged foundations. However, the idea that perhaps a huge logjam might build up in a river, become overgrown with turf, then simply break away to become a free-floating raft fifty or sixty acres in area seemed just that bit remarkable.

A hundred yards away I saw a copse of triffids, their leaves swaying in the breeze. They were otherwise unmoving, content perhaps to stand with their roots dug in and to wait. Was this great flexible raft their invention? Maybe they had brains in their woody boles, after all. Perhaps they had evolved at such a rate that in the past twenty or thirty years they had developed intellect; that individual plants had already acquired specialist skills. Triffid warlords? Triffid technicians? Triffid engineers? Engineers whose role it was to plan, to build and even to navigate a craft like this that would carry their race to hitherto unconquered lands.

Too fabulous a concept?

I didn't know. But ask a farmer how quickly a common thistle can colonize a wheatfield. Or invite a gardener to testify how even the lowly daisy can invade, conquer and dominate a garden lawn. Then ask yourself whether a plant that can walk, can communicate – and can kill – could invent such a craft to seek pastures new. I, for one, now realized how the triffids had effected their landing on the Isle of Wight at Bytewater just a few hours ago. I didn't doubt for a moment that our people would find a mat of vegetation such as this washed up on the beach. One that would have carried the advance shock troops of a triffid invasion.

The question that occurred to me now was: where would the currents take this triffid vessel?

Time would tell, I told myself grimly. In the meantime, I noticed a group of low mounds rising from the northernmost end of the raft. Rather than skulk in the hidey-hole of the jet's cockpit I decided to investigate what further secrets this singular vessel might yet conceal.

CHAPTER EIGHT

A Haunted Isle . . .

What I found among those humps and bumps confirmed my earlier suspicions. Beneath a shroud of bindweed, ivy and moss I saw remnants of a jetty; perhaps one that had lain in the upper reaches of Southampton Water or on the River Avon.

Still wearing my helmet, its visor down against any triffid attack, I picked my way across the debris. Here and there I saw timbers of a pier lodged in the mat of vegetation. Nailed to one hefty post a sign stated *Moorings For Permit Holders Only*, the barely legible lettering long since faded to stencilled outlines around mere speckles of black paint.

Elsewhere I saw the remains of a thirty-year-old shoe entangled in weed, and what I recognized as the shell of a television set, *sans* glass screen and tube, inside which squatted a handsome crab with the biggest pincers I'd ever seen. When I approached he snapped a claw in the air; he wasn't going to quit his bakelite home without a fight.

Above me, the red sun still shone bleakly in a rust-coloured sky. Seagulls cried, the sound so hauntingly sad that it served only to emphasize the mournful atmosphere. What a world — what an exquisitely mournful world. Light the colour of rust; the flotsam and jetsam of a nation now extinct; a near-supernatural sense of loneliness.

Moss, moss, moss — the last king of Angkor Wat is dead . . .

Moments later I walked between weed-covered mounds that were larger than houses. To my surprise, I saw that these were the hulks of small cargo freighters, tugboats and fishing smacks. All had been fused into this vast mat of vegetable matter and then, at some point, the mat had been torn free to drift away downstream to the open sea.

Almost hypnotized by this fabulously desolate scene — a scene that appeared to me like a graveyard of all that Man had once held dear — I picked my way over boats that were tilted this way and that, half submerged by malignant greenery. Here, a corroded funnel poked through. There, I glimpsed an open porthole behind jungle-like creepers. And inside the craft were shapes that looked like crews' bunks. I moved on, pulling aside swathes of weed, perhaps to reveal a name painted on a bow or another porthole that was overgrown with a skin of moss.

Repelled and fascinated equally by this fusing of man-made artefacts and nature I was still not prepared for what I saw next.

Sweeping aside some hanging ivy from the flank of a cabin cruiser, I suddenly froze. My blood pounded in my ears. There at the porthole was a face. One with a pair of eyes that blazed at me, brighter than anything I'd seen since falling into this weed-scape. For only a split second we had eye contact. The intensity of the encounter made me catch my breath.

Then the face was gone.

Recovering from my surprise, I stepped back from the boat, caught my heel on a branch and sat down heavily on my rear end.

When I looked up I saw a figure appear on the deck of the boat. I didn't immediately identify it as human. Rather, I had the surreal impression of a lithe, abhuman being, a creature with masses of dark hair. Amazingly, it was clad in what appeared to be bandages that fluttered in the breeze. If anything, it resembled an Egyptian mummy, yet one that moved nimbly, very much alive, over the wrecked boat.

'Wait!' I shouted. 'Please wait!'

The figure paused and looked back. I saw now that it was a girl. She was perhaps sixteen. Her eyes were bright with shock, staring at me as if it was I who'd just burst forth from a tomb.

Then I realized that her reaction was perfectly natural. Because there I was, clad in something that to her must have looked totally outlandish, with the helmet and perspex visor concealing my face.

In a second I had pulled off my helmet.

'Don't be alarmed,' I told her. 'I won't hurt you.'

At the sight of someone apparently removing their head the girl gave an audible gasp and raised two trembling hands in front of her face.

I spoke as soothingly as I could. 'Don't worry. Don't worry, please. I'm not going to hurt you . . .'

I could now see her a little more clearly. She wasn't

clad in bandages after all, only in clothes that had been worn to shreds. Although her face was clean, even looking well scrubbed, her mass of hair was a shock. I'd seen no human like this before. Moreover, there was a feral quality about her. Like a wild cat.

'I'd like to speak with you, if I may . . . please . . . I won't harm you. My name's David . . . I'm here by accident. Like you.'

That seemed the obvious assumption. That somehow she'd become marooned here. But heaven knew how she'd avoided the deadly attentions of the triffids for so long.

I smiled. 'Believe me, I won't harm you. I'll stay down here on the ground. I'd just like to—'

'Mm . . . merm-urr.'

'I'm sorry, I—'

'Merm-urr. Ah! Ah!'

Her eyes were bright. They seemed to express vitality and intelligence, but was she mute? Or . . . I felt a tingle of something, I'm ashamed to say, that came close to disgust. I'd heard stories of abandoned children in the triffid-haunted wastes of the mainland being raised by animals like the legendary Romulus and Remus. I'd written these off as mere fairy stories. Although certainly there were persistent accounts of survivors reverting to complete savagery. Even to the extent of losing the power of human speech entirely.

'Merm-urr. Ah! Ah!' With a flash of her eyes she made a claw of her hand and pushed it against her mouth. 'Merm-urr. Ah! Ah! Ah! Ah!'

'Food . . . you mean, do I have food?' Realization dawned. 'You're hungry?'

She tilted her head to one side, not understanding.

'Food.' I mimed eating.

'Ah! Ah!'

She understood.

I smiled and nodded. The poor wretch might have been here for weeks; certainly she must be starving. I reached for my satchel.

But she was quicker. Like lightning she sprang down from the deck of the boat, her bare feet lightly slapping against the turf. Then she advanced towards me, nodding and smiling while unwrapping something covered with what looked like a piece of sailcloth.

I paused, because I realized what she was doing. *She* was offering *me* food.

Now she nodded and smiled, her teeth a dazzling white; then she spread the cloth on the ground before me as if setting out a picnic. There in the centre of the cloth were two crabs – and a large rat.

She picked up the rat and mimed gnawing at its belly, while emitting a hearty 'Mmm, mmm.' Then she held it out to me so that I might enjoy the fruits of her labours.

The smile I put on my face was forced.

The rat was most definitely not appetizing. Blood trickled from its nostrils; its fur was matted; its prominent teeth were a sickly yellow.

I didn't want to offend my new friend by refusing her proffered delicacy. Instead, still smiling warmly, I broke a square of biscuit from my survival pack and offered it to her.

She seemed satisfied by our little ritual, for she replaced the rat in the cloth, quickly bundled it up, then tucked it under her arm. But she didn't decline my offer. As if plucking a hot chestnut from a fire her hand moved with lightning speed to pick the biscuit from my fingers.

It wasn't greed, or savagery; just her way of moving. Fast, yet graceful.

She looked at the biscuit. Clearly she'd never clapped eyes on baked confectionery before. Then she sniffed it and rubbed it experimentally with her thumb. When she was satisfied, she licked it.

'Mmm-mm!'

Her eyes locked back onto mine. They blazed with delight as she crammed the biscuit into her mouth and crunched it loudly – and with obvious pleasure. Once she'd swallowed it she sucked each finger and thumb in turn. 'Mmm . . . mmm!'

'You like that?'

'Mmm!'

I smiled. 'My name is . . . David . . . Da–vid.'

She gave me a quizzical look. 'Da . . . Day . . .' She tried again, framing her lips with an effort. 'Da . . . d . . . der . . .'

'David.'

She shot me a bright smile. Then, surprisingly, she said: 'Daddy.' Her voice became girlish. 'Daddy-daddy-daddy-daddy.'

At that moment I had a sudden mental vision of near-supernatural clarity. I saw a community on the mainland, struggling for survival. There, a family. Father, mother, little girl. Then disaster strikes. All die, with the exception of the girl. What horrors the little girl endured to survive to adulthood would fill a book of their own. Growing up wild and alone, beset by constant danger.

'Daddy, daddy, daddy.' She repeated the word delightedly. 'Daddy, Mummy, Aunt Sue, wash-face . . . Daddy mer-murr. Wash-face!' Beaming, she mimed washing her mouth and chin.

Then she laughed. And it was such a beautiful laugh that I found myself laughing, too. I tried to stifle it. But it was one of those laughs that couldn't be suppressed; it sprang from the depths of my stomach and roared out through my lips.

It would have made a strange picture. There's me, dressed like a spaceman from one of those precious Old World children's comics, the silvery helmet under one arm. The girl, looking like a savage, dressed in rags, fed on rat flesh. We're standing in a red-lit world of weed and wrecked ships, laughing like a couple of giddy children.

In that moment, too, I felt a kind of helpless love for the creature. She was beautiful, vital, graceful, indestructibly healthy despite her environment. And there we were: two human beings thrown together in adversity.

I knew there and then that I had somehow to find a way to rescue her from this floating mat of weed. After a while she would acclimatize herself to life on my homeland. There, trained people would care for her. She'd learn to speak English; perhaps she'd even become part of a family once more.

A shape lurched into the periphery of my vision.

In one fluid movement I drew my pistol and fired two shots. They smashed into the trunk of the triffid as it approached. My third bullet found the stem of the stinger as it curled ready to strike. The .45 calibre slug shattered plant flesh to fibre.

The girl gave a piercing shriek. Then, clamping her hands over her ears, she bolted.

'Wait!' I called after her. 'Don't be frightened!'

She ran, fleet as a young fawn, across the jumble of planks.

I ran after her, calling reassuringly, but the girl was terrified. She could never have heard the noise of a gun before.

She ran blindly. In front of her lay a dense thicket of triffids, standing with their roots in the turf.

I thought she'd swerve.

She did not.

I thought she must surely stop.

Still she did not.

She ran and ran. The sound of the gunshots had scared her witless.

'Please stop! Don't go in there . . . don't!'

For one lunatic moment I actually considered trying to put a bullet in her leg to stop her running into a death trap.

But at the last second I lowered the gun, shaking my head despairingly. All I could do was watch stunned as the screaming girl ran full-tilt into the heart of the triffid grove. Leaves and stems shook and dozens of stingers uncurled to whip through the air. The group of vile plants had all the seething menace of a nest of cobras.

As the triffids closed in on the girl she vanished from sight. After another savage flurry of movement the ugly monsters were abruptly still.

The girl's screaming stopped.

I stood. Stared. And I felt as if something had died inside my heart.

My next week was miserable. I returned to the jet; tried to sleep as best I could; ate survival rations; watched night follow day. I felt dogged by a kind of tiredness I could not shift.

On several occasions I pulled on my helmet and gloves and prowled my fifty or so acres of floating island. Crabs scuttled to and fro. Seagulls cried like lost souls.

My little world continued to be lit by the same dull red glow. It did nothing to lift my spirits.

Again and again I walked to the 'shore' and stared out across the sea. There was no land, no ships – nothing. Merely bleak, rust-coloured waters without end. For all I knew I might have been entering the straits of Hades.

On occasions it rained. Water collected into the bowl-like depressions I'd hammered into the plane's wings with a piece of driftwood. I'd carefully scoop this water into my water bottle to enable my mechanical existence to continue – eating, drinking, sleeping – but the truth was that neither my heart nor my spirit was in it at all. Triffids had killed two people to whom I'd only briefly become acquainted. But as the days passed my hatred for the plants changed to a quiet acceptance. Sailors drown at sea. Nevertheless, the sons of sailors, as often as not, follow their fathers into seafaring. So I came to accept what fate meted out. In a little while, moreover, the triffids became a lifeline. Protected as I was by the helmet and pressure suit I'd topple a triffid and hack away the stinger with my knife. Then I'd harvest its more tender shoots and leaves and chew them with that same mechanical action. Bitter-sweet — so very bitter-sweet — but they supplemented my meagre diet.

Once I'd eaten I'd settle back into my seat with the canopy locked down, gaze into the red sky above and think about the girl I'd met here. I'd wonder about her name. And whether she herself had still remembered it from the days when she had had a mother and father.

The nights were darker than I'd ever known them to be before. Even though I suspect some were cloudless not a single star revealed itself. The moon lay entirely hidden.

I sat beneath the perspex canopy and slept fitfully.

Sometimes I opened my eyes to see a wide-eyed face peering down at me, watching me as I slept.

Although this shook me, by morning I discounted these visitations as nothing more than dreams. Yet, as I briskly walked around my seaborne estate and tried to forget, in my mind's eye I could still see the wild girl's laughing face.

My father once wrote that there is in humanity an inability to sustain a tragic mood. The mind has a phoenix quality, rising again and again from the ashes of despair.

After a while my mood did indeed lift. I thought more about escaping the floating island. I began to work with my knife on the creepers that twined around a sturdy-looking yacht. I reckoned that in a couple of days I could cut her free and perhaps somehow strike a course for land — due north should take me either to the Isle of Wight or at least to the mainland coast. As I worked I had to keep my wits about me. Triffids constantly skulked nearby. The moment they closed in I'd slip on the helmet and snap the visor down. Working thus was stuffy and uncomfortable but at least the damnable plants could not harm me.

For my first few days on the 'island' I'd often hear the staccato drumming of triffids. Gradually, however, they fell silent. Later, a sleepless hour in the cockpit brought to mind one of Oscar Wilde's aphorisms. Didn't one of his quips go something like: 'There's only one thing worse than being talked about . . . and that's not being talked about'? Perhaps the triffids had said all they had to say about me. Maybe they found me uninteresting. Or, on the other hand, beyond their reach when I was safe either in my plane or in my pressure suit. For whatever reason, it seemed that they chose to ignore me, which lent them a surly rather than a sinister air.

At first, the sudden silence made me uneasy. But as they continued to ignore me I can't say I felt that snubbed. Besides, I was receiving attention from elsewhere. There was no shortage of rats. I fancied they saw me as breakfast, lunch and tea and so made a few sorties against me as I worked. But I dug out a five-foot length of chain from the bridge of a tramp streamer. This made a highly effective weapon when I whirled it around my head. Quickly the rats scuttled back to their bilges where, no doubt, they glared at me with hungry eyes.

Occasionally high seas would send spectacular convulsions through the triffid raft. These could be so powerful that the 'ground' would rise and fall to the height of my head. Then standing became impossible and I'd be bounced about the turf like a jumping bean.

Rain clouds brought darkness. Then I'd be forced back to the cockpit of the jet. There I dozed or chewed the triffid leaves that would flood my mouth with their bitter-sweet juice. Or I'd while away half an hour or so by cleaning my revolver and checking the distress flares.

Hope is a fragile creature at the best of times. Even though it might be guarded closely, cherished and nourished with tit-bits of optimism, it can so easily expire. I continued, nevertheless, to have my hopes. One of them was that I wouldn't be very far from land. I knew the currents off the southern coast of England would sweep me in a south-westerly direction for a while. Then they would merge with those of the Atlantic's Gulf Stream that would then bear me north, past the tip of Cornwall and towards the Irish Sea. Home and family couldn't be *that* distant. Or so I hoped . . .

As time went on I began to develop the sneaking suspicion that I was no longer alone. I've already mentioned that some nights I'd wake in the cockpit to see a face looking in at me. I fancied I saw a wild mane of hair and two blazing eyes. In the morning I'd convince myself that this night-visitor was part of a dream.

However, bit by bit I began to discover a little more objective evidence. Two rats with broken necks lay on the plane's wing when I returned from work on the yacht. They were laid neatly side by side as if they were an offering. One morning I heard what sounded like a distant human voice. It sang in a soft, rhythmic voice. 'Dad-dad. Dad-dad-dad . . .'

Seagull cries distorted by distance? Maybe.

So I conducted a little experiment. One afternoon I tied a piece of biscuit to a length of bandage from the first-aid kit. I hung this from the guard rail of the yacht. There it should have been noticeable — while being beyond the reach of even the most athletic rat.

Then I took a walk on my undulating promenade by the sea. When I returned an hour later the bandage fluttered lightly on the breeze; the biscuit had gone.

After that, the rust-coloured sky no longer seemed quite so oppressive. And within a few moments of beginning my work on the yacht again I noticed something that took me by surprise. I was whistling. Actually whistling! And the light of optimism had begun to glow somewhere inside of me.

By the tenth day I'd become quite the Robinson Crusoe. I'd found enough driftwood to light fires. From the tail of the jet I'd torn away a sheet of metal that I'd beaten into a pot shape in which I could boil water.

Into this I dropped triffid shoots and crabs selected from among those that constantly scuttled across the island. I didn't even have to catch them: they walked up to the cooking pot by themselves. The flavour of the resultant stew might be best described as 'raunchy'. A blend of sweets and sours with an overlying salty sharpness. With a better diet, I enjoyed a better frame of mind. My work went faster. I even derived a good deal of satisfaction from my efforts. The yacht would soon be cut free.

Moreover, I now harboured a deep-rooted belief that I was not alone on the island. Somehow — by some miracle that puzzled me yet that also delighted me more than I could say — I knew that the feral girl had survived the plunge into the thicket of triffids. True, she was still shy of me. And too fearful of the gun to reveal herself. But I would work on that. Just as I worked on cutting away the thousands of vines that held fast the yacht. A little tact and some gifts of biscuit should rebuild some bridges.

So I made my plans for my homeward journey — one with an astonishing passenger on board.

However, the best-laid plans of mice and men . . .

On the morning of my eleventh day as a contemporary Crusoe I looked up from my labours to see a steamship running alongside the island.

I knew then that I'd never complete the job of cutting free the yacht. It took only one quick moment to find and fire off a distress flare.

The ship quickly reversed its engines and pulled stern-on towards the island. I saw the faces of strangers looking at me from the decks. For them this was evidently an interesting sight: what might have been a spacesuited — and shinily helmeted — figure brandishing a blazing flare on a raft of vegetation. While my attention, in turn, was taken by an unfamiliar flag that fluttered from the steamship's mast.

It is trite to say that life is full of surprises. However, I knew that, once again, events had taken an unexpected turn.

CHAPTER NINE

Embarkation

There was a welcoming party. A large one. It crowded the ship's deck — a curious, if oddly silent throng.

Still panting from the exertion of climbing the rope ladder, I unbuckled my helmet at last before pulling it free of my head. A heavily built man of sixty or thereabouts, with broad Herculean shoulders, stared at me from beneath a pair of eyebrows that bristled fiercely with thick white hairs. From his stance — feet wide apart, hands together behind his back — I had no doubt I faced the ship's master.

At last the man spoke. The depth and power of his voice made the helmet vibrate in my hand. 'Welcome aboard, sir.' His gaze fixed on me, his glare powerful. 'Some of these folk — those who've read too much Old World trash, I reckon — took you for a spaceman. I did not, sir. Good thing, too. Bosun here was minded to put a bullet in your belly.' With a lift of his bearded jaw he indicated a man with a rifle. 'For safety's sake, you understand?'

'Then I'm glad you persuaded him to hold his fire.'

'I did not, sir. *I* favoured placing a bullet in your *leg*. But I have passengers who did their darnedest to steer me on a different course.'

'Passengers?' Now I was as much bewildered as breathless. My sudden rescue from the floating island, then being confronted by a bunch of tough harum-scarum seamen had left me more than a little bit disorientated. Moreover, the captain's heavily accented tones made understanding him properly an uphill struggle.

'My name, sir,' continued that formidable man in his booming voice, 'is Sharpstone. Master of the steamship *Beagle Minor*. And I take it you weren't on that scrap o' flotsam through choice?'

Come on, David, I told myself. *Get up to speed. He's asking you what happened.* Feeling decidedly light-headed now I said, 'Er, no. I had to make a forced landing several days ago.'

'Forced landing. You're a pilot then?'

'Yes.' I nearly added bitterly: *A damn' unlucky one. Two forced landings in as many days.*

Captain Sharpstone continued: 'Any passengers?'

'Ah . . . there was one, but—' I explained how I came to be stranded on the island and told Sharpstone about the death of Hinkman.

'That's infernal bad luck,' the captain told me, his voice softening a little.. 'Infernal bad luck.' Briefly he turned to the man with the rifle and, it seemed to me, issued a string of orders. But because of that heavy accent of his I couldn't make out more than a word or two.

Then he turned back to me, saying breezily, 'I dare say we can offer you a few creature comforts – could you use a shower and a square meal?'

Yes, I told him, I could, and I thanked him.

'But first, for the log, another formality or two. Your name and where you hail from, sir?'

'The name's David Masen. I'm from the Isle of Wight.'

'How would you be spelling "Masen", sir?'

I told him.

'Thank you very much, Mr Masen, and welcome aboard.' Gravely, the big man shook my hand. The grasp, as I had anticipated, was of steel. 'Now, if you'll excuse me I have my duties to perform. However, my passengers will attend to your basic needs. I dare say they will also ask questions of their own.'

As he turned to go, I felt the throb of the engines coming up through the deck to the soles of my boots. Smoke poured from the ship's single blue funnel, a glaring white plume against the red of that eerie sky. We were leaving.

'Wait,' I said, all of a sudden. 'Wait. We can't go yet.'

Captain Sharpstone turned to give me a stern yet questioning stare. 'Indeed, Mr Masen? I was given to believe I was still master of this ship.'

'I'm sorry,' I stammered. 'I – it's just that there is someone else on the island.'

'You told me there were no surviving passengers on your aircraft.'

'That's right . . . but there was a girl. She—'

'A girl?' He raised a knowing eyebrow, glancing

towards his men who were standing nearby. 'What kind of girl?'

At that moment I'm sure he had me down for a raving lunatic, babbling about imaginary girls, mermaids perhaps, who sunned themselves on that floating weed mat.

'Look, Captain. I'm sorry I'm not explaining this at all well. But I found a girl living on that island. She's around fifteen or sixteen years old. She doesn't seem capable of speaking.' I saw him turn his gaze to the island, looking for some glimpse of the girl. 'She's taken to hiding herself away.'

'Hiding herself?'

'I frightened her – unintentionally – when I fired my revolver at a triffid.'

'But we saw no sign of a girl, Mr Masen. We observed yourself and a crop of triffids, but little else.' He turned to a middle-aged man. 'Set a course, Mr Shea. South-east. Ten knots.'

'Yes, sir.' The man headed off briskly towards the wheelhouse.

'Now, Mr Masen.' The captain looked me up and down, with what my mother would have described as 'an old-fashioned look'. 'You have that hot shower, then the ship's medic will run an eye over you.'

I all but yelled at the man. 'Captain. There's a young girl out there. Stranded with nothing but filthy rats to eat and blasted triffids for company! She will *die* if we do not find her!'

Captain Sharpstone did not flinch at my outburst, any more than if he'd been hewn from granite. But his eyes told me I'd end up clapped in irons or some such nautical restraint if I continued in this vein.

'Mr Masen. You've endured an unpleasant ordeal. I recommend you take a moment to simmer down, then accept our hospitality.'

By now the ship was drawing away from the floating island. Triffids stood there in the bleak light. I thought of the beautiful, lively girl watching the ship – her only hope of survival – disappearing into the distance.

Fuming, I swung the helmet down against the guard rail with a crash. 'No. You can't leave her here!'

'Mr Masen, I—'

'Return me to the island; I'll bring her back myself.'

'There is no girl, Mr Masen. Now, for your own good my men—' his gaze caught that of a pair of burly deckhands '—will escort you down below.'

Two men, both with hands the size of shovels, grabbed me. This was insane. Why wouldn't the man take me seriously?

I tried to struggle free of their grasp. A futile effort. The men were walking slabs of muscle. Without much effort on their part they hauled me in the direction of a doorway. Nothing I could do, nothing I could say would alter what would happen now. The girl would remain on the island. There, from starvation, from cold, from a triffid sting, she would die. No doubt about that. No doubt at all.

'Put Mr Masen in a cabin,' the captain ordered. 'See that the door is locked.'

'Captain Sharpstone. Just a moment, please.' The voice I heard couldn't have been more different from the sailors' rough accents. This was soft, educated and, most definitely, female.

'Take a look back at the island for a moment, Captain,' continued the female voice. 'There is something you ought to see.'

Hardly a dignified arrival on my rescue ship, you'd allow. But after leaving a short trail of corpses in my wake over the last week or so I was determined that I wouldn't be responsible for another death so quickly.

At least now I could stand aside as the deckhands released me. I watched with a fair amount of satisfaction as the crew raced around the deck, making ready to turn the ship around.

The captain issued orders with practised ease. 'Turn her one-eighty, go in sharp end first. Dead slow, Mr Shea. I don't want any of that rat-tat muck fouling the screws. Get ready with the rope ladder once more, Mr Lieberwitz. Steady as she goes.'

I leaned forward over the rail. Above me hung the sun – a grim red disc at its zenith. There was precious little light. Just enough to make out the sinister, lurking forms of the triffids and the humped mounds that were the weed-smothered graves of yachts and tugboats. It should have been a desolate, depressing scene. But at that moment, by heaven, I felt a surge of triumph go crackling through me, from the tips of my toes to the roots of my hair.

Hair standing out like a huge dark dandelion clock around her head, there stood my feral girl. Her gaze, bright with excitement and – I dare say – fear, was fixed on the ship with its funnel belching smoke, its propellers churning the water white. A sight, I imagine, that she'd never witnessed before.

I was so pleased to see her. My heart surged with a simple, idiotic happiness. I was right. She hadn't died in the thicket of triffids. But God alone knew how she'd survived.

She stood as close to the water's edge as she could get, poised nervously on that dangerously fraying mat of vegetation. Clutched to her breast was a briefcase. She waited for the ship to nose its way slowly towards her.

I willed her not to lose her nerve and bolt back to her hidey-hole again. The sight of the monstrous ship looming over her would have been as awesome as it was frightening. But she must have realized that it was her only hope of survival. So, despite her evident terror of it, she stayed rooted there, hugging the case to her as fiercely as a mother protecting her baby.

'It's good to see you smiling, Mr Masen.'

I looked back to see the owner of the soft female voice.

She was around twenty-five, I suppose. Slim without being skinny. A wash of hair that was somewhere between red and blonde floated lightly around her shoulders in a style that I'd never seen before. Her eyes were clear, intelligent and a curious shade of green, while her fresh complexion was ever so slightly dusted with freckles. She wasn't there to handle the deck machinery: I could tell that from her well-shaped and far from callused hands. She radiated that indefinable quality some call 'breeding'. Yet she was dressed in workman's blue denim, a checked shirt and sturdy boots. Her down-to-earth choice of clothes was mitigated by the softening effect of a pink scarf.

She smiled, amused. 'It's not every day that someone stands up to the fearsome Captain Sharpstone. Congratulations.'

'I just wanted him to believe me. Although I made a ham-fisted job of it.'

'But you got the result you wanted.' She nodded down at the waiting girl as the ship inched its way towards the floating island. 'Who is she?'

'I don't know. She must have been swept out to sea on that thing when it broke free of the mainland.' I looked back at the young woman beside me. My mind must have been working particularly slowly that day because only then did I place the accent, despite having watched hundreds of old Hollywood films in the faded splendour of Sandown's Imperial Picture Palace. 'You're American,' I said, surprised.

'You Brits are one heck of a perceptive race.' Smiling still, she ran her hand lightly over my arm that was still clad in the rubberized pressure suit. 'Is this what all the fashionable young men are wearing on your side of the Atlantic?'

I found myself smiling back. 'Hardly. I'll actually be glad to get this off my back after ten days. Uh, and sorry about that, by the way.'

'Sorry about what?'

'Stating the obvious. That you're American. I didn't mean to sound so blindingly dense. But it's been an unusual few days, to put it mildly.' I turned to watch the sharp prow of the ship press against the floating weed mat, splitting the vegetation with the ease of a knife blade cutting through a cabbage. At that moment the engines reversed, halting the vessel. A deckhand lowered the ladder. Almost to myself I said, 'Floating islands, triffids, feral girls, days that are darker than nights. It takes some getting used to.'

'It sounds,' she said gently, 'as if you need a square meal and a good night's sleep.'

'I'll second that. And maybe a shot of rum if the ship can muster one?'

'I'm sure we can rustle up a tot or two. Now I'm the one with the bad manners.' She smiled at me with those bright green eyes as she held out her hand. 'Kerris Baedekker. New York City.'

I acknowledged the introduction with a nod and a smile — albeit a tired one. 'David Masen. Isle of Wight.'

Then we turned to look back over the rail as the girl in her rags climbed up the ladder. Even with the briefcase under one arm she moved with extraordinary agility.

I said, with feeling, 'I'm glad she's safely away from those triffids.'

Then Kerris said something that puzzled me a good deal. 'Yes,' she mused, gazing thoughtfully at what I took to be fearsome specimens of the plant. 'But they're scrawny little things, aren't they?'

CHAPTER TEN

Q&A

I had expected to find myself eating alone in a cabin. What I got was a little more than I had bargained for.

I'd showered – a wonderful hot shower at that Then I'd changed into trousers and a shirt of thin denim lent to me by a crew member of near enough the same size as myself. With no shoes yet available for me I was offered a pair of stout woollen socks that had been darned with enough black thread to give them a comical Dalmatian look.

Now, an hour after picking up the feral girl from the floating island, I could feel the throb of the powerful steam engine carrying the ship across open ocean. As I tidied up my hair with a borrowed comb a sailor stuck his head round the door. 'Chow's up, buddy,' he said cheerfully. 'Passengers' saloon, down the passageway, first door on your left. Can't miss it.'

Thanking him, I took a moment to appraise my now smoothly shaven jaw. The healthy but limited diet of the last few days had left my cheekbones a little more prominent than before. But I didn't look overly starved, considering.

The passengers' saloon smacked of unostentatious comfort, with well-upholstered seating in a room boasting a small but heart-warmingly well-stocked drinks bar in one corner. On one table stood a bowl full of stew that swam with vegetables and medallions of beef.

I saw that I wouldn't be alone. The strawberry blonde, Kerris Baedekker, was there, with three other men. There was a shining eagerness about them. Like children awaiting the arrival of the conjuror. They beamed at me as I walked across the carpeted floor in my stockinged feet.

'Don't stand on ceremony,' a tall black man told me, indicating the bowl of stew. 'You must be hungry.'

'I won't pretend I'm not. I'll be happy if I never taste triffid again.'

This seemed to surprise them and they shot questioning looks at each other.

Kerris stood up. 'I'll get that rum I promised you. But please make a start on lunch.' She crossed the room to the bar where she poured a generous jigger into a glass. 'By the way, I hope you don't mind some company?'

'No, not at all.'

With the bottle of rum still in one hand, she held out her free hand, indicating each man in turn. 'These are my fellow colleagues in adventure – Gabriel Deeds.'

The black man stepped forward. Tallest of the three men, he had the easy loose-limbed movement of an athlete. Smiling warmly, he shook my hand. 'Glad to have you aboard, Mr Masen.'

'David, please.' I corrected him, smiling

'The gent with the blond beard is Dek Hurney,' Kerris said breezily. 'Don't let him persuade you to play chess with him. His games last for days, and he smokes a pipe that's so evil-smelling you'll never be able to concentrate in a month of Sundays. If you ask me, those smoke screens are part of his strategy.'

Dek Hurney struck me as an amiable if shy man of around twenty-three. Grinning, he blushed at Kerris's banter.

'And last, but far from least, Rory Masterfield. He plays the meanest duelling banjo on the boat.'

Rory was sharp-eyed, with a nose that came out to a point. He smiled readily enough but there was waspishness there, along with a sharp inquisitor's eye. I completed the handshaking ceremony with Rory. 'That was some suit you had there, David. What kind of machine were you flying?'

I told him. He gave an impressed whistle. Then he blinked, as if storing the information for further use.

'Eat, eat,' Gabriel urged. 'There's plenty more if you need it, too. Ah, Dek, would you grab the bread on the table behind you? We gotta build this guy up.'

Dek passed me a plate piled high with bread.

The stew smelled delicious. The taste didn't disappoint, either. I found myself marvelling at the medallions of meat: it looked as if whole beefsteaks had been cast into the stew with careless abandon. There were yellow vegetables the size of peas that I didn't recognize but that tasted wonderfully sweet.

I'd eagerly wolfed down a few mouthfuls and had

begun to wonder how to tackle those huge cuts of beef with a humble spoon when I noticed that the four of them sitting round the table were watching my every move with all the intensity of an audience waiting for a magician to pull a rabbit from a top hat.

I paused, wondering if I'd forgotten something or made an unwitting social blunder. Instead, Kerris flushed. 'Oh, do forgive us. We're staring.' She smiled apologetically. 'Only the last thing we expected to pick out of the sea was our very own Robinson Crusoe jet pilot.'

Dek grinned. 'Especially one who'd make a stand against the formidable Captain Sharpstone.'

Despite everything, I couldn't help but wonder about the feral girl. This altogether new and alarming experience of human company must have been overwhelming for her. 'The girl you brought on board—' I began.

'Don't worry,' Kerris told me. 'Kim So's with her in a cabin. She's happily eating a whole plateful of cookies. How's the stew?'

'Amazing,' I said with feeling. 'You don't know how good this tastes.'

'More bread? Here, help yourself.'

'And the rum?' asked Gabriel.

'Wonderful, absolutely wonderful. I'm starting to feel human again.'

Rory had been thinking for a moment. 'You had a run of bad luck, having to ditch your plane like that. What happened?'

I told him how we'd tried to find the extent of the cloud cover that we'd first supposed had caused the darkness, then how we'd learned – the hard way – that the thunderstorm must have knocked out our radio link with the airbase. I rounded the story off with an account of the crash landing on the mat of weed. Of course, this led to some discussion about nature's little trick of apparently not allowing the sun to shine as it should. A problem, I gathered, that they also faced in New York, suggesting that the problem was global rather than merely local.

I looked round at their eager faces as they watched me mop up the last of the gravy with a piece of bread. 'What brings you across here? It's the first time I've met any Americans or even heard of any crossing the Atlantic to Europe since The Blinding.'

'The Blinding?' Kerris nodded. 'Back home we call it The Beginning.'

'The Beginning?' Gabriel chuckled dryly. 'And I call *that* enforced optimism.'

'Come to that,' Rory said, 'no Europeans have made the trip west.'

'At least, none that we've heard of in recent years,' Kerris added.

I resisted the urge to lick my fingers and settled for draining the rum from the glass. 'I guess that's understandable; we've been so busy surviving this last thirty years or so that international travel's had to take a back seat.'

'Well, we're putting that to rights now,' Gabriel beamed. 'We're taking this tub down from the Arctic Circle and all along the coast of Europe and Africa, as far as the equator.'

'We're mapping, collecting specimens – animal, vegetable and mineral,' Dek added.

'Assessing the extent of the spread of the triffids, as best we can,' Kerris said. 'More rum, David?'

'Thanks, but I'd better say no. It's gone to my head as it is.'

'Oh, by the by,' Rory said, as if remembering a small but significant detail. 'We're calling on folks on the way to say hello.' He smiled. 'It's time we started getting to know our neighbours. Now, tell us about yourself, David. What's life on the Isle of Wight like?'

What followed was a fairly intensive question-and-answer session. The four of them started by asking me questions and I supplied answers to the best of my ability. Somewhere along the way I managed to establish that the ship was already bound for the English Channel and they all agreed to join me for a pint or two of beer in Shanklin as soon as possible. After that, I gleaned a little information about my companions. They all hailed from New York. They formed a scientific research team on the *Beagle Minor* — you've guessed it, the ship was named after Darwin's vessel, the *Beagle*. Indeed, there was a big sister ship, *Beagle Major*, steadily working its way south down the American coast on a similar mission — basically, to ascertain what survived of the Old World, to map the extent of the triffid conquest and to contact scattered fragments of humanity with the long-term aim of uniting them into a cohesive global organization.

'Some just aren't interested,' Kerris sighed. 'A community on the coast of Norway answered our request to come ashore with a few well-aimed rifle shots.'

'Which cost us a couple of crewmen.' Rory's glassy look told me he was remembering an unpleasant event.

'That's why the captain was a bit prickly when you came on board today.'

As we talked I became in near awe of these young people. Their vitality, their sheer energy was extraordinary. I recall telling myself: *Plug 'em into the power supply and they could electrify every circuit in the ship.* They moved constantly, whether they sat or stood, gesturing expressively and talking with a swift confidence that I'd never witnessed before. At times I felt like the classic dim-witted country cousin. What's more, there wasn't a detail about life on my island that they didn't want to know about.

'Where do you find your coal?' Dek asked, polishing the lenses of his spectacles until they flashed like a heliograph. 'The Isle of Wight has no "native" coal mines, does it?'

'Er, no—' I said between mouthfuls of biscuits, which they called 'cookies'. 'We hardly ever use—'

'You don't use coal?' This surprised them. 'But for heat and light? And you have steamships?'

'We have, but they've been converted to burn oil.'

'Oil? You have oil wells?'

'No, but—'

'Surely you're not still drawing on old stockpiles?'

'No. The oil comes from triffids.'

'*Triffids?*' Rory's eyes widened as if I'd babbled nonsense. 'But how on earth do you refine it to produce combustible fuel?'

'Well, we have built a refinery that processes triffids on an industrial scale. My father and a man called Coker invented the system twenty years ago. It's possible to distil the oil to produce a light spirit with similar properties to petroleum and—'

'Just listen to that,' exclaimed Gabriel. 'These guys are squeezing gasoline out of those damn' plants. Incredible!'

'And heavier oils for lubricants, cooking and pharmaceuticals,' I added with a kind of bewildered pride. 'The fuel for my jet was triffid spirit; it's different from our oils for internal combustion engines or—'

'Jeepers.' Kerris looked astonished. 'The question is, will your people share your technology with our people?'

I grinned somewhat naively. 'I don't see why not.'

Rory rubbed his jaw. 'And you people have a fleet of jet aircraft?'

'Yes. Mainly fighters and light bombers.'

'Jeez.' Dek and the other three suddenly sat back in their seats, looking at each other. There seemed to be a fair amount of communication going on through eye contact alone. Suddenly, I had the notion that they wanted to go away into a huddle to chew over what I'd shared with them out of earshot of me.

At last Kerris said to me in a studiedly careful manner that made me a bit uneasy for the first time: 'David. You mean to say your island maintains a military air force?'

'Yes,' I said, a little more guardedly now. 'For defence purposes.'

'Do you see yourself threatened by — for want of a better phrase — a foreign power?'

'Not as such. But in the past pirates have targeted us. The smaller islands in our group have been particularly vulnerable.'

'So you've used the jets aggressively?'

'On occasion.' A little voice in the back of my head warned me to rein in my wagging tongue.

'I see.' Kerris reflected for a moment. 'You do appreciate why we might be concerned when we hear that an overseas community has such an effective force of combat aircraft?'

'They're purely defensive.'

'But as quickly offensive?'

'True.' I smiled and shrugged. 'But believe me, our people aren't hell-bent on world domination.'

Rory let out a breath, then fixed his gimlet eyes on me. 'But you see the dilemma, David? We — I mean, our people — are really going out on a limb here. Yes, we are going out to communities all over the world, extending the hand of friendship, offering to set up trade links — to trade knowledge as well as goods — but we are also advertising that we have a viable, self-supporting society with access to raw materials like coal and timber.'

I nodded. 'And you're concerned that some community here in Europe might try and invade and take it all away from you.'

'That is a danger.' Gabriel's expression turned serious. 'We've had pirate raids, too. We've lost friends and family.'

'So you see why we might get a tad nervous when we hear about someone with fleets of jet bombers and fighters,' Kerris added.

'After all—' Rory looked at me levelly '—you might decide not to trade but merely to bomb us all to hell and just take what you want.'

'We're not like that,' I said firmly. 'We are peace-loving. We too want to build bridges between communities.'

Gabriel relaxed a little. 'Then I'm glad to hear it.'

'And we too only want to make friends,' Rory smiled. 'Not enemies.'

'Besides,' I pointed out, 'none of our aircraft, even the jets, have the range to reach New York.'

'You don't have any aircraft carriers, then?'

I laughed. 'No. That's one luxury we don't have.'

Suddenly they were all smiles again.

'Then we're all going to be the best of friends,' Gabriel said, rising to his feet. 'I think this calls for at least a shot of something in celebration.'

He returned with a whiskey that was as fiery as it was potent. A couple of those and the alcohol went singing through my veins and right to my head. After sleeping in a cramped cockpit for eleven days straight I suddenly felt dog-tired. Kerris noticed the way my chin had started to droop down to my chest. She told me that a cabin was ready for me and led the way lightly along the corridor to a small but comfortable room where a freshly made bunk waited.

'Oh, David,' she said as she stood smiling in the doorway. 'The skipper says we should reach the Isle of Wight in the morning. In the meantime feel free to make yourself at home.'

I managed to thank her before I slipped away into a beautiful, dreamless sleep.

CHAPTER ELEVEN

Night

From the ship to a far distant shore radio signals flashed, back and forth, racing across the ether. Information dispatched. Questions asked. Orders transmitted.

I knew none of this then. I slept in blissful, peaceful ignorance in my bunk below decks.

Engine notes changed in pitch. Pulsing tremors from pounding pistons ran through the ship, growing stronger and stronger. Stokers, roused early from their bunks, were ordered below without breakfast, where, no doubt, they stoked not only boiler fires but also the very air around them with fiery curses. But needs must. They had to raise as much steam as that old ship could. They fed the furnaces with coal and yet more coal. The ship sped faster and faster through the night-time ocean.

Again, I knew none of this. I slept on.

Above me sparks cascaded from the funnel to flicker against a sky that remained starless and deathly dark. Anyone standing on deck would have seen the wake running out astern, like a luminously white chalk line across a blackboard. At first it would have been straight. Presently, however, degree by degree, the observer would have seen the line begin to curve as the ship turned, adopting a new course. She carried a treasure on board. One of such huge value that the ship's master had been ordered to stop for nothing. Or for no one.

It was in that same cosy envelope of blissful ignorance that I climbed from my bunk, donned those comical Dalmatian-patterned socks, pulled on my clothes and went to the passengers' saloon where I breakfasted on a concoction of crisped bacon, eggs and toast, all drenched in some sort of extremely sweet syrup. What was more, I didn't give two hoots when Gabriel Deeds strolled in, taking mighty swallows from a coffee mug, and commented, 'Anyone know why the skipper's driving the old tub so hard? She's shooting along like a speedboat this morning.'

The others shrugged before carrying on eating. Kerris asked me about the Isle of Wight's infrastructure.

Infrastructure? I'd have to take a couple of runs at spelling the word, never mind going into detail about how many miles of rail track or water mains we boasted.

Ignorant fool that I was then, I thought we were only an hour or so from home. Kerris had already requisitioned film stock from the ship's stores and had loaded a handsome German-made 8mm movie camera. I couldn't help but watch her slender fingers, working the film round guiders and sprockets before delicately inserting it into the lens gate. The mechanism might have been forty years old but the camera still ran sweet as a Swiss clock. The first meeting for thirty years between our two peoples would be recorded for posterity.

After a while I went on deck. The crew had their heads down, working hard. I saw Captain Sharpstone on his bridge, hands behind his back, standing four-square to the approaching horizon, his iron gaze fixed bow-ward.

I noticed too a four-pounder artillery gun on the foredeck, along with a couple of mounts for heavy machine guns. These people certainly weren't going into dangerous waters unprepared.

The sun was now well above the horizon. Or rather, the feeble excuse that passed for the sun in these darkened times. Once more it reminded me of a disc of orange foil. It hung there indifferently, as if merely pasted to the sky. We were in for another gloomy day and, despite its being June, it felt distinctly chilly. Whatever was filtering out most of the light up there so many miles above my head was doing an equally efficient job of blocking the sun's heat. Day by day the air felt more and more wintry.

Perhaps what Mr Hartlow had told me just before he died had been right. Maybe this *was* the beginning of the end. One prophesied by so many of the world's religions: the onset of the end of the world would begin with a supernatural darkness.

Without light there would be no photosynthesis. Plant life would die. Without plants herbivores would die. Soon the food chain would be shattered, link by link.

These thoughts worked a shiver through my bones, chilling me more than the cold air.

I stood leaning forward, my elbows on the guard rail, gazing from the tumbling wake in the rust-coloured sea to the horizon, searching for the first rounded humps of the Isle of Wight. At that moment my greatest pleasure would be simply to walk along the harbour wall into town. See familiar faces. Hear the voices of the children in the schoolyard. I even imagined settling into a comfortable armchair at home where I'd tell my parents and sisters what had happened to me. I pictured their wide-eyed faces as they drank in every word of my adventures. All this followed by a cathartic night on the town with Mitch Mitchell. As I gazed dreamily homeward, I sensed a figure standing behind me.

'Oh, Kerris. Sorry, I didn't notice you there.'

'I didn't mean to disturb you.'

'I was just looking for a first glimpse of home.'

'See anything?'

'Not yet.'

'We must get you some boots. You can't stand out here in your socks, it's freezing.'

'I hadn't noticed,' I said, not altogether truthfully. It was actually damn' cold. 'Be ready for a big reception committee.' I nodded toward the horizon. 'I wouldn't be surprised if the whole population doesn't turn out to greet you.' I smiled. 'It's not every day a ship full of Americans steams in.'

'I'll be ready with the movie camera.' She grinned. 'I'll catch that handsome profile of yours as we dock.'

'Handsome? What, a lens-cracking phizog like mine? Hardly.'

'You'll be too busy looking out for your wife on the quayside.'

'No. Not me. I'm not married.'

'Oh,' Kerris said. Then she turned to look forward, her

long hair fluttering back in the breeze. 'Gabe's right. We're really moving today. Skipper's in a hurry to get you safely home.'

'You're sure that he's radioed ahead on the frequency I gave you?'

'Of course. They were relieved to hear that you were safe, I can tell you.'

'I'm only sorry I can't say the same for my passenger.'

There was a pause, filled only with the hiss of the ship's wake.

'You saved the girl,' Kerris said at length, fixing me with those green eyes of hers. 'You'll return a hero.'

'I don't feel like a hero.' I shook my head. 'In fact, I feel bloody sick about what happened to Hinkman.'

'Well, be ready with a speech when you get home. Those folk on your island consider you to be some kind of hero already.'

'That's probably an accident of birth, rather than any qualities of my own.'

Kerris pulled back her hair from her face as the wind blew it into a rippling mass that now shone red in the sombre half-light. 'David. You're either very modest — almost insufferably modest — or there's some great family secret.'

I leaned forward, elbows on the guard rail, watching the foam at the bow. 'No big family secret. My father is, I suppose, when all's said and done, seen as some kind of demigod at home.'

'And you kinda feel that great things are expected of you?'

'Sort of.'

'And it rankles?'

'Not really.' I smiled at her. 'My father's a great father and my family don't expect me to be Bill Masen mark two. But there are public expectations.'

'Maybe you won't disappoint them.'

'Kerris, so far my only significant achievement has been to crash two of the island's aircraft in two days. So even if I am expected to step into a giant's shoes, it looks like my feet just aren't damned big enough.'

I turned to lean back against the rail, noticing for the first time how white Kerris's teeth were, framed by those full lips. 'That wasn't supposed to sound too self-pitying, by the way. And your family – do they pass muster?'

'They do. But they're kinda difficult to keep track of.'

'A big family?'

'I guess so.'

'A chap I know, Mitch Mitchell, has eight brothers and two sisters. I don't know how he remembers all their birthdays.' I grinned. 'Or even all their names, come to that.'

'Your buddy Mitch has got it easy.'

'You've got more?'

'Hmm.' She nodded at me, smiling. 'At the last count, one hundred and fifteen brothers and exactly one hundred and twenty sisters.'

I laughed out loud, then waited for the joke's punchline. Then I saw this wasn't a leg-pull. 'Crikey.'

'And you thought Mitch had his hands full.' She smiled and touched my chin. 'If that jaw of yours drops any further it's going to dent the deck. Now . . .' She leaned forward over the rail, her hair streaming back in the breeze. 'Any sign of that island yet?'

Then a minor revelation struck me. In isolation, societies evolve quite differently from one another. We had the Mother Houses. New York boasted families of more than two hundred children – just how that was achieved goodness knew. But one thing I did know: all our minds would have to broaden to an astonishing degree. We would have to embrace the philosophy of *vive la différence*. Or be faced with the birth of some potentially dangerous prejudices.

Even as I wondered how this shipload of Americans would handle the culture shock of encountering our homely community on the Isle of Wight, my eyes strayed to the dim sun. It was only then that I saw there was now something else wrong with it. Something very wrong indeed.

CHAPTER TWELVE

Contretemps

'David? What's wrong?'

I shot Kerris such a savage look that she recoiled. 'It's the ship,' I snapped. 'It's going the wrong bloody way!'

'How do you mean, the wrong way? We're taking you home.'

'No, you're not, damn it . . . how could I have not noticed?'

'David—'

'The thing's been staring me in the face for the last twenty minutes.'

'David.' Kerris shook her head in confusion. 'I don't understand what—'

'Look at the sun.' Shaking with anger, I pointed at the bloody red disc there in the sky.

'What about the sun? I don't see—'

'No, I didn't see either.' I took a breath. 'Look, Kerris. It's before midday. The sun's still rising. But it's rising over the stern – behind the ship! It should be rising in front of it. That means we're heading west – *not east!*'

'I don't understand. We're supposed to be—'

'*Supposed to be taking me home.*' I shot a grim glance at the bridge. 'But it looks as if there's been a change of plan.'

'David?'

'I'm going to talk to Captain Bligh or whatever his name is!'

Furious at being taken for a sap I strode up to the bridge.

'Good morning to you, Mr Masen.' Captain Sharpstone stood there with his hands behind his back. His gaze was not on me but the red horizon. 'Slept well, I trust.' Then he turned to an officer behind him. 'Take her up to eighteen knots, Mr Lehman.'

'Captain Sharpstone,' I began. 'What's happening?'

'We're making a damn' good speed, Mr Masen. That's what's happening.'

'Yes, but in the wrong direction.'

'There's nothing mistaken about our direction.'

'West?'

'North-west, Mr Masen.'

'But why? You're supposed to be taking me home to the Isle of Wight.'

'Change of plan, sir.'

'But why the hurry? Couldn't you take me home first?'

'Orders, Mr Masen.'

'But you couldn't have been more than a dozen hours away from the island. Why not—'

'When your commander issues an order, Mr Masen, you obey it, don't you? I have my orders from the highest authority to turn this ship round on its tail and make all speed for my home port. I have no option but to obey them. Or did you have me pegged as some kind of mutineer, sir?'

'Perhaps if you were to radio your HQ and explain the position? If you're running short of supplies my community would happily—'

'Mr Masen. It may be acceptable in your profession to question a commanding officer's orders but in mine it is construed as insubordination. And therefore unacceptable.' He regarded me from beneath those fierce eyebrows. 'I don't doubt that arrangements will be made to return you safely home to your family as soon as is practicable. In the meantime, however, our course is north-west.'

'New York?'

In lieu of an answer he gazed steadily through the bridge windows.

I felt fingers touch my sleeve. Kerris indicated with a tilt of her head that I should leave the captain.

Still grinding my teeth, I followed her below to the passengers' saloon where, I'm sorry to say, she had to listen to my views on the captain's orders. All of them, in the considerable heat of the moment, were well and truly peppered with some very basic English slang.

What do you do in such a situation? When you find that instead of being taken home you are to be carried away to a foreign land? Stage a one-man mutiny?

Hardly.

Nevertheless, I paced the deck for the better part of that day, scowling at anyone who caught my glance. Kerris, Gabriel, Dek, and the oriental girl Kim So were sympathetic. They also acknowledged that the captain had his orders. Captain Sharpstone, however strict, was fair. After lunching on a beefsteak of eye-popping dimensions I was invited to compose a message to my HQ.

With a twinge of homesickness I wrote that I was well, that there had been a change of plan, that I should return in the not too distant future. After that, there was little to do but make the most of the voyage.

Soon I became so accustomed to the background *thrumm* of the engines that I no longer noticed them. My first full day ended with the sun, now no more than a brick-red splotch, fizzling out into the ocean.

In new boots I took a turn around the deck with Kerris. We didn't brave the cold night air long before returning to the cosy saloon where Gabriel sat at a table, writing up notes, while Rory idly picked at his banjo's strings. I played cards with Kerris for a quiet hour or so, oblivious to a surprise that awaited me just around the next corner.

At a little after nine, Kim So entered, a smile on her face. At first I half suspected some practical joke. She shot quick little glances back over her shoulder. The movements set her thick, lustrous plait swinging.

She looked at each of us in turn, smiling yet more broadly, then:

'May I introduce a new guest to everyone?'

Kim So turned and held out her hand to someone out of sight.

Tentatively, a girl of fifteen or so appeared in the doorway. A broad smile lit her face, while her eyes darted from person to person. When she saw me, the smile became a vivacious grin. She pointed with a finger, laughed, then called out: 'Bang-bang man! Bang-bang man!'

How my wild child of the island had changed.

I hadn't recognized her. The dark dandelion clock of her hair had been tastefully cut. She'd bathed and put on new clothes. The transformation astonished as much as it delighted me. Kim So nodded encouragingly to the girl before turning to us again, smiling proudly. 'Everyone. I would like you to meet Christina.'

The once-wild child patted her own face. 'Kiss-Tina. Kiss-tina.'

'Chris-tina,' Kim repeated slowly. 'Chris—tina.'

'Kiss-tina!'

Kim smiled at us. 'Well, we're getting there. If not by giant strides then by baby steps.'

Kim had spent a night and a day gaining the confidence of the girl. She told us how readily Christina had taken to the shower, and to changing into new clothes. Kim added that in infancy Christina must have been raised in civilized surroundings since washing her face and brushing her teeth and hair weren't alien to her. Now she'd bounced back into society with a vengeance. In a matter of hours she was touching furniture, pictures, articles of clothing and striving to remember what they were called.

I too felt a surge of something very much like pride as Christina ran round the saloon looking at everything with childlike curiosity.

'Chair . . . table. Table!' She rapped the table with her

knuckles in triumph. 'Table. Sit. Eat. Aunt Sue there.' Pointing at one end of the table, she mimed pulling something out of her mouth. 'Huff-huff . . . Ayah!' She wafted a hand in front of her face while coughing.

Kerris looked at me. 'I take it Aunt Sue smoked like a chimney.'

'Maxie – gerrunder . . . gerrunder . . . Maxie naughty.' Now she mimed a dog with his paws on the table.

Rory looked at Christina. 'She'll be able to speak properly? I mean, her vocabulary won't be restricted permanently like this?'

'She's learning at a hell of rate. This is one smart kid.'

Suddenly Christina put her finger in her mouth to make popping sounds. Then she mimed pouring drink from an imaginary bottle. When she spoke again it was in a surprisingly deep voice, like a man's, with what to my ears sounded like a Scottish accent. 'To another year of life . . . God save the King.'

'Good Lord.' Gabriel shook his head, admiringly. 'I've heard of a photographic memory; I figure she has a *phono*graphic memory.'

'I dare say,' began Kerris thoughtfully, 'if you're suddenly left alone at the age of four or five those early memories of home and family are going to be etched so deeply you're never going to lose them.'

Gabriel nodded. 'Poor kid. What she went through I don't *ever* want to know.'

'So far, she won't sleep in a bunk,' Kim told us. 'She pulls off the blankets to make a kind of nest in the corner of a cabin. But, as you can see, she's in good spirits. She's lively, intelligent.'

Beaming, Christina moved from person to person, patting them on the arms and head while repeating, 'Hello . . . hello . . . hello . . .'

When she reached me she pointed again, then repeated the words she'd said when she first walked into the room. 'Bang-bang man.'

'So you're the bang-bang man?' Kerris said, amused.

I nodded, still smiling at Christina, and still marvelling at her transformation. 'She's remembering when I startled her with a gun. I took a pot-shot at a triffid that came too close for comfort. The noise scared the stuffing out of her.'

'Well, no harm done,' Kerris observed. 'She's taken to you again.' Her smile broadened as she looked at me. 'Bang-bang man.'

Suddenly Christina bolted from the room.

My smile faded. 'Maybe you spoke too soon, Kerris.'

'Don't worry,' Kim reassured. 'This is all new for Christina. It's bound to get a bit much for her at times.'

I'd supposed that Christina had retreated to her nest of blankets in her cabin. Yet she returned a moment later, glowing with pride.

'Saved it,' she told me, then held up the briefcase in both hands. 'Saved it . . . you . . . *you!*'

She pushed the briefcase towards me.

'You want me to save it for you?' I shrugged, puzzled. 'But it's yours, Christina.'

'You it,' she insisted. 'You it!'

I shook my head. 'Sorry, Christina. I don't under-stand.'

'*You . . . it!*'

I looked round at the others helplessly. They shook their heads, puzzled too.

'Ah! Ah! Ah!' The sound came gutturally from deep in her larynx. More like a bark than a human sound. 'Ah! Ah!'

Suddenly she snatched up a piece of paper on which Gabriel had been writing. Then, moving it from side to side against her face, almost as if she were wiping her eyes with it, she chanted, 'You it! You it! You it!'

'Oh . . . you mean *read it!*'

A look of triumph blazed in her eyes. Nodding vigorously, she said excitedly, 'Read it. *Read it.*'

'All right.' I smiled. 'I understand, Christina.'

She sat down close beside me on the upholstered seat, hugging her knees in a delighted childlike way while she watched me unbuckle the clasps of the case.

The briefcase with its scars and stains – even what seemed to be animal teeth marks – looked like it could have told of its own adventures down through the years. For reasons best known to Christina she'd guarded it carefully ever since she'd been forced to fend for herself as a little girl. With something like reverence I opened the case. Then, one by one, I removed the contents, laying them carefully on the table in front of me. A small Bible. Opening the cover, I read what was inscribed there. 'Presented to Christina Jane Schofield on the occasion of her Christening. From her loving Aunt, Susan Tourraine.'

Eagerly Christina watched me setting out her treasures.

'One doll,' I said, placing the doll beside the Bible.

'Becker,' said Christina, touching the doll's face.

Then came a lump wrapped in paper that I initially took to be a stone. But: 'Bread – very dry, very stale bread. Probably years old.'

Then came a few items of clothes for a little girl of around four or five. A sense of inevitability began to creep over me. I realized I would find clues here to the girl's past. For a moment I didn't want to continue with this ritual with Christina watching me.

Christina touched a cotton garment. 'Bl-owzer.' She thought for a moment, then corrected herself. 'Blouse.' Memory was returning. I could see it in the sudden distant look in her eye. 'Naughty dog, Max . . . plant bit him.' Her air of animation deserted her. She sat still. 'Plant bit him. Max in ground.'

An atmosphere settled over the room. I think everyone there looking at that bundle of belongings had started to supply their own mental scenario about what had happened to Christina those long years ago. I saw a little girl running through a darkened forest clutching the briefcase into which someone had placed a few basic items. A chunk of bread, never eaten; a Bible that she could not read but that would remind her of happier times. Should she survive, that was.

In the briefcase were a few more items. String. A pocket knife. Pencils with broken points. An empty box of matches. A gold locket with a curl of fair hair inside. The inscription read *Margaret Anne Schofield*.

The girl's mother?

In the bottom of the bag lay the final item. A metal cigar-container complete with its stopper. From the size of the tube the cigar must have been a Havana, or something equally large. Maybe a reminder of her father? All in all, a piquant clutch of clues.

I'd started to replace the items in the bag when Christina stopped me by taking hold of my wrist. She guided my hand over the table to the cigar tube, then pressed my fingers down against it.

I glanced round at the others. They watched expectantly, the room silent save for the faraway *thrum* of the engines.

'Read it,' Christina insisted.

There were no markings on the outside of the cylinder. I unstoppered it. Inside, tightly rolled, I could see a piece of paper.

After teasing it out, I took a moment to unscroll the sheet then hold it down flat with two hands against the table. The handwriting looked hurried, but it had come from a once-elegant hand.

I looked at Christina. She sat still, eyes bright, expectant.

There was nothing I could do to postpone the moment further. I read the letter aloud:

To Whom It May Concern:

The girl who handed you this letter is my daughter. Her name is Christina Jane Schofield. She is five years old.

There is little time to detail what has befallen us. For twenty years we lived in a stockade on the Cornish coast. We were a mixed community of sighted and unsighted. In my estimation, we were comparatively successful, farming mainly, with a little fishing to supplement our diet.

Then a year ago a fleet of yachts approached the coast. We had no time to defend ourselves before we were attacked. The women who were sighted, together with our children, were carried off by the raiders. The remainder were butchered. More by luck than by design, I escaped with my daughter, Christina. We wandered for months. Living hand to mouth. Sleeping in ruins. Ever avoiding the triffids, which started to follow us as wolves trail a wounded animal. Which wasn't far from the mark. I was an old man when we left our community. Now I am ill. Walking more than a mile a day became an ordeal. The more slowly we moved the more the triffids gained on us.

During our travels over the last twelve months we have not encountered a single person. Not one. We are, I conclude, the only people in the whole of the county. The triffids have either destroyed them or driven them out. Now those blasted triffid plants are intent on making a meal of us.

I sit writing this letter to you, a stranger whom I shall never meet. Christina and I have found a temporary refuge in a boathouse on a river. It is dark. Even though I cannot see them, I can hear them. The triffids — beating at their woody boles with their little fingersticks, signalling to more of their kind that we are trapped here.

Christina sleeps unperturbed. She does not know that this is our last evening together.

Although I am no medical man, I understand that my time is drawing to an end. I can feel a hard, fixed mass in my stomach. My skin has turned a sickly yellow. A tumour, I suspect. In any event, I am too weak to move more than a few steps at a time. Soon even that ability will be lost.

However, that doesn't trouble me. My only concern is for my little daughter. My heart breaks at the thought of leaving her alone, unprotected — undefended against those bastard plants.

Even now I wonder if reason is leaving me. I am so drowsy I have difficulty in remaining awake for more than a few moments at a *time. This evening Christina slipped out of the boathouse. I half remember asking her where she went. She replied she was looking for apples but other plants kept hitting her with their sticks. Naturally concerned, I asked her if the plants had struck her with their stings. She said they had, that it stung a little, but didn't bother her overmuch. Indeed, there were pink marks on her face, but no evidence of swelling, let alone of poisoning.*

But maybe I was dreaming after all. Ah, I'm writing this letter as a retreat from reality. I'm avoiding reaching the end and doing what I must do to my beautiful child.

In a moment or so I will put her in a dinghy I have found here in the boathouse. I am giving her food, water, and this letter, then sending her away into the darkness alone. I can do no more. I can barely move. And I know I have not the strength to climb into the boat with her. My dear child must do what she can to survive alone out there.

It will be the most painful thing I've ever done to watch her go, knowing I will never see her again — and that I might be sending her to her death. But is there another way? Is there?

From the bottom of my heart I can only beg you to care for her. She is a good girl.

Yours faithfully,

Benjamin Schofield

When I had finished reading the letter I didn't say anything. Nor did anyone else. We sat quietly for a while with our own thoughts.

CHAPTER THIRTEEN

Onward

'How long will the crossing take?'

'New York? Another three days, I figure.'

'Glad to be going home early?'

'Orders are orders. But it'll be nice to walk on solid ground again. Say, you're pretty good at this, aren't you?'

'I get lots of practice, waiting around in mess rooms for good flying weather.'

Gabriel Deeds played, as the saying goes, a mean game of table tennis. Such was the black man's strength that more than one ball exploded beneath the force of one of his devastating forearm smashes.

Papering the walls of the R&R room were pin-ups of starlets. Crimson lips pouted on painted faces framed by elaborate platinum hairstyles.

'Wowee, Masen, where you learn that back spin?'

'Cricket.'

'Cricket?'

'My bowling's better than my batting.'

'What's this cricket? Other than a squeaky little bug.'

'You've never heard of cricket?'

Shaking his head Gabriel cracked the ball back across the table at what looked close to a million miles an hour. The ball struck my bat before cannoning away to ricochet off the ceiling. While I retrieved it I explained the bare essentials of cricket to him. A game that my old school master, Mr Pinz-Wilks, lovingly referred to as God's own. When I'd finished explaining the rudiments, Gabriel's expression spoke of his deep and lasting bafflement. Eventually, after much deliberation:

'And both teams can get through their batting innings in a match of, what? Two hours?'

'Oh no,' I told him, smiling. 'Cricket matches last a bit longer than that.' When I told him *how* long he shot me a look of such deep suspicion he must have thought I was giving his leg a good long pull.

'Two days?' He echoed. '*Two days?*' Pushing a dent out of the table tennis ball with his huge thumb, he shook his head. 'You English guys must have real stamina. How do you play so long without food or sleep?'

'Oh, the teams have breaks for lunch and tea.'

'Tea?' Again the mystified look rolled through his eyes. I went on to explain that in England the word 'tea' not only meant a beverage but a meal eaten in that temporal borderland between afternoon and evening.

Gabriel nodded as he served the ball. 'Churchill was right. We're two nations *divided* by a common language.'

Once more I realized that cultural and even language differences between American and Englishman, superficial though they might at first seem, could cause more than one or two headaches along the way.

But I got on famously with Gabriel. His warmth and friendliness did much for my spirits. So we played table tennis, drank coffee (real coffee – not the acorn-brewed stuff I'd been raised on, that for some reason was known as 'French coffee') and we batted conversational subjects back and forth along with those celluloid balls that had such a pronounced tendency to shatter at Gabriel's touch.

He told me more about the research team aboard the SS *Beagle Minor*.

'The crew are a tad suspicious of us,' he told me. 'They call us Ollies.'

'Ollies?'

'It started as "Ologists", then they shortened it. But I think they might see us a bunch of Oliver Hardys as well.' He grinned. 'But then, when we first came aboard maybe we did seem on the snooty side with our books and lab stuff. Good shot, David! But that didn't last long. We'd barely gotten out of the harbour before we had our heads over the side, calling for Hugh.'

'Calling for Hugh?' I smiled. 'Oh, I see. *Mal de mer.*'

'That's it . . . darn it, I'm sure that net keeps moving. Then the *mal de mer* gave way to a bout of *mal du pays.*'

Mal du pays? His using the unfamiliar French term for homesickness revealed a fair bit about Gabriel. His education was certainly first-rate.

'I take it the crew called the team the Ologists because of your professions?' I said.

'Nail on the head, David. Nail on the head. I'm a biologist specializing in the plant side of things.'

'And Dek?'

'Geologist. If we do happen anywhere near oil or useful ores we want to know about it. Kerris is the zoologist. She's trying to establish how animal life is faring under all those beautiful swaying triffids.'

'Badly, I guess.'

'Rats aren't doing so badly.'

'You mean they tidy up the scraps after the triffids have done with the bigger chaps?'

'Got it in one, David. Hell, I'm sure that net's growing before my eyes. You'll have to show me how you do that backspin, buddy.' Gabriel pulled the ball from the net, then tossed it to me to serve. 'Kim So's line is anthropology. Assessing how we poor Joes who are left are managing to survive.'

'And Rory?'

'Odd man out. He's strictly diplomatic service. A kind of roving ambassador to make contact with — and, ideally, allies of — the communities we find.'

'Which can't always be the easiest of jobs?'

'Absolutely . . . ah, my point, I think, old man.' He served again. The ball whistled by my ear. 'Match point coming up.' He picked up the thread of the conversation. 'You've probably encountered the same kind of thing. People get scared that what little food they grub out of the soil is going to be taken from them by bandits, so they lock themselves away in their communities and get all insular and secretive.'

'That's understandable.'

'Yeah, but it's time to break down those barriers. We can't continue living on our iddy-biddy islands with our iddy-biddy farms in our own iddy-biddy worlds. We've got to start communicating so that we can form an international federation.'

'United Nations mark two?'

'Why not? But some of these guys tucked away in their European enclaves don't even dare use a radio transmitter in case it draws attention to them. But you can wager big money that they're all listening to *their* sets, finding out all that they can about *their* neighbours.'

'We didn't know about New York,' I said, 'so you must have your own radio blackout?'

'There! Match point.' The ball struck my bat with such force that the little celluloid sphere split into two neat hemispheres. Then, with barely a blip, Gabriel continued the conversation. 'Sure – we use low-powered transmitters, so broadcasts don't carry much more than thirty miles or so. We've suffered pirate raids, too. What's more, we were in deep trouble until we got a new administration around twenty years ago that beefed up the defences. Anyone planning a hit on our town better think twice because we can hit back so hard the bad guys will stay hit for keeps. Coffee?'

I couldn't say no to that wonderful coffee. So we perched on the end of the table, sipped from paper cups, and chewed the fat. About the possible cause of the darkness that still had planet Earth wrapped up good and tight. We swapped stories about family, childhood: the stuff you do when you're getting to know someone properly. I told him about my exploits flying the model planes I'd built, even down to the time when I'd finally got my prized rocket plane airborne. And how the verger rang the church bell in panic on hearing the sound, thinking that the doodlebugs of Hitler's war had returned.

That tickled Gabriel. He laughed long and loud, and slapped his thigh hard enough, I reckon, to raise a bruise or two.

He ran a huge thumb reflectively along the edge of the table-tennis bat. 'It's easy to forget all those good times when you're a kid. I kept rabbits, lots of rabbits. They kept multiplying so I didn't notice when one or two went missing. You see, my daddy would harvest them from time to time for the pot.' He smiled. 'And my vice? That was the movies. Every Saturday I'd be first in line at Loew's. That's a big underground cinema on Broadway. I loved the slapstick. Y'know? Buster Keaton, Laurel and Hardy, Arkina Rossetta? Although I was never one for Chaplin, too much *schmaltz*. And I liked the cowboy flicks, too. The more shoot-outs the better. But I lost my appetite for watching folks killing folks.'

'Oh?'

'Yeah, you see, my Daddy shot my Mom. *Pow* . . . straight in the heart.'

Genuinely shocked, I said, 'I'm sorry, Gabriel. I didn't mean to—'

'No, David.' He waved a hand, looking apologetic himself. 'It happened a long time ago. They say he reacted badly to the chemi-shot.'

I didn't feel it right to cross-question him about what a chemi-shot was. He must have seen the puzzled look in my eye, however.

Easily he said, 'Chemi-shot. That'll be a new one on you, too, eh?'

I nodded, unsure what to say that wouldn't sound resoundingly insensitive, but the friendly smile had returned to Gabriel's handsome face. 'Chemi-shots are a method of male sterilization by injection.' He mimed putting a hypodermic into his arm. 'I reckon at twenty-six my Daddy was too old for the procedure. Sent him a tad off balance.' He tapped the side of his head. 'It didn't bother *me* at all. But then, I didn't miss what I'd never had, do you follow?'

I did follow. Secretly, I was horrified.

Still smiling he added, 'And once I'd got the Pink Card it got me into what we called Neuter High.' He chuckled, amused. 'And I got the damn' finest education someone like me could hope to get. Now I've got a nice apartment along with a job that's second to none. Hey, David. You've spilt some of your coffee. Can I get you a drop more?'

I thanked him. No . . . I wanted to go up on deck to get some air . . . I complimented him on his game . . . I got a promise of a rematch. Then, without my face betraying what I was thinking, I left the room.

The time passed. There were times when night couldn't be differentiated from day. Heavy cloud had rolled across a diminished sun, reducing the already meagre light to nothing. Still the ship thrummed on, screws churning the waters of the Atlantic, the prow pointing westward. At times the wind blew fiercely cold. From out of the darkness raced flurries of snow. Someone once said that a snowflake in June was an evil thing. I saw that wasn't far from the truth. On what should have been a warm summer's day I watched streams of snowflakes flashing by the porthole. Maybe there would be no let-up. And maybe after a few grim years the whole world would be encased in thick, dead ice.

But then, who knew? For a thousand years, a million years, or for all eternity the Earth would circle the sun — locked inside a coffin of ice. Without so much as a microbe remaining on its face.

I wiped the condensation from the porthole glass. Beyond it lay utter darkness, sullied only by those spitting white flecks of snow.

The long-dead poet was right. A snowflake in summer was an evil thing indeed.

'Hello, bang-bang man!'

Christina beamed brightly at me from across the passenger saloon. She'd been drawing stick men with a fat wax crayon.

I smiled back, then touched my chest. 'David.' I drew out the vowel into a long 'aaay' sound. 'Daaay–vid.'

'David Masen,' she said brightly. 'Yes. David Masen. Suppertime?'

'No,' I said, taken aback by her progress. 'Supper won't be for a while yet.'

Kerris looked up from her report-writing. 'Christina's coming along in leaps and bounds. Give her a year or two and I think she'll be signing up for our research team.'

'She's going to be an Ollie, too?'

'Ollies? Oh, you've been talking to the crew, have you?'

'No. Gabriel told me. Truth be known the crew tend to steer clear of me.'

'Don't worry. They do that to us as well. Oh well, a little mutual suspicion never did anyone any harm. Whiskey?'

'Well – er, if you think—'

'Oh, come on, join me. The sun must be over the yardarm by now. Even if we can't see the blasted thing.' Lightly she swung her long legs from under the table before walking across the room with that interesting swaying walk of hers. (Gabriel had described it as 'sassy', before giving me a knowing wink.) 'If you ask me,' she said, scooping ice into a pair of tumblers, 'the crew are a little bit jealous of our refreshments.' She waggled the whiskey bottle in my direction. 'They're required to be "dry" when they're at sea. Seeing us with a reviving glass of something or other really gets them miffed. That enough for you?' She held up the glass: it held a more than generous splash of spirit.

'Yes – ample. Thanks.'

Christina gave me a stern look. 'Mucky beer.' Then she pulled a face, crossing her eyes while wobbling her head from side to side in a fair imitation of someone who'd tippled just that bit too self-indulgently.

Kerris smiled, 'Something tells me that within a few months our feral child here's going to be very much like a typical New York teenager . . . cheers!'

Within a couple of days I had my sea legs. What's more, I'd settled into the ship's routines. Meals were incredibly generous. Coffee on tap all day. Often I talked to the Ollies. Kerris Baedekker and Gabriel Deeds were the friendliest. (Although Gabriel took great delight in beating me hollow at table tennis — even so, I did pull one or two games back. I also showed him the rudiments of cricket with a cardboard tube and a pair of tightly rolled socks. Ah. Revenge, sweet revenge.) Kim So spent most of her time tutoring Christina, so I didn't see much of them. But I did notice that Christina's vocabulary had acquired musical American accents, peppered here and there with a phrasing that was pure Highland Scots. Dek, pleasant but painfully shy, tended to retreat into his work. He'd spend most of his waking hours writing detailed reports on geological findings at the various landfalls the ship had made so far. As far as I could gather there was a pressing need to find new oilfields that were readily accessible *and* triffid-free. No mean task. The team member I warmed to least was Rory Masterfield. I found a certain sharpness in his eyes off-putting; and, though he masked it behind a chummy smile, I sensed a lurking prickliness.

To my surprise, I realized I was looking forward eagerly to my arrival in New York. My spirit of adventure had been reawakened. I wanted to explore. Naturally, when I returned to the Isle of Wight I'd give a full report on whatever I might find in the American city. I'd already flagged up one area of unease. Gabriel Deeds had been quite candid about the fact that he'd been chemically castrated in return for certain privileges. On my island, where fecundity was celebrated, the notion of neutering a healthy young male created an instant, reflexive abhorrence in me. But then, the creation of a eunuch class in society certainly wasn't anything new. Ancient Rome,

Byzantium, the Ottoman Empire and many Oriental cultures had practised male castration. Often regarded as an elite within society, eunuchs performed many specialist roles, ranging from guarding the Sultan's harem to priestly duties to high office in the Byzantine civil service. As a horse is blinkered to enable it to perform that bit better, so a boy would sacrifice his manhood in order to concentrate on his duties with no hormonal distractions.

Whether I found the practice detestable or not, clearly the New York eunuch was a fact of life in Gabriel's world.

On the evening of the second day, with the sun nothing more than a brick-red smear above the horizon, the deck suddenly exploded into a frenzy of activity. Sailors raced up from hatchways wearing expressions that were as determined as they were tense.

Captain Sharpstone called down to me where I stood on deck, his voice calm yet forceful. 'Mr Masen. Get down below, please.' In the near-dark he was no more than a dark silhouette on the bridge.

My curiosity got the better of me. 'What's wrong?'

'Nothing we can't handle. Now, I must ask you to go below deck.'

By this time some crewmen had tugged protective tarpaulins from the big deck gun, while others were hoisting machine guns onto their mountings.

'Now, Mr Masen,' the captain insisted. 'Otherwise I shall be obliged to have you escorted below for your own protection.'

Reluctantly I quit the deck for the passenger saloon below.

There the mood of the research team was tense. No one spoke. Gabriel twisted his fingers into complex tangles while gazing out through the porthole.

'What's going on?' I asked. 'The crew have manned the guns up there.'

'Just a precaution,' Rory told me. 'There's nothing to worry about.'

Well said – but I noticed Kim and Dek's worried expressions.

'Does this kind of thing happen often?' I asked. It occurred to me that these people had enemies. That out there in the darkened ocean their foe might now be stalking them.

I sat quietly, too, waiting for the sound of the first gunshot.

Supper, understandably enough, came late. Only after a hurriedly prepared omelette meal did a whistle sound over the ship's PA system.

When I heard the relieved sighs of the team I guessed that this was the 'all clear' signal.' The sound of tramping feet came along the corridor as sailors returned to their usual quarters.

Whatever it was, it was over without a shot being fired.

Still, seeing that flurry of activity around the ship's guns gave me plenty of food for thought. When I retired to my bunk that night. I was still wondering what

Captain Sharpstone had expected to encounter on the high seas.

Morning didn't so much break as leak upward from the eastern horizon: a slowly spreading dull-hued stain like blood seeping through dark cloth.

I'd woken up cold. Over breakfast I learned that in order to increase our speed Captain Sharpstone had ordered that every cubic centimetre of steam should be directed into driving the engines even harder, leaving no surplus heat for the cabins. So, bundled up as warmly as possible against a bitterly cold morning, one that had left a frosting here and there on the deck gun's tarpaulin, I stood looking forward into that wintry gloom. Behind me the smudge of red slid higher into the sky. Slowly – too slowly – it grew a little brighter. By mid-morning it had attained the lustre of red foil once more. Yet it still cast precious little light.

I leaned forward, my elbows taking my weight on the guard rail. The sea, flat calm, had the look of congealing blood – a kind of viscous reddish brown. Once more I wondered if I was bound for some grim underworld.

From the distance came an eerie cry. Lonely, plaintive, ghostly with lost and dying echoes. I looked for its source. It didn't require much effort to imagine that it came from the phantom mouth of a long-dead sailor. But reason told me it must be a gull, gliding somewhere out there in that twilit world. I looked for a long while, yet never saw so much as a single seabird. The plaintive cry came again.

Between sea and sky a pale line ran as far as the eye

could see. *Mist*, I told myself. Probably due to the cold air touching a slightly warmer sea. Then, as I gazed at it, there came a subtle transformation.

In the distance tiny shapes emerged. They were clustered densely at the centre, then thinned out toward the edges. There weren't many. Moreover, they didn't seem that large, but as I watched they became that little bit more distinct. There, emerging slowly from the mist like some enchanted Babylon, were spires and towers reaching towards the sky. A magic citadel, floating above the waves.

So taken was I with the vision that I didn't notice Kerris as she came to stand beside me.

'Quite something, isn't it?' she murmured. I turned to see her green eyes shine as, nodding, she softly said, 'Home.'

CHAPTER FOURTEEN

Metropolis

Photographs, sketches, film, even a picture on a biscuit tin – I'd seen many images of the place. But this vision of buildings floating mysteriously and quite magically out of the mist filled me with wonder.

Beside me, her hair rippling in the breeze, Kerris too watched entranced. This had to be a sight you never tired of. No matter how many times you experienced it.

At length Kerris said, 'She looks quite something, doesn't she?'

I had to admit 'she' did.

Misty towers resolved themselves sharply into sky-scrapers. Even at a distance of fifteen miles or so I easily recognized the streamlined symmetry of the Chrysler Building while the more aggressive neo-megalithic lines of the Empire State Building towered alongside. Long ago, H.G. Wells wrote: 'What a funny place New York was – all sticking up and full of windows.' I didn't think the great man had done this enchanting vista justice. Not by a long chalk.

Despite the bone-deep cold, we, by some mutual yet unspoken agreement, decided to stand there in the prow of the steamship and watch. Up on the bridge, sensed rather than seen, was the formidable presence of Captain Sharpstone, guiding his ship and crew safely home to port. Presently I glimpsed fishing boats standing like inkspots on the sea, while a destroyer, bristling with big guns and missiles, stood guard in the final approaches.

The colour of the water changed to silty brown as we passed from the open sea to the confluence of the Hudson, Harlem and East Rivers. The ship's engines slowed as the ship drew ever closer to the city now rearing hugely before us.

Moments later that famous bronze lady, the Statue of Liberty, moved past our port bow. Still a greenish hue in this meagre light I noticed with some sadness that she'd suffered a savage act of mutilation. Her eyes had been dynamited from her face, leaving the great statue blinded and monstrous-looking. On the island itself half a dozen field guns pointed out to sea, their barrels gleaming dully.

Turning to look at the city of Manhattan, I saw that the skyscrapers now towered above us, their windows reflecting that same sombre sun – a million dull red eyes seemingly glaring down at me, David Masen, a stranger in a very strange land.

There were many different kinds of boat moving around the port – tugs, fishing vessels, river pilots, police launches, barges, as well as a great number of sailing ships – which indicated much about this resource-hungry nation. Now I could see roads running away straight into the heart of the city, through canyons of steel and concrete. And there were cars, thousands of cars, trucks, buses, vans of all shapes and sizes, sounding their horns and filling the air with engine sounds that sounded like a continuous low thunder. Headlights, switched on even though it was noon, shone brilliantly.

By this time Kerris had a relaxed smile on her face. For her this was home. For me . . . well . . . I'd seen nothing like it before. My chest felt tight. My head moved left and right, right and left as I tried to see everything at once.

This was a land of wonder, of amazement, of near-supernatural splendour. A strange animal passion blazed within me at that moment. I wanted, no, I *craved* to plunge into the heart of that vortex of movement, light and sound.

After what seemed like a whole string of delays the ship at last tied up alongside a quay. Moments later I walked down the gangway to see what this strange new world had to offer.

An official reception of sorts awaited us. A group of men and women spirited Christina away with Kim protectively holding her hand. In a way I still felt responsible for the girl and I asked Kerris where they were taking her. Kerris reassured me that Christina would be well cared for. 'The only danger is that she's going to become a celebrity; the same goes for you, too, David.' Her eyes twinkled. 'Now. This wharf we're walking along . . . the *Titanic* would have docked here in 1912 if it had made it across the Atlantic . . . of course, I don't know if you'd take that as a good omen or a bad omen.' She smiled as a group of uniformed men appeared. 'Well, it looks as if there will be some formalities before we can get you to the hotel.'

For an hour I completed forms in the Customs office. My photograph was taken in profile and full face for an immigration record. Then a man in a gold-braided uniform shook my hand, welcomed me to New York and invited me through a gate to where a car waited.

With Kerris by my side I sat in the back, marvelling at the city as the car nosed its way through traffic. What could I say? The sights, sounds, even the smells of exotic food – all of it was nothing less than an assault on my senses. Eyes wide, head ducking, twisting, bending this way and that I tried to absorb everything. People of all different races on the streets; the road signs with mysterious-sounding names – TriBeCa, Chinatown, Little Italy, fabled Broadway. Bars, shops, cafés, restaurants, all teeming with life. Everyone walking with a rapidity that spoke volumes about the population's vitality and sense of purpose.

Even the sun had brightened in the once dingy sky. It filled the city with a soft red light, buildings glowing with every shade of red from deep copper to gold. In that confused mêlée of first impressions I formed a single strong sense of a clean city: well ordered, prosperous.

At that moment I shared an affinity with the ancient Briton who'd travelled in his animal skins to stand in the Imperial Rome of the Caesars. How that man must have marvelled at the heroic statues, huge temples, soaring columns and finely dressed citizens in their silks and jewels.

· Suddenly I thought of my old island home. A rural backwater of winding lanes along which trundled horse-drawn carts. A hotchpotch of quaint villages, populated by sleepy yokels. It seemed a poor place in comparison with this.

Presently the car pulled up outside a towering building.

'Your hotel,' Kerris told me, then smiled at my no doubt perplexed expression. 'Don't worry, David. They're expecting you. New clothes should have been delivered, too — I telegraphed your sizes ahead. Although we still need to fix you up with more suitable shoes . . . sea boots in Manhattan just won't do.'

I was like a child at Christmas, wide-eyed with excitement, rushing from one surprise to another. Even so, I felt a twinge of disloyalty to my old home on that quiet island thousands of miles away. It had been a safe refuge for the Masen family. What grew and grazed upon its lush landscape had fed me, clothed me. Its society had done its best to educate and entertain me. But this pulsating metropolis offered so much more.

'What's that?' I asked the barman in the hotel bar.

He grinned. 'That's television, sir.'

Instantly I burned with embarrassment. I knew full well what television was. I'd seen enough of the dusty glass-fronted boxes dumped in garden sheds. But I'd never seen one, well . . . for want of a more appropriate word . . . *alive* before. On the set bolted high on the wall behind the bar coloured pictures flashed. In the space of what seemed like five seconds but was obviously longer came images of a dance troupe dressed in shocking pink and kicking their long legs to a brash rhythm. Then came a blonde girl saying how much she loved Pop's Poppercorn. Then a lady claiming that she always shopped at Macy's. Hard on the heels of that were shots of soldiers marching, then firing flame-throwers at triffids, and finally crushing the steaming plants to pulp with their boots. 'Jobs don't come any tougher or hotter than this,' boomed a deeply serious male voice. 'That's why I like nothing better than a long, cold drink of Rheingold. The beer that heroes go home to.'

The barman served me the beer I'd ordered as I perched myself on a stool. For the next hour I watched as a blond-haired man with an incongruously precise hairstyle rescued a succession of children and blushingly grateful young women from fifth columnists of some sort who'd hijacked a passenger liner. Infuriatingly, just as it appeared that the blond man would be blown to smithereens by a hand grenade or forced backwards over the ship's guard rail into a shark-infested sea, the suspense would be interrupted by more jangling exhortations to buy a coat of a certain cut, to acquire shoes that promised wearers would find themselves 'walking on air' or to purchase 'the gum that gets the gal'.

'Now don't go getting square eyes on me,' said a bright voice.

Kerris sat briskly beside me and ordered a beer. She wore trousers of an eyebrow-raising fit with a powder-blue sweater; around her neck she'd loosely tied a silk scarf shot through with flashes of gold and electric blue.

After exchanging a few pleasantries with me she handed me an envelope.

'What's this?'

'Just some cash.'

'Kerris, I can't accept this.'

'Of course you can. You'll need money. Oh, and I've included a pass for the subway.'

'But I won't be able to pay you back.'

'Nonsense.'

'But—'

'Anyway, the money isn't mine. Consider it a welcoming gift from the city of New York.' She smiled a vivacious smile. 'Right, drink up. I can't let you waste your days alone in a hotel bar.'

'Where are we going?'

'Sightseeing.'

CHAPTER FIFTEEN

The Grand Tour

Kerris Baedekker didn't stint when it came to the tour. Even riding the subterranean railway system was a thing of wonder for me. Huge steel carriages thundered through tunnels that were vast enough to make me think of cathedrals. She showed me the Empire State Building with a 'That's where my father has his office'. From there we went into Greenwich Village with its much smaller buildings and an exotic bohemian atmosphere that I found strangely exciting.

Sometimes she slipped into a tour-guide role, quoting facts and figures. 'Manhattan Island is a twenty-two-square-mile slab of rock three billion years old. Fresh water arrives through a one-hundred-and-twenty-five-mile-long tunnel from three reservoir systems. Power stations are coal-fired. The name "Manhattan" comes from an explorer celebrating discovery of the island with a local group of Indians. After the rather boozy party the island was named "Mannahattanink", which means "the island of general intoxication".'

'Really?'

'Well, it's a rather fanciful story. In truth, no one really knows how the name originated. Hungry yet?'

We ate at the homely White Horse Tavern on Hudson Street, an establishment that wouldn't have been out of place alongside the pubs of the Isle of Wight.

More than once I noticed the skyward-pointing muzzle of an anti-aircraft gun on the flat roof of a building. More evidence of a defence-conscious society? Or was there a more specific threat? If there was, however, these bustling natives made no show of it affecting their nerves.

Once more we rode the underground express train. This time north to Central Park, now under cultivation with potatoes and corn. But I did notice that the lack of natural daylight had taken its toll. Plants had turned a pale green. Stalks wilted miserably.

Kerris looked at them unhappily. 'Unless there's a return to normal daylight we're in big trouble. The crops will be dead within a week.'

We crossed what had once been an elegant formal park for the eastern side of the island. Even in that gloom I could see a pale wall running east to west. Standing perhaps twenty feet high, a number of guard towers were also clearly visible at regular intervals.

'Kerris, what's kept in there?'

'Oh, that's the 102nd Street Parallel. It cuts Manhattan Island in two.'

'Oh? Why?'

'It goes back twenty years or so.' She spoke a trifle vaguely. I waited for her to elaborate. Instead she said,

'Come on, there's lots more to see.' She took my arm, guiding me between fields of drooping corn.

The lady was right. There was lots to see. Art galleries. Museums. Libraries. Civic monuments. At one point a car pulled up on the street with a painful-sounding crunch. It appeared that its engine had suddenly and ruinously seized.

'That's a sight you'll get used to,' she said, still walking arm in arm with me. 'You can guarantee a breakdown in every street.'

'There's a shortage of engine parts?'

'No, we're manufacturing replacements now. We run our engines on wood alcohol. It's combustible, but it plays havoc with the pistons. Ideally an engine should be stripped down and rebuilt every two thousand miles.'

'It would be more convenient, more economical too, to switch to refined triffid oil. Of course, you'd have to convert the cars' engines but we find they're pretty good for a hundred thousand miles or so.'

'Good Lord.' Kerris sounded genuinely impressed.

At the risk of boasting I added, 'My father invented the refining technique, together with a chap called Coker. To date we have three Masen-Coker refining plants producing around five million gallons of fuel a year.'

She let out a breath. 'I think it must be providence that blew you our way, David. If your people would show us how to build one of these Masen-Coker machines it would solve our fuel problems over night. Or as near as dammit.'

'All you'd need then would be a lot of triffids.'

'Triffids? We've got plenty of those.' We'd followed a

road that ended at a river. This was narrower than the Hudson, maybe little wider than two hundred yards.

She touched my arm. 'Just take a look at them.'

I looked where she pointed. Across the river the land ran uphill to a line of ruined buildings.

'Brooklyn Heights,' she explained. 'A place we seldom visit. For obvious reasons.'

There, in that grave red light, I saw them. Triffids. Millions of the blasted things. Silent. Unmoving. I'd never seen such an intense concentration of the plants. Nor beheld any of such prodigious size. They covered every square inch of land as far as the eye could see. Triffids crowded down to the water's edge. The ones nearest us even stood with their roots in the water, giving the impression of some evil-looking mangrove swamp.

I knew why they crowded there. Between them and what amounted to a breadbasket of more than three hundred thousand people was a mere narrow barrier of water. Whatever senses they possessed strained toward the noisy city, sensing those sweet morsels of humanity . . . hungering for them.

I shivered, imagining an invasion by so many triffid plants. I had a nightmarish vision of them pouring onto Manhattan's streets.

After a moment or so I commented, 'You've no shortage of raw material there, I see.'

'No. And it's like that all around us.' Kerris leaned towards me, squeezing my arm, needing a sudden human closeness in the face of that implacable foe. She gave me a weak smile. 'That's right. We're under siege.'

✳　　✳　　✳

That evening I walked with Kerris to a restaurant near the hotel. She automatically slipped an arm through mine, a simple, human act that I found extremely pleasing.

Gabriel hailed us on the street, genuinely happy to see us.

'We're just about to eat,' I said, nodding towards the brightly lit restaurant. 'Why don't you join us?'

His gaze met Kerris's. For a moment there was an awkwardness that was almost palpable.

'No, I've got to dash. Thanks, anyway. I just dropped in to the hotel to see how you were settling in.'

'That's very civil of you, Gabriel. Thanks.' A thought occurred to me. 'Give me your telephone number. It's time I gave you another thrashing at table tennis.'

He laughed. 'You can't get enough of those beatings, can you? Here's my card. Ignore the telephone number at the top. That's the office. My home number's underneath.' With that he turned his collar up to the cold night air, before hurrying away.

'Come on, David. My feet are like ice.'

We headed for the welcome warmth of the restaurant. For a moment I wondered why there had been that sudden awkwardness between Kerris and Gabriel when I'd invited him to join us for dinner. Had he and Kerris been entangled romantically at some point in the past? As it was, I had only a moment to reflect on this before I reached the restaurant and saw the sign on the door. *Whites & Sighted Only.*

I gritted my teeth, then followed Kerris inside.

My appetite had been blunted by that unsettling prohibition on the door so I just toyed with my food. Kerris gave no indication that she'd seen me notice the sign. Instead, she cut a piece of veal and moved it to the centre of her plate so that a pool of gravy surrounded it.

We'd been talking about the triffids that surrounded Manhattan. She assured me that they weren't as menacing as I'd first thought.

'Excuse me for playing with my food a little,' she began. 'But let's say this long sliver of meat is the island of Manhattan. Three rivers cut it off from mainland America. The Harlem River, which you looked across today, is the narrowest, so that gives you the best view of the triffids. But it's the same on the far banks of the Hudson and the East River, too. It was once calculated that there are nigh on seventy million triffid plants crowding on land that was once Queens, New Jersey, Brooklyn and The Bronx. They form a rough horseshoe cluster round the island. Luckily we have that water barrier between us and them. Needless to say, the bridges and tunnels that connect us with the mainland have some pretty substantial barriers in place.'

'Phew.' I whistled. 'With tens of millions more triffids further out on the mainland.'

'Right. The whole country's a no-go area.'

'Are there many human settlements this side of the Atlantic?'

'A few. None that we know of on the mainland. Most are on islands further to the south. With a few scattered on the Great Lakes.'

'Do you have much contact with them?'

'Hardly any. For the last thirty years folks have gotten more insular.'

'How do you get logs for processing into wood alcohol?'

'There are teams of loggers up the Hudson. Well guarded against triffid attack, I should add. They float the logs downriver to an industrial distillery in the north of the island.'

'You said you have a population of over three hundred thousand?'

'And growing fast.'

'But how on earth do you feed everyone?' I looked round at the other diners. 'Veal, pork, beef, oysters, cheeses. Vegetables galore – not to mention coffee and tobacco. How can you produce it all in a place that's nine-tenths concrete?'

'The answer is, of course, we don't. We import a good deal from the Caribbean.'

'Oh?'

'We've managed to clear some islands of triffids down there.'

'Must have taken a heck of a lot of manpower.'

'What's that Latin phrase?' She thought for moment. '*Labor ominia vincit.*'

I took a brave stab at translation. 'Where there's a will there's a way?'

'Close. Work conquers everything.'

We chatted on. I must confess, however, that that notice on the door, *Whites & Sighted Only*, had shocked me. I'd never seen anything like it before: it was a man-made barrier between sighted and unsighted, black and white. When I'd arrived in New York it was like being offered a wonderful, beautifully decorated cake that promised ineffable sweetness. Yet just a couple of bites later it was as though I'd found an ugly fly squashed into the topping. But, I told myself, this was a different land. They had different customs. Not all of them might be to my taste. Could I sit here in judgement when the ways of my own land might appear questionable to outsiders?

In any event, my opinion of this glittering metropolis and my plans for the future turned out to be irrelevant. It might have been right then, as I sat talking to Kerris over dinner, that a cold, harsh intellect focused on me. As a master chess player considers the layout of the board and sees in a new light a piece that he once ignored, so this entity now looked with its mind's eye at me. I would become a significant element in another's future strategy. Without knowing anything about it, I had become a very important chess piece in this individual's game.

Perhaps, as I ordered coffee and shared a joke with Kerris, it at last made its decision and issued the necessary order. Then it sat back to see what happened next.

CHAPTER SIXTEEN

Rhythms of the Night

After the restaurant Kerris suggested a bar with live music. I anticipated a cocktail or two while a pianist played discreetly in the corner. Instead, I experienced another very different aspect of this culture. At the end of a long bar musicians played on a raised stage. The instruments — guitars and drums — were electrically amplified. And the noise was phenomenal. It felt as if an avalanche of sound struck me the moment I entered the bar. On the dance floor people gyrated with wild abandon.

Kerris shouted something in my ear. The shout must have been loud since my eardrum tickled outrageously but, against the decibel level of the music, I still couldn't hear what she said.

I gestured, grinning, that I hadn't heard.

She shouted again, so close that her lips brushed my ear.

'*Manhattan Blues!*'

Whether that was the name of the song or the band or

the style of music I just didn't know. But there was something thrilling about being so close to the pounding rhythm of drums, while the guitar seemed to sing, uncannily imitating a human voice. It came as a complete surprise to see that the guitarist was none other than Gabriel Deeds.

I stood entranced at the sight of the swaying dancers in a room that was so hot it was oven-like, crammed with perspiring people and vibrating to those infectious rhythms. The music ran for twenty minutes or so, with Gabriel's amplified guitar flowing seamlessly from a beautiful lyrical tenderness to alarming shrieks and howls that reminded me of a jet flying low overhead. Gabriel's soulful brown eyes gazed at some point above our heads while he played, as if the far wall had melted away, allowing him a vision of paradise. The more I listened to the guitar the more I heard some deep and powerful yearning running through the music.

After the band finished, Kerris seized my hand to pull me through the crowds to the stage. Gabriel propped the guitar against an amplifier the size of a tea chest and began to wipe the back of his neck with a towel before chasing away glistening drops of perspiration from his dark forehead.

'Kerris? David?' He grinned. 'Did you catch any of that?'

I told him I'd been completely bowled over by it. I'd heard nothing like it before.

'Great,' he responded, pleased. 'This is the finest way I know of blowing the cobwebs away after a day locked in the office.'

'I knew you'd be here,' Kerris said. 'I thought I'd show David the kind of music you play.'

We chatted for a while, eventually turning to the subject of the perpetual twilight; Gabriel had attended a conference earlier in the day where various hypotheses (and a number of sheer guesses) had been aired. 'The most plausible,' Gabriel said, 'is that the reduction in light is a result of comet debris running between the earth and the sun.'

'That would certainly account for the sunlight being obscured,' I said, 'But it's been nearly a month now; surely we should be coming through it soon?'

'That's what they're figuring. Sunlight strength's up; average daytime temperatures have increased a couple of degrees.'

'Then we might get a return to normal daylight soon?'

'Maybe, but if you ask me a lot of fingers are crossed. I don't think we're out of the woods yet. And another thing.' He draped the towel round his neck. 'It may be these dark days, or it may be something else we don't know about, but it's got the triffids all jittery. They say you can even hear the noise they're making across the East River. They're rattling the old talking sticks away like their lives depend on it.'

I nodded. 'If the lack of daylight is killing ordinary crops triffids will be suffering, too.'

'It's not before time,' Kerris said with feeling. 'I hope the filthy things rot.'

'But we do know that deprived of natural light they either become comatose after a while—'

'Or they step up their nutrient intake.'

Gabriel shot us a sober look. 'Which means they'll need meat.'

'And having seventy million of the things as neighbours means they won't be needing just a cheeseburger or two,' Kerris said dryly. 'They'll be wanting the whole banquet.'

'Right.' Gabriel glanced at his watch. 'Time for the next set. You people sticking around?'

'Just you try tearing us away.'

As the band played crowds of happy people surged back onto the dance floor to surrender with blissful abandonment to that soaring music. They looked as if they hadn't a care in the world.

'Thank you for a very pleasant night out,' I began as we walked back toward the hotel. 'But, well . . .'

'But what?' She turned to me, her eyes suddenly wide.

'Well, I'm starting to feel guilty imposing myself on you so much of the time, when—'

'Guilty for imposing,' she echoed. 'That sounds very English to me. What's it really mean? So long, I'll give you a call sometime never?'

'Pardon? Oh no. Not at all.' I'd offended her. 'No, but if you've been instructed by your superiors to keep me company it doesn't seem fair that—'

'I haven't been ordered to do anything I didn't want to.'

'So you don't mind? It hasn't been an imposition?'

'Imposition? My . . . you say the funniest things, David.'

For a second we paused to look at each other, standing

like two little islands there in the flow of pedestrians who still thronged the streets even at that time of night. Street lights reflected in her eyes, while above us skyscrapers soared, their electric lights transforming them into jewelled columns.

She smiled, tilting her head to one side. 'It's true that I was asked to help you get settled in and to show you the sights.'

'Well, that's my point. If I'm intruding—'

'But.' She held up her finger. 'Point number one, I didn't want to see you rattling round in a big place like this alone. Two, believe it or not, I genuinely enjoy your company.' She smiled. 'Maybe it's your quaint turns of phrase, or your accent or something.'

'In that case, it's safe for me to say—' But instead of saying what I intended I found myself making a kind of surprised grunt. 'Uh . . . who switched out the lights?'

I looked round as the street lights, the building lights; in fact, every light in the city suddenly went out, leaving only the car lights. In an instant the cars stopped sharply. Though from the sound of a tinkling crash one did not stop quickly enough. Then, in scarcely two blinks of an eye, for some inexplicable reason drivers switched off their lights, too.

Immediately an eerie darkness descended on Manhattan. Smokers even nipped out the glowing tips of cigarettes. An equally strange silence fell, accompanied by a sense of people holding their breath in expectation.

A hand clutched my arm. I heard Kerris whisper, 'Quick. Into the doorway.'

I couldn't see Kerris in this utter darkness but I felt my

way into a recess in the wall. Then my shoulder bumped against a closed door.

'Oh, damn . . .' she whispered. There was a note of regret in that mild curse.

Initially, it seemed that a power failure had blacked out the city. But why had the car drivers so quickly extinguished their lights? Barely had the question run through my head when a searchlight's beam sprang from the top of a building. Then another. And another, until a dozen great beams of searing white light were playing in the sky. For a moment they danced, seemingly at random, throwing splashes of brilliance onto the clouds.

From another building came a sharp crack that made the door behind me rattle. Kerris pulled in a sharp breath. There was another cracking sound. This time I saw a blue-white spark fly skyward. A moment later an explosion echoed across the city.

Another anti-aircraft gun spoke from the direction of the Empire State Building. At first it was all fairly hit-and-miss. Searchlights shone in different directions; odd bursts of ack-ack fire were either aimed at a wildly shifting target or the gunners were shooting blind.

But then, as if the searchlight operators and gunners had begun to receive coordinating instructions, the lights drew together so that they formed a massive tripod of dazzling columns converging at a single point overhead. Almost simultaneously a dozen different anti-aircraft guns fired at this apex.

For a full ten seconds balls of flame thundered up towards the illuminated area of cloud while shells detonated thunderously five thousand feet above the city. Soon, however, the guns fell silent. And only for a little while longer the searchlights made a sweep of the sky, hunting a target that had either retreated or never been there in the first place.

The city's lights remained out for nearly an hour. In that pitch dark there was no way we could move. Not that it mattered. Because for much of that time Kerris was in my arms, and I was only conscious of one thing. Her soft lips against mine.

CHAPTER SEVENTEEN

Paradise Found

For the next two weeks the sun grew just that little bit brighter every day. Early morning and evening still painted the sky as red as hellfire, but by noon it was usually blue. Meanwhile the sun strengthened from dull red to brilliant orange. Normal sunlight had not yet returned fully, but it seemed like a start – a definite, heart-warming start.

I saw Kerris Baedekker regularly. And soon, in a no-nonsense kind of way, we were what some call an *item*.

There was no repeat of the air raid. The morning after the blackout, newspapers and TV carried reports that could be summarized as 'Air bandits sent packing' and there were references to past atrocities, such as bombing attacks on defenceless fishing boats by something known as 'the Quintling faction'. A mood of self-congratulation took hold of the populace for a while but the drama was soon forgotten. Normal life resumed.

I was free to continue exploring that great city, often with Kerris, sometimes with Gabriel Deeds and Christina. My former wild child of the island had come on in leaps and bounds. With the cut of her hair and the style of her clothes she looked very much like any other New York girl of fifteen. Her vocabulary had expanded at a tremendous rate, too, but she still couldn't help grinning mischievously at me sometimes, pointing her finger and saying 'Bang-bang man'. And so we went to funfairs, rode subways, toured galleries, or visited bars where Gabriel Deeds and his fellow musicians played their hypnotic music.

Every now and again I'd have to remind myself that this wasn't really my home, that home for me was a small island on the other side of the Atlantic. Truthfully, though, that island had become indistinct to me, as if the first three decades of my life had been spent asleep and I'd only woken up fully the day I set foot in New York.

Much of that was due to Kerris. Even after this short spell of time I found it hard to accept that I'd have to leave her here when I returned to the Isle of Wight.

And if my thoughts could have travelled through the air like radio waves and reached that cool, Machiavellian mind that I mentioned before, its owner would have nodded with satisfaction. A telephone call was made. Soon everything was arranged.

'David?' Kerris turned a wineglass between her fingers in the cinema bar during the interval. 'Can I ask you something?'

'Of course,' I said, smiling. 'Fire away.'

'This sounds a bit old-fashioned, but would you like to meet my father?'

'Of course. I'd be delighted.'

She'd not mentioned her parents much so this was a bit of a bolt — a very small one, admittedly, — from the blue. Nevertheless, I readily accepted. 'And will I get a chance to meet your mother, too?'

'Ah, I'm afraid not.'

I'd clumsily stepped on toes. 'I'm sorry, Kerris, I didn't mean to—'

'No, no.' She waved away my apologies. 'She died when I was born.'

'I'm terribly sorry.'

'Don't.' She tapped my knee. 'You weren't to know. Now finish your wine. The movie's about to start.'

The poster in the subway carriage spelt out the following message in large, shouting purple inks: *NEW YORK — Home to the brightest minds, the most brilliant men, the world's greatest structures!*

Gabriel Deeds noticed me reading the poster. He smiled. 'Just in case we forget.'

'Are you hinting that some of the trumpet-blowing is a little strident?' I asked.

Gabriel's smile broadened. 'Why, Mr Masen. I think it's just perfect.'

'And I think I detect a hint of irony, too.'

He simply shrugged, then looked out of the window as the train rushed into one of the brightly lit subway stations. The train wasn't particularly crowded. Only a few passengers got into our carriage. Three black women and two blind men. I could see through connecting doors into adjoining carriages where the passengers were all white and sighted. Initially, I hadn't noticed the sign on the window of our carriage: *Coloureds & Unsighted*. I did notice, however, the curious glances the black women were giving me.

'Don't worry, Mr Masen.' Gabriel spoke in his customary soft tones. 'There's no bar to you riding in this particular carriage.'

Suddenly feeling awkward, I said, 'Gabriel, the name's David, don't forget.'

'In some public places, it's best that I address you as Mister.'

'Then I'll call you Mr Deeds.'

'Then, Mr Masen, that would get you a slight scolding from the cops and me into a hell of a lot of trouble. You do understand, Mr Masen?'

'I understand . . . Gabriel.'

'Don't worry. It's just one of our local customs. You'll get used to them.'

They weren't pleasant customs, but I didn't say anything.

The train hurtled into Columbus Square station. Everyone in our carriage, with the exception of Gabriel and myself, disembarked. The two unsighted men walked briskly away, tapping canes against the ground.

When the doors had slid shut again Gabriel turned to me and said under his breath, 'So what's your take on paradise?'

'It's got a lot to offer. But I don't care for the segregation of blacks and unsighted people.'

'I believe that's just a . . .'

'Aberration' was the word I thought he'd use. Instead: 'I believe that's just a *transitional* custom.'

'I call it horrible.'

He allowed me my view, shrugging. 'When the blindness came to New York there was chaos, as you'd imagine. Out of a population of seven million probably ninety-eight per cent were blinded. They starved in their apartments or on the streets. Only the local wildlife didn't go hungry.' He gave me a significant nod. 'Triffids moved in over the bridges. Killed most of who was left, but it has to be said, they did a good job clearing the dead from the sidewalks. Then, around twenty years ago, an armada of ships sailed into the Hudson. "Miracle of the Hundred Ships", they call it. We even commemorate it with an annual holiday every April. Well, those people cleared up the place with the help of communities clinging on by their fingertips along the coast, here and on Long Island.'

'It must have been a heck of a mess.'

'It was. But those guys who saw Manhattan Island as a great stronghold of civilization were true visionaries. They did the impossible. The millions of corpses that the triffids couldn't get to in buildings and so on were buried at sea. They restored power, fresh-water supplies, wiped out the triffids. Rounded up people from far and wide, brought them here, put them in nice apartments, gave them jobs, and – more importantly – hope.'

'So who does run this place?'

'The Tetrarchs.'

'Tetrarch – sounds Roman, if I remember rightly?'

Gabriel nodded. 'You do remember right. It's where a province was divided into four with a governor, a Tetrarch, assigned to each part. Here the divisions aren't geographical but administrative. Each Tetrarch is responsible for a certain area of government — General Fielding looks after the military, foreign affairs and triffid control. Policy and Resources is Dr Wiseman's responsibility. Population Recovery is Valerie Zito's, and Joe Garibaldi takes care of Industrial Recovery.'

'They're elected?'

'Are your bosses?'

'They will be.'

Gabriel gave a little smile. 'Ditto.'

'You consider them an effective government?'

'*Very.*'

'Do you like them?'

'Like them? I respect them.'

'But do you *like* them?'

'Is that a material consideration when it comes to assessing whether they can do the job or not?

I smiled. 'Point taken.'

'Have you asked Kerris the same questions?'

'Do you think I should?'

Gabriel shrugged. 'I'd be curious to hear her answer . . . particularly concerning General Fielding.'

'Why General Fielding?'

'Didn't she tell you?'

'Tell me what?' Now I was puzzled.

'General Fielding is Kerris's father.' He nodded to the door as the train slid into the station. 'Our stop, Mr Masen.'

CHAPTER EIGHTEEN

Discussion

'I didn't think it was that important,' Kerris answered lightly as we strolled through the evening sunlight.

'That your father is the leader of a whole city? It's not something that most people would keep secret.' I grinned. 'Just imagine what it could do for your career prospects.'

Kerris smiled. 'It *can* get complicated. Being the boss's daughter, so to speak. Your workmates tend to treat you a little gingerly. In any case—' She took my arm. 'He's one of four leaders. Not the *sole* leader. He's also from England originally, so you two will have something common.'

'I know this makes me sound a bit dim but why are you a Baedekker instead of a Fielding?'

'"Baedekker" is the name of the nursery complex where I was raised. You have to realize that my father isn't a father in the traditional sense. He never pushed me around the park in a baby carriage or took me to the movies. He was my father in a strictly biological sort of way.'

'Oh.'

'But I have met him several times. In fact, just last week he telephoned me. That was when he invited us to a drinks party tonight.'

I reflected for a moment. Kerris didn't seem unhappy about the arrangement. It was merely the natural way of things for her. I was reminded of our own Mother Houses on the Isle of Wight. In a world where getting more human beings onto the planet with as much speed as possible was all-important, I realized this society in New York had adopted a similar procedure. In the Old World before the Blinding, it would have been unthinkable for many reasons — social, political and emotional. Now, no one batted an eyelid.

'We're here,' she said, with a bright smile. 'Pop's place.'

I looked up at the building which shone reddish gold in the evening sun. The columns flanking the base, with their suggestion of papyrus and palm fronds, had a distinctly Egyptian air, while the doors were 'guarded' by carved eagles. My eyes were drawn skyward — up, up, up — but still I couldn't see the top. Fallpipes glittered like precious metal as if the whole building were an inlaid jewel of fabulous dimensions.

'Ready?' she asked.

'As I'll ever be.'

Arm in arm we entered the grand doorway beneath letters in gold that spelled out the words EMPIRE STATE BUILDING.

Through an ornate lobby. Across a marble floor. Between statues of Greek and Roman heroes (including a magnificently brooding bronze of Alexander the Great). To an elevator plushly carpeted in purple. The lift attendant swung a brass lever. The elevator sped upward smoothly. Kerris, taking my hand, squeezed it and kissed me on the cheek. 'Relax, David.' She smiled. 'He won't eat you. Honest.'

I smiled back. 'Meeting the father of one's girlfriend is always a little unsettling.'

'Surely you must have lots of practice? A handsome guy like you?'

I felt a flush spread up from beneath my collar at a velocity like that of the elevator.

If I'd expected a small family gathering I'd have been wrong. For the elevator disgorged us into a vast room that was only a little smaller than a football pitch. Beneath chandeliers elegantly dressed men and women chatted over cocktails. Many recognized Kerris. They greeted her warmly with kisses on her cheek. Until now I'd seen this city as vibrantly pulsing with almost entirely young people. But there seemed to be a lot of grey heads gathered in this room. These, I surmised, were New York's ruling class, mature men and women who'd been spared The Blinding to inherit, if not the Earth, at least this small and splendid corner of it.

Confidence pervaded the room like cigar smoke. This was where the good and the great discussed policy, formulated priorities and complex plans, issued decrees. This was the court of the King of Manhattan.

Kerris steered me to windows overlooking the city spread out below that, with the fall of darkness, had become an ocean of lights. A waitress appeared with a tray full of drinks. I accepted a dry martini. Kerris chose champagne. In the corner a string quartet played soft music. How I wished my father could see this! A cocktail party at the top of the tallest building in the world!

At that moment I promised myself I would bring my family to New York. As I basked in this warm glow of optimism Kerris touched my elbow.

'My father's across there,' she told me. 'Come on, I'll introduce you.'

I saw a tall man in profile. Aged around sixty, he stood ramrod straight, with short cropped hair that was turning gracefully from red to silver. He was speaking intently to a balding man of around the same age.

'Father,' Kerris said politely. 'I'd like you to meet David Masen.'

'General Fielding,' I said, holding out my hand.

The moment he turned to me I nearly flinched with shock. The clean profile I'd first seen had been handsome in a classically heroic way. The left-hand side of his face couldn't have been more different.

His right eye gleamed the same shade of green as Kerris's. His left eye, however, was yellow — the same bright yellow as an egg yolk. There was no iris: that shocking yellow filled the whole socket, leaving a fierce black pupil in the centre. Radiating from the eye were a series of white scars that extended to his hairline.

I masked my surprise as, smiling, he said, 'David Masen. Believe me, I've been looking forward to meeting you. What do you make of our city?'

As I told him I thought his city was extraordinary he

extended his own hand. Despite his military title his handshake felt more like a politician's.

He turned to the balding man. 'Allow me to introduce you to Dr Wiseman.'

Dr Wiseman's accent clearly put his origins well south of the Mason-Dixon Line. 'Good to meet you, Mr Masen. We're delighted to have you as our guest here. And we're hoping that when you get home to England you'll have plenty of good things to say about us.'

General Fielding looked at me, his yellow eye peering into my face with burning intensity. 'David Masen brings us an opportunity to solve one of our direst problems,' he said.

'You don't say,' Dr Wiseman replied jovially.

'There's something called the Masen-Coker Processor that refines triffid oil into a high-grade gasoline. Isn't that so, David?'

I agreed. But a small voice in the back of my head told me that I'd been too generous to my American friends with information about my homeland's assets. If this community had no access to petroleum or its associated products then the Processor would be like the goose that laid the golden egg. Nevertheless, I'd already opened my trap (reticence was never my strong point): The truth was out. I sincerely hoped that I wouldn't come to regret my earlier careless talk on the ship.

Dr Wiseman tactfully withdrew to freshen his drink. This left Kerris, her father and myself chatting over cocktails. The general waved a hand towards a pair of plush sofas that faced each other across a coffee table. The moment the men occupying them saw General

Fielding moving towards them they vacated their seats quickly. Kerris and I took one sofa, General Fielding sat in the other. And so we chatted, facing each other. Meanwhile, the sweet strains of Strauss floated through the air.

By now I had recovered from my surprise at seeing the general's ruined eye. In fact, I had seen the same condition before. Yellow Eye is caused by a splash of triffid poison, a fate that had nearly afflicted my father thirty years ago. Only prompt first-aid treatment and irrigation of his eyes with a saline solution had saved him from permanent damage. Fielding had not been so lucky, clearly. He would, I knew, be blind in his left eye.

Meanwhile, his good eye scanned my face constantly, as if he was reading words on a page. Here was someone who would assess a man's character in seconds, then judge him according to what he thought he saw.

'Tell me, David,' General Fielding said. 'You have a family on the Isle of Wight?'

I told him I had a father, a mother and two sisters.

'In good health, are they?'

'Extremely. My father has his work, which is something of a holy quest for him.'

The general appeared keen to know more about my father. I told him something of his background, how he had managed to survive the Blinding and the wholesale triffid takeover of thirty years ago. In a way that reminded me of the questioning I had undergone on the Atlantic crossing he asked me about the economics of the Isle of Wight and its infrastructure. Then he asked casually about its military capabilities.

The small voice in my head spoke again. *Play your cards close to your chest. Don't reveal too much.*

'Oh, we have a number of warships as well as military aircraft,' I said, smiling with a deliberate vagueness that a clergyman would have envied.

'Yes, I heard you had to crash land your jet. A fighter, wasn't it?'

'A fighter-bomber.'

'And you burn triffid oil in the engine?'

'A refined version, yes.'

'But I dare say spare parts and ammunition must be scarce these days.'

'We are able to manufacture spare parts,' I pointed out, 'as well as ammunition and bombs.' That voice in the back of my head, small though it was, was wise. It prompted me to implant the idea in the general's mind that the Isle of Wight was no mere helpless farming community: that we had teeth and could bite.

The general nodded, absorbing the information before asking bluntly, 'How many jet fighters do you possess?'

'Oh, enough for defence.' Again I gave him my deliberately vague smile.

'Ah, I see; you want to be discreet about your weaponry. Fair enough. After all, we don't know each other's intentions yet, do we?'

I acknowledged his point with another smile.

'Here, let's refresh our cocktails.' With barely a nod of his head he attracted the attention of a waitress who quickly brought more drinks. 'Can I get you anything else, David. Cigar? Something to eat?'

'No, I'm fine with this, thanks.' I indicated my glass.

'Now, David. I hope I can speak quite frankly with you. Kerris has, no doubt, told you that our aim here in New York is to establish contact with other communities, no matter where they are in the world?' Without waiting for my reply he pressed on. 'We shall establish trade links, exchange knowledge, personnel.'

'But some communities aren't interested in talking.'

'Precisely. Several of our people have been brutally murdered. Even when they approached those places under a white flag. Which is one reason why we have to maintain an effective military force.'

'So you will *compel* communities who are, let's say, a little on the shy side to come to the negotiating table?'

'No, of course not, David. But we must be able to defend our city here as well as our shipping lanes.'

'If it doesn't sound too impertinent, General Fielding, what is your ultimate aim?'

'To conquer the world, of course.'

He watched for my reaction. I allowed myself none.

A smile creased his face, tightening the scarred skin around his yellow eye.

'Or, to be more precise,' he told me, 'I should say reconquer the world. For all of us. For the human race. And wipe out the one true enemy.'

'The triffids?'

He nodded.

'That's going to be quite a tall order, isn't it?'

'I have a weapon, David. A wonderful weapon.'

'The atom bomb?'

'Oh, we certainly have *those*,' the general said crisply, 'but that's too crude a device. A damn' sight too mucky as well. What's the point of incinerating the triffids only to be left with a million acres of contaminated soil? No, I'm talking about the *ultimate* weapon. The weapon that is the oldest known to mankind, as well as being the most powerful.' He smiled a rather hard smile, then inclined his head, inviting me to guess.

'I'm intrigued. This weapon sounds something pretty special.'

'Oh, it is.' He leaned forward, enjoying this moment of revelation. 'The weapon is Man himself. Or rather men. And not just men by the dozen, or the thousand. But men — and women! — by the million.' Enthused, he spoke in hushed tones. 'Imagine, if you will, that this city is a huge factory. What it produces, David, is people.'

'And people are your secret weapon?'

'Yes, of course. Look, New York is manufacturing people at such a rate that our population will explode.' His yellow eye appeared to burn with a light all its own. 'Within ten years the population will be so great that even a city as great as this will not — *cannot* — contain it. Its boundaries will burst and people will spill out, hacking and trampling triffids into the dirt where they belong.'

'But aren't you in danger of expanding the population beyond the limits of self-sufficiency?'

'Then that threat of famine becomes the spur to drive mankind on.'

'But surely a slower, more controlled expansion would be a safer—'

'Safety be damned, man. This is war. Man against triffid. Survival versus extinction. Of course there will be casualties, but with huge reserves of men and women our losses can be replaced in an instant. Wherever a man falls against a triffid, there will be a dozen men to fill the gap.'

'But isn't increasing the human population going to be a long job?'

'That's why we have turned procreation into an industrial process,' the general said. 'We bring techniques of mass production to the business of birth.' He touched his fingers, ticking off each point in turn. 'The notion of a woman expending nine months of her valuable child-bearing years to produce just one child is unthinkable in the world of today.'

'You're suggesting that women have litters of babies – like animals?'

'You call such births litters, which is rather deroga-tory. We would describe such women as bountiful.'

'But is it possible to find women capable of bearing twins to order? Surely—'

'Not twins. I'm talking about triplets or even quads being the norm. In fact, that *has* been the norm for the last twenty years. Woman receive fertility drugs to produce multiple births.'

I felt an increasing unease. Hearing this man jubilantly describing how women had been reduced to the level of battery hens had taken quite a lot of the gloss off this community for me.

'Listen, childbearers are spared the tiring and time-consuming business of raising children. That role is undertaken by women who are either infertile or above childbearing age or suffer some other bar to mother-hood.' The general's sharp single good eye read the distaste on my own face. 'You don't approve. Yet I hear your people have their own methods of increasing the birth rate.'

I thought of the cheerful Mother Houses brimming with happy, much-loved children. 'We do,' I allowed. 'But the manufacturing process is less scientific.'

'You mean it's more haphazard? That you're unable to eliminate birth defects? That one woman squanders nine precious months to produce one child?'

'It may seem haphazard but it works for us.'

'And your population is thirty thousand?'

'Thereabouts.'

'With, what? – hmm, let's see – fifty per cent of the population being under twenty-five?'

I nodded.

'Here,' he said, '*ninety* per cent of our population are under the age of twenty-five. So you see, we have an energetic, lively people. Young people with the ambition and the need – yes, the *sheer need* – to create living space for themselves.' Sighing, the general clasped his hands together in his lap. 'Look at the history books, David. Empires flourished when they had a strong birth rate. On the other hand, empires failed when their birth rate declined. Now, consider how various societies increased their birth rates. In some cultures birth control was banned, in others women who produced large families were handsomely rewarded. Everyone, from pauper to king, did their bit. In short, people equal power. One man can move a stone. A thousand can move a mountain.'

By the end of this, it had become less a conversation than a political speech delivered by General Fielding. Kerris sat quietly throughout. I wondered then how many she was destined to become mother to? Twenty children? Thirty?

What's more, I knew General Fielding wanted the Masen-Coker Processor. In turn, I wondered if he'd export his philosophy of population growth, along with his fertility drugs, to my people. That, I can tell you, gave me ample food for thought for the rest of the evening.

CHAPTER NINETEEN

Omen

'OK, David. Why the long face?'

Midnight. We walked along Fifth Avenue arm in arm, the endless traffic producing a dazzling – even dizzying – river of light. A car motor seized with a *clang*, stopping it dead in the traffic. Horns sounded.

'David?' Kerris prompted.

'Oh, nothing.'

'Clearly you find *nothing* disheartening?'

'Well, it's all this business about . . .' I began peevishly, then trailed off with a shrug.

'Didn't you like my father?'

'No . . . I mean, it's not your father. He's an extraordinary man.' I stopped short of saying that I actually *liked* him. I had sensed an icy ruthlessness behind the professional smile. 'It's just this production of human babies on what amounts to an industrial scale – which I find unusual, to say the least.'

'I can't say I've ever really thought about it. But then, this is a foreign land to you, Mr Masen.'

'And foreigners do things differently, Miss Baedekker.' I smiled. 'Yes, but it's just the thought that one day you . . . well, dash it all, Kerris, I simply don't like the idea of you mothering Heaven knows how many children.'

She stopped suddenly and looked at me with those green eyes. Then she put her hand to her mouth and laughed.

'What's wrong?' I asked, puzzled.

'David . . . oh, David. You've a lot to learn. Me with dozens of children? That's ridiculous.'

'Why? Your father said—'

'No. David, listen.' She wiped away tears of laughter. 'I don't have the Mother Card.'

'Mother Card?'

'Yes. Girls are assessed at thirteen, then they receive their Life Certificates. I have a Career Card, which means I went to college to study for, as the name implies, a career suited to me. Other girls become professional mothers.'

'Oh.'

'And they have comfortable rooms, eat well, watch TV until it comes out of their ears. It's not a bad life, being a professional Mother, you know?'

'I see.'

'Another thing you should know.' She gave my arm a squeeze. 'When I decide the time is right to have children of my own. I'll get 'em in the old-fashioned way.'

Here was the rub. General Fielding's vision of what amounted to a tidal wave of human beings sweeping away the triffid menace had made me uneasy. Especially when I heard about multiple births promoted by the intensive use of fertility drugs. After all, a bitch forced to have litters of pups too frequently is destined for premature death. But, distasteful as the general's strategy was to me, I knew it had its merits. It made what I'd hitherto considered the Isle of Wight's impressive birth rate look paltry by comparison. If we were to wage war against the titanic number of triffids, we would need an army of equally titanic proportions. More importantly, General Fielding was driving his community to expand into the triffid-held mainland; to reconquer the world for the human race. While we, on our little island off the coast of England, were content to slumber away our days in blissful ignorance of what was happening in the outside world. We were static, some might even say slothful; we had no plan to re-establish communities on the mainland. My mind returned to the conversation with my father on that fateful evening just a few weeks ago. When he had warned that the island community that he had helped to found faced the real danger of withering away. Although veiled from the population's eyes at the moment, the truth was that the Isle of Wight's peaceful isolation would one day become its nemesis.

Kerris noticed my gloomy expression. Gently, she tugged my arm. 'Time for coffee and some very gooey doughnuts,' she said firmly. 'Then bed.'

Time passed pleasantly. However, I began to feel a twinge of guilt at my idleness during those days with Kerris. I decided that I should tackle the question of my return to the Isle of Wight. I also decided that I would invite Kerris Baedekker to come with me.

But, as happens so many times in life, plans were overtaken by events. My lotus-eating days were drawing to an end. In that great city minds coolly devised their strategies. And, like a pawn on a chessboard, I would be moved yet again.

On the afternoon after my first meeting with Kerris's father, General Fielding, I was busily trying to settle scores with one Gabriel Deeds. Some hope! Again his massive forearm smash sent the table-tennis ball ricocheting from the table to smash against the ceiling of the YMCA hall where we played.

In that gentle voice of his he said, 'My point, I think, Mr Masen.'

'Your point,' I agreed, breathless.

I told him I planned to request a lift home at the earliest possible opportunity.

'That would depend on sailing schedules,' Gabriel told me as he pulled a fresh ball from a carton to replace the one now lying shattered on the floor. 'Atlantic crossings aren't at all frequent yet.'

'But I saw some big flying boats in the harbour. They'd get me home in less than twenty hours.'

Gabriel looked round to make sure we weren't overheard. 'Those flying boats . . .' He dropped his voice to a whisper, as if sharing a risqué joke with me. '. . . They're for show.'

'For show? They looked perfectly serviceable to me.'

'With the right fuel, maybe.'

'They're not converted to run on wood alcohol?'

'They are, but the fuel isn't sufficiently refined for an airplane engine.' He served. 'You could get one of those babies into the air, then do a circuit of the island. Just.'

I returned the ball with a deceptive spin that caught him by surprise. 'Good stroke, Mr Masen.' He gave a little shrug. 'But it would be suicide to attempt an Atlantic crossing in one of those planes. You've seen how our cars run on a wing and a prayer. That fuel's so rough it's got teeth. Plays merry hell with the cylinders. Two thousand miles and – *bang*.' He timed the word to coincide with the return stroke of the bat. 'The pistons lock up tight.'

My only alternative now was to press for a crossing by boat. But as it was, fate dealt its coincidence card.

Kerris breezed into the hall. 'Hello, Gabriel. Good afternoon, David. I was told I'd find you here.'

'And good afternoon to you. You must have spies everywhere,' I added jokingly. 'How did you know I'd be here?'

'Ah, simplicity itself. I telephoned your hotel. The desk clerk told me that she'd seen you leave with a table-tennis bat in your hand and a rather desperate look in your eye.' She shot a grin at Gabriel. 'Is he losing terribly?'

Gabriel shrugged. 'This young man is a mere six games down now.'

'The gap is closing,' I protested with mock hurt.

'Slowly it is, David. Slowly.'

'David, listen.' Kerris looked flushed, as if she'd been hurrying. 'I've some news for you. There's been a meeting at the Research Department and the director has author-ized a new trip to Europe. It's also been decided to include a diplomatic mission to the Isle of Wight.' She smiled. 'You're going home, David. The ship sails the day after tomorrow.'

Surprised, I looked at her. 'So soon?'

Gabriel nodded at me. 'You got your trip after all, David. Congratulations.'

This was, as New Yorkers say, a whole new ball game. Something in my expression gave me away. Kerris tilted her head to one side. 'Aren't you pleased?'

'Yes. Of course . . . only I hadn't expected things to move so quickly.' I met her gaze. 'But I'll only go on one condition, Kerris.'

'And that condition is?'

'That you come with me.'

It was Gabriel Deeds who suggested the farewell drink. The night before the sailing Kerris and I walked into a blues club that looked out across the water towards the Statue of Liberty. Silent lightning flickered around the metal giant. Electricity charged the humid air. Kerris commented that a storm was brewing out at sea. Her stunning dress of some shimmering red material complemented the climatic fireworks offshore.

Finding a vacant table, I ordered drinks for Kerris and myself and had one sent to Gabriel on stage where he was busying himself, plugging cables into amplifiers and tuning his guitar. He looked across the room, acknowledging me by raising the glass.

People thronged the club. Conversation bubbled in a lively fashion. For the first time since General Fielding had enthused to me about the process of multiple births I noticed a pair of identical twins in the club. Having noticed one pair, suddenly they seemed everywhere and I quickly counted a dozen sets. Not that it affected the merry air of the club. In the corner a pair of twin teenage girls, together with their companions, celebrated their shared birthday with champagne.

'Aren't you going to miss all this?' I asked Kerris.

'I'm sure I'll adjust,' she said, smiling, her green eyes gleaming at me in the gloom of the club. 'Besides, I'm looking forward to seeing how you live across there. This is going to mark a new beginning for both our peoples.'

'I'll drink to that.' We clinked glasses.

At that moment the band started to play. At that volume speaking became impossible. Instead, my eyes flitted from the musicians to Kerris's face, shining with a beautiful glow in the lights of the stage. And all the while that magical music soared and dipped, with Gabriel's guitar sounding by turn angelic or demonic. I allowed myself to be transported by it. As I closed my eyes, it took me on a cosmic sleigh ride. Once more I discerned the soulful yearning in the guitar notes. A sense of uttermost longing.

I felt a hand close over mine. I opened my eyes to see Kerris's hand resting on mine on the table as she watched the band, her head nodding gently to the rhythm of the music.

Once more I closed my eyes. As the blue notes wove their magic, I relaxed into a state of complete and utter bliss.

After the concert Gabriel walked us out to where the taxi waited. Lightning still flickered over the sea in great airbursts of blue and silver.

He opened the door for Kerris. 'Bon voyage, Miss Baedekker,' he told her, reverting to the formal mode of address once we were back on the street. 'Mr Masen. Take care of yourself.'

'I will, Gabriel. You, too.'

I shall always remember that moment. His broad friendly grin. The way he pumped my hand up and down as we stood beside the open door of the taxi.

Because that was the moment when the man stepped out of the shadows with a gun in his hand. He pushed Gabriel back against the car, stood back, then fired at his chest.

Gabriel slumped down, the top half of his body falling into the back of the car where Kerris sat. Desperately, I moved forward, trying to catch him as he fell.

But before my outstretched hands reached him an arm tightened round my throat, catching me in a strangling neck-lock. A sharp, burning pain shot through the side of my neck. Far away, it seemed to me, Kerris was scream-ing.

Suddenly, the harbour illuminations smeared with flashes of lightning ran into a single swirling vortex of light.

Round and round, faster and faster. It swallowed me into darkness. Absolute, fathomless darkness.

CHAPTER TWENTY

Jonah

I had been swallowed into the belly of a whale. I sensed undulating movement. I heard liquids hissing through pipes. The rush of expelled air. The deep thump of a mighty heart. A spectral voice intoned, 'Ten fathoms . . . eight fathoms . . . five fathoms . . . four fathoms.'

I opened my eyes. I saw metal bulkheads. A door opened, revealing a corridor studded with electric lights. At that moment a figure loomed over me. My eyes focused on liquid squirting from a syringe. Then the needle plunged into my arm. I heard a strange bellowing cry. Dimly, I realized that it came from my own mouth. Lights swirled; the vortex returned. Once more I was sucked down into darkness.

On opening my eyes I immediately sensed a change in my environment. The air smelled different. Like herbs, it seemed to me. The dimensions of the room I lay in were greater, the bed wider. Sounds were different, too. I heard a distant rattling sound, as if someone was playing a muffled xylophone.

I should have identified the sound straightaway, I really should. However, my head seemed to have been packed with cotton wool and my eyes streamed incessantly, while my tongue had glued itself to the roof of my mouth. Feeling as if I'd enjoyed one hell of a bender (and was now paying the head-thumping price), I pulled myself into a sitting position on the bed.

On the floor sat a tin cup beside a jug of water. I stared at it for a long time. I knew I wanted, desperately wanted, to pour that cold, clear water into the cup, then drink to my heart's content. But somehow the link that connected this understanding to actually moving my arms and doing something about it was broken. My streaming eyes looked at the glass, then at the water. After a long time, I managed at last to exercise a modicum of motor control. In a dopey, uncoordinated kind of way I succeeded in sloshing water into the glass. I picked it up, managing to spill every last drop down my shirt-front before it reached my lips.

Blow this for a game of soldiers. I picked up the jug instead and gulped down its contents. Believe me, that water was the sweetest thing I'd tasted in a long, long time. After downing a quart or so of liquid I didn't feel nearly as groggy as before. The headache eased and I began to take a little more interest in my surroundings.

Right, I told myself dizzily. *Examine your environment, Masen. Walls? Timber. Windows? Count 'em. None. Beams run below an angled roof . . . corrugated iron. Yes, sir . . . corrugated iron that's rusted and patched. Floor consists of compressed earth. Light provided by one wee electric bulb, hanging from a beam. And you're sitting on a camp bed . . . no blankets.*

So far, so good. Unsteadily, I reached a door that looked as if it had once belonged to a fashionable house but had now been pressed into service in a building of far more modest aspirations.

A locked door. *Not so good.*

My dope-addled mind cleared sufficiently to understand that I was a prisoner. I returned shakily to sit on the bed where I dozed, sitting upright. At last the door opened. In stepped a lithe black woman of twenty-five or so, wearing a yellow headband. In her hands was a sub-machine gun that she casually pointed at my face. I did not move. I just watched with a dreamy detachment.

A young man with dark Latin looks filled my water jug from a larger container, then placed a tray bearing fruit and bread on the bed beside me.

My captors spoke not one word. Neither did I. With the solemn and silent ceremony over, they withdrew. My stomach feeling more than a little twitchy, I didn't trust myself to eat. Instead, I downed the jug of water in long, thirsty gulps.

The water ceremony repeated itself at four-hourly intervals. The same couple entered: the woman with the sub-machine gun, the man carrying the large jug to replenish my small one. Again, no one spoke. Moments later I was left to conclude the ceremony by once more drinking the water in one go.

After a while I grew a little more sensitive to my surroundings. A spider the size of a saucer prowled along one of the roof beams, no doubt regarding the interloper below through his multiple eyes. For a few moments a drumming roar rose outside. Rain, I figured, rain beating on my corrugated-iron roof. The downpour was a short one, stopping as suddenly as it had begun. Almost immediately I could smell the cloying aroma of wet earth. Above my head the spider lost interest in me, choosing instead to suck the vital juices from a large fly.

Food . . .

I looked down at the tray beside me. The bread looked a mite too dry for me, but the slice of pink watermelon looked appealing. I bit into it. Sweet juice filled my mouth along with a good many pips, but my appetite came roaring back. With my eight-legged dining companion enjoying his own meal above my head I ate everything on the tray.

Once more I heard the rhythmic rattling sound. I cocked my head to one side, listening. Little sticks beating steadily against a larger body of wood. I frowned, trying to place the once familiar sound.

Then my drug-soaked brain at last lurched into gear. The word I had been grubbing for reached my lips.

'Triffids.'

With no windows and a watch stopped at half-past three I had no notion of the time. Presently, however, I saw the strip of light beneath the door growing increasingly dull until it vanished. For a while the clicking of triffids grew louder with the coming of night. Crickets, too, chirped more loudly. Also, I fancied that I could hear the croak of frogs somewhere nearby. When I pressed an ear to the door I caught voices, only they were far too muffled for me to make out individual words.

I returned to the bed. By this time my eyes had stopped their constant streaming; they felt, however, unpleasantly gritty, so I used a little of my drinking water to rinse them. After that I examined my right forearm. Six needle pricks clustered around a vein. I touched the side of my neck. A sore patch beneath my left ear made me wince. Outside the blues club I'd clearly been held in a neck-lock while someone had driven a hypodermic into an artery. At least my kidnappers had been at pains to deliver me in one piece.

And yet I recalled only too vividly Gabriel Deeds falling onto the back seat of the taxi as the gunman fired. Kerris had been screaming. For God's sake, what had happened to her? Was she hurt? Was she here? Captive in some neighbouring hut? If so, what were they doing to her? A sense of foreboding oozed through me.

Presently the sound of triffids beating their sticks against their woody boles subsided. Silence weighed down on the hut where at last I lay down on the bed

With thoughts of Kerris Baedekker running through my head I closed my eyes.

I was woken by the bang of the door opening. Sunlight streamed in. For a moment I thought there'd be a reprise of the water ceremony. Instead the girl in the yellow headband motioned with the sub-machine gun.

'Come on. Don't do anything silly like trying to run away. I won't shoot you but you'll only get yourself stung to death.' The voice had a surprising Irish lilt.

'Where are you taking me?'

'Someone will speak to you.'

'Who?'

She must have been rationing her words because she didn't reply. Instead, she stepped back through the doorway with the gun muzzle pointing at my face.

This wasn't the moment for any sudden or unpredictable movements. I simply raised both hands to shoulder height, while trying my darnedest to appear relaxed in the hope that my posture would convey to her that I had no intention of making a run for it. Even so, a vivid mental image wouldn't leave me. I saw myself being marched out to a bloodstained post. There, a line of figures carrying rifles would be waiting for me. I blinked the grim notion away, took a deep breath, then stepped out through the door.

The sunlight blazing down had to be the strongest I'd seen for weeks. The heat, a humid sort of heat that clung to the skin, struck me immediately. For a moment my eyes struggled to cope with the glare. I had to shield them before I could make out my surroundings. Then I saw that I was standing on a gentle slope that ran down to a broad river of muddy brown water. Away to my left and right were a series of huts that made the place look like a military camp. My companion seemed impatient to take me to my destination. She gestured with the sub-machine gun for me to get a move on.

Well, she had the gun. I obeyed without hesitation.

Nevertheless, I still had a chance to take in my surroundings as we walked towards a modest timber house. I saw men and women in uniform. They were either working on vehicles or carrying boxes towards a timber jetty. Moored there I saw the dark, sleek forms of two submarines side by side. One of those, I reckoned, had brought me here.

Moored slightly further upriver was a handsome collection of flying boats, ranging from single-seater float-planes to big passenger seaplanes that could carry fifty people or more. With a full tank of decent fuel one of those beauties could carry me across the Atlantic and home.

I had to take a few paces more before I reached the house. I glanced up the hillside, searching for the source of the sound of those sticks on woody boles. And, yes, sure enough, there they were. Triffids. Thousands of them. Fortunately a stout wire fence, perhaps ten feet high, separated them from the camp. There were signs of burning, too. No doubt these people discouraged the plants from cuddling up against the fence too tightly with a burst or two from a flame-thrower. I had the distinct if irrational impression that those sinister plants were watching me pass by. An impression that was reinforced when the dark green leaves began to quiver, the cones on top of the trunks began to rock and there came a sudden rattling of sticks against bristle-covered boles. Triffid Morse code?

Triffids beware . . . the son of ace triffid-exterminator Bill Masen has been sighted . . . pass the message on . . . prepare to attack . . . kill on sight . . .

I wiped a trickle of perspiration from my forehead. Yes, an irrational fancy. Maybe a slight hallucinogenic after-effect of the drug that had been pumped into me. Yet the impression was compelling. Unnerving, too.

But as it was, I didn't have time to dwell on it.

The girl with the gun motioned me round the corner of the house. I stopped, surprised. For there sat the most idiosyncratic vehicle I'd ever seen.

'Sam.' The girl addressed a figure leaning forward into the machine through a hatch. 'Sam. This is Masen. What do you want me to do with him?'

CHAPTER TWENTY ONE

Excursion

The man slithered backward from the hatchway of the strange-looking vehicle. With a swing of his long arms he shut the hatch – it clanged noisily – then stood back, wiping his oily hands on a rag.

I can only describe the machine as looking like an iron elephant. Painted a pale shade of grey, it had two large rounded cabins side by side that gave the impression of an elephant's extended ears. From the front of the vehicle something very much like an elephant's trunk but made of metal, protruded. The whole bizarre arrangement, complete with air intakes, exhaust pipes and an iron-grey body, sat on a pair of caterpillar tracks. In size, it was perhaps a shade larger than a battle tank.

The machine's resemblance to the animal hadn't escaped its owners. One of the long grey flanks carried the word JUMBO in large letters. While just behind one of the glass-panelled cabins I noticed a colourful painting of a Red Indian warrior in fierce profile, his chin high, gazing towards some far horizon. Beside that, in what can only be described as a sassy script, were the words *Give 'Em Hell!*

There were more notices stencilled on the lower part of the machine, although these were more prosaic instructions like *Compressed-Air Inlet* and *Service This Vehicle With 100 Octane Fuel Only.*

'Good morning, Mr Masen.' The man who'd been working on the motor offered me his hand. He was tall, gangling, with blond hair and bright blue eyes. I put his age at around thirty-five. His accent had the courteous drawl of the Southern States. He noticed more oil streaked on the back of his hand, wiped it on the seat of his combat trousers, then offered it to me again.

I didn't respond.

He smiled. 'Can't say I blame you, feller. I'd be a mite too sore to shake hands as well.' The voice was as bright and as friendly as his blue eyes. 'You're feeling all right? No cramps or nausea?'

I shook my head. 'I feel well enough . . . considering.' I spoke a trifle stiffly.

'Good, good! Say, Jazmay.' He gave the girl a relaxed grin. 'I don't know what Mr Masen here thinks about you pointing the gun like that but I'm getting a tad nervous . . .' He turned to me. 'Say. You're not going to slug me or run away, are you? No. No, of course you won't. Jazmay, stow the gun away and fire up old Jumbo, will you?'

The girl opened one of the cabin doors of the vehicle, slotted the gun into a rack, then climbed down into a sort of well that contained the driver's cockpit beneath the cabin. With a preliminary whirring the motor fired into life. Twin plumes of blue smoke spurted from behind the elephantine 'ears'.

'Sounds great, doesn't she?' The man spoke enthusiastically, patting the machine. 'I fitted new plugs on the old gal in your honour . . .' He started off to the vehicle. But almost immediately turned back to me. 'The name's Sam Dymes, by the way. Different spelling but pronounced the same as that old coin from way back when.' He held out his hand again to shake mine, then gave a bashful smile. 'Oh, you don't shake, do you? Sorry about that. And sorry about the . . .' He mimed injecting himself in the arm. 'We figured it'd be the best way of bringing you here without damaging you.'

I stared, a hundred angry questions jostling to be vocalized. But I was too downright astonished to spit them out.

'Sam Dymes,' he repeated, touching his chest, as he backed towards the vehicle. 'Now, if you can jump aboard, please. I need to show you something.'

As the vehicle rumbled on its caterpillar tracks along a roadway, it passed more of its kind. Big, grey elephantine machines with JUMBO painted on the side. Each one bore a different signature painting behind the driver's cab. There were renditions of champing shark teeth, cartoon characters, svelte girls. Each vehicle had its own personalized name: *Lucky Lady*, *Wild Thing*, *Fire-Eater* — while one right at the end of the line rejoiced in the name *Munchin' Martha*, its painting depicting a formidable woman eating whole triffid plants like they were celery shoots.

I sat in one of the front two bucket seats alongside Sam Dymes. Jazmay, who drove the great metal beast, sat below me, her head level with my feet.

The jolting had one positive effect. The questions that had been choked back were suddenly free.

'Why the hell have you brought me here?'

Sam Dymes shot me a look of wide-eyed innocence. 'For one, I need to show you something. Hang on tight, we'll be through the gates in a moment. It gets a little bumpy down here.'

'No . . . hell . . . damn it! Why have you brought me to this place? Why did you have to shoot my friend? And what in God's name have you done with Kerris?'

'Kerris?' He rubbed his jaw reflectively. 'She's fine.'

'How do you know that?'

'You're going to have to trust me on that one.'

'She's here?'

'No. She's back in New York City, Mr Masen. Safe.'

'But your thugs had no qualms about killing my friend.'

'I'm sorry. I didn't know about any fatalities. Believe me, that wasn't our intention.'

'What *was* your intention?'

'To bring you safely here?'

'Whereabouts is *here* . . . exactly?'

'South of the Mason-Dixon Line,' he said guardedly. 'You don't need to know precisely where.'

'OK, Mr Dime. *Why* am I here?'

'The name's Dymes. Why are you here? I hope that's going to be as plain as the nose on your face.' He awarded me that shy smile again. 'Excuse me. Time for a little pest control.'

Through the front windows I saw that the truck had reached a hefty gate that took four men to swing open. We were through it in a second. Behind me I saw the gate being shut, then firmly secured with chains.

'Jazmay, can you switch on the flow for me? Thank you.'

Ahead triffids crossed our path, moving in their jerking way, the cones on top of their trunks whipping backwards and forwards.

Despite my anger, I craned my neck forward for a better view. At that moment Sam Dymes gripped a joystick in his hand, then depressed a red button on top of it with his thumb.

A ball of orange flame shot from the end of the metal 'trunk'. A second later three triffids were caught in that rolling fire ball. Green leaves blackened, wilted, cones shrivelled. One plant flopped down to the trackway.

Sam Dymes smiled back at me. 'This is one thing we've got that those darn' weeds don't have. Fire. *Glorious fire!*' He gave them another blast for good measure. A lot of triffids began to resemble Old Testament burning bushes. Sam called out: 'These guys are getting smart. As soon as you burn a couple up the others get out of your way.'

The lumbering vehicle crunched over the smoking remains of triffids that had been hit by the flame-thrower. The rest of the plants, even though there were thousands of them, no longer tried to get in front of the vehicle. A few, though, popped away with their stings at the cabin's glass panels as we passed, leaving the characteristic smear of poison.

'Safe as houses.' Sam gave the panel a good rap with his knuckles. 'Toughened glass.'

The triffid pattern around the base had all the old characteristics. Close in near the fence the triffids had packed tight, testing it with their strength, no doubt hoping deep in their botanical brains – if, indeed, that was what they had – that their combined pressure would break the wire. The further you moved away from the picket fence, however, the sparser the plants became. Perhaps in the triffid armies these outliers had the role of reserves or sentries. Of course, these days you would rarely be free of the plant entirely. As the vehicle rumbled across an open plain I could see solitary triffids dotted here and there. Mostly they remained unmoving. However, as the truck approached and they 'heard' the roar of its engine, they shuffled their stumpy legs so that they could turn to the source of the sound. They certainly looked like predators watching their prey go by.

Sam Dymes sat back in his seat now, his hand only lightly on the joystick that controlled the metal 'trunk' of the flame-thrower. All in all, this was an impressive machine. I knew how valuable an all-terrain triffid-destroyer like this would be to my people back home.

Meanwhile, though, I hadn't solved the mystery of why I'd been brought here.

'Thanks for the ride,' I said coolly. 'But you're still being niggardly with the answers.'

'I'm sorry, Mr Masen, truly I am.'

'Who are you exactly . . . your community, that is?'

'Your former hosts refer to us as the Quintling faction.'

'Yes, I've heard of you.'

'Nothing good, I'd wager?'

'That you're a bunch of outlaws,' I told him. 'That you steal and murder.'

'Joshua Quintling was one of the original founders of the New York community, but General Fielding came along to introduce some more . . .' He shrugged. 'More vigorous methods, shall we say. So, twenty years ago, Quintling left with his family and other families who wished to live in a more humane way.'

'So the Quintling faction wound up here?'

'Not exactly. General Fielding ordered one of his warships to go after Quintling's unarmed steamer. The warship shot Quintling's boat to hell. Quintling's wife and baby son were killed, along with a dozen others. Quintling only avoided losing everyone else on board by running the steamer aground in an estuary that was too shallow for the warship to sail up. Otherwise . . .' He gave an expressive shrug. Then he looked at me, the blue eyes serious. 'But you don't believe me, do you, Mr Masen?'

'I suppose I'll have to take your word for it.' But my coolness towards him must have conveyed my scepticism.

'Have it your own way, Mr Masen. I'm hardly likely to instil belief with the butt of a rifle, am I?'

'As far as I can see I'm very much at your mercy.' Though I didn't voice it I began to wonder if at some point the vehicle would stop and I'd be simply turfed out onto the ground and left to fend for myself in this triffid-haunted waste.

He regarded me for a moment. 'Do you really think we've invested so much time and fuel – valuable fuel! – to bring you here just so we can harm you?'

'Search me.'

'Why, that's preposterous.' He actually looked hurt by my implication. 'We went to a whole lot of trouble to rescue you.'

'Rescue me?'

'Sure.'

'Did I look as if I needed rescuing? If you could have seen me you'd have known I was having a great time. Besides, I was due to sail home the next day.'

'Yes, we know that.'

'Then what the hell were you playing at?'

'We knew you were sailing to England.' He looked at me levelly. 'We also knew that sailing behind you – just a little way over the horizon, out of sight – would be a battleship with a couple of destroyer escorts.'

'You're telling me that General Fielding plans to invade the Isle of Wight?'

'That's our information, Mr Masen.'

'But what's the point? We'd welcome friendly contact with open arms.'

'Are you sure of that?'

'Of course.'

The man took a deep breath, allowing his eyes to scan the sunlit landscape and its triffid sentinels.

'It seems you've been in the dark, Mr Masen. A metaphorical dark as well as a literal one.'

'Go on, surprise me.'

'You know the New York community under General

Fielding doesn't have access to oil wells or gasoline reserves?'

'Yes. They run cars on wood alcohol.'

'Which is so rough it chews motors to hell after a couple of thousand miles.'

I nodded.

'Well,' Sam Dymes said, 'We've a couple of oil wells, plus a refinery that produces around a million gallons of gasoline a year – it's not much, I grant you. But it means we can run this old girl.' He patted the seat affectionately. 'And we have good clean aviation fuel for the boat-planes.'

'Which New York doesn't have.'

'Correct, Mr Masen. So they can only tootle around the oceans in their coal-fired steamers. You see, therefore, that if they can get their hands on your Masen-Coker . . . uhm, what do they call the thing, now?'

'Masen-Coker Processor.'

He nodded. 'The Masen-Coker Processor . . . then General Fielding can refine that darn' triffid sap and have as much fuel as he wants for his automobiles, transport planes – and warplanes.'

'And the consequence of that?'

'The consequence of that for *us* is that we'll be wiped off the face of the Earth. Up here in the river estuaries we're safe from his warships. But if he has bombers and fighters . . . well.' Sam Dymes whistled. 'He'll bomb us all to hell and back.'

'Make peace with him.'

'You mean surrender?'

'No,' I said earnestly. 'Send a delegation. Negotiate.'

'He won't accept it. Soon he'll have the whip hand. Yes, he'll take our women and children to fuel his population drive. But our men? Why, they'll be shipped off to the coal mines or the logging camps, or those damn' slave farms in the Caribbean where they work night and day to clear the triffids and grow all those fancy crops to keep his followers happy.'

'You really think he's so unreasonable?' I pictured Kerris's father, General Fielding — the man with that burning yellow eye. OK, so he appeared to me to be a firm leader, even a visionary one. But a murdering tyrant? No, I didn't see that.

Sam Dymes looked at me, his fingers tapping his lips, assessing me. Then, after an interval:

'Yes, Mr Masen. I *do* think General Fielding is totally unreasonable. I also think he would stop at nothing if he could conquer us, as well as invading the Isle of Wight. Moreover, I believe he is a brutal dictator.'

'But that's only your opinion.'

'Not only my opinion, Mr Masen.'

'Oh? Who else's?'

'Can't you guess?' The man smiled, enjoying keeping me in suspense.

I shrugged. 'Whose?'

'None other than that of your own father, Bill Masen.'

'My father? He's never met General Fielding.'

'Oh, but he has. Long ago. You, too — when you were a child.'

I shook my head, frowning.

With a smile Sam Dymes reached down towards his feet. His hand returned holding a briefcase. Opening it, he pulled out a book and showed me the cover. I read the title, then the name of its author below – *William Masen*. 'You'd be surprised where your father's book turns up. We traded twenty gallons of gasoline to get this from a Portuguese fisherman five years ago. I hope your father won't come chasing us for royalties, but we ran off a thousand copies for distribution to our own people.' Briskly Sam continued, 'Your father knew General Fielding by another name – Torrence.'

'Torrence?' I knew that name well enough and sat up straight. 'My father escaped from Torrence twenty-five years ago.'

'That's right. Your father and mother plied Torrence and his henchmen with drinks when they invaded Shirning. While Torrence slept your father sabotaged their vehicle, then slipped away. Torrence woke up to find his birds had flown. Worse, the house was surrounded by triffids, but resourceful feller that he is he made protective triffid gear from chicken wire and canvas sheeting. Only, as he left the house, a triffid cracked its stinger at his head and venom sprayed through the chicken-wire helmet, blinding him in one eye.'

'Then somehow Torrence turned up in New York with a new name?'

'And a helluva chip on his shoulder.'

'But he must have known I was Bill Masen's son.'

'Of course. He intended using you.'

This cleared things up a bit. But I knew it would take some thinking through.

'But I know Torrence's daughter. I know her very well.'

'Precisely,' Sam Dymes said emphatically. 'That's why she too is a pawn in the old man's strategy. Right. We're here.'

'But—'

'You'll have to stow the questions for later. There's something you need to see.'

CHAPTER TWENTY TWO

Algonquin

Jazmay brought the vehicle to a halt at the edge of the plain. In front of us a valley dropped sharply away to a river shining in the midday sun. Sam stood on a steel bar that ran between the two seats, unbolted a hatch in the ceiling of the cab, and pushed it open. For a moment his blue eyes looked earnestly around the Jumbo. Then he beckoned me.

'All clear. The nearest triffid's five hundred yards away.' He hauled himself through the hatch and onto the vehicle's roof. 'It's easy enough, Mr Masen. Stand on the bar in the middle, then pull yourself up the rest of the way.'

In a moment I stood beside him on the machine's metal back. Behind me I saw where the caterpillar tracks had crimped the turf in a line as far as the eye could see. As Dymes had indicated, a lone triffid stood some way off. It had divined that we were there with whatever senses it possessed and had begun its lurching walk towards us on its three stumpy legs.

Sam noticed the movement too. 'We've got plenty of time before it gets here. But there's something important you should see. Then what I have to tell you next becomes a whole lot clearer.'

He handed me a pair of binoculars.

'Say.' He looked round, relishing the view. 'It's great to have real sunlight again. You know, we had darkness ten days straight. It made the triffids so antsy they were climbing over each other to get into our camp . . .' He breathed in deeply. 'Sun, glorious sun.' Shielding his eyes, he pointed into the valley below. 'See anything, Mr Masen?'

I looked. 'A river. Trees. Probably about a thousand triffids . . . gathered in three copses.'

'Use the binoculars. Anything now?'

'Yes, smoke. About half a mile away. From a settlement?'

'You've found it, Mr Masen. Look closer.'

Through the binoculars I saw a U-shaped bend in the river. 'A couple of canoes on a beach, and . . . and I can make out four, five . . . let's see eight timber cabins, with . . . Good Lord.' I took a surprised breath. 'What the hell's going on down there? They're going to be killed!'

Calmly, Sam gazed down. 'So, what do you see — exactly?'

My initial shock had graduated to amazement. 'There are people down there,' I told him. My eyes returned to the marvellous yet impossible sight. 'They're living in a camp with no perimeter fence. I can see children playing in a grove of triffids. They're not even paying any attention to the plants.'

'And the plants don't notice them, either.' Dymes took the binoculars to look for himself. 'And there's an old man sitting in the shade of a triffid.'

'Wait a minute here . . .' I pinched the bridge of my nose between finger and thumb and closed my eyes. 'This isn't right . . . this is . . .'

'Impossible?'

'Absolutely. Unless it's some kind of after-effect of that dope you pumped into me.' I looked at him. '*Am* I hallucinating?'

A smile crinkled the corners of his eyes. 'Those people in the valley below, Mr Masen, are American Indians from the Algonquin tribe. Round about a hundred years ago missionaries came along and *civilized* them. By the time The Blinding came the tribe had all but died out. What was left of them was a bunch of unhappy alcoholics. But look at them now.'

Children ran, laughing, through the triffids. One child of around eight, naked to the waist and with olive skin and long black hair, scampered up the hairy bole of the killer plant to swing round the stem, while calling mischievously to his playmates below.

From what I could see there in the valley, a happy people lived by the bend in the shining river.

'But,' I said, having difficulty taking on board the true implications of what I saw, 'the triffids are making no attempt to strike at them. Have their stings been docked?'

'No. The simple fact is that those people are immune. Triffids can't harm them.'

That took some absorbing. Then I persisted with my questioning: 'Not only that, the triffids are paying no attention to them. Don't they *ever* attempt to sting them?'

'I imagine they tried in the past. But when they realized that their stings were useless against those people they stopped wasting their venom.'

'The triffids *realized*, you say. So you attribute intelligence to those plants?'

'Of course. Don't you?'

I remembered my father's words of just a few weeks ago. In his greenhouse he had told me that those sinister plants could communicate with each other: that they could plot strategies, plan invasions, then march in a coordinated way to wage war against us.

But what Byzantine twist in nature's skein had brought about the change down there in the valley? Where men, women and children peacefully coexisted with triffids. What should have been a killing field for the likes of us had become a safe playground for the happy children of the Algonquin.

'Just imagine,' Dymes said. 'If we were as fortunate as those folks. Well, we could stroll right back out there into our world again. But we just can't get close enough to them to find out the secret of their immunity.'

We stood there on the roof of the vehicle, gazing down at the settlement. At that moment I felt as if I'd scrambled over some great divide that allowed me a peep into Eden. Equally, I understood, with a feeling of unease, that the miracle I was now witnessing was a fragile thing. One that in clumsy hands could so easily be broken.

'Ah, Mr Masen. We have company.'

I glanced behind us. The lone triffid had lurched its way over the intervening space. A few more seconds would bring us within striking distance of its fifteen-foot sting.

Dymes indicated the open hatch at our feet. 'After you, Mr Masen.'

By the time the rumbling Jumbo had reached the gates of the camp – letting fly with its flame-thrower at the clustering triffids for good measure – I had a clearer impression of my new hosts.

Sam Dymes, an engineer by training, was halfway through his tour of duty as 'manager and general dogs-body' of this military outpost of the Foresters. (A name, Sam explained, derived not from any propensity to cut down trees but because his people lived among the triffids. 'Our proper name is the United Liberty Con-federation, but as you can see – or hear, rather – that's something of an ungainly mouthful') Unlike the New York community where the population was concentrated at a single geographical point, the Foresters consisted of several hundred semi-independent settlements that pep-pered the eastern seaboard from Maryland to the tip of Florida. 'We first settled on islands and on the coast,' Sam told me. 'But Torrence, under his new name of General Fielding, sent gunboats to blow us to smith-ereens. So we moved inland along rivers, where his gunboats couldn't find us. And, of course, he couldn't send armies overland because of the triffids.' He nodded at one such plant as it lashed its sting against the window. 'Those devils have wound up as our allies. Funny how things turn out, huh?'

When the Jumbo halted I climbed out, noticing that one of the two submarines had left its moorings. I saw that Sam had noticed, too, but he made no comment.

'I reckon you'll be ready for a good square meal, Mr Masen.' He smiled. 'Get yourself a wash-up and a brush-down or whatever. Chow's served across there in the canteen — the hut with the red roof.'

I stood uncertainly for a moment as Sam headed away towards another building. Jazmay had lost interest in me, too, and was talking to a couple of unsighted men who sat at typewriters beneath an awning.

Noticing me standing there with a lost look on my face, Sam called back, 'There're no more armed guards for you, Mr Masen. Make yourself at home.'

I'd tackled two bowlfuls of a spicy dish, along with a heap of bread, when I heard the crackle of a PA system. A female voice announced the arrival of a flying boat, and invited a group of waiting passengers known as the Everglades Team to assemble at pier three.

In due course a large silver flying boat came in low and smooth over the river to make a perfect landing on the water. This stirred the pilot's blood in me. What wouldn't I have given to get behind the controls again, with a pair of beautiful Rolls-Royce engines humming sweetly and the blue sky beckoning.

'Penny for your thoughts, Mr Masen.'

I looked up to see Sam Dymes carrying a tray with a plate of steaming vegetables on it.

'Mind if I join you?'

'By all means.'

'Starting to get your bearings round here?'

I said that I was.

'Good, good,' he responded in that slow, easy drawl of his. 'We'll get you fixed up with a bunk later. And it looks as if you could use the loan of a razor.'

I ran my fingers over my jaw. Bristles were softening into a full beard. 'I could use a change of clothes as well, if that can be arranged?'

'Consider it done, Mr Masen. Say, is that chilli? I never noticed it was on the menu.' He turned back, calling good-naturedly to an unsighted woman who was serving food behind a counter. 'Say, Irene – any of that fire-cracker chilli of yours, left?'

'The young gentleman cleaned out the last drop.'

'Say, Mr Masen, you've a mighty appetite there . . . but then, we did starve you for a while.'

'How—'

'How long were you out? Two whole days. So, here, have my cake; I figure that's the least I can do for you.'

As we ate, something that I'd been dwelling on unconsciously for the best part of a fortnight at last surfaced into my conscious mind. 'Mr Dymes, when I—'

'Sam. Call me Sam, please.' Grinning, he thrust his hand across the table. 'Pleased to make your acquaintance . . . oh, you don't shake hands, do you?' He cocked a suddenly roguish eyebrow at me.

'Sam.' I allowed myself a smile that said something along the lines of *OK, you win*. I shook his hand. 'Drop the "Mr Masen", my name's David.'

'Sure thing, David. Now, what were you going to tell me? You were looking pretty serious back there for a moment.'

I nodded. 'I don't think the Algonquin we saw this morning are unique.'

'You don't say?'

'I believe there are others who are immune to triffid venom.'

'What makes you think that, David?'

As Sam tucked into a huge wedge of apple pie I told him about my forced landing on the triffid raft, then my encounter with the feral girl called Christina Schofield. He listened without comment, seemingly more intent on the apple pie, as I told him about her startled flight into a copse of triffids. How the stings had lashed out at her. How I'd been sure she'd been killed. I finished off with her miraculous return, completely unharmed.

'Well?' I invited his opinion as he swallowed the last crust of pie.

'Any more of that delicious pie, Irene?'

For a moment I wondered if he'd even heard my story, but straightaway he turned back to me. 'Christina Schofield. Yes.' He looked serious. 'And you are right. Triffid poison doesn't harm her.'

'You seem to know a lot about what goes on in New York.'

'Inside information is worth a dozen gunboats, don't you think?' he said as the matronly woman placed another slice of pie in front of him. 'Thank you, Irene. Oh, that looks wonderful.' Despite his earlier enthusiasm for dessert, his appetite seemed a little blunted now as his expression grew more serious. 'David, I'm afraid Christina's future doesn't look that rosy.'

'Why's that?'

'The latest information we have is that Torrence has ordered a huge operation, code-named Avalanche.' Sam pushed the pie aside. 'Female human beings are born with two ovaries. Each ovary contains thousands of egg cells. And, as you know, each egg cell, if fertilized, has the potential to develop into a human being.'

'Go on.'

'Torrence's medical people have perfected the use of fertility drugs to stimulate multiple births. Again as you know, his aim is to create a population explosion in his community, so that the sheer weight of people drives back the triffids, and his community can start to reclaim Long Island and New Jersey and so on. In fact, he still sends out raiding parties to kidnap women and children from other communities.' He sipped his coffee. 'Now that he has Christina who is immune to triffid stings you can see what's going through his mind, can't you? With a million like her they can simply walk back onto the American mainland and begin building Torrence's empire.'

'Let me get this straight: you mean to say that surgeons will remove Christina's ovaries, fertilize the egg cells, then implant the embryos into other women?'

'And it will be on a colossal scale. Every woman physically capable of bearing a child will become a host for one of Christina's fertilized embryos. And I mean *every* fertile woman, young and not so young. That goes for Kerris Baedekker, too, if our sources are reliable – and they generally are. In short, Christina Schofield will become "mother" to hundreds of thousands of children. Naturally, Torrence hopes that these new babies will form the backbone of a super-race that will be immune to triffid poison. That, in turn, will make him the most powerful man on the planet.' Sam took a breath. 'In addition, Christina will be dissected as a living specimen in what amounts to the laboratory version of the death of a thousand cuts, in order to learn about her natural protection.' His hand made a slow chopping action to emphasize what he said. 'David, Torrence is fanatical about this. Rabidly fanatical. He now knows how to get what he craves. In fact, he's ordered that all already expectant mothers are . . . well, rendered otherwise, so they'll be ready to receive Christina's egg cells.'

'My God . . . that's monstrous. If – if I'd had any idea what would happen to Christina I'd never have brought her to New York; I would . . .' I fell silent for a while, seething at Torrence's ruthless inhumanity. And knowing only too well now why the ship that had rescued me had been ordered to New York with all speed. 'By heaven,' I murmured at length. 'I wish I could do something to make this right for Christina. Poor kid . . . she raised herself from the age of six. Even though she's immune to triffid poison she's already gone through hell. Now she's going to go through worse.' A foul taste flooded my mouth. 'If I could only get my hands around Torrence's neck.'

Sam regarded me with his bright blue eyes. 'We may not be able to get Torrence. But we are trying to do something.'

'Oh?'

'We know that Christina's been taken to hospital. There's a lead-in time to Operation Avalanche of around four weeks while the first tranche of host mothers are prepared, so that gives us a fair interval before they operate on Christina.' He nodded out of the canteen window in the direction of the empty submarine bay. 'We've dispatched a snatch squad to bring her back here. All being well, she should be here safe and sound within the week.'

'You believe you can do it?'

'We're going to try, David. We're going to try our hardest.'

CHAPTER TWENTY THREE

Revenant

'One radio message. Just one. Surely you can give me that?'

I was up against a brick wall.

Sam Dymes shook his head, genuinely regretful.

'But,' I argued, 'I need to send a message back to my people on the Isle of Wight. You can see why?'

'Of course.'

'Then let me warn them that Torrence is still alive. And that, what's more, he's planning to send an invasion force.'

We were standing on the banks of the river as this discussion took place, while a sun that was nearer purple than red slipped down beyond the horizon.

'The weather conditions will be perfect for short-wave transmission,' I insisted.

'Sorry. I really am. But no can do.' Sam spoke in his relaxed Southern accent despite my bluster. 'David. Torrence has ships out looking for us. If he picks up our broadcast and gets a fix then he's going to come storming up that river, spitting fire and fury like nothing you've ever seen before.'

I ran my hand through my hair. Frustrating, damned frustrating, yet Sam had a point. In the secrecy of their location lay the heart of the Foresters' survival. During the three days I'd been here I'd heard ample tales of Torrence's banditry and slaughter.

I sighed. 'You see my concerns? I could be sitting here in the sun while Torrence's invasion force rips into my people back home.'

'David, listen to me. That won't happen yet.'

'How can you be so sure?'

'Because he's going to divert his manpower into Operation Avalanche. He's going to need all the medics he has to work in the hospitals on the mass fertilization programme. He'll also require the services of his ships' crews, too. After all, egg cells won't fertilize themselves, will they?'

I sighed again. 'Point taken.'

'In any event, from what you say the Isle of Wight has quite a formidable force of aircraft. Torrence can't risk losing his ships on the off chance your people won't fight back. No, he'd planned on using you as the Trojan horse to bring ashore a team of saboteurs and commandos in civilian clothes. It doesn't take a lot of figuring to see that they would seize airfields, then hold them until Torrence's warships brought in reinforcements. You follow?'

'I follow.'

'Ready for that cold beer yet?'

And that, as they say, was that.

Nevertheless, my time at the base wasn't unpleasant. The amiable, gangling Sam Dymes was a good companion with his idiosyncratic way of speaking, liberally peppered with *uhms*, *ahms* and long thoughtful *mmmmms*. I found myself believing that he couldn't be responsible for the shooting of Gabriel Deeds back in New York. Moreover, I believed him when he explained to me that Torrence's prosperous community was built on the sweating backs of slave labour. Slaves felled the trees that provided wood alcohol for motor fuel. Slaves worked the coal mines until they died of lung disease or sheer exhaustion, never seeing the light of day from one month to the next. Female slaves were shackled in baby factories where they were forced into pregnancy year after year. It seemed, moreover, that slaves were selected by colour and their inability to see – or if they'd voiced any criticism of the Torrence regime. Most slaves were confined to the north of Manhattan Island in the districts formerly known as Harlem and Washington Heights, now known as the bland-sounding 'Industrial Zone 1'. This ghetto lay beyond the high wall I'd seen with Kerris and that she'd referred to as the 102nd Street Parallel. True, some men and women of colour worked in other parts of Manhattan, but they understood that they had been granted a special privilege and all, but *all*, knew that the slightest misdemeanour would mean swift and savage punishment.

Torrence and his cronies weren't so dim that they failed to understand that among the people of different skin colours and the Blind there were many exceptionally talented men and women. Those who were a real asset to the community would be exploited accordingly. However, there was a price to pay. In return for elevation in both career and social standing these individuals had to

forfeit their sex. Whether this was a symbolic surrender-
ing of power to Torrence or whether it made for a more
pliant servant class no one was quite sure. Nevertheless,
Torrence viewed a eunuch workforce as eminently useful.

During my days at the base I helped out with general
chores, such as patrolling the anti-triffid fences, chopping
firewood or peeling mountains of potatoes. And during
the warm, balmy evenings I talked and joked with these
people over a beer or two. Yet I found myself dwelling
endlessly on Kerris Baedekker. I would ask myself a
thousand times a day what she was doing at that very
moment. Did she wonder what had become of me? Was
she friend or foe now? If I could somehow spirit her away
from Manhattan Island, would she go freely? Would she
accept that her father was no better than a robber baron,
a brutal tyrant who should be driven from power?

I didn't know. I just didn't know.

Then at night, as I closed my eyes, I saw her in my
mind's eye — and sometimes she would come to me in my
dreams.

The next day, the seventh after my arrival, was a fateful
one.

Dawn crept redly from the rocky bluff across the river.
Birds called in the trees. From the hen-coop came a
cockcrow.

Triffids greeted the daylight with a rattling of sticks
against their boles. *Here comes the sun*, I imagined them
saying. *Here comes the sun* . . . Perhaps they were still jittery
after that period of near-supernatural darkness when,
maybe, they had foreseen their own extinction. Now they

applauded the rising sun with a crescendo rapping that swelled quickly to an ungodly roar.

I listened to the botanical ovation as I shaved. Beside the sink a mug of coffee steamed. The bathroom was an easy-come, easy-go affair consisting of a row of sinks beneath a corrugated-iron roof. As there were no walls I could see the triffids shaking down their dark green leaves for the start of another day. Which for them would consist of standing pressed tight to the fence in their thousands. On their part this must have been an act of blind faith. That one day, like the walls of Jericho, the barriers would come tumbling down. A little way off was the shower block, which for decency's sake did boast walls that met the roof and from which I could hear the splash of water, accompanied by a deep male voice singing surprisingly melodiously.

I'd scraped away about half my stubble (with a merciful lack of razor nicks to my chin) when I realized that people were hurrying past the alfresco bathroom, all going in the same direction. The volume of their voices rose to shouting level — whether from alarm or excitement I couldn't tell.

Grabbing a towel, I wiped away what was left of the soap on my face. Then, with my curiosity straining like an eager dog at its leash, I joined the stream of people hurrying towards the river. I looked around, searching for the focus of this excitement. Then I saw it. Gliding round the bend in the river came the dark, sleek form of the submarine that I'd noticed earlier had left its moorings.

From the rising shouts I realized that all wasn't well. Even now I could make out that the submarine was listing to one side and the conning tower itself had a frayed appearance. The call went up for medics.

Limping in like some wounded leviathan, the submarine swung out in an arc across the river. Then, once it had aligned itself with the timber jetty, it came slowly forward.

Now, in that reddish light of dawn, the damage was all too visible. Shell holes pocked the conning tower: the uppermost part of it had been reduced to shreds of metal. The periscope and radar housing had been blasted to nothing. But the sub's hull seemed to have escaped the worst of the damage. People surged forward as a weary crew clambered out of the hatches onto the deck, then onto the jetty itself to be greeted with hugs.

The way the crew members hung their heads didn't suggest just weariness alone.

Confirmation came quickly. 'They'd moved Christina from the hospital,' Sam told me later. 'I'm sorry, David. You must be bitterly disappointed.' He turned back to watch the wounded being stretchered from the sub. 'We lost some good people, too. Only half the commando squad made it back. Then the sub took a pasting from shore batteries before it could submerge. If it hadn't been able to hide in a fog bank offshore it wouldn't be here at all.'

'What now?'

'Now?' Sam Dymes looked worried. 'Plan B.'

'What's Plan B?'

'You know something, David? I haven't a clue.'

With that he moved off to offer a few words of comfort to the injured men and women as they were loaded into ambulances.

*　　*　　*

Within a couple of hours of the submarine's arrival calm had returned to the camp. The sub's captain and Sam Dymes began a damage assessment of the vessel. Meanwhile, the more seriously injured of the crew and commandos were airlifted by flying boat to the large settlements to the south where hospital facilities would be better.

I returned to chopping more firewood. Here I wasn't far from the triffid fence. The plants beyond were silent. Unmoving. I sensed that they were watching events unfolding within the camp with an air of cool detachment. The downbeat mood of the base affected me and I found my thoughts about those bloody plants taking a morbid turn.

Triffids were evolving. They moved. They heard. They killed. They were carnivorous. They were beginning to develop sight, of a kind. Many scientists also credited them with intelligence. How long before they leapfrogged over humble humanity to add yet more abilities to their repertoire? The power to read our minds? The ability to simply *will* objects to move? I had a feeling we only had to wait long enough. Then we'd experience first-hand what new and diabolical tricks these things could play.

And so I worked on my pile of logs, chopping them down to manageable pieces for the cooking fires and water-heaters. Meanwhile, the sun climbed higher. However, it had lost some of its recently restored lustre. Today it refused to grow any brighter than a blood orange as it hung there in the sky; while all around the horizon a gory-hued mist settled.

*   *   *

Early afternoon, and with enough firewood cut for the day I sluiced my top half down with water from a bucket, then headed off towards the canteen for lunch. Now workmen swarmed across the sub's chewed-up superstructure. Already I could see the blue-white flash of an acetylene welding torch as the difficult job of repairs got under way.

At the entrance of the canteen I walked past a figure, one so familiar it didn't seem out of place.

'Hey, mister, know any place where a guy can get a game of table tennis round here?'

I stared. 'Gabriel?'

'I was beginning to think you didn't recognize me any more, David.'

'Yes. Of course . . . but, good grief! I thought you were dead.'

'An Oscar-winning performance, wasn't it?' Gabriel Deeds beamed broadly, holding out one of his huge muscular hands. I shook it, wincing at the formidable grip.

'Say. So you two fellers know each other.' Sam was sitting at a table, a hefty portion of apple pie in front of him. His smile, weary but warm, spoke volumes.

I flexed my tingling fingers. 'OK, Gabe. I guess you're not here by chance?'

Sam Dymes paused in mid-chew. 'You're not wrong.' He pointed with the spoon. 'David. Meet our man in New York. Now I'm going to finish off this incredibly delicious pie while Gabriel tells you some news you've been waiting to hear . . . Say, Irene . . . Irene? You don't have any of that fine apple pie left, do you?'

CHAPTER TWENTY FOUR

Reversal

Over lunch Gabriel told me what had happened, beginning with my abduction from New York more than a week ago.

'I set it all up,' he confessed. 'I knew that General Fielding, the guy you now know is Torrence, planned to return you to the Isle of Wight with a diplomatic envoy. Or what you'd be told was a diplomatic envoy.'

'But really I'd be giving safe passage to an invasion force. Yes, Sam filled me in on *that* scam.'

Gabriel continued, 'So it seemed clear to me I either had to get you away from New York – or kill you with my bare hands.'

I glanced at those massive hands, then back at those soulful brown eyes that were now strikingly grave. He wasn't joking about the second option, I realized.

'Believe me, David. I went down on bended knees to beg them to spring you from New York.' He sipped his coffee. 'However, you do realize that our motives in bringing you here and so sparing your island an invasion weren't entirely noble or selfless?'

I nodded. 'If Torrence seizes the Isle of Wight he also gets the Masen-Coker Processor.'

'Which then gives him high-octane fuel for his aircraft to bomb the stuffing out of the Foresters. Along with any other settlement that is reluctant to accept his – for want of a better word – *protection*.'

'And Kerris?'

'She's safe,' Gabriel assured me. 'I made sure she was in the back of the taxi before the snatch squad came close.'

'How is she?'

'Distraught that you've gone. But bearing up well, considering.'

'She doesn't know that you're a—'

'—A spy? No, she knows nothing about my other role in life. Unfortunately, she doesn't know whether you're alive or dead. Naturally, I had to exercise extreme discretion.'

'Don't you trust her?'

Gabriel looked pained at my outburst. 'I'm sorry, David. She *is* Torrence's daughter, after all. I can't take that risk. We have more operatives working in New York. If our cover should be compromised, then—'

'Yes, yes, I get the picture,' I said. 'But tell me this, Gabriel: did Kerris know about Torrence's intention to invade the Isle of Wight?'

He looked at me levelly. 'I'm convinced that she did not know. Like you, she was going to be a pawn in Torrence's plan.'

I sighed with relief. This separation, unpleasant enough as it was, would have become downright bitter if I thought she'd duped me.

As we ate, Gabriel told us about the recent mission to rescue Christina. Although there was little to say that we didn't know by now. Mainly, we knew that just moments before the snatch squad tore into the hospital, brandishing sub-machine guns, Christina had been whisked away to a secret location.

'Bad luck,' Sam said with feeling. 'Dashed bad luck.'

'In the words of the old blues song,' Gabriel commented, 'if it hadn't been for bad luck, real bad luck, we wouldn't have had any luck at all. After I drove the snatch squad back to the Hudson River who should I see but Rory Masterfield staring right at me. I knew he'd recognized me, that my cover was blown. I had no option but to get the hell out of there. So I jumped onto the sub with our guys. That should have been that. Submerge, then slip out down the Hudson and away. But a shore battery caught us with a searchlight. We were sitting ducks. However, the first bit of good luck we had that night was that the big guns on the islands didn't have our range. The shells came down half a mile away. We weren't so lucky with a couple of howitzers on the TriBeCa battery. They were good, I'll give them that. They drilled so many holes through the conning tower that there's more air than metal there now. Then they rounded that off by carving up the periscope and radar pod. That and a few too many punctures in the hull meant we couldn't submerge. All we could do was run hell for leather for the open sea. By sheer chance we dove straight into that fog bank where we gave the gunboats the slip.' He shook his head. 'Believe me, I don't want a repeat of *that* trip, thank you very much.'

The last word of Gabriel's sentence still hung on the humid air when *it* came. A sound that wasn't a sound. It was more a concrete-hard invisible wave that struck the canteen, sweeping plates from the tables, then the diners from their chairs. Windows shattered one after another. A boom echoed back like thunder from the bluff across the river. Immediately, I heard shouting. A siren sounded its rising wail.

I picked myself up from the debris of chairs, plates, spilled food. Sam and Gabriel were already running from the canteen. Gabriel stopped at the trackway but Sam continued to make for his office, his long legs pumping like an athlete's.

'Damn them,' Gabriel hissed, full of fury. '*Damn them.*'

I looked down to the river. Surging vee patterns of foam spread across the water.

'Torpedo boats.' Gabriel had seen them, too. 'How the hell did they follow us here?'

I watched the torpedo boats turn towards shore. They were small, sleek vessels, barely longer than the launch tubes that they carried at either side of a central cabin. Like speedboats they raced towards the camp before spitting out their deadly cargo.

As the torpedoes raced towards the shore I pulled Gabriel by the arm. 'Get back. We're too close.'

Those torpedoes were fast. Too fast for us to run back more than a few paces – although Gabriel's rage was such that I half anticipated he would run *forward* and try to deflect them somehow with his bare hands.

All we could do, however, was sprint a few yards before turning to witness the inevitable. Two torpedoes struck the remaining seaworthy submarine. It exploded in a geyser of white foam. With its back broken, its two distinct halves floated briefly apart before sinking to the river bed.

The third torpedo slammed into the mud bank, tearing a crater twenty feet wide. Instantly brown river water swirled into it, bubbling and steaming like a witch's brew. Having fired their torpedoes the boats then sprayed us with machine-gun fire.

Standing there like a fierce dark statue Gabriel Deeds spat his fury. 'How did they find us? On the return trip we played it by the book. We kept a twenty-four-hour watch. We made sure we weren't followed. So how come they're here now?' He seemed oblivious to the tracer bullets zipping past him.

'Gabriel!' I yelled. 'Keep your head down.'

He ran to a nearby Jumbo, climbing quickly onto its roof.

'There!' He pointed. '*That*'s how the bastards did it!'

I joined him, though I didn't like our exposed position. Those bullets were coming awfully close.

Nevertheless, I looked where he was pointing. Some way downriver, hanging back from the actual battle, its own task now complete, a curious vessel lay in the water. Painted with a mottling of deep marine blues and greens, something that resembled a flatfish barely peeped above the waterline. A pair of glass cockpits bulged upward like gleaming eyes. Clearly the tiny vessel, lying almost flush with the ocean surface, had followed the damaged sub to its base, then radioed back its location to the main strike force.

'Damn!' Gabriel spat explosively. 'We should have realized what they were doing. That's why the big guns aimed wide when we were getting out of the Hudson. They only wanted to wing us. Then they could follow us back here and . . .' His voice trailed off into a welter of incoherent curses.

Although the water was too shallow to bring in big warships with their deep draughts, all too quickly the river filled with a whole fleet of smaller boats. With deck cannon, Oerlikons, machine guns, mortars and multiple rocket launchers blazing away, they came surging forward: a pack of water-borne hyenas closing in for the kill.

We weren't without sharp teeth of our own, however. From various points on our shore artillery pieces barked, sending shells streaking out over the river. Some of these found their mark. Three enemy launches erupted into fireballs, sending burning crewmen leaping into the water.

Gabriel jumped up and down on the metal back of the Jumbo, cheering. However, a timely machine-gun round, ricocheting from the armoured side of the triffid-killer, reminded us that our position was somewhat exposed. Quickly making our way to the ground, we watched the unfolding battle from behind the vehicle.

It wasn't going well. Despite our side's spirited counter-fire from dugouts, artillery placements and watchtowers, more than a dozen launches had reached the shore. Then, from under a blistering cover of machine-gun fire, Torrence's troops stormed up the hill.

They fired as they went, some hurling grenades into dugouts. My heart sank. Torrence had launched a dedicated attack, using crack infantry. Foresters were dying by the dozen.

Somehow at times like that the incongruous often shows its hand.

From speakers mounted on poles around the camp music began to play. A lilting female voice sang a slow ballad that echoed across the hillside. Even gunfire intermingled with the agonized screams of the dying failed to drown out the beautiful melody.

A hand shook my shoulder. 'That's our signal to get out!' Gabriel pulled open the hatch of the Jumbo. 'Move it!' Quickly I scrambled inside, taking one of the front seats. I saw a young Hispanic man slip through the hatchway into the driver's cabin below my feet. A second later the engine rumbled into life.

The vehicle had already started to roll forward on its caterpillar treads when Gabriel scrambled aboard to sit in the seat beside me.

'Have you seen Sam?' he called.

'The last I saw of him he was heading across to his office.'

Gabriel twisted round in his seat to get a better view of the control block where Foresters loaded the more sensitive documents into waiting Jumbos.

Suddenly, the clanging of bullets hitting the side of our vehicle drew my attention back towards the river. More launches had appeared, packed with men in green battledress. Some of the launches tried to run aground where the banks were too steep, leaving the invaders to leap ashore there. But the angle of the mud banking meant that they slipped back into the water where they drowned beneath the weight of the equipment that they carried.

Nevertheless, many of the invaders were making it to dry land – although not all made it as far as the camp. From the lookout towers our machine-gunners raked the earth with bullets, dropping many a soldier in mid-stride. And all the time there came the cacophony of gunfire, exploding shells and the high screaming of rocket launchers. Smoke rolled across the camp with all the density of an autumn fog.

I called to Gabriel. 'What about Sam?'

'He'll hitch a ride on a Jumbo . . . we're getting out of here.'

'Where?'

He jerked his head towards the nearest triffid fence. 'Out there. Where Torrence's men won't follow.'

By now our vehicle had fallen into line behind others thundering across the grass; one clipped the shower block, bringing the roof down onto its metal back. It carried on regardless, chewing turf to mud. From some vehicles heavy machine-gun muzzles jutted; these were brought to bear on our attackers to spit lethal streams of bullets interspersed with brilliant red tracer rounds that cut down whole swathes of invaders.

At that moment, I did harbour a distinct hope that the tide of battle could be turned in our favour. Yet a clatter of bullets on our armoured side told me otherwise. More of Torrence's men had worked their way round inside the triffid fence in an encircling movement to trap the Foresters within. Now our only hope was retreat.

What seemed at first a chaotic flight soon became a well-ordered withdrawal. Our line of vehicles split up. They each drove singly towards a designated section of triffid fence. Vehicle after vehicle crashed through, snapping wire, crushing posts to matchwood.

Gabriel flashed me a grim smile. 'This is where we leave the job of defence to the big green guys.' He nodded towards the waiting triffid plants. 'We figure that Torrence's men won't have the stomach to take on all those.'

As if on cue the first triffids moved through the breaks in the fence, eagerly seeking their prey within the camp.

'It's the music,' I called over the bellowing roar of the motor. 'They're homing in on the sound of the music.'

Gabriel nodded, his face showing grim satisfaction. 'That's why we're playing a song rather than instrumental music. Those things love the sound of a human voice.'

As we lumbered towards our breakout section of fence I glanced back. Torrence's men had perhaps three-quarters of the camp under their control now. A ring of figures in battledress was encircling the Command block. The last of the Jumbos were leaving with their precious cargo of Foresters. One vehicle, however, remained. This was a monster of its kind. Twin turrets with machine guns dealt fiery death and destruction. Torrence's men charged towards it but were driven back time and time again.

At that moment I saw Sam Dymes run from the office. In one hand he held a satchel bulging with documents that were too sensitive to be left for the invader. Beside him, firing a sub-machine gun, ran Jazmay.

Come on, come on . . . I willed them to leap into the monster vehicle and roar away up the hillside to safety. Even as I silently urged the pair to run faster I saw the invaders manhandling a long black tube into position some thirty paces from the vehicle. Within a moment it was all over. With a burst of smoke a missile flashed from the tube directly through the Jumbo's metal flank to burst inside its valiant heart.

The explosion blasted the twin turrets clean from the machine. Burning wreckage tumbled across the grass.

I stared in disbelief. The blast had knocked Sam and Jazmay to the ground, but they were on their feet like lightning, sprinting towards the canteen building for cover. Any respite they found there would be short-lived, though.

Turning, I struck Gabriel on the arm. 'We've got to go back!'

'No can do. We're nearly home and dry.'

'Sam and Jazmay are back there. They're trapped.'

His dark eyes swiftly read the situation and he thumbed the intercom button. 'Driver. Make a one-hundred-and-eighty-degree turn . . . be ready to take on passengers.' He looked at me. 'OK, David. I think it's time to say a little prayer. We're just about to shove our heads into the lion's mouth.'

CHAPTER TWENTY FIVE

Withdrawal

Careering downhill, faster now, much faster, the Jumbo thundered towards the canteen building. Jazmay was firing from a window with her sub-machine gun. From behind a door Sam aimed his revolver.

The situation didn't look good. Perhaps thirty invaders were closing in on the building, peppering the walls with shots from their carbines.

'We got to move fast,' Gabriel shouted. 'When we pull up alongside the building open the hatch, then get those two in as fast as you can. Got it?'

I nodded, holding on to the grab rail in front of me.

We seemed all too vulnerable, sitting high in those cabins at the front of the Jumbo. There seemed to be nothing but glass surrounding us. While I knew it was toughened I didn't want a bullet to put it to the test.

Our Jumbo hit level ground, its nose dipping just enough to gouge a yard of blacktop from the roadway, and then we were powering towards our target.

Success or failure was a hair's-breadth matter. It only

needed an enemy soldier to roll a grenade through the canteen doorway. Meanwhile, the number of invaders in front of us grew. Our driver slowed.

Gabriel was having none of that. He stamped on the cabin floor to emphasize the order. 'Damn' well drive!' he shouted into the intercom. 'If they don't move, run the swine down!'

The swine did move.

They leaped aside as the Jumbo roared towards them, engine bellowing, muck flying from the caterpillar tracks.

'Get ready with that hatch!' Gabriel yelled at me before returning to direct the driver closer to the canteen building.

I watched as the enemy throng parted like the Red Sea before Moses. There seemed an impossible number of them crowding the area in their drab green uniforms.

I glanced round quickly. The camp had fallen into enemy hands. No doubt about that now. Although its capture might turn out to be short-lived. Already I could see triffids moving with that jerky gait of theirs that caused the upper stem and cone to whip violently back and forth. They lurched through the smashed fences, making beelines for the dead of both sides. There'd be nourishment galore for the plants tonight.

'Damn!' Gabriel swore bitterly.

Looking forward through the glass I saw a knot of men in front of us. This time they weren't running away from our machine. Two of them aimed the long black pipe straight at us.

Gabriel's eyes blazed. 'Bazooka! Get ready to bale out.'

At times like this it's astonishing how sheer survival

instinct can make one move with lightning speed. Without thinking, I grabbed the control stick in front of me, my thumb hitting the red button.

A giant flame burst from the tube at the front of our vehicle. Spitting and roaring, it was an incandescent mass the colour of hellfire itself.

Before the enemy soldiers could fire the bazooka they were bathed in flame.

I released the trigger. The torrent of hellfire stopped. At the same moment I closed my eyes, not wanting to see the aftermath of my action.

Nor did I have to. Seconds later our vehicle passed over whatever remained of the soldiers.

'David. Open the door.'

The vehicle had stopped alongside the canteen building, just half a dozen feet from the doorway. Sam Dymes, carrying the document bag, ran from behind the now bullet-ravaged door. At the hatchway of the vehicle he stopped, beckoning to Jazmay who had slipped nimbly through a window.

She'd reached the hatch. Her gaze locked on mine, dark and intense. That was the moment the enemy bullet found her. She crumpled to the ground, her beautiful hair turning a sodden crimson, her staring eyes sightless, the light of life passing instantly from them.

Sam looked down at her with a kind of pained outrage. He snatched her sub-machine gun from the ground and at that moment he looked as if he'd run after Jazmay's killer in sheer vengeful fury.

I shouted at him. 'Sam. It's too late. Get in!'

His lanky frame swayed with indecision. He burned

for revenge. Then, with a glance at the still form of Jazmay, he gave a regretful shake of his head and climbed on board.

'Go, driver. Go!'

With the hatch closed Sam scrambled up into the cabin behind me. His expression was like an open wound. Grief, anger, outrage inflamed those normally placid blue eyes, changing his stare into something that chilled my blood.

'Thanks,' he said in a surprisingly low voice. Then he stared forward through the window, locked into some distant place with his own thoughts.

This time I displayed no qualms as the Jumbo lumbered up the hill. When any invader crossed our path I played merry hell with them with the flame-thrower.

By the time the Jumbo at last broke through the fence a burning pathway stretched back as far as the place where Jazmay had fallen. Squirming, smouldering things littered our trail. But this time I kept my eyes wide open.

Nightfall saw the surviving Jumbos parked in a circle, nose to tail. We were some ten miles from the army camp on a plain that stretched as far as the eye could see. Triffid plants lurched in the direction of the faraway camp.

Clearly word was out on the triffid grapevine.

Come to the feast.

One after another they determinedly made their way north.

A headcount informed us that little more than a

hundred Foresters had escaped from the battle. Decidedly melancholic about our defeat, we built a fire inside the triffid-free zone created by the protective circle of Jumbos. Dried-food rations and water bottles were broken out for a rather dismal supper. Then, with the guards armed with powerful flashlights as well as with carbines, we attempted to make the most of the sleep available to us.

I lay on the grass, looking up at the stars. Orion, my favourite constellation as a child, looked a dull thing these days. His once sparkling belt no longer sparkled. Whatever was out there creating the foggy barrier between Earth and the wider cosmos still ebbed and flowed in some great space-seas tide. Sometimes it dimmed the sun to a blood-red disc. At other times it thinned, allowing near-normal sunshine through. Now it drew a grim veil across the stars, allowing only the brightest to gleam dismally through with all the allure of teeth in a dead skull.

I lay there for a long time, gazing up at a sadly diminished night sky, before I drifted off to sleep, my dreams populated by burning men, screams, terror-stricken faces. Looping images of Jazmay falling to the ground. Instead of blood, triffid fronds sprung from the head wound, growing out and out in endless tendrils of green that swarmed ivy-like over buildings, consuming whole countries to enshroud the whole world . . .

I woke with a jolt. A figure sat beside me in the near-dark. Smoke trailed from a cigarette held between his fingers. So preoccupied was he that he'd forgotten to knock the ash from the cigarette; it crumbled away in grey flakes across his knuckles. Sam looked as if he had the troubles of the world crushing him.

Even though he didn't move he must have sensed that I was no longer asleep.

'It's been a bad business, David,' he said, barely whispering. 'A bad business.'

Moving limbs stiffened from sleeping on the earth, I sat up.

'She told me yesterday she was going to have a child . . .' He spoke in a rambling, disconnected kind of way. 'Tomorrow she was due to fly home to her husband on maternity leave. Jazmay was a good kid . . . well, a kid no longer . . . a woman. I knew her from the time her family came over from Ireland on a sailboat that seemed to be held together by string and brown paper. It's a funny thing life, isn't it . . . not funny ha-ha. It — it just leaps out and bites you sometimes. She was chatting, all happy and excited about being a mom. A couple of hours later she's lying dead on the ground . . . kinda makes you think, doesn't it? Fate. Destiny.' His tone changed as he suddenly switched tack. Although he still spoke in that soft Southern whisper he sounded angry with himself. 'How could I be so stupid, David? How could they take us by surprise like that?'

'Those torpedo boats were fast. They came at us before we even knew they were there.'

'But we had observation posts downriver. All I can figure is that they jumped the lookouts before they had time to sound the alarm.'

'I guess so.'

He turned this over in his mind for a while. I could imagine his blue eyes like two cold flames there in the darkness. 'You know what really riles me? The way I underestimated Torrence's obsession with revenge. Sure, I knew he was ruthless. He eliminates anyone who opposes him. But I never thought he'd mount a raid like this. He can't spare the manpower or the resources, but that man's capacity for vengeance is . . . is *infinite*. He must have thrown every single soldier he had at us, burned up most of his fuel reserves and half his fleet. But he wanted something bad . . . so bad he'd nearly bankrupt his nation doing it.'

'But what was it that he wanted? From what you say the base back there is only one of dozens you people have.'

'Come on, David, don't be so naïve.'

'Pardon?'

'Take a good look at this.' Crushing out the cigarette, he pulled something from his jacket pocket. 'I took this from one of Torrence's men . . . no, he didn't mind, he was just embarking on a new career as a deceased person. Here, what do you make of that . . . no, wait . . . you can't see it in the dark. Let me get some light on that for you.' I heard the click of his lighter. 'From what I could see, all of Torrence's men had these stuffed into their pockets or taped to their helmets. That, David, is what Torrence wanted so badly.'

In the wavering flame I saw a photograph. I sighed as I understood. 'Me,' I told him.

'Got it in one. While you were back in New York Torrence's spies were watching you.' He pushed the photograph back into his pocket. 'They were taking snaps, too.'

'But why risk the lives of his best men to go after me?'

'Torrence wanted you back. Dead or alive would have been fine by him. Remember, Torrence holds your father responsible for him losing his eye, as well as causing a lot of hurt to his ego. Torrence would cheerfully have sent your head pickled in a jar to your family if you'd been killed. Or if he'd gotten you back to New York alive he'd have used you as a hostage. Either way, he'd exploit you to make your father suffer for what he'd done.'

'You know how this makes me feel now? Dozens of your people were killed this morning.'

'Any way you look at it, there's only one man to blame. That's Torrence. He's responsible. He's the one with blood on his hands.'

'What now?'

'We'll camp out here for a few days. When that mob have gone we'll go back, clear the base of triffids, repair fences, rebuild. Bury what's left of the dead. It'll be a long job but we'll do it.'

'But you have military aircraft. You could hunt down Torrence's ships and bomb them to pieces.'

'We could,' Sam allowed. 'But you see, a lot of our people will have been taken prisoner today. They'll be on those ships. One day, we hope they'll be free again.'

'But until then they'll be used as slave labour?'

'Yes, they will.' He nodded, thoughtfully running a finger along the bridge of his nose. 'And the women who were captured will become part of Torrence's grand scheme. They'll be forcibly impregnated. They'll have babies.' He sounded tired. 'I'm going to turn in now.' He patted me on the shoulder. 'You try and get some sleep too. We're going to have some busy days ahead of us.'

He ambled away to sit with his back against one of the vehicles. I doubted very much if Sam Dymes slept at all that night. Even if he did, I had the feeling that nightmares would torture that good-hearted man until daybreak.

CHAPTER TWENTY SIX

Sight & Sound

The next morning I'd barely pulled on my boots when Gabriel Deeds tapped me on the shoulder. 'David. Come take a look at this and tell me what you think.' He looked like a man who'd just uncovered a treasure chest.

I followed him to the edge of our camp, marked by the line of Jumbos. They looked even greyer in the misty dawn.

'I didn't think it would be long before we had the neighbours round,' I commented. For already triffids had been shuffling towards the camp. So far their way was blocked. Even so, we'd have to be careful of their stings.

'Stand up on that tree trunk, so they have a clear view of you'

'Gabriel.' I looked at him quizzically. 'Gabriel, I've seen those things before, you know?'

'Of course. But stand up on the trunk. Trust me on this, I'm going to show you something.'

'But they're—'

'No, listen to this,' he said quickly. 'There's something different about them.'

'What do you mean?'

'Unless I'm very much mistaken I think they've just gone and learned a brand new trick.'

I stood on the tree trunk, which gave me a platform about four feet from the ground. The nearest triffids were hidden, with the exception of their uppermost stems and sting cones, by the bulk of the Jumbos. However, a hundred yards or so away a slight bump in the ground meant that a few triffids were elevated enough for me to see them root to stinger. From those triffids came a tapping as they rapped their sticks against their hairy boles.

I gave Gabriel a questioning look.

'What do you hear?' he asked.

'Nothing, apart from the triffids tapping their finger sticks.'

'You mean you missed it when you climbed onto the tree trunk?'

'Missed what?'

'Now. Stand very still for five seconds.'

'Gabriel—'

'Trust me, OK?' He looked serious, but charged-up somehow. As if he was onto something important.

'OK, now what do you want me to do?'

'All right. When I say "Now" stand as still as possible for five seconds. Then quickly put your arms straight up above your head. Only, as you do so, listen carefully to those triffids across there on the mound.'

I did as instructed.

When I stood still I heard a slow rattling sound, almost like a man drumming his fingers meditatively on a table top. When I moved my arms there came a sudden manic burst of tapping, which slowed back to its previous rate when I stopped moving.

'Did you hear that?' he said expectantly.

'Yes, but what does it mean?'

'The triffids nearest to us, the ones that are hidden behind the Jumbos, didn't increase the rate at which they rattled their sticks. Yet the ones that were in full view of us suddenly went crazy; the tapping became so rapid it was like listening to a . . . a woodpecker or a machine gun . . . not a dit-dat-de-dat sound but a rapid *brrrrrr*.'

'You're saying that they responded to my movement? But we've always known that.'

'Yes, but something's changed here. They're responding from a greater distance. And can you see that the ones on the hill all have their cones pointing at you — targeting you — like radar dishes?'

'You're telling me that they've undergone some kind of evolutionary change? But why now?'

'Why not? When environmental conditions change, life must adapt too or go stand in line with the dinosaurs, dodos and Tasmanian tigers in extinctionville.' He rubbed his jaw reflectively. 'My guess is that when the sun stopped shining for a spell it triggered some quantum leap in their evolution.'

'But evolutionary change takes thousands of years.'

'Normally, yes. But we're not dealing with your normal beastie here. Those plants have torn up the laws of nature and are rewriting them to allow triffids to meet their goal. Namely, to inherit the Earth.'

I moved my arms again. This time I heard it. The triffids on the hill rattled their sticks so fast the sound became more a buzz than a rattle.

'But only the ones on the hill made the sound. The ones just behind the Jumbos didn't do anything different.'

'That's because they can't see you,' Gabriel answered, a note of triumph in his voice. 'But I use the word "see" between inverted commas.'

I smiled. 'Something tells me that if my father was here you two would have a wonderful conversation. My own knowledge of botany inclines to the scant.' I jumped down from the trunk. 'So, Gabe, how does the process work? After all, there's still no physical evidence of eyes.'

'I don't think it is optical.'

'Not optical? I don't follow. Surely—'

'No . . . no.' He held up his finger. 'Not all animals see using an optical system. And remember, I said I used the word "see" in inverted commas.' He took a breath. 'Take dolphins. They have eyes like we have, but they rely on sound to track fish, or to avoid rocks and boats.'

'You mean a kind of natural sonar?'

'Only it's infinitely more sophisticated than the crude electronic sonar equipment we have. A dolphin fires out clicks at a rate of around three hundred a second. The click bounces back from a fish, the echo enters through the dolphin's lower jaw where it shoots through to its middle ear, then on to the part of its brain where the sound is processed. But the remarkable part of this is that the dolphin doesn't hear the sound, it "sees" it in a way that we don't entirely understand. But we do know it "sees" a three-dimensional image of the fish it's hunting. And because sound travels through soft tissue it not only sees the outside of the fish, like we would, it sees the fish on the inside, too — its skeleton and some of the denser internal organs.'

'Hang on there, Gabriel. So you're telling me that the triffids are "seeing" the echoes of the sounds they make with their sticks?'

'Sure. I reckon they're catching the echoes in the cones at the tops of the stems. Think about it: they'd make the perfect natural antennae.' He nodded across to the vehicles. 'But the ones screened by all that armour plate can't "see" us because of the obstruction to their clicks. But if we were to move those vehicles they could see not only our outer forms but our bones and probably what we ate for supper, too.'

'All of which is pretty depressing news. A plant that can walk and hear and kill is bad enough. Now it can see in the dark?' I shrugged. 'That tips the scales in their favour, doesn't it?'

'I agree.' Gabriel's eyes were troubled. 'But the question I ask myself now is this: what kind of surprise are they going to spring on us next?'

If the triffids were harbouring any unpleasant surprises they kept them well hidden. More triffids did, however, join the growing throng beyond our circle of vehicles. For most of the time they did little but sway and rattle their finger sticks, while no doubt carefully scrutinizing us inside and out (assuming that Gabriel's sonar hypothesis was correct).

We gave the plants a wide berth within our enclosure, ensuring that we stayed beyond the range of their stingers. Apart from that exercise in self-preservation there was little to do but talk among ourselves, eat our dried-food rations and, on occasion, leave the safety of the camp to gather firewood, suitably attired, of course, in protective triffid gear complete with large cylindrical helmets of plastic 'glass'.

Sam Dymes lived beneath a cloud of his own pre-occupation for the first couple of days. His speech came in halting fragments as if self-doubt had completely destroyed his confidence. But by the third day he was largely back to his old self. The hesitant speech was still there, freely decorated with those *uhms*, *ahms* and long thoughtful *mmmmms* . . . but every so often, just when you thought his speech would grind completely to a halt, the words would suddenly pick up speed until they were tumbling out after each other. He was a man who lived on nervous energy. When he was animated his whole gangly frame would come to life and he'd walk up and down, gesturing enthusiastically. That was when the words would come flying from his lips like those of a man close to speaking in tongues.

Already he'd dispatched one of the Jumbos with its crew to keep a discreet watch on the camp. They would return as soon as it looked like Torrence's marauders had quit the place.

It was late on the third day after the invasion that we had more visitors — of sorts, that is. Three men came across the plain. They walked with the easy rhythm of those who travel great distances on foot. Instantly the Foresters were alert to danger, watching the approaching men with their guns at the ready. But the three made a point of giving our encampment a wide berth.

From what I could see there were two young men walking with an older man. Each one wore his long hair in a single ponytail. Clad in clothes of brightly woven cloth, they carried heavy backpacks stuffed full, I imagined, with game or skins. On their shoulders they carried bows with quivers full of arrows.

And these people, as I'd seen before, simply walked among the triffids as if those sinister plants were no more deadly than apple trees.

The Algonquin hunters paused for a moment to look at us with somewhat suspicious eyes. But once they'd decided that we weren't there to make mischief they continued on their way without a backward glance at us. Their easy stride took them effortlessly through the assembled triffid plants.

Although the triffids knew of the Indians' close proximity (I'd seen the plants' cones turn towards them) the plants never made even one attempt to strike at them. Gabriel Deeds watched the men dwindle into the distance across the plain. Then, turning to me, he said softly, 'Now, if we could learn a trick like that life would look a whole lot rosier.'

Little more than an hour after our 'visitors' had walked on out of sight the Jumbo came lumbering back to the camp. After a brief conversation with its crew Sam Dymes strode towards me. 'They've gone.' A grim expression made his face like stone. 'It's time we went back.' With that terse speech he waved his people to the vehicles.

We were returning to the camp. I didn't relish the prospect of what we'd find there.

CHAPTER TWENTY SEVEN

The Return

The return journey to the Foresters' camp was made in an atmosphere of grim expectation. What we found was even grimmer.

Torrence's invasion forces had gone. Even now they were probably steaming north for New York. A shambles – a macabre shambles met our gaze. The elephantine vehicles grunted their way into the camp through gaps in the fence. Naturally triffids had filled the vacuum. They were busy feasting on the fallen soldiers of both sides. Littering the river banks were the remains of the landing craft that had been destroyed by the Foresters' artillery. While a little upstream, partly submerged, our flying boats had been hacked to pieces by the invaders before they left. Clearly they had wished to make life difficult for us on our return. Similarly, food and fuel stores had either been looted or spoilt. Buildings had been reduced to sooty smudge marks on the earth.

A little while later, after a corner of the camp had been cleared of triffids, and with a line of Jumbos forming a temporary barrier against them, Sam Dymes stood upon the back of one of the vehicles to address the survivors.

He told us that a grim task lay ahead. But we wouldn't short-change the men and women who had died defending the camp. They would be buried with full honours. A memorial would be raised to them. That was the moment when the full import of the death and the destruction hit the survivors. Many went to their knees. Concluding the address Sam said, 'Torrence gave us a bloody nose. But he has not beaten us. And this . . . this barbaric attack on our camp did not achieve its aims. He sent his men here to snatch back David Masen. They failed. That means Torrence's wider strategy has been stopped dead in its tracks. Without Masen he can't invade the Isle of Wight because he knows those guys over there have an air force that can bomb his warships out of the water. And if Torrence can't seize the Isle of Wight, he can't grab the machine that turns triffid oil into fuel. Without that, he doesn't have a viable air force of his own. So . . .' Suddenly Sam turned to face north and with a genuine burst of hatred he shook his fist at the northern horizon. 'So you can stay in your skyscraper palace, Torrence! You can rot there for all we care! Because all you've succeeded in doing with your treachery and your brutality is to build yourself one hell of a prison. And you can't do squat about making your stinking, filthy, cockamamie empire one square yard bigger.' For a moment I thought he'd draw his side arm and in the white heat of rage fire off the whole magazine in the direction of distant New York City. But suddenly the rage vanished. In low, even tones he turned back to us. 'OK. We've got work to do.'

Squads moved out across the camp in protective triffid gear, the clear fish-tank helmets gleaming in the sun. They docked the triffids of their stings, then felled them. Soon the whine of chainsaws filled the air. Post-mortem teams collected the dead, identified them, tagged them. Torrence's men were given burials as decent as those accorded the Foresters' dead.

As I donned the stout canvas protective suit prior to repairing the fences, Gabriel appeared. He showed me a bucketful of syringes before dumping them into a trash barrel. 'These came from Torrence's soldiers.'

'Morphine?'

He shook his head. 'Amphetamines. His men were pumped so full of this junk that they came ashore feeling they were running on rocket fuel.' He wiped his hands on a rag as if they'd come into contact with something unclean. 'The poor devils were so high they never even felt it when a bullet hit them. Torrence, huh? Don't you just admire and respect the man?'

The fence was a mess. Perspiring inside my suit I made a start with wire-cutters, clearing the tangled strands ready for the fencing gang to come and string fresh wire along the posts. A hundred yards to my right another figure — its appearance rendered androgynous by the protective suit — clicked away with wire-cutters, too. Far from comfortable, I tugged at this spaghetti supper of wire while triffids either lurched by me into the camp (where the anti-triffid squads would deal with them) or chose my head for a spot of target practice. Every so often a stinger would snap against the glass helmet with a chiming *trringg*. Something that never lost its power to irritate me deeply.

Nevertheless, I laboured on, cutting wire and then dragging it free of the tangle of triffids that had been crushed during our escape. I wondered if the Foresters' headquarters, based several hundred miles to the south, knew of Torrence's attack on one of their military camps. These days communities were so reluctant to surrender knowledge of their whereabouts that they were inclined to avoid radio transmissions altogether. Instead, they tended to rely on something akin to the Pony Express, namely a written communication delivered by hand. With this deep mutual suspicion bordering on paranoia it was hard to see that the disparate communities scattered across the globe would ever make contact with one another, never mind actually get together to form alliances for trade and mutual support. Maybe my father was right. Humanity would be destined to exist in scattered fragments that would eventually shrivel and die out completely.

Even at that time, when Torrence's evil handiwork was so obvious not only to my eyes but also to my nose as warm days and legions of bacteria did their work on the corpses, I did wonder about the man. Yes, he was brutal. Yes, he was a warmonger. Yes, he was undoubtedly Draconian. And yet . . . and yet, a genuine vision of the future drove him. Although his methods were wrong, his goal was right.

As my cutters snapped through the glittering wires I immersed myself in my thoughts. I was so immersed, in fact, that I never saw them arrive.

One moment I saw only the hairy boles of triffids, together with a mass of dark green leaves. The next, I realized that four individuals stood there, watching me.

In a reflex action, I immediately looked for the shotgun that I'd left leaning against a fence post. Instantly, one of the four, a young woman with raven hair, drew back the string of a bow and released an arrow. With the sound of air being cleaved apart the arrow blurred past me, striking the wooden stock of the shotgun and splitting it neatly in two.

I froze, staring at the four through my transparent helmet, their bodies distorted slightly by imperfections in the material: they looked more like phantoms than real people. Yet I saw clearly enough when the girl notched another arrow against the string of her bow and then raised the bow so that the projectile pointed directly at my chest. She pulled back the bowstring until it stretched taut.

CHAPTER TWENTY EIGHT

Some Came Calling

My father once wrote: *That's the kind of warning I don't debate.*
Wise words. His son remembered them only too vividly,
expecting that the arrow would come thudding into his
chest at any moment.

To signify surrender in the time-honoured way, I
raised both my hands. For a moment we looked warily
at each other. Me, in my protective suit complete with
transparent helmet, and the four American Indians who
were dressed in brightly woven tunics. The Indians, of
course, didn't wear any protective clothing at all. They
stood side by side in the thicket of triffids; one had lifted
a hand to push aside some of the thick green triffid leaves
that obscured his view of me . . . and a strange sight I
must make, I surmised. Three of the Indians were scarcely
teenagers. The other, a man who was anywhere between
fifty and seventy, watched me levelly for a time. His dark
eyes assessed me. Then:

'Naome, you can put up your bow now.' He nodded
towards me. 'We're not here to make trouble.'

I continued to stare.

The old Indian smiled. 'Surely you didn't expect me to say something like "Me scalpum white man", did you now?'

With the polished courtesy of a professional diplomat he bowed his head slightly and said, 'Good afternoon. My name is Ryder Chee. This is my daughter Naome, and my sons Isa and Theo.' His voice had the precise tones of a cultured man.

'My name is David Masen.' My breath misted the clear material of the helmet. 'Do you mind if I lower my arms?'

'By all means, David Masen. I am sorry that we damaged your shotgun. But we wanted to ensure that you didn't shoot first and ask questions afterwards.'

Recovering my composure, I asked if I could help them in any way.

Chee smiled. 'We're here to offer some small degree of help to *you*. After all, you are our closest neighbours.'

I thanked them. Then I invited them to follow me down into the camp where I found Sam Dymes poring over hastily written work agendas with Gabriel.

Once inside the triffid-free corner of the camp I could relieve myself of the burdensome protective suit. The fresh air smelled unbelievably good. With a lungful of good, sweet air I introduced our four visitors to Sam and Gabriel.

Chee nodded towards Sam. 'You are the leader.' It was a statement rather than a question. 'Forgive our intrusion at what must be a harrowing time. However, we understand you have a number of wounded people here.'

'Yes, that's right.' Sam sounded a little cagey. 'You'll

be aware that things got a little rough round here a few days ago.'

'We saw that there was fighting, yes.' Softly the old man spoke the names of his children. Quickly they slipped the backpacks off and laid them on the ground. 'We discussed your plight. We decided that in view of the wholesale destruction you might be short of medical supplies. Therefore we have brought clean dressings, antiseptics, soap and penicillin.'

'Penicillin?'

'Yes. We make it solely in a tablet form since we don't have access to hypodermic needles. There are also opiates to relieve pain.'

Sam appeared suddenly moved. For a moment he looked incapable of saying anything. Then the words tumbled out. 'Why . . . thank you. Thank you a million times. You don't know what this means to us. We're flat out of first-aid kits. All our medical supplies were burned up with the clinic.' He pumped their hands enthusiastically. 'Again, thanks a million. Thank you – I'm going to use that word so much it's going to get all worn out . . . You people have saved lives today, but then I guess you know that, don't you? Gee! I can't begin to say how grateful I am that you fellers called over today.'

'We are your neighbours. We saw that you needed help.'

'That's really Christian of you. If you don't mind the phrase. Now, come on, where are my manners? Please take a seat . . . yes, yes. There on the cushions, we're still a little informal due to necessity round here yet. You must have coffee with us . . . and I think we have some fresh bread . . . we found an oven still in working order. Thank heaven for small miracles.'

'Coffee would be lovely,' Chee said in his educated tones. 'I would, however, if it's at all possible, more than welcome a cup of tea.'

'Tea. Say, Gabriel, do we have any tea? I don't think we've . . . wait a minute . . . wasn't there a tin of the stuff in the back of the truck we rode in on?'

Gabriel smiled. 'I'll get someone onto it.' He had a word with a youth who nodded before hurrying away. 'Coffee and tea are on their way,' he said. 'And the medics will find a good home for the medical supplies.' He nodded towards the backpacks.

Gabriel and I squatted beside the already seated group. The old Indian's heavy-lidded gaze took in the scene of desolation around him with undisguised sadness.

At last he said, 'Will there be a way to resolve your differences peacefully?'

Sam gave a regretful sigh. 'One day we hope to start working on it. It's just that the other feller won't parley.'

Gabriel said, 'You've got yourself a neat operation if you can manufacture medical supplies.'

'We can make a small amount. Of course, that's sufficient for our day-to-day needs. Ah, but by that . . .' Chee smiled, his eyes twinkling. '. . . you are really fishing for information about us?'

Sam nodded. 'You're right. We're curious about you; darn' curious.'

Chee didn't seem perturbed in the slightest by the curiosity. 'That's perfectly natural. Well . . . I am from the Algonquin tribe. I began training as a medical student, then switched to psychiatry after hearing a brilliant lecture by a Swiss psychologist. Indeed, after corresponding with him for some months he invited me to work with some other young disciples of his at his home on Lake Basel in Switzerland. I spent a whole winter there. Inspirational it was, too.'

'Wait a minute.' Gabriel raised a surprised eyebrow. 'A famous Swiss psychologist? You're not talking about Carl Gustav Jung, are you, by any chance?'

'Indeed, yes. He was particularly interested in recording the dreams of aboriginals, as they were called then. And I fell into that category. However, I learned more from him than he from me, I think. In that April of thirty years ago I returned to America, to my home reservation, only to find that a very old and cantankerous medicine man had a bee in his bonnet about something. At the beginning of May he browbeat the whole of the village into going down into a disused silver mine where, he insisted, we must retreat from the coming of Doom. Most obeyed him. We stayed there for three days and three nights. During that time he drew his signs on the earth in coloured soils and grains of wheat. He told us that these foretold a catastrophe. That we must remain in the mine workings until the danger had passed. Yes, I believed him. Not because of my people's old beliefs but because of something that Jung was fond of repeating at the dinner table. He would quote these words of Goethe: *Coming events cast their shadow before*. Before The Blinding, I believed I could sense a growing agitation among animals. A local herdsman was trampled to death by cows. We noticed flocks of birds migrating when it was the season to nest. Fish moved into deep water as if it were winter, not spring.' He raised his hands, fingers splayed wide. 'The medicine man was right. Doom *did* come – in a form that you know well. During that fateful night three decades ago green flashes lit up the sky. This was reported back to us in the tunnel by a pair of youths who foolishly disregarded the old man's warnings and went to look outside. In the morning they were blind. However, out of our population of three hundred men, women and children, two hundred and eighty were spared The Blinding.'

'You people certainly seem to have prospered,' Sam told him. 'You have a fine family here.'

'Ah, these are my babies. These three have nephews and nieces older than themselves now.'

'So you returned to the old ways of your tribe?'

'Some of them. But when the white man supplanted us we lost not only our lands but our self-delusions. You see, for thousands of years we believed that we were the guardians of the sun. That our rituals maintained the sun's light and heat for the rest of humanity. We were very proud of that responsibility. However, missionaries managed to rid us of, as I said, our self-delusions but they did not successfully instil in us any new ones. At best we suffered disillusion, even disappointment . . . at worst many of our people began to suffer from depressive illnesses that often deteriorated into psychosis. You see, we had lost the will to live. So, with the coming of The Blinding we found we could rediscover ourselves. And even though we could no longer embrace our old gods, we were able to reinterpret and reinvent them, using

Jung's teachings. We therefore crafted a new, stronger faith based on spirituality rather than dogma.' He looked at us through his heavy-lidded eyes. 'I suspect this isn't important to you. But you must remember we live in a new age. The Blinding swept the Old World away. And a new age demands a new faith. Look at the societies of old. They flourished when they discovered new gods and embraced new religions. Their cultures declined only when their faith crumbled.'

'Are you suggesting that we should adopt a new religion?' Gabriel frowned. 'It sounds like just another tool of oppression to me.'

'Why not? But don't confuse God with religion. They should be discussed separately. Instead, consider, if you will, religion as a design for living. Much as a body of rules forms a nation's constitution.'

A youth brought mugs of tea and coffee. Gabriel Deeds couldn't hold back any longer. 'There's one thing we'd all like to know . . .'

'Ah, I doubted if we could avoid that question.' Chee nodded. 'How can my people move freely among the triffids without suffering harm?'

Sam clasped a hot mug in his hands. 'That, sir, is the big question.'

'If you'll permit me to touch your face?' Chee held out his hand towards my chin. Puzzled, I nodded. His dark fingers, tough as leather, lightly touched my chin.

'Stubble,' he said. 'Now, please touch mine.'

I did as he asked. 'Feel that?' He smiled. 'Smooth as the skin of a watermelon. No stubble.' Instead of answering the original question directly he said,

'Twenty years ago triffids claimed their last victim of our tribe.'

'And after that?'

'Some of us were stung from time to time. But the poison was never fatal. By fifteen years ago the sting had no effect on us beyond the force of the blow.'

Gabriel frowned. 'Why do you think you became immune?'

'I believe the answer lies partly in the demonstration just now. I see stubble on your jaws. Which is something of a novelty for us. You see, I am fifty-five years old and I've never had a single hair on my chin. You'll recall there are significant biological differences between American Indians and Americans of a more recent African or European descent. I'm sure you're aware of the facts. Look at our features: straight black hair, heavy-lidded eyes; Asiatic appearance . . . broad faces, red skin.' He pointed to his face. 'Look deeper and you find more. Among us you will find few adults with body hair, there is a high frequency of shovel-shaped incisors, an absence of blood type B, low levels of blood group N with a high incidence of the Diego-positive blood type. In short, gentlemen, Mother Nature has brewed our blood a little differently from yours.'

'That's the answer?' I found myself almost disappointed. I'd been expecting what amounted to a cure for triffids. 'That there's some difference in your blood or your chromosomes that means you're immune to the triffid sting where we aren't?'

'Perhaps.'

Gabriel's thinking was sharper than mine. 'But you

indicated this was a gradual process. That more than twenty years ago your people were still dying from triffid stings. But then, after a few years, suddenly you became immune.'

'That's true,' Chee allowed. 'I suspect a latent natural bodily immunity was stimulated due to our people ingesting large amounts of triffids. I remember as a young man dining regularly on a potage of vegetables flavoured with the shredded flesh of the sting. A dish that was invented on our reservation because of economic necessity rather than any culinary adventurousness.'

'So a gradual exposure to triffid poison over a long period of time triggered an immune response?' Thoughtful, Gabriel pinched his bottom lip between thumb and forefinger. 'And now that freedom of movement gives you an advantage over everyone else.'

'A rare advantage.' Without any malice Chee added, 'And sometimes that affords us a degree of satisfaction.'

There wasn't much of a reply we could make to that. Here was a man with a healthy family from a self-confident and manifestly independent community that shared a new faith. One that gave them strength, purpose and self-respect. Indeed, here were people who hadn't suffered from the coming of The Blinding or the triffid invasion. For them the cataclysm of three decades ago hadn't been the disaster that it had been for us. It had been their salvation.

When the four Indians had left we continued with our work. I snipped away the ruined sections of fence. By nightfall it was ready to receive the new wire. Exhausted, I crept beneath a blanket within the barrier of Jumbos. On top of one of the vehicles a guard gently stroked blues notes from a guitar that were as melancholy as they were sweet. Between wakefulness and sleep I found myself replaying the conversation with Chee, seeing again in my mind the wise eyes gleaming beneath the heavy lids. He'd talked about biological differences in their blood that rendered them immune from the triffid sting. I thought of him and his children strolling through the triffid groves with impunity.

And at that moment I sat bolt upright with a single word on my lips: '*Christina.*' The thought leaped unbidden and shining with all the power of a Biblical revelation into my head: *Christina ran among the triffids. I saw her. She's immune to their poison, too. But I'll be damned if she has one ounce of Red Indian blood in her veins . . .*

CHAPTER TWENTY NINE

Reconstruction

On the banks of the river Gabriel said to me, 'Didn't he strike you as a little smug?'

'Ryder Chee?'

Gabriel nodded. 'He talked about creating a kind of Jungian religion for his tribe to give them a new faith, but it struck me he was only instilling in them another self-delusion.'

'But don't we all self-delude ourselves to a certain extent? Don't they say that civilization's only an illusion in itself? That if we stop believing in it, it ceases to exist. And if civilization is just one form of illusion that is . . .' I groped for the word '. . . expedient . . . that does the job for us, why should Ryder Chee's variety of self-delusion be any worse?'

'The man isn't confronting reality head on. He himself must know that Jung said that the delusions of a psychotic were the psychotic's attempt to create a new vision of the world. Therefore, Chee has, whichever way you look at it, created a society that is essentially psychotic.'

'Maybe I'm dim, Gabe. But my view is that if it works, if it produces a community that's energetic, optimistic and basically happy, then why not indulge in a modicum of self-delusion?'

Gabriel looked at me, his gaze hard. 'You know something, David?'

'What?'

'You know the problem I'm having with Ryder Chee?' His face softened into a grin. 'I'm envious, David. I'm as green as those triffid leaves with envy. Because deep down I know Chee and his people not only have a natural immunity from those monsters.' He nodded to the triffid plants beyond the fence. 'He's also got the mechanism of his society running as sweetly as a Rolls-Royce motor.'

'Wouldn't it make sense to borrow some of his ideas?'

'It might.' He shot me a toothy grin. 'New gods for old, eh, David?'

Out on the river a woman in a canoe waved a hand above her head.

'That's our cue, David. Pull the rope.'

He handed me an end of rope, then took a grip of it further down towards the water's edge. Forty paces upstream two men picked up another section of rope. Together we began to pull. I'd expected the job not to be overly taxing. But that rope felt as if it had been anchored to the river bed.

'Tarnation,' Gabriel panted, the muscles bulging in his arms. 'Who would've thought fishing could be such damn' hard work?'

We continued to pull hard. At last we made headway. The line of the net broke the water's surface, making a horseshoe shape as we drew the net to shore. Five minutes later we hauled the net onto the bank. Perspiring so freely that beads of moisture stood out on his forehead as big as pearls, Gabriel regarded our catch with more than a hint of disgust. 'All that effort for those?'

Barely a dozen fish of dubious nutritional value flapped in the netting. After contemplating our sorry-looking haul we began to disentangle the fish from the net, returning the tiddlers to the water while dropping their bigger brothers into a basket.

'Fish and shoot of triffid soup.' Gabriel wrinkled his nose in disgust. 'Great.'

As he pulled away some of the waterweed he suddenly cursed. Then, grimacing, he pried the pincer of a crayfish from his little finger. Once he was free of the claw he sucked his finger, then said with a wry smile, 'Am I getting paranoid, David? Or is Mother Nature out to get us?' He dropped the crayfish into the basket. (The freshwater crustacean would no doubt wind up in the soup pot together with whatever else the cook could scavenge.) 'Oh, for a juicy steak. A heap of potato salad. Golden French-fries. Creamy mayonnaise. Crisp lettuce. Sweet tomatoes. A jug of ice-cold beer. How much—'

'Shh.' I held up my hand. 'Can you hear something?'

We stood for a moment, listening. I looked up along the river towards where the sound seemed to be coming from. All I could see was the silvery stretch of water between the banks. A flock of birds, disturbed by the sound, took to the air from a line of willows.

Gabriel's face hardened. 'Hell. Not again.'

The others moved back quickly from the water's edge.

Men and women ran to collect their guns. Further along the bank the gun turret on the back of a Jumbo swivelled to point its twin machine guns upstream.

I listened to the note of the engine. It didn't sound as it should, but there was no mistaking it. 'Wait!' I shouted. 'Hold your fire!' I ran down to the water's edge to get a better look upstream.

Gabriel called out to me, 'David! Get yourself into a trench before the shooting starts.'

'No, those are aero engines. It's a plane.' What puzzled me, however, was that the note of the engines was all wrong. The plane wasn't flying but taxiing.

A moment later I got visual confirmation. From round a bend in the river came a big four-engined flying boat. The sleek lines of the formidable Boeing Clipper were instantly recognizable to me — which was hardly surprising since I'd slept underneath a handsome technicolour print of the aircraft for years as a child. The picture had been pinned to my bedroom wall.

The flying boat, engines roaring, its propellers blurring discs of silver, surged towards what remained of a jetty. The white vee of its wake washed up the river bank, almost reaching my feet.

Now the Foresters cheered the return of the craft.

With the arrival of its crew on dry land we learned that this was the only aircraft based at the camp to have survived the attack. By chance, several pilots had been chatting to a maintenance crew near the plane when the torpedo boats came storming upriver. With great presence of mind they'd leaped into the flying boat, started the engines and got away. The intention had been to make for the next military camp of the Foresters and return with reinforcements. That was until the pilot checked the fuel gauge, which told her that there was barely a splash of juice in the tanks. So after a hop of three miles she had brought the plane down into an offshoot of the river where, like us in the Jumbos, they had sat tight for a few days until they'd judged it safe to taxi the flying boat downstream to the camp once more.

Sam digested the news before speaking. 'Well, thanks to some quick thinking, we've got one aircraft intact. It strikes me that we need to do two things. First, fly pilots up to Columbus Pond to get hold of replacement aircraft. Second, we need to get word of the attack to headquarters. Central Command still don't know that we failed to bring the Christina girl out of New York.' He added a little sourly, 'I guess the top brass will be hopping mad about that. But . . .' He shrugged. 'Those are the fortunes of war.'

While the ground crew refuelled the surviving flying boat with whatever drops of fuel could be squeezed from sundry jerrycans I caught up with Sam Dymes. 'Sam,' I said, 'what's this Columbus Pond?'

'It's a lake about a hundred miles upstream. We keep aircraft in reserve up there.' He nodded at the blackened ruins around him. 'Just in case we were ever to suffer a situation like this one.'

'How many spare aircraft?'

'A good half-dozen, I'd say.'

'But you've only four pilots?'

'Go on.'

'Then it'd make sense if I went up there, too,' I told him. 'I can help out with some of the flying chores.'

He looked at me with his clear blue eyes. At that moment I sensed he was forming a different judgement about the man he'd first seen bleary-eyed and still cranky from his involuntary trip from New York to this Southern backwater. 'So . . . you're offering to help us?'

'Yes. Why not?'

'It's just that . . . well, let me tell you what I'm thinking now, David . . . I'm thinking this is a crucial time . . . I guess you might say a pivotal moment in our relationship. More precisely, in your relationship with us – the Foresters.'

'I'm not sure I follow. I thought you could use some help to—'

'Yes, and I'm very grateful . . . thankful, too, that providence brought us another experienced pilot. But what I'm going to ask you, David, is this: are you joining us?'

I saw how Sam's mind had been working. He'd reached the stage where he needed me to express my allegiance to the Foresters and all that went with it: a commitment to help them, and a clear rejection of the Torrence regime.

'Yes,' I told him firmly. 'I am an ally, there's no doubt in my mind about that.'

'And Kerris Baedekker?'

'What about Kerris?'

'She's not only a citizen of our enemy's regime, she's also his daughter.' He watched my face. 'And she and you were romantically attached.'

'And I bitterly regret that she's still in New York. But my allegiances are to you and to my own community on the Isle of Wight. I don't doubt for a moment that our two peoples will be allies in the short term and the best of friends and trading partners in the long term.'

'Well said.' Sam allowed his face to break into a slow smile. 'David Masen. I'd be honoured if you would shake me by the hand.'

So I shook his hand.

'OK,' he said. 'I suggest you grab a quick coffee. We're flying out of here in half an hour.'

CHAPTER THIRTY

Columbus Pond

Within thirty minutes we were airborne. Our flying boat was a combination mail, freight and passenger craft. Sam, Gabriel and I sat in a fair degree of comfort in the midship cabin while the surplus aircrew grabbed some well-deserved shut-eye in the sleeping berths aft.

After taking off downstream the plane doubled back over our camp. What had for a while become my whole world now revealed itself as little more than a small clearing containing a few black smudges marking the positions of burned-out buildings.

The plain droned higher into the sky. The sun shone steadily. Below us the river described a thick snaking line of silver to a distant ocean. There were no towns to see, even though I knew there must have been some down there once. In the intervening years, territory so painfully won by humanity had been reclaimed by nature. Now vines, trees, bushes, thistles and vast seas of nettle had drawn a green shroud over roads, railway lines and cities.

And, no doubt, that triffid army of occupation would have its sentinels posted down there.

After sitting on the ground for the last few days it was a pleasure to settle into the armchair comfort of the cabin seats.

Following a lengthy contemplation of this land now devoid of human beings Sam Dymes said, 'That's going to take some reclaiming. It'll keep our children and their children busy for a long time to come.'

'At least you're an optimist, Sam,' commented Gabriel. 'You see a time when we can start kicking those damn' triffids out.'

'Sure, I'm an optimist. After all, what would be the point of struggling on, working and planning and fighting, if I didn't believe we were making any progress?' He grimaced. 'Why, if I thought otherwise, I'd open that door across there and step into the wide blue yonder.'

We talked for a while, mainly about what we saw unfolding beneath us on the plain, including what looked like a glimpse of a vast factory complex now engulfed by a lake. Blocked drainage ditches would mean a return to old water levels before any land reclamation. On those lowlands we could plainly see the remains of factories, schools and houses showing as oblong islets set in an expanse of water.

The plane flew on. I gazed out at the silver wings shining in the sunlight. Four massive sixteen-hundred-horsepower engines carried us effortlessly through the air. We could cruise comfortably at two hundred miles per hour at an altitude of fifteen thousand feet. Flying solo, this machine could get me home to the Isle of Wight in fifteen hours. For a while I ran through more calculations in my head. I was still pondering the logistics of such a flight when the plane glided in to land.

A perfect touchdown. My professional pilot's eye noted the angle that the flying boat's belly kissed the water, sending out a plume of spray at either side of the craft. Instantly the note of the engines dropped as the pilot closed the throttle. The plane coasted along, slowing gradually.

For a moment I thought we'd landed on an ordinary lake, even though it did boast the decidedly funny name (considering its prodigious size) of Columbus Pond. I soon saw, however, that it was one of the 'new' lakes formed by the failure of the artificial drainage systems. The flying boat taxied slowly across the water towards what could only have been the brick tower of a church rising some twenty or so feet above the surface. The top half of the clock showed above the lake. Its hands had stopped at ten to two. To the right-hand side of the tower a few rotting roof timbers jutted out of the water to mark the remains of the main body of the church.

Moored incongruously to the church tower, an old riverboat of some antique vintage bobbed, complete with an array of rear paddle blades. Moored to that were a pair of barges and what appeared to be a timber raft held afloat by several dozen oil drums. Then, in a line beyond that, sat three large flying boats, comparable in size to the one we'd just arrived in. There were also several float-planes of more modest dimensions.

Our crew quickly opened the aircraft's doors. Then, as

the plane nosed its way closer to the raft, they leaped onto the boards where they moored the plane expertly. With a splutter its engines died.

We stepped out onto the raft boards to be greeted by an eerie silence. Thin sunlight danced on the water. There was no movement from the old paddle steamer that served as the crew's quarters. A slight ripple on the lake caused a bell to chime somewhere nearby. The dreary tolling rolled across the water to be swallowed by the vast emptiness that surrounded us. It spoke of desolation. A dead sound that induced shivers.

Gabriel looked grim. 'What, no welcome party?' The emptiness robbed his voice of its usual depth.

Sam's puzzled blue eyes regarded the assortment of vessels moored to the church tower. 'Now, that's odd. There should be a team of seven manning this depot. Where the heck has everyone got to?'

By this time the others had disembarked from our aircraft to stand with the same bewildered air on the raft.

Sam cupped his hands around his mouth. 'Hello! Anyone there?' That greedy void swallowed his call. 'Hello!'

No reply. Even the sound of the bell petered out, leaving only a cold, goblin silence.

'Oh no.' Sam murmured the words. He'd sensed something ominous. 'Oh no, oh no, oh no.'

A swirl of water rocked the raft gently, setting off an array of wet sucking sounds that came from somewhere beneath it. Sam walked to a gangplank that ran across to the nearest barge. There he paused, touched his lips to caution us to silence and drew his revolver.

Water swirled, and again the greedy sucking sound came from the underside of the raft. The chiming of the bell started again, too – a hollow, ghostly sound that rolled across the water. This time I saw that it came from a red-painted bell fixed to a kind of gallows set beside the gangplank. Painted on a sign beneath it were the words: *Ring me, then run like hell.* Clearly an alarm system for the depot crew.

Gingerly making his way up the gangplank, Sam signalled us to follow. Now I noticed a few clues that did suggest something had gone seriously wrong. An axe had been driven into a timber guard rail. A shattered china mug lay on the deck of the barge. This was one of the workshops where mechanics serviced the aircraft engines. One engine lay partly stripped. A spanner rested on the fuel-pump casing as if the mechanic had only this moment taken a cigarette break. Elsewhere there were signs of violence alongside those of a normal working day. In the workshop stood a coffee cup half full of the now stale beverage, while near the guard rail glittering lines on the steel deck suggested that someone had attacked it with an axe, scoring gashes in the metal.

'Hell,' Sam grunted. 'What in damnation happened here?'

'Torrence's men.' Gabriel stood with his automatic at the ready.

'I can't see how. They don't have the planes to fly in. We're twenty miles from the nearest navigable river with an outlet direct to the open sea. Even if they'd learned where this place was, they'd have had to haul small boats for miles overland through triffid country before they could reach this place out on the lake.' Mystified, he shook his head. 'It doesn't add up.'

Gabriel picked up a rifle. 'Someone used this as a club. Look, the stock's all busted.' He checked the magazine. 'But it's fully loaded.'

'Probably jammed.'

Gabriel pointed the muzzle out across the lake and pulled the trigger. The report rang in my ears. Once more the sound died without the ghost of an echo.

'Perfect,' he said. 'You have a gun full of ammo that's in working order. So why use it as a club?'

'And there are no spent cartridge cases on the deck,' I commented. 'There's been a fight, but not a shooting fight.'

We moved from one linked barge to the other. Soon we reached the paddle steamer moored to the church tower. Close up, it towered over me, boasting two storeys of cabins with wide promenade decks and ornamental ironworks. This had once been quite a Southern Belle among riverboats, luxuriously transporting millionaire gamblers along the rivers. Once the decks must have been awash with music and laughter, maybe along with the odd contretemps over a game of poker or the favours of an aristocratic femme fatale. Now it had become a ghost ship.

Cabin doors creaked with each ripple of the lake. Uneaten meals had dried and stuck to plates in the mess room. A kettle had boiled dry on a stove and the bottom had melted out. Beds lay neatly made.

'Whoever attacked the depot must have come during the day,' I said. 'The beds weren't occupied. And unless

I'm very much mistaken that looks like lunch on the plates, rather than breakfast.'

'I agree.' Sam looked as if a bad taste had filled his mouth. 'But there are no bodies. No bloodstains. Yet they were alerted to the attack and had time to fight back.'

'And they chose to fight with axes. They wielded rifles like clubs, even though the guns were loaded.'

We searched the riverboat from top to bottom. No sign of the men. Or, for that matter, an attacker. I reported this to Sam as he stood at the ornate deck rail, gazing down at the water between the church tower and the hulk of the riverboat. Down there I fancied I could see the skeleton of a truck below the water, its dead headlights staring like eye sockets in skull. Flood waters must have carried it there years ago, hard up against the church. Now it lay rotting. Long strands of bright green weed streaked the water like hanks of goblin hair.

Sam lit a cigarette. 'OK, David. I give in. What's gone wrong with the world? How come it's gone so topsy-turvy?' Grim-faced, he drew on the cigarette. 'How come thirty years ago folks saw green lights in the sky, lights that sent them blind? How did we get overrun by a bunch of shuffling plants with goofy leaves? And why doesn't the sun shine like it used to? And in God's name how do a bunch of grown men suddenly vanish like they've been spirited away by phantoms?' He looked at me. 'Tell me you've got the answers to those questions, David, and you'll make me one hell of a happy man.'

As much as I wished that I could help Sam in this way, I regretfully told him the truth: I had no answers.

He threw the cigarette into the water where it died with a hiss. 'Well, that makes two of us, David. I tell you something. I wish I were home with my wife and family right now. Then I wouldn't have to wake up every day and be confronted with another mystery bigger than the last. I'd be able to enjoy a lie-in Sunday mornings, with a pot of coffee and the newspapers and a good woman by my side.' For a few seconds his gaze was distant. He wasn't seeing the drowned church, or this ghost ship we stood on. It only lasted a moment, then his eyes came back into focus. He took a deep breath. 'OK. We better file all this——' he gestured towards the deserted vessels, '——under *Marie Celeste* and leave it at that.'

If only it could have been so easy.

For the next hour or so we went about the chores necessary to ready the flying boats for the flight back to the camp. Support crew pumped aviation fuel into empty tanks, checked oil levels and wiring, untied restraining cables. Pilots, myself included, settled into flight cabins to run instrumentation checks.

Sam watched for a while, a little out of his depth. Eventually he cupped his hands to his mouth and shouted from the riverboat. 'Coffee's on. It'll be ready in ten minutes.'

Certainly whoever had abducted the depot crew hadn't even touched the food stores. By the time we assembled on the deck of the riverboat Sam had set out jugs of wonderful hot coffee and a canister of oatmeal biscuits. 'You might as well tuck in,' he told us, his expression sombre. 'Something tells me the original crew aren't coming back.'

One of the pilots appeared on deck to tell Sam he needed to fly out now if he was to reach HQ before dark.

'OK . . . look, here's my report and a letter to the boss. Ask her if she can let you have a reply and my new orders by tomorrow morning.'

After the pilot headed off in the direction of his plane Sam lit another cigarette. Then he addressed us all, as if some facts had been weighing on his mind. 'You know we had a complement of exactly one hundred men and women at the camp. Thirty were either killed or captured during the raid. And there's still half a dozen with wounds that are going to keep them hospitalized for a time yet. How do you replace good people like that?' He shrugged. He wasn't expecting an answer. These wasn't one. I knew that, in all, the population of the Foresters in their scattered communities numbered no more than a hundred and fifty thousand. That meagre population was already overstretched simply feeding and clothing itself, not to mention expending precious resources on the never-ending job of culling triffid armies and repairing hundreds of miles of anti-triffid fence. Gabriel chewed thoughtfully on a biscuit. 'From what I can see the Boss is going to have to strip personnel out of the other camps to make up our numbers again.'

Sam nodded. 'I guess so. But that's not going to leave much in the way of reserves . . .' He gave a tired smile. 'Reminds me of the old army joke. If your bed sheets are too short, cut some off the top and sew it to the bottom . . . only it isn't a joke any longer. To all intents and purposes that's what we're doing.'

Gabriel looked at me. 'Maybe we can negotiate some form of Lease-Lend with David's people? We could certainly use—'

'Gabriel – sorry.' Sam held up a hand for quiet. 'Did anyone hear that?'

We looked at each other and shook our heads.

Sam walked to the guard rail. The way his head suddenly jutted forward told me he'd seen something awry. 'Michael's down . . . he's flat out on the deck.'

I followed Sam along the interconnecting gangplanks from riverboat to barge, then to the next barge. In front of us, at a lower level, was the big platform of the raft. The pilot lay flat on his back in the sunlight, his arms flung out straight to either side of him. The envelope containing Sam's report lay beside him.

A babble of voices rose around me. Confusion. Anger. Concern.

People began to surge forward to help their fallen comrade. But my old schooling from years ago came back to me.

If you find someone collapsed on the ground, stay back. Look round carefully. Then carefully examine the patient's face and neck for telltale signs . . .

I did. And I saw them.

'Wait!' I yelled as men pushed by me, ready to run down the gangplank to the deck of the raft. 'I said *wait!*' I pushed myself forward, blocking the way.

A thickset man said, 'Move yourself, buddy. Can't you see he's ill?'

'No!' With an effort I pushed the man back. 'Stay there. Don't you see what's on the side of his neck?' I touched my own neck, just below the ear. 'There's a red mark.'

'So?'

'Don't you recognize it?' I shouted, desperate to avoid further loss of life. 'It's a triffid sting.'

'Triffid sting? Buddy, you've got to be out of your mind. Do you see any triffids out here?'

I looked round. I saw what I'd seen when I'd arrived here. A motley collection of vessels, a few flying boats; a drowned church. Apart from that nothing but a vast lake glittering somewhere between grey and silver in that dulled sunlight.

'So?' The man's face flushed with anger. 'Do you see any damned triffids?'

'Believe me, that's a triffid sting.'

Sam gave me a puzzled look. 'David. I'm sorry, you must be mistaken. Now, we've got to help the guy.'

'He's dead; you can see he—'

'Move it, buddy.' It was understandable. The thickset man wanted to help his friend. It was also fatal.

Grunting, he pushed me back against the guard rail. A moment later he ran across the deck to the fallen man. Before he'd even reached him the lake alongside the raft swirled and rippled as if hungry fish were feeding just below the surface. Simultaneously I heard a swishing sound.

I don't think I actually saw them. In retrospect I told myself that I did see the *blur* of something long and very slender.

The thickset man groaned. His hand shot up to his forehead. Then it was over. He spun round and his knees buckled. Then he slumped forward at the edge of the raft, one arm swinging down so that his fingertips reached the water.

'Now stay back!' I thundered at the surprised men. 'Get right back into the workshop.' I chivvied the men back until they were through the door. They'd be safe these, behind the timber walls.

Sam shook his head, dumbfounded. At last he took a steadying breath. 'What was *that?*'

'He was brought down by a triffid sting,' I told him.

'But out here? In the middle of all this water? I – I mean, do *you* see any triffids?'

I recalled the triffid raft of logs and driftwood held together by turf on which I'd crash landed. I looked out over the water but I saw nothing even remotely resembling it.

I shrugged, deeply puzzled. 'Believe me, Sam. There's a triffid here. Somewhere. Only I just don't see it, for some reason.'

Gabriel moved forward, his great height giving him the ability to look down into the water from our otherwise restricted vantage point. In his low tones he said, 'I know where they are.'

'Where?'

'In the water.'

Sam stood on an upturned pail to look down into the lake, still wary of another attack. 'No, Gabe,' he said at last. 'I don't see them. Where are they?'

'Under the water . . . you see, it's all a question of mutation.'

'Say what?'

'Mutation. Those monsters are changing at a hell of a rate. They walk, they kill, they communicate with their buddies. They "see" by using a kind of sonar.'

Sam stammered. 'Now – now you're telling me these filthy plants can actually swim?'

'No, not swim,' Gabriel murmured, almost as if he was afraid the triffids would overhear. 'An entirely new species . . . an aquatic species. What I'd taken to be common waterweed out there in the lake must be the upper fronds of the triffids.'

'That clears up the mystery of the depot crew, I suppose. They were picked off by those new water triffids.'

'Not picked off one by one,' I told him. 'It was a planned attack. They killed all the depot crew in the space of a few moments.'

'An *ambush?*'

Gabriel nodded. 'I reckon David's right. Those triffids kept the depot crew under surveillance, then chose a time when the entire crew were exposed to attack.'

'Shoot.' Sam shook his head. 'We've got to get word of this to Central HQ fast. Why . . . these plants might already be on the march underwater, up rivers and streams right into the middle of our towns. Damn the things.'

Gabriel looked out. 'But first things first. If anyone goes out there, they're going to be killed before they get anywhere near the flying boats.'

'Good point.' Sam stroked his jaw. 'Very good point. So how do we reach the planes?'

CHAPTER THIRTY ONE

Necessity's Child

A ten-minute search provided the materials. Crowded though we were into the workshop, with Sam at the door keeping watch for any more unpleasant surprises, I set to work. I fashioned a helmet from galvanized mesh. I'd have preferred welded seams but settled for strong twine. This, laced in and out of the mesh, held the sections together into a box shape, open at the bottom. A little trimming with wire-cutters ensured a close fit around the shoulders. The search had also revealed an ancient pair of leather flying gauntlets. Hardened with age, they'd do the job. To protect my eyes I found some flying goggles. Covering the rest of my body was a leather flying jacket, while over that I wore a poncho cut from a sheet of very stout canvas. I completed the mongrel outfit with sections of canvas tied around my legs like a horseman's chaps. Fetching it wasn't. But it should work.

I asked for and was given a bowie knife by one of the surviving pilots. I tucked this into my boot top; for additional weaponry I chose a hand axe.

Thus armoured I went to the workshop door. Outside, all appeared calm. However, as we'd worked something had happened to the body of the thickset man who'd pushed by me.

I stared at the empty deck boards. The body had been there ten minutes ago. Now it had vanished. But there was no time to dwell on that. We needed to get this group of men and women onto the aircraft, then take them safely back to camp. Somewhat gingerly I stepped through the doorway, then walked to the gangplank. My makeshift anti-triffid suit was, I hoped, adequate, but I knew only too well it was untested. I kept my lips pressed shut. If a stinger hit the helmet there was still a chance that droplets of poison would spray into my face. However, at least my eyes were well protected by the flying goggles.

Looking and listening all the time I moved down the gangplank onto the broad deck of the raft. It bobbed slightly beneath my feet, setting up a sucking sound under the timbers.

One glance at the pilot told me that he was dead. The flame-red mark still burned on his neck where the sting had found him. I planned to pull the flying boat alongside the raft by its mooring lines, then climb aboard to start the engines so they'd be warmed sufficiently for take-off. What was more, if I brought the flank of the machine hard against the edge of the raft, leaving no gap through which the aquatic triffid could strike from the water, then people could safely board.

I'd begun the strenuous job of pulling on the rope, drawing the massive flying boat slowly, slowly towards me, when I felt the first strike. A stinger cracked against my chest. I prayed that the canvas would be thick enough. Another stinger struck the helmet. I flinched at the fine spray of venom on my bare skin. My lips stayed firmly closed as the venom began to itch and burn on the exposed flesh. As the poison wasn't lethal unless it was injected through the skin and into the bloodstream by the hypodermic-like hairs on the sting, a rinse with water would cure it — once I'd completed the task at hand, that was.

More stingers lashed out from the beneath the lake. Now I saw the water ripple as they broke the surface. A series of whiplike blows struck my gloves, arms and helmet.

You're starting to lose your aim, I thought. *Your frustration's getting the better of you.*

So I told myself. However, then I noticed the stingers that apparently missed had fallen just beyond me. Yet somehow, I found, they were getting tangled around my legs.

I told myself that these aquatic triffids were simply getting themselves into a snarl-up. But presently the stings began to pull against my legs. A moment after that they were taut as guitar strings, vibrating so much that droplets of water flew from them.

I stopped hauling on the mooring line because I realized that the pull the triffids were exerting had become fierce. Looking down at my legs I saw that perhaps a dozen stingers had wrapped around each limb. This was no accident. Those stings were prehensile. The strength behind their pull was enormous and at that moment I realized they were attempting to drag me into the water.

So *that* accounted for the disappearance of the thickset man as well as that of the depot crew. Killed, then hauled into the water where they'd become triffid food.

Quickly releasing the mooring line, I tried to snap the stings. No good. Far too tough. Now I had a clear vision of myself being dragged struggling into the lake. I could almost feel the water closing over my head. They'd pull me down. Drown me. Then they'd start feeding.

Cursing under my breath, I pulled out the knife. The bowie blade flashed. Thankfully, it sliced through sting after sting. As soon as I was free I redoubled my efforts.

'I thought you could do with a hand.'

I glanced sideways. 'Gabriel?'

He grinned through the wire-mesh helmet, his eyes obscured behind goggles. 'Here,' he said, 'don't keep all that rope to yourself.'

Now the task became a little easier. We pulled the flying boat alongside the raft. With only a foot or so of clearance between propellers and deck boards I saw that I couldn't risk starting the engines after all. At least now, though, the bulk of the flying boat would provide a barrier against triffid stings. In a few moments we'd boarded the people from the workshop.

Soon the flying boat, along with its sister aircraft, had taken off, leaving the vessels below to the care of the water triffids.

The rest of the day was taken up with the routine of going back and forth between camp and floating depot.

One of the pilots collected a small floatplane and headed south on the four-hour journey to Central HQ. Beside him on the seat was the envelope containing Sam's report, his warning about the water triffids and a request for fresh orders.

The rest of the pilots and myself ferried tents, food, ammunition and aviation fuel from the depot back to camp.

Despite the traumas of the day it felt good to be flying again. I relished the feel of the joystick in my hands, the comforting familiarity of routinely checking the gyro-compass and altimeter, trimming the mixture control. And the sound of four engines running sweetly was sheer music to my ears.

As I made the return trip with the plane almost full to bursting with much-needed supplies, I looked out of the windows at the setting sun casting long shadows across the ground three thousand feet below me and I sang under my breath.

It occurred to me then, flying solo as I was, that I could have ditched those supplies and swung the plane's nose east. The fuel tanks were full and by mid-afternoon, local time, of the next day I could have been gliding that plane down to land in an Isle of Wight bay. But I knew I wouldn't do that. And it wasn't entirely a question of loyalty to Sam Dymes and his people. No. I had made other plans. But for the moment I would have to keep them to myself.

CHAPTER THIRTY TWO

A Little Forward Planning

Work. And more hard work. That was what filled my day following the trip to the floating depot that lay as eerily as a ghost ship out there on the lake. Helping to clear the incinerated remains of accommodation huts, I found myself breathing dust and eating soot. What made this mess more appalling were the human remains lying like blackened sticks in the debris. It wasn't long before I had a handkerchief tied across the lower half of my face to avoid inhaling the worst of the debris.

At least now we saw progress. Anti-triffid squads had made short work of the plants that had surged in through the broken fences. The fences themselves had been repaired. There were minor miracles, too, for which everyone was sincerely grateful. An apprentice mechanic had been pulled alive from a well where he'd bolted once the shooting had started. Later that morning a pair of women in protective suits had limped in through the triffid groves. These were survivors from an outlying observation post, which had been surprised by the enemy before the attack.

With the return of order to the camp — the setting-up of tents, the provision of open-air kitchens — our prospects seemed so much better. Things looked brighter still with the return of two of the big four-engine flying boats that had left at first light.

A squad of heavily armed men and women disembarked on what remained of a jetty. I counted fifty of them. They unloaded kitbags from the plane, along with boxes of ammunition. For the rest of the day the flying boats shuttled back and forth between the camp and Central HQ.

At a well-earned lunch break I washed myself thoroughly, marvelling at how the water running off my body had become inky black from the ash. Then I sat down to the now-customary fish-and-triffid stew.

Gabriel joined me. 'Reinforcements have arrived,' he announced as he broke bread into his bowl. 'Crack troops. So that should tell us HQ have something up their sleeve.'

'Such as?'

'Sam received sealed orders from the Marines' commanding officer about twenty minutes ago. He's going to hold a meeting this afternoon.' He looked at me. 'You're invited, by the way.'

I spooned some of the spicy food into my mouth. 'Will there be any more reinforcements? I mean, fifty's a start but we lost more men than that.'

'Manpower's overstretched as it is. The rest of the Marines have their hands full with counter-insurgency operations down in the Florida Everglades. And the air force and gunboats are working non-stop to keep a bunch of pirates out of our waters down in the Gulf of Mexico. That's before HQ even begin to think about taking on Torrence.'

Once more my mind went back to my home island. More than ever it seemed a peaceful out-of-the-way spot, untroubled for years by either triffid or human enemies. It seemed to me that the Foresters had their backs to the wall. Bandits, pirates, even run-of-the-mill poachers seemed to be threatening every border.

'And the sad thing is,' Gabriel said, 'we're not talking about swaggering brigands here. We've noticed that whenever there's a bad harvest or a hard winter raids on our own communities triple — whether it's to rustle cattle or steal a couple of sacks of potatoes. The truth is that those people who are raiding us are simply ordinary folk like ourselves who are driven by the threat — and the reality — of starvation. After all, if your child is dying of hunger do you just sit back when your neighbours have a full larder? You do something about it, right?'

'Who are these people?'

'Often we don't know. The only thing we're sure of is that they have nothing to do with Torrence. They seem to be small independent settlements, scratching a living — a pretty meagre living — up in the highlands.' He shrugged. 'When times get hard for them they come down and make life hard for us.'

'Surely something can be done about them?'

'We've expended a lot of fuel and pilot time trying to spot them from the air. But even if we do find their settlements the idea of bombing hungry families sticks in my craw.'

'No, I mean start talking to them. When times are bad give them food.'

'Give them food? Would that be a kind of welfare programme? Or like paying protection money to the Mafia?'

'If you give them enough to stop them starving then you'd take away their reason for raiding Forester settlements.'

'Good point, David. But we've tried that. When it comes down to it everyone views everyone else with mutual suspicion. It's like Ryder Chee and his family. We've lived cheek by jowl with those people for the last twenty years, as near as dammit. But when they came visiting two days ago that was the first time we've exchanged so much as a word with them.'

'They've taken the first step,' I said. 'They brought medical supplies.'

'And I thank them from the bottom of my heart for their assistance.'

'Gabriel, I'm sure—'

'And *I*'m sure that one of the reasons those guys came here, strolling through the triffids like they're no more venomous than cherry trees, was to indulge in some self-satisfied gloating.' His eyes had a hard glint to them. 'But my guess is that once we normalize our situation here we won't see hide nor hair of Ryder Chee or his clan again.'

I swallowed the last spoonful of stew. 'I see what you mean about mutual suspicion,' I told Gabriel before returning to work.

*　　*　　*

That afternoon I got word to attend a meeting in Sam's tent at three o'clock sharp. Gratefully, I left the blackened mess of roof spars I had been clearing, washed, changed my clothes and then presented myself at Sam's makeshift office with a minute to spare.

Sam tended not to stand on ceremony. Without a word he waved us in as he poured coffee from a jug. I glanced round the table. Sitting there were the camp's surviving pilots, Gabriel Deeds, the commanding officer of the newly arrived Marines and a couple of Sam's team who provided secretarial support. Still without speaking he took a letter from his briefcase and spread it out in front of him. Then, without meeting our gazes, he said matter-of-factly, 'Lieutenant Truscott delivered this letter a short time ago. I'd like you to listen to this, please.' He began to read. 'From Central HQ, Chapel Hill. To Commanding Officer Samuel J. Dymes, Fort Comanche. By Direction of the Committee of Central Command you are instructed to secure original objective as stated in order 93C/1. Namely, deliver Subject "C" to Central HQ by Monday the twenty-first. You are reminded to devote the highest priority to this objective, and to achieve it at all costs. Reinforcements, together with supplies, sufficient to meet your objective accompany this communiqué. Transportation logistics are a matter for your own initiative. You are fully aware of the importance of this mission. In closing, I stress that I have absolute faith in your abilities as leader and your team's competence to deliver a prize of incomparable value to our people. Sincerely yours, Major General Cordelia Ramirez'. He took a deep swallow of coffee. 'For the benefit of people who haven't seen order 93C/1, subject "C" is Christina Schofield. Something you've no doubt already figured. Now . . . these orders tend to err on the side of brevity but I think we're all clear what the Boss is telling us to do. We are required to spring Christina from New York and deliver her safely to Central HQ by a week Monday, which by my reckoning gives us exactly ten days.'

Gabriel put his hands over his eyes briefly as if in disbelief. 'Impossible,' he declared. 'We don't know where Christina's being held. What's more, we only have around fifty Marines to do the job.'

Lieutenant Truscott took this as a slight. 'Mr Deeds, my men are perfectly capable of executing those orders.'

'Look.' Gabriel's fist clenched on the table. 'No offence intended. But New York is still a heck of a big place. It's well defended with artillery and rocket batteries. It has radar, picket ships, a standing military of fifteen hundred men and a civil-defence force of close on ten thousand.'

'Gabriel,' Sam broke in. 'No one's saying we're going out there to conquer New York. This is going to be a snatch raid. Once we have Christina we're outta there. And this might be a good time to remind people why we need to do this: Torrence intends to use the eggs in Christina's ovaries to create an army that will be immune to triffid venom. With that army he will crush us, as he will crush every community that will not surrender their freedom to him. In short, we either rescue Christina or . . .' He shrugged. 'We might as well sign our own death warrants.'

'Excuse me, do you mind?' Gabriel nodded at the letter.

'Be my guest.' Sam handed him the sheet of paper.

Gabriel scanned it until he found a sentence that caused his eyes to widen. 'It says here that, "Transportation logistics are a matter for your own initiative."'

Sam gave a weak smile. 'That's a fancy way of HQ saying, "We don't know how you're going to get the Marines to New York, but we're sure you'll think of something".'

Gabriel jerked a thumb in the direction of the wrecked submarines. 'Our boat strength is down to a couple of canoes and a dinghy.' He looked at myself, then at the other two pilots. 'But I guess you've other plans?'

'Indeed, Gabe. We can fly the snatch squad up to New York in three hours.'

'Tell me you're kidding, Sam. Tell me this is a big joke, then we'll all have a side-splitting laugh. After that we'll get down to the real strategy.'

Sam shook his head, his blue eyes serious. 'No joke, Gabe. That's what we're going to do. We've got three pilots and three good planes. We can easily transport a force of ninety up there and then bring them back safely.'

Gabriel looked appalled. 'Come on, Sam. You've just heard me say that New York is protected by radar, searchlights and about a hundred anti-aircraft guns. Those big old flying boats will be sitting ducks.'

'I didn't say I had all the answers, did I?' Sam's face crinkled into a grim smile. 'That's why I've invited our pilots. They're going to tell us how to beat the radar.'

Gabriel let out a heartfelt sigh. 'It looks as if I've been

given the role of devil's advocate here . . . and far be it from me to shoot down your plans in flames, if you'll excuse the ominous metaphor, but we only have two pilots.'

'Two plus David Masen makes three.'

'But the sheer sweat and effort it took to get David away from Torrence! You'd have to be mad to send him back there.'

Sam smiled. 'Welcome to the lunatic asylum, Gabe.'

'But for crying out loud, why? If David falls into Torrence's hands we're back where we started. Worse. Torrence will lock David away until he can use him as a hostage to get hold of the Isle of Wight and that hoo-hah machine that turns triffid oil into aviation fuel, gasoline and a whole lot else. Then we're all dead and buried.'

Sam knitted his fingers together. 'Needs must, Gabe. We need to spring Christina from New York. As well as those fifty Marines we need engineers and sappers with demolition expertise. That makes a force of ninety.'

'So they can be carried in two planes, not three.'

Sam turned to me. 'I'm no flyer, David. Explain the problem to Gabe.'

'Two planes can carry ninety people between them, but the more passengers or payload you carry the faster you use fuel. You need to split those ninety people between three planes for that kind of distance or you'd simply run out of fuel on the return journey.'

'Then fly in a pilot from another base.'

'You know that's impossible, Gabe,' Sam told him. 'They're overstretched as it is.'

Gabriel accepted this with an expansive gesture. 'OK.

Granted. Even disregarding that I think we're crazy to send David back into the lions' den, there are still fundamental problems. One. We don't know where Christina Schofield is being held.'

'We do: the Empire State Building. Ninety-third floor.'

'So you found a replacement for me on the inside fast enough?'

'He or she,' Sam replied cagily, 'was already in place. You were the best, but we needed to know we had a substitute.'

'Just in case?'

Sam admitted it with a nod. More coffee appeared on the table; Sam lit a cigarette. And so the talking went on throughout the afternoon. Outside the meagre sun did its best to illuminate the world. A flock of geese flapped steadily southwards overhead, their honking cries filling the air. Beyond the fence, evicted triffids rattled their sticks, twitched their leaves and did their best to flaunt their sinister presence.

One by one the points of Sam's plan were worked through. Fuel requirements. The range of the aircraft. Their capacity to hold demolition explosives. Types of ammunition. Food rations. Duration of mission. Route. And so on. It was the real nitty-gritty where the devil was truly in the detail. For a tiny item overlooked could result in a catastrophic failure of the whole strategy.

I confess. During a lengthy debate between Sam and Lieutenant Truscott on whether hollow-point or solid-point ammunition should be used my mind wandered. As they talked I made a series of little sketches on a bit of paper I found under the table.

There was a break for sandwiches and the roast beef that had been flown in that morning made its appearance between slices of bread. The respite from fish-and-triffid stew was enough to lift spirits a little at least.

Reconvening the briefing meeting, Gabriel raised the problem of what he considered was an insurmountable obstacle to any progress we could make with the plan. 'Radar,' he said. 'New York is protected from every point of the compass by an extensive network of radar stations. How do the aircraft approach the place undetected?'

I raised a finger. 'I've been putting some thought into that one,' I said. 'Firstly, we have to make our approach at night. There's a half-moon over the next few days that should be enough for us to see by.'

'OK.' Gabriel shrugged. 'We fly in by the beautiful light of the silvery moon. But radar can detect us as easily by night as it can by day.'

'This is the tricky bit,' I told him. 'To avoid detection by radar we need to fly in at a very low altitude. Probably no more than a hundred feet.'

'But even flying that low over open water still won't be enough for us to escape radar detection, will it?'

'No. Like I said, this is the tricky part.' I placed my roughly sketched map on the table. 'That's Manhattan Island. Running north from it is the Hudson River. If I remember correctly the Hudson is flanked by steep hills and cliffs over a hundred feet high. We need to fly down the river, keeping below the tops of the cliffs.' I pointed at my map. 'That's the only way we can reach New York without being detected by its radar.'

This time it was one of the pilots who all but choked on his disbelief at my suggestion. 'This is *crazy*. You're seriously telling us that we have to fly a big four-engine plane along a river valley just a hundred feet above the water? And in the *dark?*'

'It can be done.'

'It's suicide.'

'We'll make it.'

'But an altimeter isn't accurate at that low an altitude. How can you judge that you're just a hundred feet above the surface?'

I put sketch number two on the table. 'We fix small lights on either wing. Here, on the port and starboard float struts. If you point these downward at a carefully calculated angle, the focused light beams will fall on the water, showing as two spots of light. In a mirror set against the cockpit window the navigator will see these spots of light gradually move closer to one another as the plane descends. As I've said, these lights will be precisely angled. And, giving the pilot a continuous commentary, the navigator will sing out when the two spots of light merge into one on the surface of the water.' I tapped the paper with my fingertips. 'At that point – with the convergence of the lights – that's when the plane will be travelling precisely one hundred feet above the water. Which will be low enough to get us under New York's radar without being detected.'

Sam clapped his hands together. 'And that, ladies and gentlemen, is how David Masen has just earned his keep.' He turned to me. 'Now, David. Added to my congra-

tulations on your invention – let's call it—' he gave a wry
smile '—the Masen Height Indicator – is my suggestion
that you start work on it straightaway. We leave for New
York in two days.'

CHAPTER THIRTY THREE

Night Journey

Whether the following words come from a song, a play, a folk legend or are some ancient Oriental proverb I just don't know: *Softly, softly, catchee monkey!*

The words, however, ran freely and unbidden through my head as the three flying boats lifted from the smooth surface of the river before turning northwards for the three-hour flight to New York.

Softly, softly, catchee monkey! A proverb (if it was a proverb) that urged stealth, and perhaps a certain delicacy of action, if you wanted to catch your primate. For, as I raised the nose of the aircraft, the engines humming sweetly in my ears, I knew that I had an ulterior motive for making sure that I was piloting one of the New York-bound planes. When I arrived there I would find Kerris Baedekker. Then I would take her to my homeland. You must understand that it was as though this conviction had embedded itself in every nerve, sinew and bone of my body. I knew I would rescue her. We would be reunited.

But, to be completely candid, it was *how* I would achieve this outcome that completely mystified me.

Softly, softly, catchee monkey! Naturally, no one else knew of my plan. A poor half-formed plan at that.

'Coffee?'

'Please.' A co-pilot was a luxury the mission could not afford so Gabriel Deeds occupied the seat beside me. He poured steaming coffee from a thermos.

'So far, so good?' he asked, handing me the cup.

'So far, so good,' I agreed. 'And now comes the magical part that passengers prefer not to think about.' I flicked a switch on the control panel in front of me. Then I took my hands off the joystick.

Watching a little uneasily as the joystick continued to respond as if to a ghostly controlling hand, Gabriel said, 'Automatic pilot?'

'The pilot's best friend.' I smiled. 'Now I can go and get some shut-eye until we're ready to land.'

Gabriel's eyes widened.

'I'm kidding, Gabe. I'll stay here in the hot seat, but at least I can relax – well, *try* to relax – for a while.' I sipped the coffee.

'Quite some sunset.' Gabriel nodded through the window at the flaming reds and golds bursting on the horizon. 'But I'd prefer it if I was watching it with the ground beneath my feet.'

'Not down there. That's triffid country. Just look at the beggars. There must be thousands.'

He swallowed. 'I'd still rather take my chances down there.'

'You're not a devotee of air travel, then?'

In a rather dry voice he said, 'First time I've ridden in a cockpit.'

'Don't worry . . . in ten minutes you'll get used to it. In half an hour you'll love it. In two hours you'll be bored stiff.'

He nodded. The look in his eye, however, told me loud and clear that he didn't believe one word.

I turned back to the navigator. 'How're we doing?'

'Right on course. Before it gets dark the planes will switch on their tail lights. The leader will show a green tail light. The middle plane will display a blue one. Follow the blue.'

'OK.' I returned to gaze through the window as mainland America rolled out beneath me in a carpet of green. A green, I knew, that contained the sinister dark hues of triffid leaves. Masters of their territory, they would be settling for the night, their roots anchored firmly into soil that was once part of fields, parks and gardens. I could see them in my mind's eye. On top of their stems the cones would detect the sound of our planes passing high overhead. The cones would move as one, tracking the source of the sound. Perhaps the finger sticks would rattle. They'd be comparing notes with a triffid neighbour or sending a message that would alert farther-flung comrades.

Although I could see perhaps thirty miles there were none of the tell-tale smoke trails that would indicate human occupation. Down there the triffid was king.

Even though the hydraulic system of the autopilot kept the plane efficiently in trim while maintaining an economical two hundred miles per hour, my eyes would repeatedly flick to the gauges, checking altitude, airspeed and so on. A little ahead of me I could see the other two planes in our formation. Wings glinted gold in the setting sun. To a seasoned pilot like myself it made for a heart-warming sight.

This part of the flight would – gods of the air willing – be reasonably straightforward. Landing undetected near the island of Manhattan would be another matter entirely. With the help of a pair of electricians I had rigged up the light system that Sam Dymes had jokingly named the Masen Height Indicator. Test flights over the river showed that it did work. Thankfully. Because in a couple of hours we were going to have to put it to the test.

Gabriel must have become a little more accustomed to flying because he unbuckled his seat belt, commenting that he was going back to check on our passengers. These consisted of twenty Marines, the elite troops of the Foresters' army, along with an eight-strong team made up of sappers who were expert in demolition (their huge store of plastic explosives was crammed in the forward hold), a couple of radio communications technicians and, for some reason, a television engineer. While an expert in televisual broadcasting did seem a mystifying requirement to me, I guessed Sam Dymes simply wouldn't have been so frivolous that he'd asked the lady along just for the ride.

These planes had been built to transport civilian passengers in some degree of comfort. They certainly hadn't been intended as troop carriers. So for now our passengers could enjoy the benefits of electric-razor points, hot and cold water and well-appointed 'bath-rooms' – as the Americans called toilets – with a similarly well-equipped galley that boasted hot plates, a toaster and thermos compartments for hot meals. If any of them had the stomach for food, that was. For the previous night I'd seen those men and women writing letters that would be delivered to their families if they should fail to return from the mission.

Gabriel returned with the news that our passengers were in good shape. Many were fast asleep, although how they could sleep at a time like this was beyond me.

Beyond the windows the sky darkened quickly as night fell. Whatever had dimmed the stars and the sun had affected the moon similarly. Certainly it wasn't as bright as it should have been. It showed itself as an orange semicircle above my port wing.

I glanced at Gabriel. He was taking a more objective interest in the business of flying now. I noticed his dark eyes flicking from the artificial horizon to the airspeed indicator, then to the altimeter. His quick mind made sense of the apparent confusion of dials.

'Do you fancy having a go, Gabe?' I asked, nodding at the joystick in front of him. 'It's fairly straightforward.'

'I'll leave it to you this time round.' He smiled. 'To tell you the truth, the thought of all that explosive down in the hold is making me a mite nervous.'

'Thoughts about it keep popping up in my mind, too. Either that or the fifteen tons of fuel we've got stuffed into the tanks . . . So I hope no one's calming their nerves with a cigarette back there.'

Gabriel's smile looked a tad more forced. 'I hope so, too.'

I voiced something that had been on my mind. 'I hear Sam Dymes is in the lead plane. I thought that, as commander of the camp, he'd have stayed behind?'

'Top brass are pushing hard for this mission to be one hundred per cent successful. I'm not belittling the skills of those guys in the back but Sam knows he has to put everything he's got into this one.'

'You know, Gabe, I've been thinking . . .'

'Oh?' He gave me a sideways glance.

'There's a few details about this mission that have been nagging away at me.'

'It's going to be a tough one. No doubting that.'

'I know the prime objective is to spirit Christina Schofield away from Torrence.'

'That's it in a nutshell.'

'But the Foresters aren't thinking of breeding their own super-race, are they? After all, if you have people who are immune to triffid poison then you're going to have the edge over everyone else.'

'True. But we're not going to do anything as radical as remove her ovaries and then implant our womenfolk with the eggs.'

'Really?'

'Do I detect a note of disbelief, David?'

'Maybe after my experiences of the last couple of months I'm becoming a more suspicious person.'

'David, our community prides itself on its humanity. That's why we split with Torrence's junta in the first place.'

I gazed out at the coloured tail lights of the other two planes. 'But surely the same thought must have gone through the minds of your leaders. I imagine that they've required Sam to come up with some contingency plan, too.'

'And what would that be?'

'That it would be in the interests of national security that if Christina couldn't be rescued then she should be killed. And her body destroyed so that her ovaries would be useless.'

Gabriel's expression hardened. 'You think Sam Dymes would be capable of something as brutal as that?'

'Desperate times call for desperate measures. You know that, Gabe.'

'You *are* developing a suspicious streak, David.'

'I agree. But right now I'd describe that as a useful survival trait.'

'Oh?'

'Maybe being entrusted with piloting this plane to New York has given me more confidence in my own position among your people, and maybe I'm saying more than I ought. But it occurs to me that it would make perfect sense to order the Marines to ensure that I didn't fall into Torrence's hands under any circumstances.'

'You really think we'd do that to you?'

I shrugged. 'What I do think is that it would be very wise to make damn' sure I took a bullet in the head rather than become Torrence's hostage.' I looked at Gabriel. 'After all, I remember that when I was snatched from New York there was a contingency plan if it seemed my rescue might be in doubt.'

'That is perfectly correct.' Gabriel nodded slowly. 'All

I can say is, trust us: we'll keep you safely out of harm's way once we're in New York.'

'That's not going to be easy.'

'There's another fundamental reason to trust us, isn't there? We need you to fly us back out of there once we've gotten hold of Christina.'

'You've brought false moustaches and dark glasses for everyone, then . . . I know, that sounds flippant, but I'm still wondering how we're going to melt into the brick-work.'

Gabriel rubbed his jaw. 'Maybe we shouldn't have been so mean with the information.' He poured more coffee into his cup. 'You know we're going to put these people in the northernmost part of Manhattan Island. And you know that's in an area north of what is known as the 102nd Parallel?'

'Yes, I know that. But I don't know what that place actually is.'

'Oh, that's simple. That whole northern tip of the island is one godalmighty prison.'

'Then it's going to be full of prison guards.'

'Not entirely.'

'Sounds a pretty relaxed prison.'

Gabriel glared at me. 'If you knew what it was like there you wouldn't say that.' Now he sounded angry. 'You wouldn't say that at all.'

'OK. Then tell me what it is like. If there are no guards why don't the inmates escape?'

'Because Torrence is clever. All he needs is a good high wall running from one side of the island to the other like the Berlin Wall, cutting Manhattan in two. One half is the city, all bright lights, cafés, movie houses, luxury apartments. Everything above what was 102nd Street is a slum: a ghetto for people who are the wrong colour, or who cannot see, or who didn't care for Torrence's so-called glorious administration. They can't climb over the wall, which does have guard towers and dogs and land-mines, by the way. And they can't swim across the river to the mainland because there are a million triffids waiting there.' He pressed on, thoroughly in gear now. 'In those rotting tenements families live on just enough food to keep body and soul together. It only looks like they work willingly in the sweatshops and the factories. The truth is that they *have* to work or they don't get their daily food ration. Without that they and their children would starve. And what makes the whole thing tick along just like clockwork for Torrence and his cronies is that ten years ago they hit on the idea of injecting some of those people with heroin. Now that was a stroke of genius.' Gabriel's eyes blazed with anger. 'You see, heroin dulls awareness. So the slave workers no longer appreciated the sharper edges of their miserable reality. In turn, that meant Torrence could force them to work longer hours. But it doesn't stop there. Heroin is addictive. So after a few shots the slave workers became addicts. Then Torrence ordered that the injections should be stopped. Of course, all these new addicts were crawling up the walls, craving a fix. So what does Torrence do?' Gabriel didn't wait for my reply but steamed on. 'He offers his slaves another shot if they meet their productivity targets. And hey presto! Manufacturing output goes up because his slaves work their hearts out for another fix. And, yes, that eases the craving for a few hours. But then it comes back, so they have to work all the harder for their next shot. Simple, huh?'

For a full minute Gabriel sat, fists clenched, his jaw working as he struggled to contain his fury. Then at last: 'So you see, David, the neighbourhood above the 102nd Street Parallel isn't a nice place to be.' He took a deep swallow of coffee. 'It's a prison that's run by its inmates. It's brutally efficient. And it works night and day to keep Torrence and his favourites in a style to which they have become accustomed. What it means for us, however, is that there are few guards to worry about. Also, we have allies there. While our teams do what needs to be done they will provide us with safe houses until it's time to fly home . . . God willing. See, David?' He gave me a grim look. 'I promised you'd be safe, didn't I?'

After that we travelled without talking for a while. A good long while at that. A little more reflective now, I ran checks on the instruments while making sure that I still had the tail lights of our two sister planes in sight. When I glanced at my watch I saw that we were a mere hour from landing. This time my mouth really did go dry. In a few moments we would adopt a radio blackout, otherwise we'd be in danger of being picked up by New York's powerful detector antennae even though the power of the aircraft's radios had been deliberately reduced. Before radio silence was imposed I asked the pilots of the other planes to check the lights that would measure their height above the water. A pair of beams suddenly shone down from each plane. Placed towards the end of the wings, the lights blazed downward at a precise angle to cross at exactly a hundred feet below the plane. For a moment it looked as if the hundred-ton aircraft were actually supported on twin beams of light that formed an elongated 'X' design beneath them.

Within a second of confirming that the lights were in working order and requesting that they be shut down again, Sam Dymes came on the radio, speaking from the lead aircraft. First of all he asked that his transmission should be switched through to the passenger cabins, too.

'Just a couple of minutes to radio silence,' came Sam's characteristic voice, still shy-sounding as if the microphone awed him. 'I just wanted to wish everyone good luck and good landings. I know that with our pilots we are in good hands. And – and you know this mission scares me . . . truly, it scares me a lot. And I'd be a darned liar if I didn't tell you all that I wish I were at home with my wife and children. Because I know there's a chance that not all of us will be coming back. Those that do will be acclaimed as heroes. But those that don't make it will be more than that. The gift of their lives will become a bridge to a better future for their friends, families, children, grandchildren . . . we won't forget you. And I wish there was more I could say about that, and about the importance of this mission, but the truth is that I don't have words that are clear enough or powerful enough to do you justice. But I can certainly tell you that there are going to be thousands of people praying for you tonight. Good luck.'

Static hissed from the speaker. After that, a click. Then silence.

* * *

Flying according to plan we followed a curving route that took us close on a hundred miles north of New York, thus making sure that we were well out of radar range. Then, our way lit by that dull moonlight, we turned south. In Indian file the planes headed towards the Hudson River: the great shining road that would lead us down from the Catskills to New York itself.

For a while, anyway, we could afford to fly at an altitude of three thousand feet. Soon, however, if we were to avoid radar detection, we'd have to drop until we were skimming just a hundred feet above the surface of the river. Those bluffs and hillsides looked all but black in the moonlight. I only hoped we could differentiate a black cliff face from a patch of harmless shadow.

Flying level, I checked the instruments. Gabriel watched me, then he cleared his throat. 'Now might not be the best time to tell you this, David.'

I looked at him.

'Your suspicious nature didn't steer you wrong,' he told me. 'If we should fail to rescue Christina – then we do have someone on the inside who will make sure she's no use to Torrence.'

'Oh?'

'If Christina isn't in our hands within seven days, Kerris Baedekker has orders to kill her.'

'Kerris Baedekker! Then she's—'

'One of us.' Gabriel nodded, then gave me sidelong smile. 'Only I never knew that until yesterday. And she never knew that I was a spy, either.' This time he shook his head. 'Espionage? It's a funny old game, isn't it?'

At that moment there were a hundred . . . no, a

thousand questions I was burning to ask. Only there was no time.

Instead, I pushed forward the joystick. 'Hold on tight,' I told him. 'We're going in.'

CHAPTER THIRTY FOUR

'Some Other Hand . . .'

After rescuing survivors of the *Titanic* disaster, Captain Rostron of the *Carpathia* spoke of his ship's near-suicidal dash through the icebergs. Rostron said: *'When I saw the ice I had steamed through during the night I shuddered. And could only think that some other hand than mine was on that helm during the night.'*

That uncanny sensation came to me, too. Down, down, down through the dark I floated, following the coloured tail lights of our sister aircraft. At either side of me rose the cliff walls that hemmed in the Hudson River. Moonlight sent ghostly gleamings running across the water. Perhaps it was only the slipstream of the leading aircraft but the effect of those lights moving on the face of the water was decidedly uncanny. Distracting, too, as I found my eye following their darting movements. Nevertheless, I forced myself to concentrate on the tail lights of the planes in front. Too slow and I'd fall behind, lose them. Too fast and I'd be likely to ram them.

Nerves wound up as tight as a watch spring, I brought

all my senses into play. Sensing the balance of my aircraft; hearing the note of the engines; watching dials, meters; the planes beyond the glass, the colossal walls of rock at either side of us becoming even narrower until the wing-tips seemed only a whisker away from oblivion.

Lower. Lower. Still lower.

Then I hit the switch that turned on the lights beneath the plane.

'OK,' I said to Gabriel, my voice so calm that it surprised me. 'Look into the mirror. See the lights hitting the water?'

'Got them.'

'Tell me when the two points of light begin to merge.'

'Yes. They're getting closer together . . . wait . . . they've stopped.'

'I'll bring her lower . . . keep watching.'

'OK.'

'Tell me the second they touch and begin to overlap.'

'Will do.'

I eased the throttle back a little. The hum of the engines dropped a note.

'That's it,' Gabriel said. 'The lights are touching. Yep. Starting to overlap now.'

'Right. I'll keep her at this height. Just tell me the moment the lights separate. OK?'

'Gotcha.'

And so the planes weaved on down the valley. With the flanking cliffs and hills higher than we were, as far as New York's radar operators were concerned we might as well have been underground. The next fifteen minutes were hair-raising stuff. Too low and we'd make a heck of a splash. Too much to port or too much to starboard and we'd vanish in a blaze of flame against the valley sides.

Just when I found myself slipping into an unreal state of mind, where I could almost believe we'd flown into the Earth and were soaring through some subterranean cavern, I saw a glow ahead of me. The lights of Manhattan were even brighter than I remembered.

'So far, so good,' I murmured. 'There's no blackout so they don't know we're coming.'

All of a sudden the city lights grew even brighter. Once more there were rivers of headlights as cars surged along roads in that metropolis that never slept. Sky-scrapers showed as light-studded towers soaring up towards a blood-red moon.

Ahead of me the lead plane dropped quickly to land on the river, making only a small splash as it did. The second plane followed suit. I cut back the throttles to glide in for a surprisingly smooth landing.

'We're down,' I said, a trifle unnecessarily. 'I only hope no one saw us coming in.'

'New York is populated by people who look in — not out. They won't have heard us, either. All those cars make far too much of a racket for that.' Gabriel shot me a grin. 'Good flying, by the way, David.'

'It's not over yet. I'll be happier when we get this machine out of sight.'

I taxied the plane across the oily waters, keeping engine noise to a minimum. All I knew was that I'd been instructed to follow the lead plane.

I began to perspire. The big flying boat had become the proverbial sitting duck. At any moment I expected to see a searchlight beam spring suddenly out of the darkness to pin us down like a butterfly to paper. With that would come a hail of machine-gun fire to cut us to pieces.

But all I could do was tail the other two planes, my engines muttering so low that we approached the shore at a worryingly slow speed. Just when I'd begun to suspect a trap I saw the lead plane suddenly swing to starboard and accelerate through the water, sending a creamy wake washing out to either side.

The plane headed directly for a rounded, humped building that jutted out from the shore. Mercifully, two huge doors opened at the front of the building. In a moment the first plane was inside, followed by the second. I didn't hesitate and opened the throttle just enough to send the plane surging towards the doors. The moment we were through I cut the engines, leaving the plane to coast under its own momentum.

Inside, neon lights lit the place brilliantly. Men and women scrambled along jetties to haul the planes manually into purpose-built bays. This was no makeshift dock.

I scanned the walls. They were encrusted with years of dirt. Yet I soon made out a number of signs. *Aircrew Only. This Way To Immigration. Ocean Clipper Restaurant & Bar. Welcome To Riverside Park Sky Way*. There were other signs for Boeing, BOAC and American United Airlines. Clearly I was in a proper flying-boat port that had served New York before The Blinding. Transfixed in time like a fly in amber, it had now been quietly restored to life.

The Marines disembarked swiftly. People in civilian clothes whom I didn't recognize began unloading explosives and ammunition.

Sam appeared at the nose of the craft as I sat making my post-flight checks. He gestured to me to open the cockpit window.

'Great flying, David. Now we need to get you to a safe house until we're ready for the flight back home.'

'I thought I'd be staying with the aircraft. There's—'

'Too risky. There's no guarantee that this place won't be searched. You'll be assigned a guide who will take you to an apartment. You're to sit tight there until you're brought back here. Got that?'

I nodded.

'Make it snappy,' he said. 'We need to be away from here in ten minutes flat.'

By the time I'd left the aircraft, most of our people were already moving out. I noticed that the Marines had been divided into small squads of anything between four and eight members. Each had what I took to be a local guide. They left the hangar by a side door at staggered intervals. Gabriel had been assigned to one of the groups. From across the building he caught my glance and gave me a salute. Then he slipped away with a squad of Marines into the night. My group was the last to leave. I saw I was in the company of the television technician and a pair of sappers. No manpower was wasted. I found myself carrying a heavy backpack, as well as my own rucksack.

'What's in it?' I asked.

'Don't ask,' came the reply. 'But when you set it down on the ground treat it like you would your grandmother's best china.'

'Oh.' Now I could guess what the backpack contained.

After that I treated it with tremendous respect.

A moment later we were through the side door. Once more I had the solid ground of Manhattan beneath my feet. In the distance I heard cars mingled with a metallic clanking that could have been some factory. Ahead of me, a road separated the dockside from a cliff.

Our group now consisted of about a dozen people. Sam Dymes, after conferring with our guide, loped up to me.

'Stick close to the rest of the pack,' he told me. 'We're moving off in one minute.'

'Aren't we going to look conspicuous, strolling through the streets of Manhattan with all this on our backs?' I nodded at the team with their bulging backpacks. Several were sporting sub-machine guns as well. All of which would make us pretty suspicious-looking even to the least observant of policemen.

'Don't worry, David. We're north of the 102nd Street Parallel. This part of Manhattan's a lot different to the fancy part you know in the south of the island.' With a distracted air he looked repeatedly about him, as if afraid that we'd be spotted. This didn't inspire a whole lot of confidence. 'What's more we'll be using a rather special route . . . ah.'

'What's wrong?'

'Nothing. It's just our guide. She's here at last.'

I turned to see a slim figure step out from the shadows. There was something about the walk . . . A second later she turned her face toward me.

I stared.

'Kerris?'

CHAPTER THIRTY FIVE

Doppelgänger

'Kerris?' I repeated her name as she stepped out further from the shadows. Immediately I moved towards her, my arms stretched out ready to embrace her. She recoiled as if I was about to attack her.

'Kerris, what's wrong?'

She lifted her chin as she looked at me. At that moment I saw a cruel disfiguring scar running diagonally across her face from her right temple to the left-hand corner of her mouth. A vivid red slash that cut her face in two. I stopped dead. All of a sudden I thought: *Torrence has done this to her.*

'Oh, God, Kerris, what's happened?' Once more I made as if to embrace her. She glared furiously at me. 'Kerris—'

I felt a hand on my shoulder. 'Easy, David.'

'Sam, look what the monster's done to her. She used—'

'David . . . David, no, listen.' Sam gripped my arm. 'That isn't Kerris. It will be her sister. Maybe even a twin sister. I don't know.'

'Good grief . . . ' I turned to her. 'I'm sorry, I'm truly sorry. I thought—'

'David, I regret this.' Sam said quickly. 'It looks like a dirty trick, but it's not. I had no idea that a sister of Kerris's would be here tonight . . .' He turned to the girl. 'I'm sorry, ma'am. We mistook you for someone else.'

A small dark figure appeared beside us. 'Marni don't speak.' The man touched his tongue. 'The cops thought she was speaking too much as a kid.' His fingers mimicked a pair of scissors.

'I don't understand.' I shook my head. 'She's one of Torrence's children? And he's done this to her?'

Sam looked grim. 'Torrence has hundreds of children. Those that don't meet his criteria wind up here. I gather he's highly selective when it comes to being a father . . . if that's what you can call him. Wait, what's that, ma'am?' The scarred girl who otherwise bore such an uncanny resemblance to Kerris appeared to lose patience. She patted Sam on the shoulder, then pointed toward the cliff.

'Oh, uhm, right,' he stammered. 'Looks like we should be moving out.'

We moved in pairs across the street. The small dark man led the way, while Marni followed, clearly making sure we didn't lose any stragglers. If I slowed down even slightly I felt her hand against my backpack, urging me on. I didn't hesitate to obey her wordless instructions. I didn't know how much shoving the contents of the bag could take.

If I'd expected to find some path running up the cliff I was mistaken. Instead we turned along the bottom of the rock face where we came upon a long low building that stretched from the water's edge to the cliff. We were ushered inside (with a helpful shove, where required, from Marni.) Inside the building were sets of rail tracks. The guide lit a kerosene lamp, then gestured for us to follow.

I'd only been walking for a little while before I realized the building didn't end with the cliff. The twin sets of rail tracks continued on into a tunnel.

'The subway?' I asked Sam who walked beside me.

'No, look at the rust on the rails. This hasn't been used for years. I guess this must be the coal-transportation tunnel. In the old days coal came down the Hudson on barges, then got shipped underground by train into the city.' He looked round at the arched tunnel cut through the living rock. 'It might not be the pretty route but if it gets us to our destination without being seen then it's OK by me.'

We walked on. Even though I tried hard not to, I found myself repeatedly glancing back at Marni. Her hair, eyes, the shape of her face and ears – all her features, with the exception of the scar that daubed a blood-red line across her face, were identical to Kerris's. She was an eerie wordless doppelgänger who shadowed me as we moved deep beneath the city.

I thought: *I'm moving into a place of nightmares. I see the mutilated twin of the woman I love. I'm walking through a cave that never seems to end. On my back are eighty pounds of high explosive. Meanwhile, our guide's lamp seems to be failing. Darkness is closing in. How long before the ten million ghosts that must haunt Manhattan come swirling out of that dead tunnel?* I shivered. The air had grown much colder. All I could see were the luminous eyes of my companions. Behind me Marni's green eyes seemed even brighter. Like shining balls of glass that hung suspended in the darkness.

The weight of the explosive pressed hard against my back. A lunatic itch started between my shoulder blades. This had the resonance of a nightmare, all right. I wished someone would speak. Or whistle. Or hum some idiot tune, come to that. Instead, we toiled on in silence. While all the time the darkness settled on us like a physical weight.

Welcome to hell, I told myself. *Welcome to hell.*

This underworld journey finally came to an end. Beside a pile of rusting machinery that could only be some ancient conveyor belt that once took coal to the surface was an iron staircase. Wearily, we ascended. My eighty-pound pack of explosives now felt closer to a ton. Legs shaking, I made it to the top of the steps, then shuffled through an open door.

All of a sudden I was outside in what appeared to be a coal merchant's yard. Mounds of chopped firewood stood alongside pyramids of coal. Moving stealthily now, our party crossed the yard to a gate set in a wall. The guide moved through the gate. Quickly he checked that the way was clear and then we were beckoned forward. Behind me, the impatient Marni ensured that there were no stragglers.

The sight that met my eyes revealed a very different New York. Here, buildings were low, stunted things.

They ranged from one-storey shacks to five-storey tenements. And they were about as appealing to look at as a row of rotting teeth.

The moonlight revealed more. Open areas of ground – formerly city parks, I surmised – were given over to a kind of shanty-town industrial estate. From tightly packed huts smoke poured from stovepipes, while I couldn't help but hear the incessant hammering and sawing vying with the clatter of metal on metal and the whine of power tools.

'The night shift,' Sam told me in a low voice. 'Torrence likes to keep his workforce busy round the clock . . . yes, ma'am. I'm coming.' Marni's long arm reached out to push Sam firmly in the right direction.

Once more into nightmare. Street lights burned, casting a sickly yellow glow over the neighbourhood. Yet, oddly, though people moved about inside the houses there seemed to be little electric light in these ghetto homes. Now I passed churches that had been converted into factories. Power hammers thundered within once-tranquil havens. From what I could see, there were few motorized vehicles here. Men, women and children hurried on urgent errands with heavy loads of all kinds on their backs – animal carcasses, firewood, lead pipes, scrap metal, car tyres. Here and there, areas of road had been fenced off to provide enclosures for goats, sheep and chickens.

We hurried on. I noticed that our strange-looking squad attracted no curious glances. Here the population's eyes were dull, whether from overwork, hunger or opiates – or from all three – I could not say.

I slowed for a moment as a child crossed the road beneath a load so enormous that it sickened me. Its face was a grim mask, lined with pain. Marni moved me on with a firm push.

So on I walked, passing through that grisly assortment of buildings that housed cobblers, blacksmiths, weavers, bottle makers, potters, carpenters, barrel makers, box makers, soap makers (from where terrible smells of boiling animal fat issued). And all the time my feet slopped through waste material I did not care to identify.

We reached an alleyway. From one of the tenement windows a saxophone played. But it was a musician gone mad. A helter-skelter of notes spiralled up and down the scale, managing to be both lyrically musical and cacophonous at the same time.

This was the place for the bleak night journey of one's soul. I sensed a dark, unforgiving oppression. My stomach fluttered in a queasy sort of way and, my God, what wouldn't I have given to have been walking the gentle green hills of home . . .

'In here,' our guide said. 'In here. Quick.'

Rather unceremoniously we were bundled through the back door of a four-storey tenement where we were marched up stairwells that smelled of well-sweated cabbage. A moment later I noticed that the guide appeared to be allocating rooms. Now *that* was a welcome idea. I longed to lie down on a soft mattress.

My turn. 'In here,' the guide told me. 'You get to eat later.'

Sam slapped me on the shoulder. 'I'll drop in soon to see how you've settled in.'

I hadn't expected luxury. So at least I wasn't disappointed. I found I was sharing the room with an assortment of copper tubing and vessels that bubbled and hissed. If my nostrils didn't betray me, the smell of malt boiling in some kind of steel urn suggested that my room-mate was a liquor still. Both the smell and the heat were appalling.

I turned but the door had already closed behind me, while the sound of tramping feet told me my comrades were still being shown to their rooms. At one end of the room a curtain ran from one wall to the other. Thirty years ago it had been the plush velvet drape of some wealthy homeowner. Now . . . well, suffice to say that it had seen better days.

I'd just decided to have a glimpse at what lay beyond the curtain when the door opened behind me. Glancing back, I saw Marni enter. The scar on her face gave her a permanently fierce expression. But then, her eyes were fierce, too. So maybe she really didn't like me. Perhaps she'd misinterpreted my earlier attempt to hug her.

After giving me a long, furious stare she went to the still. With surprising violence she kicked a cauldron. In turn that sent liquid gurgling through the pipes. She then took an empty bottle from a cupboard, set it down under a pipe and turned a screw. A clear liquid began to drip into the bottle.

Ignoring me now, she made more adjustments to the still, mainly with the toecap of her boot. Then she went to the curtain and pulled it aside.

I found myself looking at another figure. The girl sat

on a bunk bed. Her red hair had been shaved down to her scalp. Her face was thin. The green eyes, however, were no less bright. Marni turned to scowl again at me.

I looked back at the two young women. They met my gaze unflinchingly. 'Oh, dear Lord in Heaven,' I breathed. Now there were two near-perfect facsimiles of Kerris Baedekker staring back at me.

And that was that.

As my mother was fond of saying when spooning greens onto my plate. 'You've got two choices, David Masen. You can either like it or lump it.' Whether I relished the idea or not, this would be home for the night. Against the wall were three bunk beds. Marni energetically pointed at the top one. Enough said: that would be mine for the night.

Not that she wasn't helpful. In that manner of hers, which see-sawed between vigour and violence, she all but dragged the backpack from my shoulders.

'No . . . *wait!*' I stopped her just before she dropped the backpack down onto the floor. 'Nice and easy does it.' I gave her a nervous smile, then nodded at the bag. 'Boom boom.' I regretted instantly my use of baby-talk English. The fire in her eyes told me that Marni was anything but simple. Just what, I wondered, had she been saying that had provoked the police to cut out her tongue?

It was a little while before the second carbon copy of Kerris spoke. 'What is it about us that unsettles you so much?' Her voice, while resembling Kerris's, sounded very weak. Indeed, I saw that the girl looked ill. Her body appeared so fragile that it seemed a sudden movement could smash it to pieces.

'I – er – I . . . well . . . you reminded me of someone, that's all.' My attempt at conversation bordered on the inarticulate. But the truth was that seeing what amounted to two Kerris Baedekkers (albeit altered in some way) rattled me.

'Is it because we are General Fielding's children?'

'General Fielding?' Again I stammered, forgetting momentarily that I now referred to Fielding by his original name: Torrence.

The shaven-headed girl continued while Marni stared mutely at me. 'There are a lot of his offspring about.'

'They all look like . . . er, I mean, you all resemble each other?'

'Some of us do.'

'You've heard of Kerris Baedekker?'

'No. Should I?'

'She looks like you,' I said, knowing that it sounded a trifle lame. 'She might be a twin.'

'Or a triplet. Or a quad.' The girl didn't sound surprised. 'You'll find a lot of people wearing this face.' She pointed at her own. 'Especially round here.'

'You've always lived here?'

'No. I was moved north of the Parallel when I was twelve. I'd gone to a good school and I was marked out for a career in administration, but I went down with a bout of influenza and for some reason I never got over it.' She gave a tiny shrug. 'I was taking up valuable classroom space and too much good food. Cripples are a luxury we can't afford, so here I came.'

I looked at her face in the meagre light. The delicacy of bone. Her translucent skin. The light in her eyes. I didn't know what caused it . . . but there was something ethereal about it.

In contrast, her sister sitting beside her was fiercely robust.

'I'm sorry,' I said. 'I haven't introduced myself. I'm David Masen. I guess you know why I'm here.'

'Haven't introduced yourself,' she echoed with a tired smile. 'My . . . I haven't heard such courtesy in a long time. Good evening, David Masen. My name is Rowena. And this is Marni. But then, you've already met her.'

'Yes, I have.'

'Marni's a bright kid. She arranged meetings where she questioned our father's policies. The police took her downtown for questioning. When they found out the family connection they reported her to our father. He ordered them to make sure she didn't talk again. He also suggested that they should give her the ugly treatment.' She made a gesture across her own face, miming a cut with a knife. 'My father figures that if you're ugly people won't listen to you anyway.' She shrugged. 'So Marni too wound up here.'

'Dear God. But you didn't know Marni existed until you met her here?'

'No. Like I say, there're an awful lot of us about . . . as alike as peas in a pod.' She glanced at her sister. 'Unless someone messes us up.'

'But how do—'

'I'm sorry to be so ill-mannered, David. But my sister and I both need to sleep now.'

Marni nodded in agreement.

Rowena explained, 'We've both got to work tomorrow.'

'Work?' I repeated in surprise as I looked at Rowena's sickly frame.

She shrugged. 'If we don't work, we don't eat.' She eased herself under the blankets while Marni climbed into the bunk above her.

I paused.

Without raising her head from the pillow Rowena whispered, 'Be our guest, David. Take the top bunk. It's not dirty.'

'No . . . no, er, I'm sure it's fine, but the man who guided me here said there'd be food later.'

She gave a weak smile. 'He meant breakfast.'

'Oh.'

Feeling a bit awkward about the sleeping arrangements I pulled off my flying boots and jacket, then climbed up onto the top bunk. It was narrow, the mattress thin, but I immediately lay still so as not to disturb my companions. Rowena especially looked as if she needed more than just one good night's rest.

Before I drifted off to sleep myself I decided to suggest to Sam Dymes — no, damn it, *demand!* — demand that arrangements be made to smuggle medicines here. Clearly they were sorely needed. But as things turned out I didn't get that chance.

CHAPTER THIRTY SIX

Going Solo . . .

'I'm sorry, I don't understand,' I said, flabbergasted. 'Sam Dymes was here with ten other people last night. Where's he gone?'

The man who had acted as guide the night before shrugged. 'Me? I don't know.'

'He didn't say anything?'

'He only say he was leaving.' Then the man added, with a slight touch of pique: 'He had another guide.' He pulled a sheet of paper from his pocket. 'But he tell me to give you this.'

Angrily, I took the note to my room and read it to the accompaniment of the gurgling liquor still.

I'd woken that morning as the two women readied themselves for work. Before leaving, both had drunk a cup full of whatever dripped from the tap of the still. Only a little while after that did I discover that Sam, along with my other travelling companions, had gone.

I read the note.

David, this seems a lousy trick, running out on you like this, but we've got to move faster than we originally planned. For your own safety I must urge you to sit tight until we get back. You'll be safe there. If you need anything ask Benji (he's the guy who brought us in). Yours, Sam Dymes.

I glanced at where I'd left the bag of explosives. It had gone. Clearly the sappers were on their way to do whatever was required of them.

What now?

With no windows to see out of I sat on a chair and listened to the drip, drip, drip of the liquor filling another bottle.

Another hour of that infernal dripping and I would have gone spectacularly mad. I decided to take a little walk. I reached the top of the stairwell. That would be the limit of this morning's adventure, I told myself; for there, sealing off the stairs, stood a padlocked gate. As it reached to the ceiling there was no question of climbing over it. I glanced to my right through an open doorway. An elderly lady squinted suspiciously back at me. She, I took it, served as the concierge. No doubt the key to the gate lay somewhere in her lair but, short of fighting her for it, it was still beyond my reach. Besides, no doubt if I tried anything, 'She'd start a-yellin', then the posse'd come a-runnin', to quote the words of a modern ditty.

I retreated to my room. There I pondered my options. Quickly, I realized that those were fairly limited. Either stay put in this stinking DIY distillery or find some way to break out. Not that breaking out appealed. Where could I go? The obvious answer would be south into the city. But that would mean scaling the twenty-foot wall, which wouldn't be the easiest of tasks: for one thing, the armed guards would take exception to my doing so. Perhaps it would be best to sit tight until Sam Dymes returned.

If he returned.

Tut, tut, David, I told myself, *there goes your suspicious mind again* . . .

But there *was* a chance that circumstances might prevent the return of Sam and the others. In which case, I might have to take my chances, making for the flying-boat hangar and then heading for home under my own steam.

Drip . . . drip . . . drip . . .

The still did its work. The almost overpowering smell of sweating malt and barley took possession of my nostrils. At intervals the concierge broke off from her gatekeeper duties to limp into the room, remove a full liquor bottle from beneath the ever-dripping tap, stopper it, place it with its cousins (dozens and dozens of them) in a cupboard, then place an empty bottle under the tap, turn the screw and – yes – the drip-drip-drip would start all over again.

Later that morning I discovered a way of looking out onto the street. I found that if I stood on a chair I could see through a ventilation grille. Now I had a reticulated image of a road lined with four-story tenements. Sunlight revealed a busy scene. People of all ages and all races hurried to and fro. Most carried baskets or bundles of different kinds. I could see a great number of the Blind, too. They moved with confidence along the street, yet I noted, feeling sick, that they seemed to be employed as beasts of burden. They carried huge wooden boxes secured by a kind of harness to their backs. I didn't see one person dressed in anything better than the most pitiful of rags.

I continued to watch the scene for some minutes. During that time one or two people on bicycles went past. I saw a handcart, pulled by a burly man, in which were two pigs and, bizarrely, a coffin lined with satin in a delirious shade of pink. Following him came a herd of cattle driven by boys with sticks. Then, for the first time since my arrival in this zone, I saw a powered vehicle. I craned my head to see better. Trundling noisily into view came what appeared to be a metal box on wheels. What few windows it possessed were covered with steel mesh, while on top of it a perspex bubble glinted in the sun. In this gun turret sat a man smoking a cigarette.

As the vehicle turned into a side street I could see the words *INDUSTRIAL SECTOR POLICE (NYC)* stencilled on its flank.

This was important. Despite this slave camp being largely run by its inmates there were police patrols. I mentally filed the information.

The small dark man, Benji, appeared. His glance at me was rich with disinterest. 'If you come down from da chair, Marty's serving chow in da parlour.'

'Parlour?'

'Big room down da hallway. You got any cigarettes?'

'No, I'm sorry, I don't—'

'Chow's in da parlour. Make quick, or it's gone.'

In the words of Benji, I made quick. I was hungry. What was more, I didn't know when the next meal would appear. The moment I walked into the hallway the barley-and-malt stench was replaced by powerful boiled-cabbage odours.

My nose didn't steer me wrong. Cabbage soup steamed in a huge tureen. Already a dozen or more blind people had begun to eat. I joined them. The concierge in yet another change of roles doled out bread that was grey and gritty. There was a mood of silent despair in the room so strong that it seemed to percolate through my nostrils as pungently as the boiled-cabbage smells. I remember thinking to myself: *Something must be done. These people shouldn't have to live like this.* Yet, for the life of me, I could not think of a way to help them.

At six o'clock Rowena and Marni returned from their work. Some sooty material had made their skin grimy. Both disappeared into the bathroom to wash. Then, as if this routine had been established for many a year, Rowena climbed onto the bottom bunk where she just sat, obviously painfully exhausted by her labours and looking more fragile than ever. Meanwhile, the robust Marni helped make her comfortable, then brought her the cabbage soup and bread that was her evening meal. Rowena balanced the bowl on her lap to eat while Marni went to collect her own ration.

I busied myself with my remaining rucksack for a while so as to give them a degree of privacy while they ate. Afterwards, I sat on the chair opposite the bunks. 'Strictly, I'm supposed to keep this as an emergency ration,' I said. 'But would you like some chocolate?' I held out two blocks. They both looked at me, perhaps wondering what I required in return. Clumsily I said, 'Please . . . take it. I wish I could do more for – what I mean to say is . . . I hate seeing you forced to live in these conditions; to eat this food . . . it's—'

'So unfair?'

'Dammit, yes, it is!'

Rowena gave a tired smile. 'This is our life now.' She looked round. 'This is home . . . we must make the best of it. But thank you for the chocolate. I don't think either Marni or I have tasted it in the last ten years.' She took the chocolate bars and, handing one to her sister, said, 'Marni. Would you bring us all a drink, please?'

Marni moved nimbly across the room to the still. There she poured generous measures into three cups. I couldn't understand it. Rowena seemed to be completely without self-pity. With something close to serenity she simply gazed at me as I tried to disentangle myself verbally from the guilt I was feeling, telling her that Torrence was despicable and that to force people into slavery was nothing less than evil.

Marni placed the mug of liquor beside me on the floor, then sat down by her sister. For a moment both of them seemed uncertain about how best to eat the chocolate. But as soon as they tasted the first morsel they quickly devoured the lot. I wished sincerely that I had more for them.

Meanwhile I stammered on, feeling a scalding mixture of guilt and anger. 'But surely people in the rest of Manhattan can't condone keeping you here in these appalling conditions?'

'They don't know. It's as simple as that.'

'But word of what it's like here *must* get out. What about the truck drivers who move goods from the north of the island to the south?'

'Our masters are very careful. All goods are shipped to warehouses on the boundary at night, using slave labour here. In the morning free workers from south of the Parallel load the goods onto trucks for distribution in the city. Clever practice, isn't it?'

'So the two labour forces never meet?'

'Never. For all the people in the south know, the warehouses are magically filled each night by some fairy godmother.'

'But don't people in the city ever question what goes on up here?'

'Some do. Like Marni here, when she was a student. But to do that is to risk winding up here yourself. And if that happens to you, then it's like dying and going to hell.' Rowena shrugged. 'You know that you're never going to return and that you're never going to see or communicate with your family ever again.' She sipped the liquor. 'In reality, some of those in the city must have an inkling of what lies above the Parallel, that it's a prison of sorts, but when has the public ever taken a keen interest in the workings of jails? Like waste disposal or the process of getting cattle to your plate in the form of roast beef, you tend not to think about it too deeply.'

I burned with the injustice of it.

'Tell us about your own life, David,' she said. 'What is your home like?'

Two green gazes fixed on mine. Both uncannily alike. Once more I half believed that these were some supernaturally altered forms of Kerris Baedekker looking at me. One had an unearthly yet delicate beauty. The other had a face cruelly scarred by that diagonal crimson slash.

It was hard not to make life on the Isle of Wight seem like paradise when I described the rolling downs, the fresh sea air, my family home tucked away in the fertile green heart of the island. I told them about my own history. They even smiled with amusement at my account of some of my exploits as a child, which at one point had resulted in the spectacular demolition of my father's laboratory.

And, in truth, I warmed to my room-mates. As we talked I saw a lively spirit slowly revealing itself in both of them. Marni's poor scarred face had suddenly broken into a touchingly beautiful smile. Rowena's sense of humour arose from some deep interior wellspring. If only I could have spirited these two away to my home-land they would have become fully functioning human beings again. Good food, rest, fresh air and the simple freedoms we enjoyed would restore them. I was positive of that.

I watched them as they drank the liquor from the still. Whatever it tasted like it had some restorative effect. A little colour came to Rowena's face. Marni became more animated. At last she noticed my untouched cup. She pointed at it, then mimed drinking.

Nodding and smiling, I raised the cup to my lips.

Ten minutes later my eyes were still streaming. Then I heard a thunderous clanging sound coming from the hallway.

CHAPTER THIRTY SEVEN

. . . And So Like Orpheus

Raised voices accompanied the clanging. Still wiping my eyes after swallowing the fiery spirit, I rushed out into the corridor. It thronged with the Blind, demanding to know what was amiss. Down the hallway I could see the concierge hobbling towards the gate that was the source of the clanging sound. Being tall enough to look over the heads of people in front of me I could see a red-faced man in a black peaked cap. He was belabouring the gate with a staff.

'Let me in, woman!' he bellowed. 'Let me in now, or I'll order my men to fire.'

The old woman did as she was told. I could see the upper half of the gate above the milling heads swing open with a crash.

'Out of the way . . . get out of the way!'

The man in the cap forced a passage through. The Blind in front of me were forced back. A woman tripped in the crush. Quickly, I pulled her to her feet to stop her being trampled.

By this time I'd been pushed back past the door of my room. Now I could see that the men forcing the Blind back were police. These, however, only superficially resembled the neatly turned out officers I'd seen on my first arrival in New York. The officers here were brutish-looking individuals. Uniforms were sweat-stained and badly fitting. These cops carried either fearsome-looking batons or shotguns. And clearly they were in no mood to dally. As they herded the Blind back deeper into the hallway it occurred to me for the first time that they were here for me. Perhaps they'd been tipped off by one of the apartment block's residents that a party of strangers had arrived. Maybe the police were here to make a search for the mysterious intruders.

I bent my knees to bring my head lower than those around me. At the same time I deliberately allowed my eyes to glaze over as I did my best to act the part of a blind man. I groped at the walls while moving back towards the shelter of the parlour.

The police began to kick open doors in their search. Anyone straying into their way was brutally shoved aside.

'Have a good look round!' bellowed the officer in charge. 'This is the place!'

The red-faced officer reached the door of the room that I'd shared with the two girls.

'Ah,' he said, pleased with himself. 'In here, men. The snitch was right.'

At that moment I thought about trying to find some back way out of the property. Even a window would do.

Red-face stood back and waved his men through into the room. 'Go to it,' he boomed. 'But be bloody careful.

No, lad. Easy with it, easy. Unscrew the piping first. No, don't bother with the mash . . . dump it out onto the bloody floor.'

With the police now in the room I edged forward to look inside.

Red-face stood with his hands on his hips, watching his men dismantle the still.

'Careful with them copper pipes.' Then he added, with good-natured brutality, 'If anyone dents them pipes I'll dent their bloody 'eads.' Strangely, there were broad Yorkshire vowel sounds mingled with the New York accent. No doubt there was an epic yarn in how that middle-aged Yorkshireman had reached New York. But what he was doing now was clear enough. This was no legitimate liquor bust. The officer was undoubtedly appropriating the still, together with every bottle of liquor in the place, for his own purposes.

Marni didn't take kindly to a policeman helping himself to a half-full bottle from the table by her bunk. She jumped up to stop him. The big man tussled briefly with the girl.

'Leave her alone!' Rowena hauled herself from the bunk to help her sister.

Without turning his head the man shoved her back onto the bunk. I saw her forearm whip out and crack against the bunk post. Instantly, her face crumpled with pain. Marni, her eyes blazing with fury, spat at the man's face.

He swore and raised the bottle like a club above her head.

'Bloody hell, 'Arry.' The red-faced man guffawed at his

colleague who was struggling with Marni. 'What yer flaming well playing with them lasses for?'

The man looked as if he was going to make some whiny complaint about Marni but Red-face clearly didn't have time for fun and games. 'Put 'er down, 'Arry – you don't know where she's been.' He pointed to another policeman. 'Now start taking this stuff down to the truck . . . and be bloody careful with it. I don't want to hear any bangs or breaking bottles. Treat 'em like you'd treat a bloody babby. 'Arry, leave 'er! Get on wi' shiftin' them bottles . . . no, start with the full ones, soft lad.'

The one known as Harry simply pushed Marni away. Scowling, he picked up a crate of bottles and headed for the door. I moved back again, once more adopting a sightless stare.

Meanwhile the concierge wailed, 'Leave us the booze. Why can't you leave us with some bottles . . . you don't need it all. Leave the bottles!'

'Shut it,' snapped Harry, still irked by his tussle with Marni.

After that a despondent silence settled on the occupants of the apartment block. They must have experienced all this before. The police raids. The bullying.

When the last man had left with the last case of liquor I went back to the room where Marni was tying a makeshift sling around Rowena's neck. Rowena herself looked sick with pain. She glanced up as I walked across the room.

'Are you all right?' I asked.

'Oh, I've gone and broken my arm,' she said as if it

were her own fault. 'Damn. I won't be able to work tomorrow.'

'Don't worry about work. You need to get your arm seen to.'

'There's someone here who'll set the bone . . . it's just that I won't get any vouchers now.'

'I'll see that you get food,' I told her.

'It's not just the food.' Suddenly she sounded weary beyond belief. 'I won't get the vouchers for my booster shots until I start work again.'

'Booster shots?' The penny dropped. 'Oh.' I recalled what Gabriel had told me about Torrence's policy of enslaving his work force with heroin. 'Oh, I see.'

She grimaced as the pain bit deep. 'It's a pity about the still. The drink would have taken the edge off all that cold turkey.'

By this time most of the building's occupants had moved off to their own rooms to contemplate their misfortune. One elderly man, however, looked at Rowena's arm. I winced at the sight of the kink between wrist and elbow where the bone had snapped.

'Make yourself as comfortable as you can,' he told her gently. 'I'll be back in a few minutes. I need to make some splints.'

'Thank you.'

I seethed at my impotence. How could I have stood there and watched those thugs do this? But what could I have done? They outnumbered me, they had guns. I had nothing.

Marni did what she could. She made Rowena lie down

on the bunk, then tenderly positioned a pillow under the broken arm.

Once more I rummaged through my rucksack. I thought I'd seen something earlier when I'd been handed my emergency food rations. Yes, there it was — a small cardboard box with a red cross on its lid.

'David? David Masen?'

I looked up to see Rowena regarding me.

'David,' she said. 'You've got to leave here now.'

'But—'

'Listen. It's not safe for you to stay.'

'The men came for the still.'

'Even though they weren't looking for you, how long before one of the officers remembers seeing a face that doesn't belong round here?'

'I'm sure they didn't get a good look at me.'

'David, come on now. They might have been pre-occupied with our little miracle machine and not break-ing any bottles but one of them's suddenly going to ask themself why there should be such a well-nourished young man round here. Believe me, they'll be back. And sooner rather than later.' She spoke so forcefully that she accidentally disturbed her arm. The pain made her grimace. 'And if you think you'll be a hero for sticking round, think again. We'll all do the fire walk if you're caught here.'

'OK.' I said. 'Just tell Sam Dymes what happened when he gets back.' I slipped on my flying jacket. 'I'll make my way back to the flying boats.'

'You won't find them by yourself . . . Marni.' She turned to her sister. 'Take David back to his aircraft.'

Marni nodded, then gestured at me to get a move on.

'OK. Take care of yourself, Rowena . . . and you'd best have this.' I handed her the first-aid kit. 'There's a couple of shots of morphine and a hypodermic. You know . . . if you need it.'

'Thank you, David. I appreciate it.'

On impulse I stooped down and kissed her. Right then I nearly did a stupid thing. I nearly told her I'd come back and get her and Marni out of there. And kick the backsides of those thuggish police for good measure. But I knew, as sure as eggs were eggs, that those were promises I'd never be able to keep.

'Goodbye, David. Now, please hurry.'

The concierge had anticipated this turn of events. Without a murmur she unlocked the gate and I followed Marni downstairs. Soon we were outside. In daylight I stood out like a man from Mars, so she pushed me back indoors, put her finger to her lips, then ran back down the hallway. Returning in a moment, she helped me into an evil-smelling overcoat; whether it was black from filth or dye I didn't know. She stepped back, her clear green gaze assessing the result. With a shake of her head to indicate that not enough had been done she crouched down on the hallway floor. She rubbed her palms on the tiles, then returned to me. Standing close up against me in the narrow hall, she now smeared those palms all over my face, paying particular attention to my forehead and nose.

Then she looked at me again, nodded that she was satisfied, grabbed me by the elbow and propelled me to the doorway. Now, suitably disguised, I walked quickly along the street. Marni strode beside me, a determined set to her jaw.

We did the previous day's journey in reverse. With the evening sun slanting along the street we slipped into the coal merchant's yard, then down into the old tunnel that had, long ago, been a conduit for coal from the Hudson River. Once again there was that eerie walk by lamplight through the echoing cavern.

At last I emerged, thankful to have seen the back of that cold tomblike place for good. I was thankful too soon.

For there, beside the aircraft hangar, were three of the boxlike vehicles. Policemen in their peaked caps swarmed in and out of the doorway. I even recognized the red-faced Yorkshireman. He saluted the arrival of a superior and ushered him delightedly into the hangar. So much for the flight home.

I turned to Marni who was watching the police with fury in her eyes.

'Marni,' I said, reaching a decision that I should have made hours ago. 'Can you take me south – into the city?'

CHAPTER THIRTY EIGHT

Frustration

Once more into the tunnel. Marni and I retraced our steps through that grim, dead cavern. I had expected to emerge again into the coal merchant's yard but instead she urged me on past the mass of rusting conveyor belts. After walking for a further quarter of an hour, the lamplight casting a sickly yellow puddle of light around us, she climbed up onto what appeared to be a station platform. Then she went towards a set of large timber doors. She pushed one open. Rusty hinges screamed in protest. There came a scuttling of claws on concrete as rats fled.

An ancient sign on a wall read: *NO UNAUTHORIZED PERSONNEL BEYOND THIS POINT – COLUMBIA UNIVERSITY.* Putting her fingers to her lips for silence, Marni moved lithe as a cat through the vast basements of the university. In the light of the lamp I glimpsed a boiler room with long-extinguished furnaces that sprouted networks of iron pipes.

She paused for a moment, contemplating a set of

gloomy corridors that appeared to run away into dark infinity. Ancient cables hung down like black vines, while heating pipes shrouded with cobwebs snaked along tunnels before abruptly turning off to burrow into walls.

I felt Marni's hand on my sleeve and we moved off once more. We'd gone perhaps another hundred yards when she pointed to a stairwell. I climbed up after her to emerge into a derelict building where we passed doors bearing the names of long-dead university professors. A moment later we emerged onto a broad street flanked by high buildings. My cherished hope that I'd find myself on the clean sidewalks of the city vanished in an instant. Road surfaces here were as thick with detritus as those in Harlem. People in rags still hurried by, carrying bundles. A girl of around nine laboured to push a handcart piled high with animal skins that dripped blood. Once more shops and cafés had been given over to industrial use. Men and women worked furiously over lathes, metal presses, saws.

I felt a thump on my side. Marni flashed me a warning look. Deliberately, she lowered her head as she walked along then glanced sideways at me to make sure that I'd adopted the same posture.

A sign told me that we were on Amsterdam Avenue, a once prosperous street that ran north-south through Manhattan. Another junction sign indicated that we'd reached 114th Street, the next said 113th. Now the descending order of street numbers informed us that we were moving south, which meant we weren't much more than half an hour's walk from 102nd Street where the twenty-foot-high prison wall divided New York City in two. Reaching the wall was the easy part. Finding a way through would be another matter entirely.

We passed a huge Gothic structure that could only have originally been a cathedral. Inside sat rows of the Blind. With great dexterity they all hammered at silvery pieces of metal. The noise from hundreds of people hammering was stupendous. It was all I could do to stop myself clamping my hands over my ears as we hurried by the open doorway.

Now I saw that the flow of people carrying bundles or pushing handcarts all seemed to be converging on one point. I recalled what Rowena had said about warehouses at the 102nd Street Parallel being stocked by slaves by night and emptied by the city workers by day.

Worryingly, there were also more policemen. True, most rode in cars or the boxy vans I'd seen before that were topped with perspex gun turrets. There were a few, however, on foot: these appeared to be on traffic duty. They directed human beasts of burden along certain paths to various collection points. A line of barefoot girls took it in turn to empty baskets of brightly coloured clothes-pegs into a large cart. I couldn't help but notice that two of the girls bore an uncanny resemblance to Kerris. Torrence's progeny dwelled in every city block – or so it appeared to me.

While all this appeared to be their customary practice I sensed that tonight a change had been made to their routine.

Standing by the cart were a pair of middle-aged women. Their clothes and smart shoes proclaimed in an instant that these ladies weren't normally resident in the ghetto. They were talking among themselves while watching the clothes-peg girls. Still walking with my head down I began to take a closer interest in what was happening there. The two women were making an assessment of the girls. Every now and again one of the women would single out a girl who'd be ordered to the edge of the road where a growing number of similarly chosen girls already stood. Girls not selected walked away with their now-empty baskets.

A furtive glance along the street told me that this selection process was happening elsewhere. Pairs of men and women with clipboards moved along the workshops, carefully looking at the workers. Now and again a girl or woman would be called out and ordered to stand in a given place at the roadside. I noticed Marni too casting inquisitive glances from beneath her mane of red hair. Something was most definitely up. But what?

For a moment I believed the choice of girls was arbitrary. But then I realized only the post-pubescent girls were being chosen. While women beyond their middle years were being passed over.

Two words came into my mind. *Operation Avalanche.* So it had started. Torrence's medical people were selecting women of childbearing age (although some were only barely that). Torrence's race of superhumans would, I figured, be making its debut some nine months from now.

My line of thought came to a sudden end.

'Hey! Wait. You there. Redhead. Stand still, girl.' Marni obeyed. She kept her head down, her gaze fixed on the ground. I copied her submissive posture. *Good God*, I thought, *it only takes one of the women to notice the quality of my boots, then the game's up.* I cast a sidelong glance at a policeman standing on the street corner, hands on his hips, a shotgun slung across his back. All I could do was wait for the woman in her smart shoes to say what she had to say before we could move on.

Curtly the woman snapped, 'Name and number?'

Marni continued to gaze down at the ground.

'Girl, I asked for your name and number.'

I felt a sinking sensation. This wasn't going well.

'Girl. Are you being insolent? If you are, you're—'

'She's mute,' I said quickly, while making my voice sound as servile as possible. 'Her name is Marni.'

'Yes?' The woman stood poised with her pen over the clipboard. 'And her number?'

'Her number?' I repeated dimly. 'I don't—'

'Oh, for goodness' sake, come here, girl.' The woman roughly grabbed a handful of Marni's hair and pulled her head up. She wrinkled her nose in distaste at Marni's scarred face. 'Oh, the ugly treatment, was it? Tongue as well? Open your mouth . . . yes. Well, we don't need you to have the use of your tongue or your face, do we, now?' The woman ticked a box on the sheet. 'Now turn round.' Roughly again, she grabbed the neckline of Marni's sweater and dragged it down, exposing her shoulder. 'Stand still, girl. I can't read it if you go bobbing about like that.'

Now I saw a long set of figures tattooed on the back of Marni's shoulder.

After copying the number onto her clipboard the

woman indicated a cluster of girls at the side of the street. 'Go stand over there. Do not move until I tell you otherwise.'

I began to follow Marni.

'Hey,' called the woman. I turned to look at her. 'We've no use for you, big guy. Go about your business.'

I looked down the street at the policeman. He wasn't looking this way yet, but I knew that he'd come quickly enough if the woman kicked up a fuss. Keeping my head down in the same servile way as those around me, I moved off up the street. As I did so, I glanced at Marni who'd gone to stand with the other girls. I mouthed *Wait*. She gave a nod.

Just ahead of me a bus pulled up and started taking girls on board from another group. Quite obviously, it was picking up groups of girls all down the street. Now I didn't have the luxury of thinking through a clear plan of action.

The moment I reached the sidewalk I doubled back towards Marni. If I lost her I doubted if I'd ever make it south into the city.

By this time the woman with her clipboard was busy taking down the particulars of a girl with a handcart. I prayed she wouldn't look in my direction.

I reached the knot of girls where Marni stood. Behind me the bus lumbered along the street, the engine sounding louder as it neared me. Without stopping I spoke to Marni.

'Marni. Walk ahead of me. Keep walking naturally. But if I shout "Run" – *run*.'

Nodding, she walked a few paces in front of me. Once more we kept our heads down.

'Girl. I told you to wait!'

The woman's indignant voice cut like a blade through the street sounds.

On the corner the policeman looked round to see what was happening.

'Officer!' shouted the woman. 'Stop the redhead!'

The heavy-set man was quick on the uptake. He marched forward and grabbed Marni's elbow in his massive fist. 'You stay here until I find out what's going on,' he told Marni. 'And damn' well stand still.' He didn't wait for her to acquiesce. With a vicious swipe of his hand he slapped her in the face, knocking her back on her heels. I closed the gap between myself and the policeman who was still holding on to Marni. She shook her head groggily. I saw a smear of blood on her lips.

For a split second I looked round at the people nearby. I discounted one after another as possible sources of help until I saw an old lady with a burden of iron rods. In a reflex action I drew one of the rods from her basket and brought it down as hard as I could onto the policeman's head.

He never even saw it coming. With a coughing grunt he toppled into the mud. Marni looked down at the felled man in dazed disbelief.

Immediately I heard shouts, while the woman with the clipboard began a screaming fit that got shriller and shriller.

'Come on!' I grabbed Marni's arm. 'Run!'

We hared off down the street. Across the road another policeman shouted through the doorway of one of the square trucks. I saw the perspex turret on top of the vehicle revolve smoothly until the machine-gun barrel was pointing at us.

'Faster!' I yelled. At that moment several rounds whined past my head. The wall alongside me suddenly appeared to fizz as bullets pulverized chunks of brick.

The police gunner had fired high. He wouldn't make the same mistake twice.

Panic turned the street into a seething, terrified mass of people who shouted, ran, spilt the contents of their baskets. In front of me a man writhed on the pavement, clutching his head where a ricochet had caught him.

Marni scrambled through an open doorway. I followed. I found myself in a long room where the Blind had been making stuffed toy animals. Now, startled by the gunfire, they turned their heads, searching for the source of the sound.

'Keep moving,' I called to Marni. 'There must be a back way out of here.'

Once we were in the building, and out of sight, it would have been common sense for the gunner to hold his fire. He did not. He fired a burst through the open doorway. One of the toymakers fell back, his chest smouldering where an incendiary tracer bullet had ripped through his clothing. Workers shouted in panic before scrambling outside through the front doorway.

The machine gun rattled furiously. I glanced back to see bullet-torn bodies falling into the gutter.

Marni thought more clearly than me. Instead of dwelling on the tragedy she gave me a forceful shove towards the doorway at the back of the workshop.

Not pausing now, I raced through a storeroom full of

staring dolls' heads, then half tumbled out of a doorway into a rear alleyway where a dozen or so puzzled men and women walked with their bundles and handcarts. They'd heard the shooting but clearly didn't know what was happening or where the gunfire was coming from.

With the speed of an athlete Marni raced ahead of me. Whatever the destination, whatever the outcome, all I could do was follow.

CHAPTER THIRTY NINE

To The Deep

'Stop!'

We did no such thing. Before the officer who'd sprung up in front of us could bring his shotgun to bear we dodged down another alley.

This wasn't a wise choice. For lumbering towards us came another armoured truck. The eyes of the driver blazed as he accelerated, bearing down on us. Marni was ready to run away from the vehicle but I urged her to run *towards* it. I gambled that the gunner in his turret on top of the truck wouldn't be able to depress the gun muzzle far enough to hit us if we were too close.

The gun barked and a tracer round flew high enough over our heads to tell me that we were safe from the machine gun — at least, for the time being. The lumbering truck was another matter. It looked as if its driver had decided simply to run us down.

'Climb over the fence,' I called to Marni. We both vaulted over as the truck loomed over us. A moment later we found ourselves in a walled garden that was full of milling goats.

I glanced back; the perspex bubble of the gun turret stood higher than the fence. Once more it revolved smoothly to bring the gun to bear on us.

Marni needed no urging. Like lightning she climbed the wall of the adjoining garden. I followed, dropping down into a mass of potato plants as bullets hungrily chewed the coping stones. We paused for breath while the gunner took the opportunity to blast the other side of the wall and test the thickness of the brickwork. No doubt he hoped the heavy machine-gun rounds would punch clear through and kill us both.

Fortunately, some long-dead builder hadn't skimped. The wall held firm even though the bullets loosened a blizzard of mortar on our side. Marni looked at me and I nodded. We moved on, keeping as low as possible. Although I could no longer see it, I heard the police truck reversing along the alleyway as the turret gunner looked over walls and fences into the gardens for any sign of us. This time, however, we took care to remain out of sight. Using chicken coops, rabbit hutches and an assortment of bushes as cover we worked our way from garden to garden. If there were any of the tenement's residents about I didn't see them. They'd heard gunfire. Now they were keeping indoors until the trouble had passed.

Halfway along the rear of the tenement Marni noticed a passageway to the main street at the front of the block. She grabbed my hand and pulled me through.

It was much like any other street in that vast prison

camp. People carrying bundles. A road surface slick with mud. A row of workshops with the workers still at full stretch — sewing, smelting, chiselling wood, weaving rugs, boiling animal fat for candles.

Where we were I didn't know, though fortunately the streetwise Marni did. We made our way quickly along the street, then into another network of alleyways. By this time dusk had begun to slip into night. Street lights flickered on as Marni pulled me towards a large Gothic-looking pile set in a line of four-storey buildings. Upon entering it I immediately recognized it as a church that had long ago been gutted by fire, leaving the roof open to the night sky. In the shattered stained-glass windows there still remained sad fragments of angels and saints.

I followed Marni over the debris, exiting from a door at the back of the church. Now I found myself in a graveyard that had been turned over to pigs that snorted and rooted muddily at the ground. At the edge of the graveyard Marni stopped me, then pointed over a wall.

Cautiously, I looked over. For a moment the brilliance of the lights dazzled me. Then I saw it. A twenty-foot-high barrier of concrete, brilliantly floodlit, ran to my left and to my right as far as the eye could see. On this side (the prison side) buildings nearest to the wall had been razed to the ground in order to create a strip of open land running alongside it. In turn, this was fenced with barbed wire. I scanned the top of the wall. Every couple of hundred yards I could see guard towers. If I were to have hoped that those towers were unmanned, my level of optimism would have been that of a lunatic. To underline that thought I saw a police car draw up at one of the towers. Two men clambered out of the back and climbed the steps into the tower. A moment later two other men came out — time for the changing of the guard.

For what seemed a long time I gazed at the fortress-like wall. It lay perhaps fifty yards from me. Beyond that were the bright lights and creature comforts of New York City. I could even hear the traffic. Aromas from some high-quality restaurant just beyond the wall reached my nostrils. Somewhere, maybe no more than a short walk away, would be Kerris Baedekker.

At that moment the truth struck me. That city with all its lights, its noise, its hustle and bustle and its thousands of cars was a fraud, a confidence trick perpetrated by Torrence. He squandered precious resources at such a rate that it would soon lead to the city's ruin. Like a bankrupt spending money he didn't have in order to impress others, he *bought* the loyalty of its free citizens with what amounted to shiny trinkets — whether they were cars, colour televisions, radio stations galore, or the latest chic evening gown. The sounds of New York still reached me, but all I truly heard now was the hollow clang of an empty vessel.

I looked at Marni who gazed at the wall with something like awe. 'What now, Marni? Do we go underground again to get to the other side?'

She shook her head. I followed as she made off again. This time her route took us parallel to the wall. However, she took care to stay in the shadow of derelict buildings. With the absence of street sounds our footfalls seemed unnaturally loud. Time and again I glanced back, sure I'd heard footsteps following us. But it was only the echo of our own feet. After a while the urban wasteland ended. I entered the northern quarter of Central Park, which had been sliced off by the concrete wall. Here, strangely, there were tranquil fields of barley, potato and beet. A sheep bleated somewhere off in the gloom. By the time I reached the far side of the park, moving once more through urban dereliction, my legs had begun to ache mercilessly. 'How much farther?' I asked the tireless Marni.

She gave a little wave of both hands, which I interpreted as *not long now*.

Even so, I still didn't see how we were going to scale that wall. I had spotted a number of gates but they appeared to be firmly locked. What was more, guard towers overlooked every inch of the wall. If there wasn't some subterranean route then this, as the New Yorkers would say, had me beat.

The time was close to midnight when we suddenly reached the end of the wall.

I found myself looking out onto an expanse of river. The wall itself ended a few yards beyond the water's edge. However, by means of a timber boom and a heck of a lot of barbed wire the barrier had been extended some twenty yards further into the water.

I felt my heart sink. 'How are we going to do this, Marni?'

She looked at me, her green eyes bright in the reflected floodlighting. Then she gave a shrug as if to say *Do you mean you haven't worked it out for yourself yet?*

'Marni, no, not in there. I don't think it's possible.'

She nodded eagerly, then mimed a swimming action.

I bit my lip. 'I was afraid you were going to do that.'

She walked to the water's edge but I stopped her. 'No, not yet. Let's see if there's a better way.' I pointed along the river bank, away from the concrete wall that seemed as unscalable as a sheer cliff face. 'Let's see if we can find a boat or something,' I said. 'Even an oil drum would be better than taking our chances in that completely unprotected.'

She nodded, a trifle reluctantly. No doubting that the kid had guts, I told myself. She was all for plunging in and swimming round the barrier. I was uneasy, though. I recalled from my excursions with Kerris that here we were on the eastern edge of Manhattan Island, so this had to be the Harlem River near where it ran into the East River at the ominously named Hell Gate. And that was no frivolous label for an ordinary stretch of water. Without warning the Hell Gate could become a swirling maelstrom of rip tides and killer currents that could sweep even the strongest swimmer into the great watery hereafter.

Besides, I remembered the aquatic triffid plants in Columbus Pond just a few days ago. I didn't relish finding out what lurked in *these* muddy waters.

A search of the river bank revealed no boat. Once more Marni mimed a swimming stroke. I shook my head.

We headed back into the streets. There had to be something here we could use. I walked along an alleyway, peering into back gardens and yards. Presently I heard the sound of sawing. Homing in on the sound, I came to a workshop. By lamplight a swarthy man sawed at planks of wood. Behind him stood a partially assembled wardrobe.

What caught my eye in particular were half a dozen plastic sacks filled with sawdust. I signalled to Marni to hide in the shadows.

I only had to wait a moment or so before the opportunity came. The swarthy man walked to a doorway and hollered through it. 'Joe . . . Joe! You ready with that coffee yet?' The carpenter listened to a distant voice. 'What's that? Joe, you said you'd be ten minutes, man. It's closer to half an hour. I got to get this furniture done for shipment or I'm not going to get my shot. There's no way I can do that if you don't keep that coffee coming. Hell, man, I'm dryer than dust out here. If you're not going to pull your weight, then I'm going to see you don't get no food. D'ya hear me, Joe?' While the carpenter berated the unseen Joe I grabbed two sacks of sawdust. Then I returned to Marni. 'OK,' I told her. 'Let's get back to the river.'

'Just do what I do,' I said.

Marni nodded, her green gaze serious.

I emptied the plastic sack full of sawdust onto the river bank. She followed suit. Then, quickly stripping off my clothes, I stuffed them into the sack. After I'd pulled the laces out of my boots I put the boots into the sack, too.

This was no time for false modesty. Nevertheless, I made sure I looked Marni in the eye as I said, 'Now tie up the end of the sack with the lace. Make sure it's good and tight . . . no. Don't squeeze the air out of the bag. Make sure there's plenty in. It should be inflated when you tie it . . . good, that's it. Ready?'

She nodded. There was a determined set to her jaw.

I stepped into the water. It was flipping cold. I gritted my teeth. Moving deeper, I tried to ignore the sharp gravel beneath my feet. All the time I scanned the river. It looked particularly dark and somehow evil at this time of night – a deeply sinister abyss oozing with dreadful, nameless horrors.

I realized that more of those water-dwelling triffids might be lurking under the surface. Yet, somewhat rashly, I gambled that the plants either hadn't spread this far or that they favoured the still waters of a lake. From the pull that I could feel round my bare legs the current of the Harlem River was decidedly fierce.

I glanced at Marni. Her skin showed a near-luminous white in the gloom. She gasped and sucked in her stomach at the shock of the cold.

'Don't worry,' I told her. 'We shouldn't be in here long.'

She nodded.

I glanced into her face. In the dark the scar had vanished. What I did notice were her beautiful eyes. They were absolutely trusting. I gritted my teeth and asked myself what fresh dangers I was getting her into.

Something slithered round my knee. I froze instantly. The water was too dark and too muddy to see anything. But I knew I'd felt it. Something smooth and slippery had just brushed against my bare skin.

At any moment I expected to see a sting lash up from the water.

I stood there, stock-still, not breathing, my heart thudding in my chest. Whatever had brushed against me didn't return. It might have been river weed or even an eel. Then again, I didn't want to dwell too closely on what might lurk in that filthy-looking goo.

'Here goes, Marni.' I mustered what remained of my confidence. 'Don't swim yet. Just let the current carry you downriver past the wall. Now, put your arm round the sack and allow it to keep you afloat. OK?'

She nodded, smiling tightly.

'Right. Easy does it. And stay close to me. We've got to keep each other in sight.'

The cold water rising over my body made me clench my jaw. I heard Marni give a stuttering gasp as she lowered herself deeper into the river.

The plastic sack grew taut beneath my arm as it took my weight. Beside me the plastic sack that Marni held gleamed silver. I only hoped the guards on the wall wouldn't notice. A few well-aimed rifle shots would soon put paid to us.

I found I had to paddle slowly with my free arm to keep alongside Marni. And I was right about that current; in moments it had carried us out towards the middle of the channel. Some twenty feet below us would be the slick bed of the river, seething with whatever noxious things had made their home there. In no time at all we were borne downstream, past the boom extension of the wall. Now I could see the bright lights of the city itself. Cars streamed along its roads. I could even see people strolling along a riverside promenade. Night owls were having fun.

Meanwhile, for Marni and I, just fifty yards from the bustling waterfront, the river sucked at our bodies, turning us round, threatening to roll us over and pull us down.

'Grab my hand,' I panted. 'I can't keep close to you.'

Marni raised her hand above the surface of the water. I grabbed it. Held it tight. Now she nodded at the sack I clutched.

It had deflated a little and I looked down to see a stream of bubbles pouring from a nick in the plastic. Nodding, I turned the sack over and gathered the slack plastic into my fist where the gash bled air.

'We'll have to get to the shore,' I whispered. 'I don't want the current to push us across to the other side.' I didn't add that the banks across the water from Manhattan were a congested mass of triffids.

We began to swim, pushing the sacks full of clothes in front of us. Once again something smooth slid across the bare flesh of my belly, nearly fetching a yell from my lips. With a Herculean effort I kept my mouth shut. But shivers like pointed insect feet prickled up my spine and through my hair.

As I swam I expected teeth to sink suddenly into my leg or even, irrationally, a slimy hand to break the surface in front of me and clutch my throat.

But the night swimmer didn't return. We pushed on. I pointed to some bushes over-hanging the water. 'Make for those,' I whispered. 'We should be out of sight of the road.'

The last few yards took a long, long while to cover. A strong current tugged us back, and all the time I expected that invisible denizen of the river to lunge out of the water at my face.

Marni swam hard, the white gleam of the soles of her feet just ahead of me. Moments later I felt something sharp buffet my knees. It came again. I shoved my hand under the water to fend it off — and struck solid stone.

Grateful to have the ground beneath my feet again, I climbed out of the river to join Marni. Exhausted, I sat beside her as she squeezed water from her hair. I'd begun to fumble with the wet bootlace that tied the sack when Marni nudged me, then nodded out at the water.

In the gloom I saw a smooth rounded shape break the surface of the river. It was a glossy liquorice-black. I glimpsed a dorsal fin. Then there came the sound of pent-up breath being released; white vapour flickered briefly above the water.

So there was my monster, my denizen of the deep.

With a smile (and a massive sense of relief) I said, as much to myself as to Marni, 'It's only a harbour porpoise.'

Although I barely had time to enjoy any feeling of deliverance because at that moment an arm abruptly emerged from the bushes to hold the blade of a lethal-looking bowie knife at my throat. More arms appeared to seize Marni and drag her into the shadows.

CHAPTER FORTY

Something Wicked
This Way Comes . . .

Bundled from the water's edge we were dragged deeper into the bushes. I felt the knife blade pricking my skin. I sensed that any stupid movement I might make would be my last.

A hand grabbed my jaw, pulling my face up towards the light from the street filtering through the branches.

'What should we do with these two lovebirds?' whispered a voice.

'Kill them.'

'But—'

'And be quick about it. Use the knife.'

From another direction came a third whispering voice. 'Wait. I've seen that guy's face somewhere before.'

'So?'

'Hey, it's the guy who flew us here . . . the English guy . . . ahm . . . Masen. That's it: Masen.'

'Are you sure?'

'Yeah, positive.'

More muttered conferring took place. One voice whispered, 'Wait here. I'll be right back.'

'Right back' seemed to take a good half-hour. Meanwhile, our captors kept a grip on us. I saw a glittering knife held to Marni's throat, too. Still soaking wet, I felt myself growing numb with cold.

At last there came a rustling in the bushes.

A voice whispered, 'Sacramento.'

My captor replied with a hissed 'Berlin.'

More people pushed forward into the bushes. Then a familiar if surprised voice asked, 'David? What on Earth are you doing here?' The hand gripping my jaw released me. I turned to see Gabriel Deeds looking at both Marni and myself in astonishment. A slow grin spreading across his face, he added, 'And why are you naked?'

Quickly, I told Gabriel what happened, including the grim news that the authorities had found our flying boats. As I talked I gratefully pulled my clothes from the sack and put them on. Marni did the same.

Gabriel clicked his tongue when he heard about the planes. 'We'll have to find some other route home. But first things first. We'll get you to another safe house until all this is over.'

'You'll do no such thing. I'm a participant in this venture now. A full and active participant. I'm going to find Kerris and get her out of this place.'

'If she wants to leave.'

'Well, I'm going to hear that decision from her own lips.'

Gabriel nodded. 'OK. But we can't do anything until

tomorrow afternoon. All our units are lying doggo until zero hour.'

'Zero hour?'

'That's when the fireworks start. I'll explain later.'

I pulled my flying boots on over my still-damp feet. 'But how did you get down here past the wall?'

'We went underground again.' He glanced at Marni. 'But I guess your guide didn't know about that particular route.' A small smile touched his lips. 'It would have saved you getting your feet wet . . . as well as sparing your modesty.'

With that, he motioned us to follow him. 'Watch where you're walking. The sappers were setting charges down here when they saw you two frolicking in the river.' He nodded to a concrete block of a building not thirty paces away. 'Anti-aircraft installation, so *shhh*.' He put his fingers to his lips.

Once we were clear of the bushes I saw that the sappers and Gabriel were wearing casual civilian clothes, enabling them to blend in with the ordinary New Yorkers. Gabriel glanced at Marni's ragged clothes and muttered something to one of the sappers who removed his sweater and handed it to Marni. She pulled it on over her own, concealing its rips and darned holes. The borrowed sweater was absurdly long but at least she looked less like an escapee from the slave camp.

As it was, we didn't have much of a walk. We'd barely gone a block before Gabriel indicated a door beside a still brightly lit café. He tapped on the door. It opened an inch or so. Then, when the man on the other side had satisfied himself about Gabriel's identity, he opened the door fully.

Beyond lay a flight of steps. Gabriel led the way downward to a large basement room. Bales of paper filled half of it. Elsewhere there were makeshift beds on a platform of bales. In one corner someone had stacked cases of canned food and bottled water.

'Help yourself to supper,' Gabriel invited us with a wave of his hand. 'It's baked beans cold from a can, I'm afraid. But there's plenty of apple pie and cream.' He smiled. 'I thought we should buy in a good stock just in case Sam Dymes drops by.'

'Where is he?'

Gabriel gave a shrug. 'Away on business.'

I looked at Marni. She'd recovered enough from the night swim to eat a hearty supper of cold beans.

By this time it was three a.m. Over the next three-quarters of an hour more sappers returned from their missions. Straightaway they'd pull off their shoes, then retire to the makeshift beds.

Gabriel handed blankets out to Marni and myself. Then he said simply, 'Big day tomorrow, David. You best get some rest.'

I remember thinking quite clearly as I lay down on the lumpy mattress of paper bales that the one thing I wouldn't be able to do was sleep.

But barely had I closed my eyes, or so it seemed, then I opened them to see Gabriel crouching beside me. Sunlight streamed in from a glazed grating set above my head.

'There's some coffee,' Gabriel said, his face serious. 'Grab a cup, then come over to the table. There're a few details I need to share with you.'

I joined him at the table. Above my head tramping feet on the glazed grille told me that the people of Manhattan were going about their business as on any other day. I glanced to a wall where a clock hung from a nail. Chalked beside it was a message to the unit bivouacked here: *Synch Your Watches To This Time.* The clock showed that the time was just a little before ten. I'd slept late. Marni smiled and waved to me from where she sat eating from a can. Pleasingly, she'd been given new clothes, while her long red hair shone from what must have been a damn' good brushing. Apart from the scar running across her face she would easily have melted into the city's smart set.

Gabriel unfolded a map. 'OK,' he said. 'It all happens this afternoon at five . . . that's the start of the rush hour. Cars will jam the streets. Workers will be crowding the sidewalks and subways as they head home.' He pointed at the map. It showed the characteristic carrot shape of the island of Manhattan. 'We're here, on the Upper East Side. We know that Christina Schofield and Kerris Baedekker are in the Empire State Building.'

'Does Kerris knows what's happening?'

'She knows that *something* will happen. But she has no details yet. Torrence has instructed her to be Christina's room-mate to make sure she's happy and entertained before her . . .' He grimaced. 'Operation.'

'I saw girls being taken off the streets north of the Parallel yesterday. I guessed that was the start of it.'

'You guessed right, David. Any woman capable of bearing a child will be impregnated. North of the Parallel it's mandatory. Down here in the city it will just be considered patriotic . . . but I figure any woman not volunteering to play host to one of Christina's embryos will be coming under lots of pressure to do so. Now . . . after the debacle of the last attempt to bring Christina out by submarine Torrence has gone all cagey on us.'

'So Christina won't be moved out to a hospital?'

'No. Torrence has ordered that a suite of offices near the top of the Empire State be converted into a clinic, complete with its own operating theatre. Once Christian's ovaries have been surgically removed they will be shipped to hospitals and maternity clinics ready for the implantation programme.'

'So how do we get into the building to bring Christina out?'

'Good question.' Gabriel assumed a thoughtful pose, his eyes troubled. 'A very good question. We know that it isn't going to be easy. Torrence is very sensitive about his own safety. In buildings immediately surrounding the Empire State he has the bulk of Manhattan's armed forces on permanent standby. They're backed up by tanks and armoured cars. Meanwhile he has his own bodyguard – the Guardsmen – based inside his building. They're a ruthless bunch of thugs who do his dirty work for him.'

'We've got around sixty Marines. You think we're really going to be able to fight our way into what amounts to a fortress?'

'No, we can't simply hammer our way in by brute force.' Gabriel tapped a hefty finger on the map. 'Sam Dymes believes our only chance of success is to draw the bulk of Torrence's army to the far south of the island, down here in TriBeCa and Lower Manhattan. He's going to use a strong detachment of Marines, sappers and undercover operatives to strike at the shoreline gun batteries to make Torrence believe this is the prelude to a big seaborne invasion.' Gabriel gave a grim smile. 'Believe it or not, one of our secret weapons is Manhattan's rush hour. The streets will be choked with cars when we launch the attack on the big guns down there on the river banks. Torrence's tanks and armoured cars will have to travel all the way down from Midtown to Lower Manhattan. The distance is no more than a couple of miles but with luck — and a little more mischief on our part — it will take them an hour to get through the traffic.'

'But even so, our Marines are only armed with machine guns at best. They won't stand a chance against tanks.'

'That's why as soon as the Marines see them arrive they'll disengage their diversionary attack, then head back on foot to the Empire State Building. Oh, and the streets through Greenwich Village are a tad on the narrow side, and we'll leave a few sappers there to mess up the traffic a little more.'

I looked at the plan. On paper it seemed sound. But something Gabriel had said came back to me. 'You told me that the rush-hour traffic was one of our secret weapons. What's the other?'

'They don't call us The Foresters for nothing,' Gabriel said. 'For years we've used the triffids as an important line of defence against Torrence. Now we're going to use them again.'

'How?'

'See these bridges across the East River? Each one is sealed shut with a thirty-foot fence. We've set explosives to blow those fences sky-high at five o'clock sharp.'

I gave a low whistle.

Gabriel went on: 'Torrence's people are going to have to contend with a lot of mean triffid plants when they come stomping over the bridges into Manhattan. And every Torrence soldier we can draw away from the Empire State makes our prime objective that little bit easier.'

'Gabe,' I said, 'there are tens of thousands of men, women and children on this island. They are innocent people who have nothing to do with Torrence's regime. You're going to have their blood on your hands.'

Gabriel disagreed. 'New Yorkers have a contingency plan. When the alarms sound – and they will be screaming all over this damn' city, just you wait and see – then folk will, if they're away from home, take to the subway tunnels for cover. Once the electricity for the rail system is cut off they can accommodate thousands. Trust me, David. The general population will be safe.'

I took a breath. The idea of encouraging triffids to rampage through a hitherto safe area ran seriously against the grain for me. 'Anything else I should know?'

'Only that there are a few more surprises in store.'

'Such as?'

'Ah, those, David Masen, are kept secret even from me.'

Indeed, there were surprises to come. But not all of them were planned by the very able Sam Dymes.

CHAPTER FORTY ONE

Zero Hour

The build-up to five o'clock that afternoon passed slowly. A painful slowness that the leaden ticking of the clock on the wall did nothing to alleviate.

By midday most of the unit that had been camping in the basement had left for their respective destinations. I whiled away the time with Marni. She'd found a travel-chess set that had been left by one of the sappers. By the third game, when her queen, rook and bishop were again crowding my king into a corner, I didn't complain when Gabriel said, 'Right, David. Time to kit out.' He nodded towards a packing case from which an assortment of muzzles pointed at the ceiling. 'You know how to handle a sub-machine gun and grenades?'

I told him I did.

'Good. Take your pick. The Ingram's the lightest to carry but the old M3A1 packs more of a punch. Oh.' He'd remembered a detail. 'Later, when the balloon goes up, if someone you don't know shouts the word "Sacramento" at you, answer "Berlin". Otherwise they're likely to shoot you dead.'

A useful bit of information. I hoped I'd remember it when the time came.

Five o'clock. Rush hour. The sound of traffic grew louder outside. More feet pitter-pattered over the glazed grille. What I did not hear were any explosions. Nor the gunfire of Foresters attacking gun batteries down in the south of Manhattan.

Gabriel Deeds must have read my thoughts. 'We're too far away to hear any of the bridge gates being blown. Which will make life easier for us for the time being. Ready?'

I nodded.

Apart from Marni, Gabriel and myself there were five Foresters. All carried weapons concealed in a variety of ways, either in bags or musical instrument cases. Gabriel carried a sub-machine gun and a satchel of grenades in a guitar case. My sub-machine gun found a snug but temporary home in a canvas holdall.

Gabriel addressed everyone. 'OK. It's five. The attacks will have started. It'll take at least a few minutes for the news to be made public. So, for the time being, when we go up onto the street, spread out, walk in pairs . . . and I mean *walk*. Look as if you're just wanting to get home after a long day at the office.' He nodded to each of us in turn. 'And good luck. I want to see every one of you people going home. Right-oh, Benjamin, lead us out.'

Soon we were on our way. By the time we arrived at the Empire State the assault by the Foresters on the building should be nearing its objective. After that, our orders were short and simple – disturbingly so. We were to regroup, then head north to the 102nd Street Parallel. From there we had somehow to recapture our flying boats for the journey home. With a growing sense of unease, I realized that not only might we be fighting all the way back to the riverside hangar, there was also a good chance that Torrence's men guarding the planes might simply have removed the engine leads or cut the control cables, thus crippling the aircraft. If that happened we were well and truly stranded. What then? I only hoped that Sam Dymes had a contingency plan tucked up that long sleeve of his.

I turned my attention back to the street. Cars and pedestrians crowded along it. It looked like any other rush hour I'd experienced in New York. But just a few miles away, I knew, a fierce battle for control of the gun batteries had erupted.

Beside me, Marni walked with her head down, trying hard to conceal her scarred face with her long red hair. Just a little ahead, Gabriel moved with that long easy stride of his.

'Hey, Gabe!' The call came from a cab driver in his car. 'Haven't seen you in weeks . . . what ya bin doin' with yourself?'

Tension tightened my stomach muscles. Gabriel must be a wanted man in New York. If he was recognized by a cop then the shooting match might start sooner rather than later. Casually, Gabriel stooped towards the window of the cab. Smiling, relaxed, he exchanged a few words with the driver, then pointed at his watch. I guessed he was telling the man he was in a hurry. But by that time a green traffic light was showing anyway and the line of traffic rumbled away.

Gabriel continued walking. But I saw that he now paid more attention to the people in cars and to those around him on the sidewalk. He even raised the guitar case towards his chest as if ready to flick open the lid at a second's notice.

I pulled the zip down a little on the holdall. Glancing down I saw the glint of gunmetal. I eased the zip back to make sure a passer-by didn't see the gun. But at that moment I knew I was ready to start shooting if I had to.

Traffic still rumbled around us. Once more it looked like nothing more than a typical weekday rush hour. People sat over coffees in diners. A boy sold newspapers on a street corner. Traffic lights ran their sequences from red to green to red again. Illuminated signs on street corners flashed their familiar *Walk . . . Don't Walk*. We moved with the flow of pedestrians.

At that moment I told myself: *Something's gone wrong. They've called off the attack. It's all gone to hell.*

Yet still Gabriel walked about twenty yards ahead. Behind me the other Foresters walked in ones and twos, trying to look part of the crowds.

Because of the tension, my mouth had dried so much by the time we reached Fifth Avenue that my tongue felt as though it had been welded to its roof. By now, I could clearly see the Empire State around four hundred yards away. A shimmering tower in the late afternoon sun, it stood aloof and apparently tranquil above the bustling city streets.

Certainly there was no sign of an armed assault on the place in progress. All I could hear were the cars, the call of bagel vendors, music blaring through the open door of a clothes store. Still not so much as a single gunshot.

Meanwhile, Gabriel could have been a man making for home with nothing more than a cold beer on his mind. But just as I was beginning to think that I'd arrive at the base of the Empire State Building to find the place going about its business as usual there was sudden pandemonium.

I saw Gabriel react. He stopped suddenly, then looked sharply back at me. I didn't like the expression on his face. A mixture of shock and bewilderment. I hurried forward, looking for the source of the sudden outbreak of screaming. Then I saw it.

It had nothing to do with what might or might not be happening at the Empire State Building. Instead a wave of people were charging out from one of the cross streets.

A yellow cab roared down the sidewalk, sounding its horn. A truck tried to weave through traffic but struck a bus. While people on foot were fleeing from something I couldn't see, all of them running and stumbling in the same direction. I watched in astonishment as this flood of humanity streamed across Fifth Avenue to vanish into the streets opposite. This made no sense whatsoever.

I caught up with Gabriel. 'Gabe, what's happening?'

'I don't know.'

'I can't hear gunfire.'

'Me neither.'

'But what are those people running from?'

'Search me. But whatever it is, they're scared out of their wits.'

We stood watching as the cross street disgorged more panic-stricken people. They dropped their bags, brief-cases, shopping. Many had even lost the shoes from their feet in their mad dash to escape.

But to escape what?

I moved out into the traffic that had been brought to a halt by the sheer volume of cars and by the people running across its path. A truck roared crazily from the cross street and struck some stationary cars on Fifth Avenue. Now the whole road was gridlocked.

Edging a few steps further out among the cars, I looked along the street in question. New Yorkers still ran from it, some so wildly that they tripped and fell flat on their faces. More fell over them until there was a writhing mass of limbs on the sidewalk as people struggled to get to their feet, only to be knocked over again by the never-ending rush of men and women.

Then I saw the cause of the panic. My blood ran cold as I stared in disbelief at what now appeared round the corner of a building. A full sixty feet high, its stem lurching and swaying, its dark green leaves shaking with every step, the cone on top slowly turning left and right, came a triffid from beyond the boundaries of nightmare. With lightning speed its stinger shot out at the knot of fallen people. Again and again it struck like the whip of a slave-driver.

Piercing shrieks filled the air.

The triffid paused on the street corner. It was in no hurry. No hurry at all. The cone turned as if to scan the street. Then, seeming to make a decision, it moved casually on, killing with ease as it went.

'Hell,' breathed Gabriel, his dark eyes shining with horror. 'How did a triffid get so deep into Midtown? And look at the *size* of the thing.'

'You said the sappers were blowing the bridge gates.'

'But that wouldn't have unleashed triffids into the city itself. There are triffid squads to deal with them. They'd have been burning the damn' things as they came off the bridge. There's no *way* triffids could get onto these streets!'

'Well, *that* one has.' I nodded towards the plant as it continued its lurching walk on its three massive yet still strangely stumpy legs. I'd never seen a specimen that size before. Like the aquatic variety of the killer plant we had encountered in Columbus Pond, these huge triffid variants must have been growing in America's hinterland, far away from human eyes. Once more this hinted at the plant's intellect. Had triffid 'high command' concealed the variant as a secret weapon to be launched when it deemed humanity to be at its most vulnerable?

This monster must have been five times the height of its tallest brother plants. It also appeared to move five times as fast. It crossed the road and disappeared into a side street.

'Don't bother about that,' Gabriel told me. 'The triffid squads will soon burn it.'

He'd barely said it when a whole mass of greenery seemed to burst from another cross street behind us. I counted perhaps eight of the killer plants. They were easily as tall as their comrade that had just gone lurching in the direction of Times Square. Stings lashed out. More screams. Now there was *total* panic. Car engines roared as drivers tried to find an escape route, but with the traffic already at a standstill all they succeeded in doing was ramming into other cars. Many relied on the protection of their vehicles and sat cowering inside them with the windows shut tight. But they were to discover – the hard way – that they weren't as secure as they'd hoped. The sheer force of those gigantic stings shattered windscreens with one blow while the follow-up strike found the car's occupants, poisoning them with lethal efficiency within seconds.

Motorists quickly realized that the only means of escape was on foot so, throwing open their car doors, they ran for it. Many weren't fast enough. Hundred-foot stings cracked through the air with uncanny accuracy to strike exposed faces. Soon dozens of bodies lay twitching in the street.

Screaming men and women ran one way towards apparent safety, only to be faced with yet another triffid lurching round a corner. They were forced to run back the way they had come.

I looked down the street. A narrow subway entrance had become blocked with panicking New Yorkers as people fought and clawed their way to what they desperately hoped would be safety underground.

The particular timbre of this frenzied screaming attracted the attention of a triffid. It stopped moving north. The cone on top of the stem turned to – and there was no doubt in my mind about this – to *look* at the mass of humanity scrambling for the narrow staircase. Knowing where to find easy prey, it changed direction to come lurching towards the hundreds of frantic people.

And this monster of its species could move *fast*. The

stem whipped back and forth high above the trucks. I could see the whorl of the sting contracting as it tensed, ready to strike.

I'd seen enough. Pulling the sub-machine gun from the bag, I aimed, then let the vile plant have a good long burst, shredding its cone and destroying its stinger.

Gabriel's glare stabbed at me. 'You shouldn't have done that, David.'

'I'm not going to stand by while innocent people are massacred by those things.'

'David, that is not our objective.'

'Objective be damned!'

The gunfire had attracted the attention of other triffids. They came lurching eagerly along the road. Panic-stricken people surged toward us. Marni was knocked aside. I grabbed her and dragged her back to the relative safety of a shop doorway.

'OK, David,' Gabriel said. 'You've brought the big guys this way. What now?'

I looked at the swaying forms of the gigantic plants. Clearly I couldn't shoot the tops off them all.

'Hold this.' I handed Gabriel the gun. Then I turned to Marni. 'Help me turn on the car radios. As many as you can . . . turn them up full!'

Gabriel's expression indicated that he thought I'd gone mad. But Marni didn't hesitate. She ran with me along a line of grid locked cars. All had been abandoned, yet some had been left with their engines idling. It only took a moment to switch on the radios, then turn them up full. Soon a mixture of classical music, jazz and talk stations blared out of the open car doors.

Marni and I worked our way back towards Gabriel, turning up radios so loud that the cars' bodywork vibrated under our hands.

By this time the triffids should have reached us. But they stopped at each car to investigate the source of the sound. I'd just reached the cab of a truck and had switched on the radio when the bluegrass guitar music was cut off in mid-chord. An urgent female voice said: 'Attention. Attention, please. This is a public announcement. Triffids have been sighted on Manhattan. If you are at home or in a secure building, stay there. If you are in a car or hearing this in a public place, make your way north to the 102nd Street Parallel. The gates there will be opened and you can take refuge north of the wall until the danger is over. I repeat. For your own safety make your way to the 102nd Street parallel. Gates will be opened for you to—'

At that moment I had plenty to occupy my mind without thinking through the implications of tens of thousands of New Yorkers suddenly finding themselves in such a grim neighborhood north of the prison wall.

'Smart move, David,' Gabriel acknowledged reluctantly. 'You've given those people a chance to save their necks.' He handed me back the gun. 'But it's time we did what we set out to do. Come on.'

With that he led our little band in the direction of the Empire State Building. By now the streets were largely empty of people. Either they'd rushed into office blocks or they'd headed down into subway tunnels. There at least those monster triffids could not reach them.

Which was more than could be said for our own exposed position. We constantly had to weave through the jam of abandoned cars as triffid after triffid lurched into Fifth Avenue. That was when it became clear to me that this was no haphazard rampage by a few triffids but a coordinated attack. As far as I could determine, they were moving east to west, driving people before them. Then they would leave one of their number at a street corner to guard the intersection. If this continued, the triffids would soon be able to stop all movement of unprotected pedestrians. Moreover, the sheer bulk of these plants wouldn't permit you to simply shove them aside with a car. They'd have to be tackled with flame-throwers and bulldozers.

We were within a hundred yards of the Empire State when a girl with a rifle stepped out.

'Sacramento!' She aimed the rifle at my chest.

'Berlin!' The word was past my lips before I'd even realized I'd said it.

She nodded. 'OK. Stay here.' Then she turned to Gabriel. 'The Marines are going in now, sir. They were held up by triffids for a while in the south.'

'Where on earth did all these damn' monsters come from?'

'There was a change of plan, sir. As well as blowing the bridge gates the engineers managed to open up the tunnels under the river.'

'Good God . . . that means the triffids are pouring up out of the ground *inside* the city.'

'That seems a damn' cynical tactic to me,' I said. 'Those people out on the street hadn't got a chance. Or do we write that slaughter off as just another bloody accident?'

Gabriel's eyes became hard. 'There are some who would call this payback time.'

I looked back along Fifth Avenue and realized that any discussion about the morality of the Foresters' actions would have to wait. The nearest triffid was maybe a couple of hundred yards away. What was more, it seemed to be taking a particular interest in us. 'I don't think it's going to be too healthy for us to stand around here any longer,' I said.

A colossal explosion drowned out whatever reply Gabriel had intended to make.

I turned to see smoke billowing from the bottom of the Empire State. Gabriel gave me a grim look. 'They're going in,' he told me. Then he ran towards the massive building that was both Torrence's headquarters and his imperial palace.

I hadn't come this far to hide in a shop doorway. I followed – just as the shooting started.

CHAPTER FORTY TWO

Fire Fight

Squads of the Foresters' Marines emerged from behind cars or from doorways to race towards the foot of the enormous building. By now the smoke had cleared sufficiently for me to see that a pair of doors had been blasted inward. Through this opening the Marines charged. They fired short bursts from their automatic weapons, clearing whatever opposition met them.

My party swiftly pulled firearms from bags and cases as they moved forward. Gabriel Deeds flicked open the catches of the guitar case. He lifted out his sub-machine gun, then hoisted the satchel full of hand grenades over his shoulder.

I glanced back to see more of the huge triffids. These things moved with an awful majesty, their sixty-foot stems swaying with all the grace and menace of a giant cobra while their cones swept left and right as if scanning the street. With consummate accuracy the stings cracked through the air to claim yet another victim. Even as I watched a man was incautious enough to look from an open third-storey window. The sting found his face. He toppled forward to the ground, his scream echoing along the street.

It seemed that we had made an alliance with the devil himself. But I had little time to ponder the morality of the Foresters' actions in unleashing these monsters onto the streets of Manhattan. Ahead lay the shattered doorway. The bullet-ravaged corpse of a Marine lay slumped across the timbers.

Seconds later I followed Gabriel into the building. Marni stayed close by my side. This was no place for her, but at the same time I couldn't leave her to the tender mercies of the killer plants outside.

Inside the building chaos was king. People were running everywhere. Some fired weapons. Some fled for their lives. In this confined space the racket of gunfire and the thunder of grenades felt loud enough to smash my skull. Blue smoke misted the air. Beneath it men and women lay dead or wounded.

I took refuge behind a sofa. Gabriel and Marni crouched beside me.

We were in a large entrance hall. I'd been here before when I had visited Torrence with Kerris. There were the same statues of Alexander the Great, Julius Caesar and Hadrian, all interspersed with potted ferns that formed clumps of greenery.

Now I could make out the pattern of attack. Marines advanced in small teams of five or six, leapfrogging forward, as it were. One team would rush forward and secure an objective. The team following that one would then advance to secure the next, and so on.

Machine guns spat back from those clumps of ferns that must have concealed Torrence's guard. A fact confirmed when a Marine tossed a grenade into the greenery. The explosion blasted away leaves to reveal a low, thick-walled concrete structure, a pillbox. From slits in the sides gun muzzles disgorged streams of bullets.

Marines went down like ninepins. Blood flooded across carpets.

'Hell,' Gabriel breathed. 'We're taking one heck of a beating.'

'What now?'

'Push the sofa forward. Keep it square to the pillbox . . . and for heaven's sake keep down.'

The three of us wheeled the sofa forward. As a bulletproof barrier between those big-calibre machine guns and us it was more than a little flimsy. At best the gunners within the pillbox simply might not notice our advance amid the carnage.

When we were within thirty paces of the pillbox Gabriel pulled out something like a Very flare pistol that had an unusually wide gun barrel. He clicked a bulbous-looking shell into its breech.

'Keep your heads down.'

He fired the grenade pistol at the pillbox. The missile hit the concrete flank where it exploded with a fierce roar.

'Damn, I'm getting the shakes.' Reloading, he took a deep breath, then fired again. This time the missile cannoned through an opening in the concrete. I took a cautious look in time to see the detonation shake white dust from the pillbox's exterior. Immediately, smoke poured from the gun slits; the machine guns inside fell silent at last.

At that moment a hand slapped Gabriel on the shoulder. 'Good shooting, Gabe.'

I turned to see Sam Dymes giving him a grim smile. 'If we can secure the lobby then we're nearly there.' Sam nodded at me. 'I see you've joined the team?'

'I've got some business here too, Sam.'

'I'm more glad than I can say that you're here, David. It looks like we're going to need everyone who can fire a gun.' His hand went to his elbow where a red stain was spreading through the shirt material. 'Just a grenade splinter. I should have learned to throw the damn things further.' He gave a rueful shake of his head. 'Hoist by my own petard, as the old saying goes.'

From a staircase in front of us came a swarm of black-uniformed figures.

'Someone called out the Guard,' Gabriel murmured.

I raised the sub-machine gun and fired a burst at the group of heavily armed men. Several of them pitched forward to roll down the staircase. Gabriel fired another of his pistol grenades. The blast felled yet more.

At that moment I saw a flicker of green from the corner of my eye. One of our sappers lurched forward, clutching the side of his neck. With an ear-stabbing yell he collapsed writhing on the floor.

I looked back to see that a young triffid had found its way into the building. Little more than seven feet tall it was still lethal. I turned to give it a short burst, the bullets shredding the cone, leaving it and the sting in tatters.

'We've triffids coming in at our backs,' I shouted. 'We've got to get out of the lobby.'

Sam's expression was grim. 'Looks like we're between the devil and the deep blue sea,'

He was right. In front of us black-uniformed Guardsmen were pushing into the lobby. While behind us, the street outside seemed to have sunk beneath some kind of enchanted forest — if 'enchanted' was the right word. Where there had been concrete sidewalks, bare walls, and blacktop swamped with gridlocked cars now there was a swathe of jungle-like greenery as triffids engulfed Manhattan.

I pointed to a corridor off the lobby. 'There's an elevator there,' I shouted. 'Take that.'

'We haven't secured the lobby yet.'

'Leave it to Torrence's men and the triffids to slug it out. Come on!'

I ran from behind the sofa. Behind me came Gabriel, Marni and Sam. By the time we arrived at the elevator a pair of Marines toting heavy-duty machine guns had joined us.

Gabriel looked at the elevator with suspicion. 'What if this thing's been shut down?'

'There's one way to find out.' I pulled at the door. It slid open to reveal a calm mahogany interior. Mirrors reflected our smoke-stained faces back at us.

'Inside, quick.'

There wasn't a moment to lose. A door swung open nearby to reveal the surprised face of a guard. He swung up his rifle but our Marines were faster. They blasted the man where he stood. But more men appeared from inside the room, firing in our direction.

With everyone inside the elevator I pulled the door shut. It was one of the old manual lifts. Instead of punching buttons that matched a floor number, there was simply a wheel that swung either way to a stencilled *Up* and *Down*. I spun the wheel. With a shudder the elevator began to ascend at a stately pace.

A little too stately. A shadowy figure appeared at the other side of the glazed door to fire a handgun through the glass. I fired a burst back to spoil his aim.

A second later the elevator had climbed out of harm's way.

Holding his bloody elbow, Sam Dymes managed a weak smile as he nodded at the shattered mirror behind him. 'That's seven years' bad luck for some poor devil.'

Slowly, timbers creaking, the venerable old elevator took us higher and higher. A glance round told me that with the exception of Sam's elbow wound we were all unscathed. Marni looked at me, her green eyes serious yet determined. I handed her an automatic pistol. Checking that the safety was off, I told her, 'If you should need this when we get out, just point and shoot. OK?'

She nodded.

Gabriel and the Marines seized the temporary respite to reload their weapons. I followed suit, snapping a fresh magazine into my sub-machine gun.

Sam nodded up at the ascending hand that indicated the floor numbers. 'We need to make for the ninetieth floor . . . but be ready. Something tells me we might have a reception committee waiting for us.'

'Then bypass it for the ninety-first,' I told him. 'With

luck they won't be expecting us there. Then we can walk down to the next floor.'

'Good idea.' Sam grimaced as he flexed his injured arm. 'Does anyone know how to control this thing?'

Marni nodded and stepped forward to the control wheel.

'OK, we get out at the ninety-first.' Sam drew a pistol from his belt. 'But if those guys of Torrence's are in a trigger-happy frame of mind, then they might just put a whole mess of lead through the door as we pass by. So stand back against the side walls of the elevator . . . no, not at the back of elevator. Here, at either side of the door.'

Then came the waiting. The indicator above the door pointed to the eighty-first . . . slowly it moved up to the eighty-second.

Now the sounds of the battle in the lobby below had receded. In the elevator, along with the creaks of cables and pulleys I could hear the sounds of my companions' ragged breathing.

It was a strange interlude. There was no plan for the coming combat that I could run through my mind. All I could do was stand and wait for whatever happened next.

'OK, brace yourselves.' Sam's voice was tight with tension. 'We're coming up to the ninetieth.'

Through the cracked glazing of our elevator door the block of darkness gave way to a band of light as we came up to the ninetieth floor. I had expected a burst of gunfire through the elevator doors.

Nothing. The elevator rumbled upward.

Marni stopped the elevator on the next floor. The

Marines were out first, standing back to back, their machine guns at the ready. Then they waved us out. I found myself in a passageway with offices opening off. So far, the place appeared to be empty. A sign directed us towards the stairs.

On the way the Marines kicked open any door they deemed suspicious. Inside one, half a dozen office workers were hiding behind a line of filing cabinets.

'Don't shoot!' cried a grey haired man.

'We won't shoot if you don't shoot us,' Sam replied civilly. 'Do you have any guns?'

'No, sir. We're only filing clerks.'

'Filing clerks, eh?'

'Yes, sir.'

'You seen any Guardsmen on this floor?'

'No, sir.'

'You telling me the truth, mister?' Sam rested the pistol muzzle in the crook of his bloody arm.

The grey-haired man raised his hands higher, then cast anxious glances at his colleagues. 'Well . . . er, I did see some Guardsmen in the stairwell, they—'

'How many? And where, exactly?'

'Four. They were carrying a machine gun on a tripod. Er, they were taking it down the stairwell right at the end of this corridor.'

'Thank you,' Sam said with genuine courtesy. 'I'm sorry if I alarmed you and your colleagues.' Before leaving the office he added, 'Oh, and I recommend you sit tight behind those cabinets. And don't do anything stupid like making any telephone calls. Got that?'

'Indeed, sir. Thank you.'

We returned to the corridor. Sam spoke to the Marines who then took the lead as we moved in Indian file towards the stairs.

When the stairwell was in sight, the Marines gestured for us to stay back a little. Then they each pulled the pins from grenades that they lobbed underarm down the stairs. Before the crash of the explosions I heard a startled shout. After that there was only silence. The Marines ran forward to fire machine guns at some target down the stairs, then signalled us to follow them. I saw a heavy machine gun tipped from its tripod at the turn of the stairs. A number of bloody bodies lay prone.

'See that the old guy gets mentioned in dispatches,' Sam said, smiling grimly. 'He saved our bacon.'

On the marble steps we picked our way through a crimson mess that was as slippery as engine oil, all of us having to grip the stair-rail hard to prevent ourselves from slithering down onto our rear ends. Nevertheless, we were soon in the corridor below where we made good use of the expensive carpet to wipe the soles of our boots.

A sign informed us that we were on the ninetieth floor. It was uncannily silent here, too. I found myself glancing out through a window to see the sun dropping low over an apparently calm Manhattan, the evening rays reflecting redly in the windows of the office blocks.

'Keep moving,' a Marine hissed. 'I'll watch your backs.'

With one Marine in the lead and one guarding our tail we moved along the corridor. Torrence had been busy here. Offices had been converted into a self-contained hospital. I glimpsed scrubbed tiles and the massive overhead light of an operating theater.

That was the moment when points of light suddenly appeared at either side of my head, streaking away past me down the corridor.

Instantly I dropped to one knee. Looking back, I saw a pair of black-uniformed guardsmen firing automatic rifles at us. The Marine guarding our tail had caught the worst of it. His lifeless body lay face down in the corridor. Squeezing the trigger of my own gun, I hosed the men with sub-machine gun rounds. More wildly fired shots ripped plaster from the walls in clouds of white dust.

Blinking dust from my eyes, I saw the two men crumple to the ground.

'Move it!' hollered the Marine in front. He charged forward down the corridor. We followed.

A moment later he burst into a lobby. Straightaway I saw a line of black-uniformed figures manning a make-shift barricade of upended desks, filing cabinets and cupboards. Strangely, though, they were on the same side of the barricade as us, not, as you might think, on the other.

'Drop your weapons,' Gabriel shouted. '*Drop them.*'

Some chose not to.

A well-aimed shot from Marni's pistol sent one of the men rolling back against a desk, both his hands gripping his throat.

I fired in short bursts, bullets stripping away chunks of wood from the desktops. But a number of rounds found softer targets. Black-uniformed figures jerked like marionettes with their strings cut before dropping to the ground. Other Guardsmen took the second option.

Shouting at the tops of their voices, they threw aside their guns and raised their hands. Gabriel moved forward, ordering the surviving Guardsmen to lie down on the floor with their arms outstretched. I noticed that he limped, and he left a bloody footprint on the carpet. A glance at Sam Dymes told me that a bullet had nicked his chin. Gradually, a red beard formed around his lower jaw. But he didn't look too badly injured, considering, and he moved forward to talk to the Marine.

At that moment, I realized that my left ear seemed oddly cold, as if a piece of ice had been pressed to it. To my surprise its upper third had simply vanished. My fingers, when I looked at them, glistened crimson, too. I looked down at my right arm. It was dotted with tiny wounds from each of which hung a pearl of blood. Luckily, I felt no pain in the arm and when I moved it experimentally it functioned well enough.

It took some minutes to move the surviving Guardsmen and their wounded into a storeroom. I noticed a telephone in the corner and took the liberty of tearing it from the wall before locking the men in.

Once our small and increasingly blood-soaked team had re-assembled in the lobby Sam said in a low voice, 'I don't see any alternative now but to go straight over that barricade.'

'You figure that Kerris and Christina are still here?'

'That's what the most recent information tells us.'

Gabriel looked at us. 'Everyone reloaded?'

We nodded.

'OK,' Sam whispered. 'Let's do it.'

We ran at the wall of upended furniture. At that

moment my arm decided it was a good time to start hurting. Grunting, teeth clenched, I scrambled over the barricade to slither down the other side.

I was greeted by the sight of a second line of upended tables that had been pulled around the end of a corridor to form yet another barrier. *Great . . . just great*, I thought, as my nervous system settled down to flashing pain signals bright and clear to my long-suffering conscious mind. Holding the sub-machine gun in one hand, I lumbered forward. Just then the muzzle of a rifle appeared over a table, and I found myself looking along the barrel to a pair of green eyes framed by red hair.

I stopped in my tracks. 'Kerris?' I said in disbelief.

The rifle was lowered to reveal a surprised face. 'David Masen? It's about goddamn' time.'

CHAPTER FORTY THREE

Hiatus

I just stood and stared at Kerris's face. Until that moment I'd found it hard to believe that I'd ever set eyes on her again.

She smiled. 'I was beginning to think you were never going to get here.'

'As trips go, it was a little on the eventful side,' I managed to say.

A moment later Gabriel walked up. 'You'd better finish off that embrace inside,' he told us with a tired smile. 'We might have company at any minute.'

We moved deeper into the corridor. Two Guardsmen lay dead along the walls. From a side door burst Christina. 'David! David!' She lunged at me and hugged me hard enough to remind me about the state of my arm. But despite the lively waves of pains ebbing and flowing across my forearm, I gave her a delighted hug. 'Hey, it's good to see you again . . . you've not been harmed at all?'

Christina's face shone with excitement. Then, in a surprisingly articulate manner, she said, 'Kerris made us a war up here! She shot the bad men. Then built the wall.

Then we sat waiting for you . . .' She gave me a sudden scolding look. 'But you took ages and ages to get here, slowcoach.'

I smiled. 'Well, I'm here now.' I looked at Sam. 'All we have to do now is figure out how to get everyone *away* from here.'

Sam touched his jaw thoughtfully. He looked surprised when he saw the blood on his fingertips. 'I guess we can't go anywhere in a hurry. What strikes me, however, is that at some point those elevator doors will open. Then either Torrence's men or our own people will come out. So until then I better make sure there's a guard on the barrier.'

He went to have a word with the Marine, who took up a position behind an upturned table with his machine gun.

Meanwhile, Marni stepped forward. Kerris started when she saw her. Both women looked searchingly at each other. As if unconscious of the action Kerris ran a finger across her face, following the same line as Marni's scar. It was the action of someone looking at their reflection in the mirror.

'You're my sister, aren't you?' whispered Kerris.

'Marni can't speak,' I said and told Kerris briefly what I knew of her background.

Kerris nodded. She seemed stunned by the sight of the woman who stood in front of her. 'Long ago I did wonder if I had a twin. After all, I have plenty of brothers and sisters, and some of those were sets of twins. But we must have been separated at birth. Just look at her eyes. They're identical to mine . . . only her poor face . . . I'd like to get my hands on the rats who did that to her.'

'It looks like you've already made a start.' I nodded at the dead Guardsmen.

Kerris told me what had happened. She'd been staying with Christina when the attack alarm had sounded. There had followed some garbled telephone calls from the ground floor saying that what amounted to a battle was being fought down there. Guardsmen holding the ninetieth floor had told Kerris that she and Christina were being moved to another part of Manhattan. Clearly if that happened Sam and his men would then have the problem of finding the two women all over again. Kerris, therefore, had decided that the time for action had come. She knew that the Foresters had managed to infiltrate three operatives into the nursing staff stationed on the floor. So, arming themselves from a hidden cache of weapons, they had shot dead two of the Guardsmen, then managed to barricade the entrance to the corridor. More Guardsmen had made it to this floor where they built a second barricade. The ace that Kerris held – and she knew it – was that the Guardsmen wouldn't risk injuring Christina and the precious egg cells that she carried in her ovaries by trying to shoot their way in.

In turn, I told her that the battle downstairs had been further complicated by an influx of triffids onto the streets.

For a while an uncanny silence settled over the nine-tieth floor. It was neither stormed by Torrence's men nor relieved by ours. No telephones rang. The electric lights burned steadily. Beyond the windows a blood-red sun settled on the horizon. We busied ourselves checking weapons and dressing our wounds. Fortunately none of us had suffered any serious injury. Probably the worst hit was Gabriel. A bullet had smashed through his calf. Nevertheless, he continued to hop round with the aid of a broom, the brush part tucked below his arm in a fair imitation of Long John Silver.

I joined Kerris at the window.

'Can you see anything?'

'We're too high. From up here everything looks perfectly normal.'

She nodded out across the island to where the Hudson River gleamed red-gold in the sunset. 'Beautiful, isn't it?' Wistfully she added, 'It could be something out of Paradise. I once went on a fishing trip upriver. You could see what remained of all the millionaires' mansions on the hillsides, and just for a minute you could imagine what they were like before everything went wrong. In my mind's eye I could see children playing in swimming pools and moms and dads reading in deckchairs or cooking sizzling steaks on barbecues . . .' She shook her head sadly. 'Do you think those days will come again?'

'In some parts of the world they already have,' I told her. 'Back home we still have Bonfire Night. We build big fires outside, fire off skyrockets, and bake potatoes. Children love it. Adults, too.' I smiled. 'But all the adults seem to wake up with hangovers the next morning.'

'Bonfire Night? What's that?'

'An old pagan custom.' I felt a grin breaking across my face. 'Probably linked to some fertility rite or other. We burn effigies of a man called Guy Fawkes on the fire, too.'

'What a curious people you British are.' She wrinkled

her nose, amused. 'And to think I went and did something as ridiculous as fall in love with one.'

I kissed her. 'If we're going to do this thing properly,' I told her, 'you must come home and meet my family.'

She looked round the office where we were perched hundreds of feet in the sky. 'When we get out of here, the pleasure will be all mine. Then, to comply with those other Old World conventions, we'll get married too, won't we?'

I smiled. 'Why not?'

And just for a moment I felt suspended in a bubble of happiness . . . one as wonderful as it was incongruous.

Perhaps as some kind of natural antidote to that precarious time high in the skyscraper people busied themselves with trivial distractions — brewing fresh jugs of coffee, playing cards for matchsticks. Later I found Sam Dymes sitting on a desk, jotting notes on a pad.

He glanced up, noticing my bandaged head. 'Say, David, how's the ear?'

'The bit that's still attached to my head stings like crazy.' I gave a tired smile. 'As for the other chunk that's lying somewhere down the corridor, it doesn't hurt one bit.'

Sam chuckled. 'I guess that's what you English call gallows humour. Coffee?' He poured the steaming liquid into a paper cup. 'Torrence certainly doesn't stint on quality.'

'Thanks.' I took the cup. 'How's the arm?'

He raised the arm in its sling a little. 'Oh, fine, fine. Just nicked me in the crook of the elbow.' In that characteristic way of his Sam suddenly changed conversational tack. 'You know, a funny thing happened to me in the middle of all that fighting. Of all things, the answer to an engineering problem that had been bothering me for months suddenly popped into my mind. There I am, firing at living human beings and I suddenly say to myself, "Sam Dymes, why don't you run the rail track to the north of the lake, not the south, because . . ." Oh, you don't know what on Earth I'm talking about, do you?' His speech speeded up as he became enthused. 'Before my military service I was a railway engineer, and I will be again when my tour of duty is over – God willing. You see, I'd got this thorny, even downright bamboo-zling problem of running a railway line from a new harbour on a lake to town. Only there were all these hills and crags and dirty great ravines in the way . . . bothered the hell out of me. Whatever I planned it never worked out right. Then, as we came storming up that corridor, guns blazing, grenades booming away like the coming of the apocalypse, I suddenly said to myself: "Sam, why don't you run the rail track to the north of the lake . . . You'll save miles of track and months of labour . . ." Now, David, that strikes me as a mighty peculiar time to have such an idea, right bang in the middle of a blood-and-guts battle, huh? So now I'm taking a few minutes to write it down so I don't forget.'

Sam talked on for a while. I realized that, like Kerris and I making dreamy plans for the future, the gangling engineer had found a temporary refuge in his vision of a new railway line.

I glanced round. Marni and Christina had found an instant rapport. Smiling, they communicated with an impromptu sign language that both appeared to understand. The Marine chatted to female lab technicians who'd been part of the undercover team. Kerris still gazed out of the window. Now night had fallen. Lights burned steadily from neighbouring buildings.

Only Gabriel Deeds sat on the barricade. He watched the elevator doors with brooding eyes. Beside him stood a heavy machine gun that he'd taken from a dead Guardsman. I knew he was waiting for the moment when Torrence's men would rush from the elevators.

The elevators, despite Gabriel's state of readiness, remained resolutely inactive for the rest of the night. We slept in shifts. Sam, Gabriel and I took it in turns to keep a watch on the elevator and the corridor that led to the stairs. In the morning we made a breakfast from food still in the canteen. Sam made sure that drink and food reached our captives in the storeroom.

As I took my turn on guard at the barricade Sam ambled along, a cup of coffee in his hand. After gazing for a moment at the silent elevators he rubbed his now-stubbled jaw. 'You know,' he said, 'I'm beginning to take the view that our people didn't succeed in capturing the building. They'd have contacted us by now, surely.'

'But then, we haven't heard from Torrence's men, either.'

'That's true . . . that's very true.' Thoughtfully he ran his finger along the bridge of his nose. 'But we do hold what Torrence now considers his most valuable assets.'

'Christina.'

'And yourself, don't forget. You, David, are Torrence's key to the Isle of Wight and that machine of yours that turns triffid sap into gasoline. Both are of huge value to him. And both, if they were in his hands, would enable him to continue building his empire until . . .' Sam stretched out his arms as if encompassing the whole globe. 'Well . . . I don't think Torrence has set a limit on his ambitions, do you?'

'So you think it's unlikely that Torrence will send his Guardsmen in here firing off machine guns and hurling grenades?'

'Not yet.'

'So it's a case of sit tight and see what he does first.'

'Or do you think we should take the war to him?'

I shrugged. 'I'm just uneasy about giving him time to cook up some plan.'

'But sitting up here on the ninetieth floor leaves us with no place to go.'

'I agree. Maybe we should consider trying to find out what's happening on the ground. After all, there is a third possibility.'

'And that is?'

'That maybe Torrence has lost the battle too. What if the triffids have taken control of the place?'

'I guess you might be right about that.' He pondered. 'Mmm. You know, I think I'll ask Gabe if he'll take a little walk downstairs – if his leg's up to it.'

Gabriel Deeds was keen for some action. He snatched up the machine gun.

'No heroics, Gabe,' Sam told him. 'Just see if you can find out what's happening down there, then get back here as fast you can. OK?'

'OK.' He picked up a couple of grenades in one huge hand. 'But I might lay a couple of these eggs on the way.'

I followed Gabriel to the stairwell. He still limped along, using the broom as a crutch, but he wasn't going to let a little thing like a bullet wound slow him down. Reaching the stairs, he took the first step down. Quickly I stopped him descending further, then put my finger to my lips, because faintly, hardly more than a faint echo, I'd heard a stealthy footstep.

I eased back the hammer of my revolver. Then, leaning forward a little, I called down the stairwell, 'Sacramento!'

My voice went echoing downward. There followed a long pause.

I called again, 'Sacramento!'

Then came an echoing answer: 'California!'

My shot in answer to that went ricocheting down the stairwell.

Clearly Gabriel wouldn't be making his descent along *that* route. For the next ten minutes he and I hauled desks from a nearby office before shoving them down the stairs. By the time we'd finished anyone making a dash up the steps would have to climb over a messy tangle of furniture. Of course, that left the staircase ascending to the next level. I noticed that a gate could be drawn fully across it. Without a padlock we made do with lengths of electric-light flex, until the gate was firmly tied in place. I added the finishing touch with a hand grenade taped to a table leg, the pin attached by a cord to the gate. Anyone managing to open the gate would encounter a rather nasty as well as a very noisy surprise.

We reported back to Sam.

'I guess now we know,' he said in a low voice. 'Torrence must have beaten our people. His Guardsmen are in charge of the building.'

It wasn't long after that that a telephone rang. Sam looked at it for a moment, then commented, 'I guess someone wants to parley.'

That someone was Torrence himself. He confirmed that his men held the building. That the triffid invasion had been thwarted and that his cohorts had their tight grip on the throat of Manhattan once more. He demanded our immediate and unconditional surrender.

Sam suggested that Torrence might like to take a trip to hell. Then he put the phone down.

When Torrence rang back again he (through gritted teeth, I imagine) offered more moderate terms. A safe passage out of New York in return for Christina Schofield. Magnanimously, he even said that I could walk free too.

Sam said he'd think about it. Then he put the phone down again.

'Of course I don't trust the guy one inch,' Sam told us. 'He'll double-cross us the moment we walk out of here.'

'That doesn't give us a lot of options,' Gabriel said. 'So what now?'

'Well, how I see it, we either sit tight, safe in the knowledge that he wouldn't dare risk injuring Christina in an all-out attack. Or we surrender. Or we find some alternative way out of this place.' His blue eyes were grave as he looked at each of us each in turn. 'So, ladies and gentlemen . . . do you have any ideas?'

CHAPTER FORTY FOUR

In the Country of the Blind
the One-eyed Man is King

Sam Dymes pointed out that now wasn't the time to rush into making a decision. Torrence wouldn't hurry to take us by force up there on the ninetieth floor. He too could bide his time until our resolve crumbled bit by bit. Equally, we could not wait here for ever. So when Torrence telephoned again Sam began to negotiate. This went on until late afternoon.

At a little after six that evening Kerris held up her hand. 'Wait: does anyone hear that?'

'That's shooting.' Sam said.

'But who's shooting whom?' Gabriel went to the elevator doors, gun at the ready.

I joined him at the elevator. By pressing my good ear to the doors I could hear the sound of gunfire echoing up the shaft. Initially, the gunfire rattled continuously. Then, at last, it subsided to sporadic single shots. Moments later there was silence.

Sam stood, his head cocked to one side, listening for more sounds. At last he said, 'Well, what the hell happened down there?'

We moved back behind the barrier of office furniture. As we did so I heard a buzzing sound. I hunted for the source of the noise until I came across a small wooden box on which were a series of switches.

'It's the intercom,' Kerris said. 'Someone's trying to get in touch with us on the internal system.'

Sam looked at it suspiciously for a moment. 'Why don't they use the phone like they did before?'

'Maybe the telephone system is down?'

'OK.' Sam picked up the wooden box. It was attached to a cable that snaked away to the wall. 'Now, how do you switch this thing on?'

'Here, let me.' Kerris flicked a switch on the box.

Sam didn't say anything. He just listened. A faint hiss of static came from the speaker. Then, tentatively, 'Hello?'

A male voice came over the speaker. 'Sacramento.'

A flicker of hope lit Sam's eyes. Giving the answering code word, he asked, 'Who's this?'

'Sergeant Gregory Campbell, Foresters' Marines, C division, sir.'

'Is Lieutenant Truscott there?'

'Sorry, he was killed just a moment ago, sir. There's been a hell of a battle down here.'

'What's the position?'

'We regrouped with other elements of the force, sir. Then we launched another attack on the building around half an hour ago.'

'You're holding it now, Campbell?'

'Yes, sir, but we can't hold it for long. Respectfully, sir, you've got to get the hell down to the lobby so we can get away. Enemy tanks will be here any minute.'

'Thank you, Campbell. We'll be right down.'

Sam looked at us. 'It looks as if we've just got our ticket out of here.'

Here the elevators were automatic. Gabriel pressed the call button and within moments the elevator duly arrived.

As the doors closed on us for the long descent Sam said, 'Keep bunched tight around Christina when we get out in the lobby. Keep your guns ready, too.' His troubled eyes locked on the descending hand of the floor indicator. 'After all, we don't know what we're going to find down there, do we?'

I glanced at Kerris. She gave me a reassuring smile and I felt her hand rest against my forearm.

What we did find came as a surprise. The lobby was empty. I looked round, noticing blackened smears on the marble floor where grenades had exploded, along with the rust-coloured marks of dried bloodstains, too. As I stepped out of the elevator with my companions I saw the ruined furniture had been cleared away. Strangely, despite the sounds of battle we'd heard earlier, there wasn't a single spent cartridge to be seen.

In the doorway at the entrance of the building stood a lone Foresters' Marine armed with a rifle, the characteristic green bandanna around his neck.

'This way, sir,' he called. 'Please hurry.'

Even from this distance I saw that his face burned a bright red colour. Suddenly I realized he was blushing with embarrassment — or with shame.

We were halfway across the vast expanse of marble floor when I heard Gabriel mutter, 'I don't like the look of this . . . something isn't right.'

Another five paces – and then something strange happened to the lone Marine. He suddenly shot backwards. As he flew back through the doorway he gave a strangled cry. 'I'm sorry! I didn't want—'

As he disappeared through the doorway a dozen black-uniformed figures took his place. Without any fuss they pointed machine guns at us.

We aimed our own weapons back at them.

Stepping between the Guardsmen came a man I'd seen before. It was Rory Masterfield, the sharp-faced man I'd met on the steamship that first brought me to New York. Dressed in trousers and an open-necked shirt he held out his arms to show he was unarmed.

'Kerris. Ask your friends to put down their guns.'

'No.'

'*Tell them*,' Masterfield insisted. 'There's no point in you all dying over this.'

'We're walking out of here,' Kerris shouted. 'Tell your men to clear the way.'

'You know you'll not get through the doorway. There are hundreds of our soldiers out in the road.'

'You won't shoot.'

'Won't we?'

'No. Because you won't risk injuring Christina. Torrence values what she has too much for that.'

'Then we've reached an impasse, haven't we?'

As he said the words he stepped back. Then he put both arms straight up, above his head.

I interpreted that as a signal to someone. I glanced round for hidden snipers. Above my head electricians had made a start on rigging temporary lighting to replace the chandeliers smashed during yesterday's firefight.

Only no light bulbs hung down from the cables. Instead there were long thin wires from which objects that looked like candles dangled.

Sam noticed them, too. He pulled a grenade from his belt. I raised the muzzle of my gun. Seeing that blue-black gun barrel come up to bear on the Guardsmen in the doorway was the last thing I remembered with any clarity for a while.

For right then it felt as if the entire building had crashed down upon my head.

The first perception after that to make any sense to me was my recollection of looking up and seeing that wire-festooned ceiling. Hanging down from the wires, like a strange kind of fruit, had been sticks of dynamite.

I never did hear the actual detonation. (At least, I had no *memory* of having heard it – one of the effects of the concussion. I guess.) But I felt its effects, all right. When I opened my eyes all I could see were blurred pairs of boots hurrying around my head. At that moment I could still hear nothing. In fact, it felt as if my ears were stuffed with cotton wool. However, I could feel a distinct pins-and-needles sensation in my face.

For the moment I was content to lie there on the floor, because the world had taken to lurching dizzily around me. But even as I decided that standing upright wasn't really for me, hands seized my clothing to hoist me roughly to me feet. I blinked and my blurred vision improved. To my right stood Gabriel Deeds. Blood streamed from his nose while one eye was closed by an almighty swelling.

I looked to my left. Kerris stood there, her face as white as paper. My hearing came back in a rush accompanied by ringing sounds that, I guessed, came from somewhere inside my blast-addled head. Behind me was Sam Dymes, his face blackened by the effects of the explosion. And there was the rest of our dishevelled team: Christina, Marni, the Marine and two undercover operatives.

While milling all around us in a state of high excitement were dozens of Guardsmen. I saw Rory Masterfield watching me with an expression on his face that could only be described as smug.

I winced as the smarting around my eyes intensified. Being a little taller than average I figured I was paying the price for my face being nearer the explosion. Flash burns were beginning to make their stinging presence felt.

Hands grasped my arms as I was searched for any weapon that I might still have concealed up a sleeve or down a boot. Presently the Guardsmen were satisfied. One of them shouted back towards the entrance, 'Prisoners secured!'

The line of black uniforms parted in front of me.

A tall figure strolled forward. And once more I found myself looking into that resolute face with its one green and one yellow eye. Torrence looked pleased with himself. He regarded my face closely, as if I were some much-sought-after antique. 'Yes,' he said at length. 'You do look remarkably like your father, Masen.' He smiled at me. 'Now, in a little while, I'll be able to repay Bill Masen for this.' He pointed at his egg-yolk eye. 'Believe me, I will be paying him back with interest. And how is your mother, Josella Playton?'

I kept my mouth firmly shut.

'Or does she call herself Josella Masen now?' He smiled again, then brought his face close to mine so the yellow eyeball hovered in front of my own eyes. 'I'm looking forward to our reunion party. Hmm. Come to think of it, Josella won't be that old, will she? Oh, I know she'll be too long in the tooth to have children *naturally*. But I'm sure she can play host to Christina's progeny, can't she?'

Torrence didn't wait for a reply. Instead, he looked over the rest of his catch. Again he looked pleased with himself. He had every reason to be. He'd lured us down to the lobby using a captured Marine. With a stroke of brilliance his men had strung sticks of dynamite across the ceiling, using the explosive in such a way that it wouldn't produce lethal shrapnel but would generate a concussive blast wave to stun its victims. There had been a chance that we might have suffered more serious head injuries, but Torrence had gambled that the ovaries deep inside Christina's stomach would be unharmed, and that his surgeons could speedily remove them if need be. But then, my father always freely admitted that Torrence had good organizational skills, even if they were applied downright brutally. What was more, he must have galvanized his anti-triffid squads into action overnight. Through a window I could see armoured bulldozers clearing away the once fearsome sixty-foot plants that had been burned to cinders by what must have been a veritable firestorm from massed ranks of flame-throwers. With Manhattan cleared of invaders – human and triffid alike – the city was once more in this man's iron grip.

Torrence paused to look at both his daughters. First he scrutinized Marni, paying particular attention to the scar. Then he turned to look at Kerris again. 'You know,' he began, 'I think you really are twins. Of course, you don't look so identical now.' He spoke back over his shoulder. 'Masterfield.'

'Sir?'

'I want you to make sure that Kerris Baedekker once more resembles her sister. Then she can go to the Maternity Complex.'

'Yes, sir.' Rory Masterfield spoke with unconcealed eagerness. 'And the others, sir?'

'David Masen is important to my strategies for the Isle of Wight. As for the others . . . ' He gave a dismissive wave of his hand. 'I think they will have a long and uncomfortable career in the coal mines. No promotion prospects, naturally. Now, what I think is essential is—'

With a wordless bellow, Marni broke free of the man holding her. She launched herself forward, slashing at Torrence's face with her clawed fingers. He moved back. But not before I saw red lines slash across one cheek.

Before her fingers could reach his one good eye the Guardsmen had pounced on Marni, dragging her back. Roaring with fury, she turned her attention on them.

In one movement Torrence drew a pistol from beneath his jacket and fired.

Marni pressed the heel of her hand to her breastbone. Then, as her face creased with pain, she crumpled to the floor. There she lay, face down. Unmoving.

I bunched my fists and judged my chances of getting just one full-blooded punch into the man's face.

Torrence, however, decided not to take any more risks. 'Put them in chains.' Angry, he touched his scratched face, then glared down at Marni's still body. 'And throw that *thing* into the incinerator.' He kept his pistol in his hand.

Guardsmen had started snapping steel cuffs on my wrists when I heard a disturbance in the street outside. For a moment I actually hoped it signalled the return of the triffids. But these were no shouts of alarm. More a rising buzz of voices that, although quite calm, were insisting upon something.

Torrence rolled a fierce green eye in the direction of the main doorway. I followed his gaze. There in the entrance was a line of civil guards armed with rifles. I saw them look uneasily at one another. Then, one by one, they moved aside.

Curious now, I raised my head to look over the Guardsmen in front of me as a ripple of voices came through the lobby. Even the Guardsmen were distracted from chaining their captives.

By now the civil guard had moved yet further apart, and I saw, with some measure of disbelief, a curious body of people marching across the lobby. These, I realized, were the Blind. They moved with a quick confidence, their white sticks sharply tapping the marble floor. Indeed, there were so many of them that the rap of their sticks drowned out every other sound in the place.

'What is this?' Torrence asked with supreme irritation. 'Get these people out of here.'

But the Blind moved forward, and what I took at first to be dozens of them turned out to be hundreds. What a mixture they were. All the different colours of humanity were there. Some were neatly dressed, others wore rags. Clearly they'd come from both Free Manhattan and the slave camp in the north.

Torrence's expression switched between anger and bewilderment.

At the front of this strange procession was an unsighted woman of around seventy with long white hair; beside her a sighted girl acted as her guide.

Torrence let out a sudden laugh. He looked at me, then at Sam Dymes. 'I know what this is, Dymes!' Pointing back at the Blind with his pistol, he said, 'This is your secret weapon.' He laughed even louder. 'Is this the best you could do?'

'I . . . I don't know anything about this.' Sam's voice was barely a whisper.

'Oh, so you're disowning this absurd pantomime? Sanity at last!' Torrence then turned and bellowed at the Blind men and women. 'Listen to me! Don't you know that the old adage still rings true?' He pointed to his green eye. 'That in the country of the blind the one-eyed man is king!'

'General Fielding,' began the elderly woman in calm tones.

'Oh go away, blind woman. And take your rabble with you.'

'We are not leaving, General Fielding. Or should we address you by your real name . . . Torrence, isn't it?'

Torrence's humour vanished. 'Masterfield, have this place cleared, and if they don't clear out in five minutes give the order to open fire on them.'

Guardsmen raised their weapons.

The woman spoke out in a clear voice. But she didn't address Torrence. Instead she called out, 'Stephen? Stephen? Are you there?'

This was a cue for all the Blind. With a calm dignity they began to call out in clear voices.

'Elizabeth? Elizabeth?'

'Anthony?'

'Hans, are you there, Hans?'

'Joe? Can you hear me, boy?'

'Colleen?'

'Rose?'

'Aaron, are you there, son?'

'Theo . . .'

'Michael, it's your father . . .'

The slave Blind and the free Blind were calling to their sons and daughters.

'Colleen?'

'Benjamin, this is your mother.'

'Can you hear me, son?'

'Thomas . . .'

With unsuppressed fury Torrence barked at his men. 'Drive those people out of here with your fists if you have to . . . if they don't move, put a bullet in them. Shoot them down like dogs!'

I glanced round at the Guardsmen. They couldn't have looked more stunned if a whole squadron of tanks had thundered through the doors. Everywhere, faces of the armed men flushed red; they began to look to one another to see what their comrades would do.

They did nothing.

The Blind continued to call out to them.

'Joe, listen to me. Throw your gun down, my boy.'

'Colleen, put away your gun.'

'Benjamin . . .'

I looked from Guardsman to Guardsman. Their grim expressions had begun to change as powerful emotions started to build inside them.

Suddenly an officer threw his gun to the floor, where it clattered loudly.

And all the time the clear voices of the Blind continued calling to their sons and daughters.

'Pick that gun up,' Torrence raged at the Guardsman. 'Pick it up or I'll have you court-martialled!'

Shaking his head, the man lowered his gaze to the floor. After that, a rifle was thrown down, followed by a sub-machine gun.

'I *order* you to pick up those guns.'

Another gun fell to the floor, then another and another. Soon the sound of metal striking marble filled the lobby. I looked at the civil guard in the doorway. They followed suit, laying down their rifles and pistols. As quickly as the sounds had filled the lobby it became silent.

Then the elderly woman spoke. 'It's over, Torrence. Your co-rulers have been arrested. They will be tried in a court of law in due course. As you will be.'

'What? You . . . you *creatures* stand in judgement of me? Never . . . *never*.' He raised the pistol, pointing it at the woman's face.

It is sometimes said that there is no such thing as a true accident. That our unconscious desires guide our actions.

Only one of my arms had been manacled, the shackling process having been interrupted by the arrival of the Blind. Now a yard of chain hung from my right wrist. At the end of that formidable chain was a heavy steel cuff.

Before Torrence could fire I swung the chain with all my strength. I had intended to strike the arm that held the pistol. But I whipped the chain too high. At that moment, Torrence heard the sound of the approaching chain and half turned.

The manacle cracked into the side of his face. I saw only too clearly the damage caused by the open steel cuff as it embedded itself in his single good eye.

The screams, the curses, the sheer despair and fury of Torrence's inarticulate but highly vocal rage still rang around the building as the medics took the man away.

I turned to see Kerris kneeling beside Marni, holding a bloodstained hand. Tears glistened on her face. I went to her. I think I was the only one to move at that moment. Even though the lobby held perhaps five hundred people, everyone was still. As if even now, though the man himself had been disgraced and deposed, the ghost of Torrence's presence somehow still held sway there.

But formidable though the tyrant had been, the malign presence did, at length, pass and was no more. Guardsmen joined their blind mothers and fathers. From the emotions they displayed I sensed that the soldiers hadn't seen their parents for a long, long time.

That was, perhaps, the instant that Torrence's spell

was well and truly broken. Families, now reunited, began to leave in small groups.

In a little while we'd leave, too. But not just yet. Arrangements had to be made for Marni. We would make sure we did right by her.

CHAPTER FORTY FIVE

The World Beyond

On a bright October morning the flying boat's hull kissed the surface of a perfect sea. I throttled back and the engines that had powered our fifteen-hour flight eastwards across the Atlantic fell silent. The green hills of the Isle of Wight were as I'd remembered them. A mist clung to the shoreline, softening the outlines of the houses of Shanklin. Presently a motor launch fastened a line to the aircraft's nose, then towed it to the jetty where quite a crowd had turned out to see us.

It had been a long journey and there was still a lot of work to do back in Manhattan. But I thought it only right that my parents should meet the woman who was carrying their first grandchild.

We disembarked to cheers and wild applause. I'd seen nothing like it before. What had happened to that customary English reserve? I smiled as Gabriel Deeds found himself surrounded by dozens of islanders eager to shake him by the hand. The American Indian, Ryder Chee, made an impressive if incongruous figure among the crowd. But even his customary solemn expression broke into a crinkling smile as islanders surged forward to welcome him.

Christina laughed with delight, waving and clapping her hands back at the crowd, her eyes flashing with excitement.

It all became confusing, not to say a little riotous for a time. But suddenly I was face to face with my father. His strong face broke into a smile. 'Enjoy this moment, son,' he told me, putting his hands on my shoulders. 'You're getting a welcome fit for a hero . . . and you deserve every bit of it.'

Coherent speech became impossible. There were too many hugs, handshakes and kisses, too much backslapping for that. My old pilot buddy Mitch Mitchell managed to reach over the thronging people, displaying an impressive length of arm that justified his nickname of 'Monkey'. He rubbed my hair vigorously while calling out, 'White Swan, tomorrow night at eight. The beers are on me!'

By degrees we made it into the town where cars waited for us.

My father, Bill Masen, that hero of an earlier era, had learned from radio messages about what had happened to me over the last few weeks, but he was eager to learn more. 'And you say that the girl you found, Christina Schofield, is actually immune to triffid poison?'

'As are Ryder Chee and his tribe. They can walk among triffids like we'd take a stroll through an orchard.'

'You told me over the radio that you had another surprise for me.'

I smiled. 'Yes, I have.'

He grinned. 'Come on, David, what is it? You're not going to keep your old father in suspense, are you?'

'I'm afraid I will for a little while. This is something that I really need to show you.'

'In that case, I'm most definitely intrigued. Now, you take the car in front.' My father turned to Kerris who was walking arm in arm with my mother. 'Kerris, dear, you ride with David. We'll follow on.'

And so a convoy of cars headed out of Shanklin, bound for a country hotel that would accommodate our party. As we drove I thought about the revelation I had in store for my father, and I wondered how he would react.

I watched the familiar countryside pass by. It did feel good to be home. However, I couldn't help but reflect on the last few months, beginning with what at first seemed an ill-fated mission to free Christina. It was only after the blinded Torrence had been carried away that I realized what had happened. I remembered when the triffids had lurched through the streets and I'd heard the radio broadcast instructing New Yorkers to head north to safety. Now it made perfect sense why radio and tele-vision engineers had joined the Foresters' mission. On the day of the attack radio and TV stations had been seized and warning broadcasts issued, urging the population to flee north of the 102nd Street Parallel. It had been a significant element of the overall Dymes plan to expose free New Yorkers to the horrendous reality of the slave-labour camp. The plan had worked beautifully. Such was the flow of panicking humanity northwards that Torrence's prison guards had been forced to open the gates. (No doubt they had also been persuaded to do so by the march of those monstrous triffid plants through the Manhattan streets.) Consequently tens of thousands of refugees from the south of Manhattan suddenly found themselves in the ghettos of the north. There they had looked around in both horror and astonishment. As simply as that, Torrence's gaff was blown. What followed then had been the spontaneous march on the Empire State Building by the Blind, whether they were slave or free.

That was when Torrence's evil regime had died. Slave camps were liberated. Families had been reunited. Of course, the transition wasn't without its difficulties and setbacks, but progress was still being made.

At the hotel we ate dinner. Family histories were exchanged. My father talked to Ryder Chee as if they'd known each other for decades.

Then I said to my father, 'Ryder Chee would like to conduct a little test on yourself, along with the other people in the room. If everyone is willing?'

Everyone was immediately curious.

'Would you all roll up your sleeves?' I asked. All complied.

My father raised an eyebrow. 'Is this the final surprise you were going to spring on me?'

I nodded, smiling. 'It is.' I rolled up my sleeve too. 'Ryder Chee only finalized the test last week. We still need to refine it so that everyone on the island can be tested quickly and accurately. But Chee has the bones of the thing sorted out.'

'Now you really *have* aroused my curiosity,' said my father. 'What are we being tested for, exactly?'

I couldn't resist a touch of the theatrical. 'Wait and see.'

Ryder Chee moved from person to person while Christina carried a tray for him on which a dozen or so needles rested on sterilized paper. Taking a needle, he dipped the point in a pinkish solution in a glass phial. Then, working very methodically, he moved from one person to the next, pricking each of them on the forearm with a needle before discarding it, selecting a fresh one and repeating the process with the next candidate.

I gazed at the tiny pinprick on my skin. Chee told me I wouldn't have long to wait. I didn't. The pinprick began to itch, then burn as a single bright red spot appeared on my arm.

My father looked at his own arm expectantly. Then he shook his head, almost as if he was disappointed when the red spot didn't appear on his skin. Ryder Chee looked carefully at his arm. 'There is no sensation, Bill Masen?'

'None at all.' My father looked mystified.

Ryder Chee nodded with satisfaction. Then: 'Bill Masen, there are still many triffid plants in England?'

'Yes, I should say so. The whole place is infested with them. Why?'

'Because, if you should wish to do so,' Chee told my father, 'you might like to take a trip to the mainland. And walk among the triffids.'

My father looked astounded. 'You mean to say that this test shows that I'm immune?'

'I pricked your skin with a needle dipped in a weak

solution of the plant's poison. There was no reaction. Therefore the triffids cannot hurt you. But I can't say the same for your son. He can be harmed by the plant.'

'But how?' my father asked in astonishment. 'Thirty years ago I was very nearly blinded by a triffid. My face felt as if it was on fire.'

'And since that day you have eaten triffid, worked with them. You have been exposed to their poison in quantities so small that they have been harmless to you. Over the years this has stimulated your body into providing a natural immunity, in much the same way that snake-charmers become immune to the venom of the snake.' He checked the arms of the others in the room. 'A quarter of the people here have not responded adversely to the test. I imagine this sample will be representative of the local population as a whole. Many thousands of your people will be immune. They are now free to begin reclaiming their old homelands.'

My father sat there at the table, shaking his head. The truth would take some time to sink in. He'd worked so hard to find a scientific way to neutralize the power of the triffids. While he'd toiled away in the laboratory, however, his own body had done just that — without him even knowing.

That is the lasting impression that stays with me. My father is sitting next to Christina. And there is such a look of awe on his face at he gazes down at his unblemished forearm. In it he sees the key to a new world.

That was more than six months ago. Now, even though it's the last day of March today, here in Manhattan we are still in the grip of the fiercest winter I have ever known. Blizzards sweep across the city, turning the world beyond my hundredth-storey window into a maelstrom of white. Normally I would have had perfect views of the Statue of Liberty, the mouth of the Hudson where it pours out into the Atlantic, and the tiny island where the blinded Torrence still roars out his fury in his one-man prison.

While the scattered remnants of humankind followed their ancient instincts and made war on each other, the wider universe ran according to the eternal laws that govern its own celestial mechanism. As we battled for control of Manhattan, so the cloud of interstellar dust, which we now know was responsible for the great darkness that fell on the Earth, continued to drift through the solar system. At times it formed a dense veil between our planet and the sun, reducing day to the blackest of nights. During the summer months it thickened again. Frosts in August ruined our crops. By September there were five inches of snow on the ground in the Isle of Wight and America's southern states alike.

By October the dust cloud had gone, no doubt continuing its silent journey through the cosmos. For us, though, the damage it had wrought lingered on. While there were the joys – including the birth of our son, William, and seeing Rowena recover her health – there were, and still are, bitter realities to confront, too. The battle to find enough food for our people is never-ending. New Yorkers had to accept slashing cuts in their standard of living with the liberation of the slave-labour camps. Those days of gluttonous consumerism are over for the foreseeable future, – with luck, for ever. Triffids are more aggressive now than they have ever been before. They mutate faster, spawning newer, more lethal models of themselves. At least now, however, the people of the Isle of Wight, Manhattan and the communities I'd come to know as the Foresters have joined together, allies against both hunger and the triffid menace.

As I sat here earlier today at my desk, with the shrieking wind blowing snow against the glass and William asleep in the next room, I had reached the stage in this account of my experiences where it's customary to write those two simple words: *The End*. Then I planned to find Kerris and share a coffee with her before returning to our apartment. But as in so many areas of life, whether we are speaking of civilizations or individuals, it is simply not possible to say 'We have reached the end' as though everything will cease to exist beyond that point.

This was brought home to me not half an hour ago when Sam Dymes bounded into my office with the words, 'Say, sorry to bust in on you like this, David, but just take a look this . . .' He showed me a report from the people in Wireless Research announcing that they had picked up some inexplicable — and indecipherable — radio signals of staggering power. As I write this I can still see Sam pacing excitedly up and down, repeating the details to Kerris: that the transmissions are belting out from a far corner of the world; that they make the best of our own transmitters look as powerful as a tin megaphone; that already he's planning to launch an expedition to find the source of this mysterious broadcast . . .

See? There are no endings. Until a moment ago I'd been looking ahead to months spent here in this office, working on flight schedules for our airlines, calculating budgets for the airmail service and a host of other vital but mundane chores.

But now I'm seeing myself behind the controls of an aircraft once more, golden sunlight shining on its wings, engines humming sweeter than honey. And there on the horizon lie new territories just crying out to be explored.

So at the very final page, here, I know to the depths of my bones that I will have to defy convention. For I can't with any certainty write 'The End'.

Instead, on the threshold of a new world and new adventures, I can — and I will — write with total confidence:

This is the beginning . . .